THREE FEET OF SKY

BOOK ONE

STEPHEN AYRES

Three Feet of Sky
© 2012 Stephen Ayres

ISBN-13: 978-1477623237
ISBN-10: 147762323X

"When the soul suffers too much, it develops a taste for misfortune."—Albert Camus, The First Man

END OF EDEN

If Adam Eden was dead, then this was not Heaven. There was no feasting with the Gods, ready-to-wear virgins, or cloud-hopping Angels. This was a darker place. Adam was a faded entity, unaware of time or location. All that made him human was gone: memories, hopes, physical consistency stripped away. Only a tenuous feeling of death remained. Time was a fragile pattern, an indistinct reverberation. Eden's purgatory was not without form. There was almost material darkness to this lifeless limbo, a cosseting cloak of impenetrable liquid black.

An hour before his demise, Adam was celebrating. It was early November 2010, a typically wet night on the south coast of England. Portsmouth's harbour lights played through the rain, hazily illuminating the old maritime city's docks and marinas. Dark silhouettes of Royal Navy destroyers buttressed the cityscape against the deep water. On a clear night, the harbour-side roads and walkways thronged with an army of pleasure seekers, but tonight, only a sprinkling of revellers braved the rain.

The Horatio Tavern was part of a new retail development next to Portsmouth's historic naval dockyards. A typical theme pub, Horatio's boasted a plethora of reproduction maritime kitsch - any clue to the area's proud heritage gleaned by an untidy display of tourist leaflets by the entrance and a solitary portrait of Admiral Nelson near the toilets. Adam did not mind the formulaic artifice. He preferred it. He liked the familiar, safe and predictable. He never strayed out of the box.

Despite the weather, the bar was crowded. It was the third round of the evening: half a lager, three tequila shots, and a pint glass of diet lemonade. Adam sat at a table near the bar with Scarlett and Manny, as dissimilar a group as the choice of drinks suggested. As children, they attended the same school but had not been friends.

Thirty-three years old, Adam was a little under six feet and obese. His weight, along with a deep furrowed brow, dark bags under the eyes, greying hair, suggested a life of dubious choices rather than the usual passing of youth. Alcohol, junk food, unemployment and depression, each had taken a piece of Eden.

"You look deep in thought," said Manny, in his usual clipped manner.

Emmanuel Beaumont was solely responsible for pulling Adam out of his miserable five-year stupor. Known as Manny, the skeletally thin Christian volunteer had literally dragged Adam off the street, and got him into a church halfway house.

"Are you thinking about your children, Adam? They can visit you every Sunday now. I know your ex-wife swore she would kill you before ever letting you see them, but I don't think she meant it. People just say that kind of thing when they're angry. She didn't mean it, did she? I'm sure she doesn't know I was involved."

"Don't worry about Julia," said Adam taking another sip of beer. "She's not some axe-wielding murderer. I was only thinking how much I missed the taste of good lager."

Twitching nervously, staring at Adam's drink, Manny scratched a horseshoe remnant of dark brown hair. The many months weaning Adam off alcohol were an ingrained stain: months of shouting, vomit, aggression, and tears. Abstinence was not an option. Adam insisted on a new life without too many constraints. Despite the greatest of efforts and the best of intentions, they settled on compromise and moderation.

"It's alright, Manny, I'm not going back there. A year ago, I would have chugged this down in one. Mind you, then I wouldn't have bought decent lager. It would've been some cheap no-name super-strength white cider. You know, I used to carry a calculator to work out the best alcohol to price ratio. How sad is that?"

"It's very sad."

"Yeah, I knew the price of everything and the value of nothing. Although, I do miss half pound chilli burgers."

"You can still have a small burger with extra lettuce," suggested Manny, "as long as you don't have any sauce or chips. That's healthier, and much easier on the pocket."

"That's not worth queuing up in the rain for. Come on, Manny, I know I'm on a diet, but today's special. Let's go to Tabbas after this and get a chilli burger with fries. It'll be a treat for Scarlett."

"No, and you promised you wouldn't pressure me about burgers again. Remember that website? You know, the one that showed all the scary cuts of meat they put in some burgers. It made you vomit. Do you remember?"

"They're not all like that. Anyway, it made *you* vomit, not me. I've said it before and I'll say it again; I don't care what's in it, I just want it in me."

Adam knew it was futile arguing. It was best to back down before God came into the conversation, and Manny had a tendency to call on the big guy like some bullying older brother. Hoping to depressurise the conversation, Adam conceded, "But you're right. I'll just have a couple of bags of crisps."

Manny nodded sagely:

"Those half pounder days are well behind you. You weighed over 350lbs when I found you on the street. Now look at you."

"I know, I've lost 92lbs so far, but I won't be checking in to the anorexia clinic just yet."

Adam's other companion was Scarlett Slaughter, a successful freelance lawyer for several European fragrance houses. Elegantly slim, blonde hair effortlessly manageable, Scarlett usually exuded classic sophistication – her signature scent, sparkling floral aldehydes, gentle wafts of jasmine, settling on sandalwood. Now, thoroughly drunk, she fixed a disdainful glassy stare on Manny, her expensive fragrance crudely submerged beneath spilt tequila and the alcoholic sweat of intoxication:

"So, if fatty here follows your diet, he can have a body like you, eh? Hmm, that's a real incentive. And, why are you still wearing that Godboy sweatshirt? Hoping to save some souls tonight are we? You could've changed into something more casual."

"There is nothing wrong with my clothing," stuttered Manny, intimidated. "This is my Christian Volunteer sweater. Notice the sign of the fish next to the initials. It is a symbol of my devotion to Christ and the Lord God Almighty. It's by no means a source of embarrassment. I notice you're wearing the same black trouser suit you wore in court. I suspect you're even wearing the same shirt."

"This is Chanel, you bony little git. You can't compare this to that crap you're wearing. Lame retard blue jeans. And, who the Hell wears sandals with grey socks? Anyway, I'm only wearing this because I was supposed to catch a flight back to Paris tonight and didn't pack a change of clothes. Stupidly decided to stay and celebrate with Laurel and Hardy's stunt doubles instead."

"Well, I'm glad you did," smiled Adam, shrugging off the insult. "I get to spend next weekend with Charles and Emma thanks to you."

Scarlett raised her shot glass, announcing the fifth toast of the evening, "Here's to that old fart of a judge for being such a pushover. Oh ... and to your ex-wife's lawyer, that lightweight bleeding heart amateur."

Swallowing the tequila down in one, Scarlett slammed the glass upside down on the table.

Adam chuckled, raising his glass, "I'll drink to that. You blew them away. They really weren't ready for an international hotshot lawyer at the local Family Court." He took a small sip of lager.

Manny sat cross-armed, pointedly not touching his pint of lemonade.

"For Christ's sake, what's it this time?" snapped Scarlett. "Jesus doesn't approve of lemonade?"

Manny sniffed, "I just don't think it is right to celebrate others' incompetence. They are all God's children. It was perfectly correct for the judge to grant Adam access to Charles and Emma. Perhaps we could toast your skill as a legal professional. That would be a more positive thing to do."

Scarlett grinned, and raised another shot of tequila:

"Sounds good to me. I propose a toast to me: for my outstanding skills as a legal professional, my years of dedication and study," Manny raised his glass, her tone darkened, "and for being the most ruthless, savage, hard-hearted bitch ever to walk out of Hell and into a courtroom!"

Scarlett swallowed, slammed, and glowered at Manny.

"Now fucking drink that lemonade!"

Adam winced. In court, Scarlett was the epitome of effortless charm and sophisticated wit, but had already knocked back a small bottle of vodka in the taxi on the way to Horatios and was now well beyond a comfortable companion. Remembering her boasts about a Satan tattoo on her left buttock, Adam was in no doubt the little red gentleman would make a public appearance before the end of the evening, just before they were asked to leave the premises.

"Please, Scarlett, if you could get your claws out of Manny for just a moment, there's something that I've been wondering about."

Scarlett relaxed, reaching for her last tequila:

"What?"

"You know, you've never really explained why you helped me. I could never have afforded a decent lawyer, and then you come along, offering your services for free. I know we went to the same school, but I don't remember you. Couldn't picture your face or anything. Back then, I hardly knew Manny either, but I remembered seeing him around. But you … "

Scarlett put down her glass without drinking.

"Nobody knew me at school. I always looked down my nose at everybody else. I knew what I wanted to be in life, and anyone or anything that wasn't part of that I simply ignored. I just wanted to be a lawyer: studied hard, made the right moves, met the right people, took on the right attitude, and boom, here I am."

"So why did you help me?"

"Made the mistake of revisiting my past. I went on that 'Friends Again' website. You know, the one where you can find out how all your old school 'pals' fucked up their lives. I only went on to gloat at how successful I was compared to all those losers."

"Losers?" said Adam. "You think I'm a loser?"

"I found that two of the girls in my year killed themselves. One ploughed her car into a tree just because of some promotion, and the other took an overdose because of a stupid breakup. I didn't know them, but it started to bug me. Surely, someone could've stopped them. I decided a bit of charity work was on the cards. I ended up trawling 'Friends Again', saw Manny's profile, found out about your problems, and decided to help. Oh my god, Manny you look like you're about to cry."

"Can't help it. You care so much about people." Manny gently took Scarlett's hand. "I know it is not easy to open your heart like that."

Scarlett rudely snatched her hand away.

"Dry your eyes, Godboy, I did this for me, just me. Nothing like a bit of charity work to make you feel superior and ease the guilt. Adam, you haven't done any of this yourself. Manny dragged you out of the shit and got you a job, and I secured you a mortgage and access to your kids. One day you'll have to support yourself for a change. I tell you, when this is over, I'm never looking into my past again."

Scarlett drank her tequila but this time placed the glass down gently.

"So you really think I'm a loser, a charity case?" asked Adam.

"Yeah, a loser who thinks beer and burgers constitutes a good night out. You had two kids, a decent job, a house, and you let your wife and her latest fuck-buddy take the lot."

"I did it for my children. I didn't want them involved in a long drawn out fight."

"Ha, blame the kids. They didn't become alcoholic fat bastards now did they? I found out how low you fell; what kind of person you became. Hell, I mean, considering your name, you strayed so fucking far from the Garden."

Putting up her hands in a gesture of apology, Scarlett said, "Whoa, I'm sounding like a demon here. Maybe it's the tequila. Maybe it's missing that dinner engagement at Taillevent. You know, right about now I'd be enjoying Langoustines royales croustillantes."

"If you're hungry, I can get some more Doritos or cheese puffs," offered Manny. "They're very expensive here compared to the supermarket, so if you don't mind chipping in."

"Mmm, and to think you're still single, and such a catch...incredible. Adam, you might want to take Manny up on his offer of church on Sundays. It goes down well with British judges. It might just stop you losing access again. Happy clappy is fine just as long as it's not one of those fundamentalist groups."

Manny gushed with childish excitement, "Oh, don't worry, it's mainly joyous singing, uplifting sermons, and tea and biscuits. We're not at all pushy. You see, when He chooses, God will find you."

"Like a serial killer," said Scarlett.

Adam laughed, "Look Scarlett, you've just made Manny's day, don't ruin it. Now, you will have to excuse me, but I'm desperate for a leak. Next round's on me when I get back."

"Adam, let me go with you," suggested Manny, rising from his chair. "When I went earlier there was a rough looking fellow in there. He's probably a drug addict. He stared at me whilst I was urinating. Could be one of those willy watchers."

"I'd rather go on my own, Manny. The only drug I ever abused was alcohol, so don't worry. There are some things a man must do by himself."

As Adam made his way through the crowded bar, Scarlett slouched back in her chair and fixed her gaze on Manny:

"If you don't want to go on your own, then I'll come and hold it for you."

Glimpsing a movement behind Manny's trouser zipper, she smiled wickedly:

"Ooh, Jesus will not be pleased."

Once hidden by the crowd Adam headed for the entrance. One thing that neither Manny nor Scarlett could put right was Adam's genital shortcomings. He was convinced that this was the true reason that his wife left him. She always denied this but her constant reassurances only served to deepen his suspicions. The whole affair left Adam painfully penis shy. Braving Horatio's toilets was impossible, thanks to Manny's dire warning of the shady staring pervert. Deciding to find some dark spot outside and piss into the harbour, Adam inadvertently chose death over embarrassment.

Outside, the night air was cold and crisp, the rain a refreshing mist. Adam breathed a sigh of relief, noticing very few people in the immediate vicinity, and definitely no axe wielding ex-wife. A momentary glance revealed a drunken young couple in a rather sloppy sexual squeeze, and a dishevelled vagrant shouting obscenities at the distant Spinnaker Tower. Nearby a man and a young boy looked out to sea, perhaps a father and son – Adam felt a warm glow, anticipating happy days with his own children.

About fifty feet away, facing an empty retail unit, Adam spotted a promenade section still under construction. There were no lights or railings, plastic warning barriers a temporary substitute. The darkness was a beacon of hope, and Adam immediately headed to the secluded shadows to relieve himself.

After doing the deed, Adam zipped his fly and turned back to the bar. How had Manny's 'Friends Again' profile alerted Scarlett to his problems? He prayed there were no embarrassing pictures or details online - and one disgusting photo in particular.

In the distance, the Cherbourg car-ferry heaved quietly past, the array of windows a streaming fluorescent gallery. Adam noticed the father and son were somewhat nearer than before, staring in his direction. He hoped they had not seen him urinating in public. Taking a step forward, the world went black for Adam Eden. There was no warning, no obvious danger, and no ominous sense of foreboding. Everything became almost nothing. The dark place ...

TRANSITION

For Adam, any change to the darkness was unexpected. The faintest nuance of perception revealed the dark limbo evolving. Five menacingly iridescent metallic strands pierced the gloom, thrusting across the darkness like sharpened strings on an infinite cello. He sensed rising fear as the strands passed close by. Fear revealed Adam's consciousness returning, mental fragments reconnecting. He was no longer dead, just a disembodied mind, weak but again aware of his surroundings. Adam avoided the glowing threads, scrabbling frantically to hold onto the blackness. He could not cling on for long. It was futile, like clutching at oil. He slipped onto the strands, silently screaming.

If the strands looked threatening, then the reality was far worse. Tempestuously transported towards a destination unknown, waves of agony ripped through Adam's mind, constant and deep. Adam experienced feelings of traumatic physical renewal, sliced with lines of surgical precision, like a tongue lightly licking a razor's edge. He began to perceive time, the beating of his heart giving cadence to the dark limbo.

After what seemed hours of torture, a point of brightness appeared on the distant horizon, the strands aimed at its centre. Adam slid inexorably towards it, the light looming exponentially larger and more intense with each heartbeat. Go into the light, do not enter the light, Adam had no time to contemplate movie clichés before impact. The light engulfed him.

Darkness returned, though now due to tightly closed eyes. Adam became overwhelmed by a sudden sensation of gravity, feeling pressure on the soles of his feet. His arms hung by his sides, hands immobile save for the stiff movement of fingers. He was upright, standing, aware of an outer covering, clothing. A gentle warmth caressed Adam's face, and fresh air cooled his nostrils, filled grateful lungs. Like a new-born, he dared to open his eyes.

The light of the setting sun was painful, forcing him to look down, avoiding its glare. He was considerably slimmer than before, and wearing an orange jump suit. His black booted feet were visible without bending, no longer obscured by a massive belly. A jumble of thoughts raced through his mind. Was he a prisoner? Had he died and woken up in some afterlife Guantanamo?

Struggling to keep his eyes open, Adam looked up. This did not look like a prison, not even close. The view was pastoral beauty. Adam was standing in a lush, almost manicured, green meadow, rolling lazily down to a stream crossed by a high-humped cobbled bridge. A large white-plastered thatched cottage nestled by the bridge, and another meadow gradually inclined up on the far side. In the distance was a patchwork of bountiful fields, separated by neat hedgerows. Adam's sore eyes ached unbearably.

A huge mansion stood nearby—neat neo Georgian, plastic pillared portico and upvc bay windows. It seemed designed for a 1980's executive suburb rather than this rural idyll.

Hurrying towards him, from the direction of the house, were two figures. Through the pain, Adam could only identify them as hazy blurs: one male, one female. He blinked repeatedly, attempting to keep his eyes open, and tried to call out but his voice was a feeble croak. The pain became too intense, and Adam closed his eyes tight.

"It's Adam. I knew it would be Adam," whispered the woman, registering obvious disappointment. "She as good as told me so."

"We should have been waiting," replied the man brusquely. "Quick, give him the blue drink, and the shades."

"I didn't bring them."

"Oh no, how could you forget them?"

"I didn't forget."

"You shouldn't break with tradition like that. It's not right. Help me get him to the house."

Adam's hearing was as bad as his eyesight, as if underwater. The voices were young adults, vaguely familiar, though certainly not Scarlett and Manny. Supporting each arm, the couple escorted him to the house. Each step was sluggish, Adam's body stiff and leaden. They stopped after a few faltering steps.

"No, no," said the woman. "I think he should go now. Send him now."

"That's not done. We have to take him to the house first. He needs to rest. You know that."

"Send him to the concierge now."

"But … it's not done."

"Send … him … now!"

"Alright, we'll send him now, but it's your responsibility."

Turning awkwardly, they escorted Adam away from the house. He opened his eyes again, more concerned about his destination than the pain. Straight ahead, hovering just above the grass was a sleek transparent ovular pod. Human sized, a large red recliner cushion the only visible internal content.

The woman continued bickering:

"You say it's my responsibility. I was under the illusion that we were a couple. I thought our marriage meant something, even here."

"Yes, yes, I meant it's our responsibility," the man sighed. "Now, let's put Adam in the c-pod before he gets his strength back, and starts resisting."

Silently, the pod split into two halves and the couple clumsily manhandled Adam onto the cushion. Once settled, the cushion automatically moulded itself into a red cocoon, with Adam's face peering out like a swaddled baby. The couple stood back, facing Adam. He was sure he knew them, perhaps from a photo or family video.

"Well, Harry, I think you should take responsibility for this," said the young woman. "I thought you wore the trousers around here."

"Whatever you say, dear," muttered the young man wearily.

"Well?"

"I wear the trousers so it's my responsibility."

As the pod halves came seamlessly together, Adam recognized the couple. Yelling out, he only managed a garbled rasp:

"Mum, Dad, is that you?"

THE CONCIERGE

Without a sound, the pod pushed downwards, squeezing through the grass, the ground forced apart like a tight rubber membrane. Once through, the opening snapped shut, and the pod slotted into a white-walled tube. The pod accelerated, shooting along with sleek rapidity. Adam experienced little sensation of speed or distance, all points of reference screened by the frictionless silence, pure white walls, and engulfing red cocoon. After only a few seconds, the pod decelerated, squeezed through another tight orifice, and came to an abrupt halt.

The pod dissolved into a flat glasslike disk on the floor, and the red cocoon reverted to a cushioned recliner. Laying sprawled on the recliner, Adam painfully scanned his surroundings. It looked like a dingy private room in some sleazy Soho sex club: scuffed black leather seating, red anaglypta walls, and grimy floor tiles. In the centre of the room, ready to dance, a star spangled bikini girl grasped a shiny metal pole. Bleached blonde, pneumatic chest and glossy legs, she introduced herself.

"Mr Eden, I am your concierge—a caretaker—and if you ever need me, this is where we will meet. I would to like welcome you to the Environment, your new home. I will try to explain everything using terms with which you are familiar. However, you are very early. I was not expecting you so soon."

She motioned proudly towards the metal pole:

"I had planned to dance for you. I am not very good at it yet, but I can manage a few of the beginner's moves. Let me show you what I can do, and after that, we will discuss how you got here, and what you can expect from your new life."

Red and orange disco lights bounced around the walls as the room throbbed to a heavy sexual beat. Sensually swaying her buttocks, the concierge

11

ran her hand provocatively up and down the pole. The flashing lights and loud music sent Adam into an almost comical spasm.

Raising an arm, he screamed in pain, "Please, no. Stop it! Please, stop it! It hurts! It really really hurts!"

The concierge stopped her dance, baffled by Adam's reaction, and the music and lights ceased. Adam breathed a sigh of relief.

"Are you alright, Mr Eden? That was not quite the response I expected."

The concierge inspected Adam, and immediately noticed his blood shot eyes. Adam detected a distinct trace of annoyance beneath her caring expression.

"I am sorry, Mr Eden. You obviously did not rest before coming here, and have no protective eyeshades. That is most unfortunate. I must apologize." She smiled, tenderly brushing Adam's hair with her hand. "Mr Eden, this discomfort could and should have been avoided."

The concierge retrieved a pair of wraparound shades from a concealed drawer, and gently placed them over Adam's eyes:

"There, that should help."

Bringing instant relief, Adam found no problem keeping his eyes open. Holding a small glass containing a creamy blue substance up to Adam's lips, the concierge said, "Here, drink this. It will soothe your throat and sort out the aches and pains."

Adam obeyed, the liquid swiftly dowsing the fire, his body soothed and energised.

"Is that better?"

"Much better, thank you. Those people out there, were they my parents? It sounded like them but they looked younger. My mum was always a bit weighty, but that woman was slimmer, much slimmer."

Slinking enticingly over to the leather seating, the concierge sat, patting the cushion next to her.

"Mr Eden, come sit by me. I have much to tell you. We will save the pole dance for another day."

Adam leapt nimbly from the hovering recliner, but decided to sit opposite his alluring host. Smiling sweetly, the concierge pushed up her breasts with her hands.

"I chose these myself. Do you like them? Your profile suggested you would." She jiggled teasingly.

"Err, very nice," replied Adam. "Look, what the hell's going on? Am I imagining all this?"

"This is not your imagination, Mr Eden. I guarantee this is reality. The law states all communication between us must be through an avatar, surrogate, proxy, go-between, whatever term suits you best. You cannot meet the real me, so we use this robotic interface. I do not speak your language, so we use interpretation filters. Everything down here is based on your profile: my appearance, the furnishings, the wall colour, even the grime on the floor tiles."

"My profile, interesting. Look, can you stop grinning and shaking those now? It's very distracting."

Softening her expression, the concierge stopped jiggling:

"I should explain your situation, starting with the basics. First, I need to ask you whether you prefer the imperial or metric measurement system. Your own profile indicated a mixture of preferences"

"Is this still 2010?"

"Many centuries have passed since then. I am not permitted to be more specific than that. Now, do you prefer imperial or metric?"

Adam rubbed his chin and thought for a moment. All those years of metric education and he still used a mixture of both systems.

"Well, I prefer milligrams, but I also use pints, and feet, oh and miles … so I guess … Imperial."

"Good, then I will begin with how you got here. Mr Eden, you died on November 12th 2010 at precisely 9:16 pm and 13 seconds. Whilst I am not permitted to divulge the details, I can reveal the general procedure."

"I'm dead?"

"We used time channelling technology to access your final moments. Your memories were saved a few minutes before the event that precipitated your death. Next, at the point of death, we extracted those segments of the brain that concern the Self, your true being. Using your DNA, we created a new body, including a functioning brain, into which we grafted the brain segments. Finally, we mapped your saved memories into the new brain."

"Oh my God, I'm dead."

"Your new body represents the peak of your genetic physical potential. You are all you could ever be."

"How did I die? I don't remember dying. I only remember taking a piss."

Adam stood and nervously paced up and down.

"You drowned. You fell into Portsmouth Harbour, hit your head on an iron mooring, and drowned. You do not remember this because we mapped your memories a few minutes before the event."

"Why? Why cut out something so important?"

"The memory of death has proved too traumatic for most. It is the law."

"Did someone push me in? Was it was Julia? I got access to Charles and Emma, and she couldn't deal with it."

"I am not permitted to talk about what precipitated your death, nor can I discuss anyone else with you. Please sit down Mr Eden."

Adam sat next to the concierge, taking deliberate deep breaths, composing himself:

"So I died. I get it. I thought as much. And, to tell the truth, this isn't bothering me as much as it should. I used to get in a right state about the littlest things, but I feel quite relaxed about all this. I'm more confused than terrified. Oh, and please call me Adam."

"Adam, you have been chemically conditioned. It is a standard procedure to help you settle in. You suffer less stress this way. The effect will wear off in a few days. It is harmless, I assure you."

"So what was that dark place with the burning lines? I've never known such terror and pain. I guess the chemical conditioning is helping me deal with that too. Was that Heaven, or some sort of limbo before you get to Heaven?"

"Not at all. The dark place is your mind being transported across time, and stored. The painful experience of the carving lines is basically the mental manifestation of us building the new you. I apologise for the intense suffering, but our technology cannot minimise it without harm to the subject."

"No need to apologise. I'm alive, and that's gotta be worth the torture, although I certainly don't want to experience that place again"

"If you're careful you won't have to. We have the technology to bring back most of the human race. Everyone is provided with abundant resources, a safe environment, and eternal life—eternal being a relative term you understand. Your profile dictates your apparent age. You look to be in your late twenties, but it varies from person to person. The majority are between twenty-five and fifty-five, although a few are older."

"You mean people can come back as an old person? Why on earth would anyone want that?"

"We are only talking about looks. Internally, everyone is at their physical peak, so age is somewhat irrelevant."

"Will I age?"

"No, and If you encounter some fatal event, we can resurrect you again within 24 hours."

"Ha, ha, do I get another orange jumpsuit?"

"No, that happens only on your initial resurrection. In the unlikely event that you need resurrecting again, you will wake up in your own bed, wrapped in a protective sheath. Also, if you ever sustain any injuries, no matter how minor, they will be gone when you wake up the next morning."

"Is there any cost to this? Do I have to earn my keep?"

Everything is free. Food is provided on an all you can eat basis, and…"

"Free, and all you can eat," gasped Adam. "Oh yes, my kind of deal. Lethal for my waistline though. I'll be a fat Elvis within a month."

"No need to worry, Adam. You will only absorb the nutrients you need, no matter how much you eat. You will not store fat, nor suffer seriously from excess. Negative side effects from overindulgence include stomach-ache and an increase in flatulence and faeces, but nothing damaging. You will remain slim and fit."

"Excellent, and what about drink? You know, the alcoholic kind."

"You can drink as much alcohol as you like. No matter how much you drink there are no ill effects: no hangover, no liver damage, no loss of brain cells, and no violent behaviour."

"Wow, no mean drunks, that's a miracle. This is getting better and better."

Adam smiled, imagining an eternity of wanton consumption, before asking, "There's no catch is there? Nothing scary? The food's not made from our recycled faeces: you know, Soylent Brown is faeces. There's always a catch in deals like this, and I've eaten enough dodgy burgers to know the consequences."

"There is no catch, and it's not faeces. You can have almost any product that was available during your lifetime, or the lifetime of those with whom you share the Environment: food and drink, clothes, films, games, anything you want, and at no cost. They are reproductions but you won't be able to tell the difference."

"So, I'll just settle down for an eternity, enjoying anything that takes my fancy, and without anything to pay. This is Paradise!"

"I thought you would like the set-up. Your responses are all I hoped for. You might be my favourite."

Leaning over, the concierge kissed Adam on the cheek.

"Thanks. I'm flattered," said Adam, blushing.

"I'm glad to hear that. You see, even though I have only limited experience with a small number of resurrected, you are the first genuine loser I have encountered."

15

Adam's smile dropped, "Loser?"

"Your profile suggested that the word, loser, was appropriate. Would failure be better?"

"Neither," spluttered Adam, remembering Scarlett's insulting tirade in the bar.

"What about dud?"

"No…!"

"Disappointment, washout, flop, deadbeat …?"

"Look, stop it. I may have had a few setbacks in life, but things were definitely improving before my, err, accident. I got access to my kids. I lost a bit of weight. I had a small flat. At least I wasn't lying in my own vomit in some alleyway."

"Please, there is no need to take offence. In my world, people do not suffer mental and physical breakdown. Meeting someone with your lack of success and downwardly mobile imperative is a unique experience for me. I find you fascinating."

"I wasn't a total loser," Adam protested. "I was an IT consultant. That was a pretty respectable job in 2010. OK, I was mainly self-taught, but I knew my stuff, and I was going to night classes to get the certificate I needed."

"In 2010, an expert in IT could be anything from a billionaire entrepreneur, to departmental technical support, all the way down to someone who botched their family and friend's computers. Where did you fit into the scheme of things?"

Adam conceded defeat:

"I guess I was working my way up to botching computers. But, I fathered two wonderful children. I guess that counts as a success."

The concierge clapped her hands together in glee:

"Wonderful, wonderful. Just what I was hoping to hear. A prime example of 21st century loser talk. There were in excess of six billion people on the planet in 2010, and technology enabling even the infertile to conceive. I suppose you also consider your ability to breathe for thirty-two years worthy of praise, or perhaps that as an adult you masturbated an average of 1.6 times per day … yes that's in your profile too. Chimpanzees are capable of such achievements, and we don't resurrect them."

Contemplating the concierge's words about masturbation, Adam stood and unzipped the jumpsuit, hastily inspecting his groin. Eagerly expecting the 'all you can be' effect, it only took a moment to sadly realise it was all that it ever was.

"Damn, it's just the same as before. I thought you said I was at the peak of my genetic potential. For God's sake, can't you make it bigger?"

"You are limited by your genetics. There is nothing I can do about it."

"Don't you have the technology to alter stuff like this?"

"Yes, but it is not permitted for the resurrected. You are who you are."

"What if a person has a severe disability? You know, like missing arms and stuff. Do you fix that?"

"We have procedures for such cases, but your perceived lack of penile length is not a severe disability. While we are on the subject of physical size, remember I asked which measurement system you preferred?"

"Yeah, sure. What about it?"

"Adam, you are just over an inch tall."

SMALL MATTERS

"I'm an inch tall? How can I be an inch tall? I feel totally normal. Better than normal."

Adam stood and held on to the dancing pole. Unzipping his jumpsuit, he ran his hands up and down his body, but felt nothing disturbing. Glimpsing himself in a large mirrored wall tile, nothing looked out of place.

"I used to have a massive pie belly and floppy man boobs. This new body feels like solid muscle. Am I really so small?"

"Adam, everybody resurrected is reduced to about one-seventieth their original lifetime height. The Earth is no larger than when you died. How else do you think we can accommodate even the billions of people alive in 2010?"

Adam slumped back down onto the seating. "So size really does matter."

"You see, by 2010 over 100 billion people had lived. When you add all the billions that lived and died after that date, then you can appreciate the importance of shrinkage."

"You're going to bring back everyone?"

"That was the original plan, but there are exceptions. Sadly, we do not resurrect anyone prior to 814 BC. Beyond that date, the cost of successful channelling is prohibitively expensive. The absolute limit of our current technology reaches only as far as about 3000 BC, and it is a moving target so every year that passes is another year of people that cannot return."

"Ha, sucks to be ancient."

"We also rarely bring back undesirables."

"Can't argue with that. Those dictators, serial killers, and terrorists don't deserve a second chance?"

"Oh no, those types are darkly fascinating – so committed. They are highly collectable. Most are already resurrected, so when one comes to auction there is immense interest. Sponsors bid generational fortunes to obtain a known name. History's most infamous figures reside in the most lavish VIP Environments."

"Are you kidding me? What kind of world puts scum like that on a pedestal?"

"A world like ours, Adam. Your own time was no different, I believe. Throughout history, atrocity equals notoriety. Colourful characters hold our attention. They lift us from the blandness of our own lives."

"Even if their colour's blood red?"

"Especially so."

"So who are the undesirables?"

"People like you, life's failures, those who led aimless, pointless lives - not very interesting really. Nobody wants them brought back."

"Whoa, I'm an undesirable? If that's true, then why am I here? Why did you bring me back?"

Snuggling up close, running a hand lightly through Adam's hair, the concierge explained, "Understand this, Adam. I had no say in your resurrection. Your kind are the lowest priority. Frankly, I wish you had stayed dead. Your being here has seriously disrupted my finances."

"Stayed dead?"

"I cannot make any of my intended bids and purchases now. I am already committed to another major acquisition. With that, and your unexpected appearance, all my plans are now on hold."

The concierge's voice was gentle, her face serene, smiling, without a trace of malice. Adam could only guess the expression on the face of the andoid's user – if they still had faces this far in the future.

"Ok, if I'm not wanted, then why on earth am I here?"

"In your time, you had retail outlets that ran 'buy one get one half price' deals. It is a little like that. I explained to you how people are time channelled. Sometimes, very rarely, the channel will intersect the death of someone else along the way, albeit in another time and place. Since the cost of piggybacking the secondary subject is minimal, both are resurrected."

"So, I'm the parasite on the pig's back."

"The original target is put up for auction, and those who have some family connection, and can provide a good placement are given priority.

Although to be honest, huge bids often trump all other considerations. The auction is always successful."

"And in my case?"

"As an undesirable, you were offered at cost price to any suitable interested parties. There were none, so being the best placement, I was forced to accept the offer."

"Why the friendly welcome if you hate me so much? Back on the streets nobody concealed their contempt, and I had the scars and bruises to prove it."

"I do not hate you, Adam. On the contrary, your worthlessness intrigues me. I told you that you could be my favourite and I meant it."

With a girlish sigh, she kissed Adam's cheek, then motioned to a nearby doorway.

"Come, even with eternity before us, time is pressing. I have only until midnight to finish your induction."

Adam reluctantly followed the concierge into a small dark circular room. Sharp spotlights dazzled down from the ceiling, illuminating a large, open topped box on a raised platform. The concierge gestured to the box:

"This is a scale model of your new Environment. You can even see your accommodation."

Peering into the box, Adam saw the same scene he remembered from earlier: grassy meadows, a few houses, and a stream with a small bridge. Woodland bounded much of the edging, but there was no sign of the distant vistas Adam had seen.

"Is this it? I remember seeing villages in the distance, and a few hills."

"The distant images are artificially created, including the sky. We use three-dimensional retinal feedback – very realistic. Even up close, you cannot tell it's artificial without touching it. You are unlikely to wander into the boundary since there are many terrain features such as thickets, low walls, and bushes that skirt the edge."

"So I'm living in a box. I thought everyone would be roaming free. What's the deal here?"

"Billions of people from various times and places roaming free would cause many problems. There are millions of these Environments, each with its own sponsor, and an approximate 500-person capacity. Ours is almost empty, only five including you. And now my finances are low."

The concierge cast a sharp glance at Adam.

"Alright, alright, we've covered all that. How big is this box? The real one I mean."

"In reality, the Environment is 75ft long by 75ft wide, but considering the one seventieth size reduction, that's the equivalent of one square mile. Everything in the Environment is reduced in size by the same amount, so it will all seem normal to you. Everything is in proportion: people, products, landscape. The Environment is three feet high, but considering the size reduction, to you it will seem like 210ft."

Adam contemplated eternity with only three feet of sky, gazing up at wandering artificial clouds. Others may have shivered at the prospect, but with death as the alternative, Adam could see the up side.

"But what if I want to leave the box?" he asked. "What if I want to visit friends or relatives in some other box? Can I do that, or is this just a fancy free-range prison."

"Environment transfers are permitted every other day. You contact someone in the Environment you wish to visit, and if they agree to your request, you are transferred while you sleep. You wake up the next morning at your destination in a purpose built wake-up cubicle. After midnight, you are returned, and wake up in your own bed at 8 am. It's simple."

"Yeah, I get it. Like a day trip where you come back fast asleep on the mail train."

"Anything else you would like to know?"

Well, I've just been informed by my stomach, that I haven't eaten since 2010. Is there any chance of trying that 'all you can eat' deal?"

"You can have any food you want. That grey panel, next to where you entered, that is a product dispenser. There are identical ones in the Environment. I warn you though, in an hour it will be midnight, and you will sleep. Eating so late is not a good idea."

"Oh don't worry; I've always been a bit of an insomniac."

Ignoring the concierge's warning, Adam exited the circular room. He approached the dispenser. It resembled a large futuristic larder door, with a soft coloured display and flush gunmetal finish.

"No, you will sleep," protested the concierge. "All the resurrected fall asleep at midnight, you are programmed that way. You have no choice. Twenty seconds before midnight your survival instincts will heighten, you will seek a safe position to rest, and then it is lights out."

Adam shook his head:

"I still want something to eat. How does this thing work?"

"Hold up your hand in front of the blue light, describe the products you want, put your hand down, and they will be produced. If you make a mistake, make a fist. This will reset the order."

"So if I wanted a burger and fries I would just say that and it would appear?"

"Yes, although you can be much more specific if you wish. You can name a specific brand or restaurant, the date, location, anything to narrow down your choice. Be careful how much you eat Adam. Your body is not used to solid food yet, and there is a price to pay for overindulging so close to midnight. You may suffer in the morning."

"Then I'll suffer. Ok, let's give this a go."

Crudely aping the gestures of a classical conductor, Adam flamboyantly held up his hand:

"One take-out half pounder cheese burger with large fries and a supersize coke, Tabbas, Portsmouth, err … April 2009, with chilli sauce on the burger, and salt and vinegar on the fries."

Adam lowered his hand, and frowned:

"The lights turned green. What's that mean?"

"The green light means the product is an exact match to your request. If the light stayed blue it is a near match, and red means best guess. Wave your hand and the door will open."

A wave of his hand and Adam was holding his prize. The look of love was unmistakeable:

"Oh yes, even the wrapper's just like the real thing."

Wrapping discarded, large bite taken, chilli sauce contouring the chin, Adam enjoyed the meaty succulence.

"Oh this is delicious. Why did I ever let Manny talk me out of eating these?"

"I don't understand. You were criticising burgers earlier. You said they were dodgy."

Adam wiped his chin with his sleeve:

"We're always harshest with the ones we love."

Consumed in less than fifteen minutes, Adam washed down the food with the supersize coke, and slouched back in his seat holding his sated belly.

"That was so real. That was just like I remember. I know Tabbas don't do the best burgers in the world but they're what I know. They were always too generous with the sauce. I mean, just look. I've got it all over the jumpsuit. I hope I've got more clothes back at the … you know you haven't told me where I'll be living."

"Do you remember the house where you first appeared?"

"Yeah, but I saw my parents coming out of that house. You're saying I'm back living with my parents."

"I am not permitted to discuss anyone else. You will live in an annexe attached to the house. It has two floors, and full amenities. There is no interconnecting door to the main house, so you have your independence and privacy. A product dispenser is installed, although it has limited functionality for the first ten days. It will dispense food and drink but nothing else. After ten contiguous days of life, you will have full dispenser access."

"Does that mean I have to wear this jumpsuit for ten days? Is there a washing machine? I stink of chilli sauce."

"The orange resurrection suit will be gone by morning, and I promise you will always wake up clean and refreshed. You will find a small selection of clean clothes provided every day. The selection is based on your profile. As I said, full functionality is available after the ten-day acclimatisation period and then you can have any clothes you wish. I am sorry that you will not have your own detached dwelling but my funds are low ... and you are an undesirable."

"Yeah, so you keep saying. Look, it all sounds fine to me. Much better than my shoebox flat back in Portsmouth, so I can't complain."

"It is exactly a minute before midnight. I suggest you find a comfortable place to sleep. You will stay asleep for eight hours. Whilst asleep you will be transported to the annexe. You will wake up in bed."

Adam stood defiantly, shaking his head.

"I told you, I'm an insomniac, the chronic kind. You've no idea know how much time I've spent watching mind numbing gambling channels, and looping infomercials into the early hours."

The concierge just stared as the seconds ticked by. At exactly twenty seconds to midnight, a tsunami of anxiety ripped through Adam, and he stumbled around, glassy eyed, desperately seeking the safest most comfortable spot. He staggered toward the red recliner, clambered aboard and lay still. Midnight, the wave of worry receded, ebbing away with Adam's consciousness.

Before shutting down, the concierge whispered in Adam's ear, "Sleep tight, you beautiful, worthless drain on my finances."

STEPHEN AYRES

THINKING INSIDE THE BOX

A dam awoke in a king-size bed - black satin sheets and chrome frame. Normally, he stretched and yawned, reluctant to meet the day, but now he felt immediately refreshed and alert. It was as if someone had flicked the on-switch. As promised, he was perfectly clean, without any of the usual bed-sweats, toe jam, or the meaty whiff of chilli burger. Even his hair felt freshly shampooed and conditioned – silky and soft without a hint of unwashed greasiness. On a bedside cabinet, a digital clock read 8:00am. What Adam failed to notice was a tiny ten-minute timer counting down.

On the other bedside cabinet were neatly folded clothes and a silver robe. Pulling on the robe, Adam decided to inspect his new home. There were two bedrooms on the first floor, separated by a smooth-sliding wall panel. High-gloss modular bedroom units lined both rooms, many mirrored, enhancing the space and light. Adam could not help flashing open his robe to admire his new body. The friction fat-rash round his groin was gone, his chest no longer a gynomasticated mess. Overcome with joy, Adam struck ludicrous muscleman poses, and raised an eyebrow every now and then, Bond-style. He strutted confidently over to the large picture window overlooking his new Environment. The fields, woods, stream, and cottage were just as he remembered from his first awakening. Admiring the view for a moment, Adam realised his nakedness was still on show, and hurriedly pulled the robe tight.

A spiral staircase led down to a large open plan lounge area - a stylish fusion of Miami deco and modernist executive chic. Risqué, abstract paintings of androgynous nudes adorned pastel pink and blue walls. White leather and chrome Corbusier seating seemed more sophisticated than comfortable, and the wall embedded flat screen was the biggest Adam had seen. Large artificial leafy green pot-plants positioned about the annexe added a welcome softness.

Upstairs, the clock countdown reached zero. 8:10am, and the consequences of overeating so close to midnight struck with unexpected rapidity, a surge of terrible stomach pain accompanied by loud uncontrollable flatulence. Wishing he had heeded the concierge's warning about overindulging, Adam desperately searched for a toilet. In the back room, adjacent the lounge, he pulled on a chrome handle, revealing an en-suite shower cubicle:

"Damn!"

Slamming the door shut, he focused on the next handle. It proved a wise move … a toilet! Adam shot inside, raised the lid, lifted his robe, and planted his bare buttocks on the seat with skilful synchronicity. He gasped with relief as the flow ensued, but became concerned as the surge continued for far longer than seemed humanly possible. Eventually, as the stream subsided, Adam slumped back, vowing never to eat or drink late at night ever again.

At last able to appreciate his surroundings, he noticed the cubicle was agreeably equipped with elegant Victorian style fittings, including an overhead syphon with a traditional metal chain flush. It reminded Adam of the toilet in his last bedsit—his only sanctuary from a life of hopelessness and despair.

In those darkest of days, just as Adam faced homelessness and probably terminal physical decline, Manny literally heaved him off the street, bundled him into a car, and got him into a Church halfway house.

Before this timely and selfless intervention, Adam had endured a worsening selection of grotty bedsits, and desperate, often dangerous neighbours. His separation from Julia forced him to find rented accommodation, but the subsequent loss of his job limited his choices to undesirable neighbourhoods, and so the rot began. For a while, Adam held onto some semblance of dignity. Though never thinking he would fall further, there was always someone or something to rip the floor from under him. Late night drinking, to block out the desperation and hopelessness, soon became all day drinking to block out the disapproving looks of the general public and the unsolicited advice of do-gooders. His parent's attitude quickly turned from sympathy to shame, contact increasingly infrequent. Adam vowed his children would never see him in his reduced state, and so cut himself off completely from both friends and family.

Always acclimatising to the next level down, Adam stubbornly endured. His final bedsit, a ground floor back room in an old Regency townhouse, was as run-down as the building's cracked plaster façade suggested. Every room in the house had threadbare carpets and a grim jumble of dumpster standard furniture. The living experience was further spoiled by a pervasive rodent damp stink, which no amount of cleaning and disinfectant seemed to remove.

Everyday folk prayed for rain. It kept the scum off their streets. For Adam, a night indoors was aural torture. The university dropout upstairs played death-metal at the highest volume his crappy boom box would allow - Absinthe and cannabis rendering him incapable of hitting the off-switch. Worse still, was the cacophony from the bedsit beyond the kitchenette wall, a late night drunken karaoke of sea faring shanties. Sailor Sam, an old grizzled face from the streets, spent hours convincing the world that he was ... Sailor Sam. Adam knew better. Sam was an ex-rent boy, who decades ago, plied his trade amongst the real sailors who roughly docked in many, often-painful ways. There were many nights where Sam could be heard sobbing into his Tennent's Super, muttering about 'them heartless bastards', and wishing his parents would come for him. They died long ago.

Winter was worse. Heating was unaffordable, with quilts, blankets, and woolly hats poor substitutes. Wrapped up, shivering on the sofa, with only a tiny wind-up radio for entertainment, Adam was an eco-activists low carbon wet dream. On the coldest nights, the old pipework froze, and the single glazed windows frosted up. Should Hans Christian Anderson's, "The Little Match Girl' have peered inside, she would have shrieked with laughter, rapping on the windows, taunting Adam with her supply of warmth giving matches.

Any other weather was fine, and the late-night alleys and doorways filled with the many bedsit escapees and homeless, seeking companionship, booze, drugs, and food. Busy weekends usually meant discarded half-drunk cans of beer, and cider. If you were unlucky you got a can of piss, but most were too stoned to notice or care.

Everybody had a street name, and Adam became 'Prof'. This was partly due to his useless depth of general knowledge, but mainly for his ability to calculate the best value booze. Any bums with money trusted Adam to work out how far their money would go in the local drink outlets, sometimes pooling resources to take advantage of extra special offers. Was it, financial efficiency, the free market at work, or just feeding self-destructive addictions? Nobody cared as they enjoyed that extra can. Fortunately, this made Adam popular, and helped him avoid many of the petty, and usually bloody, feuds that were a nightly occurrence.

Even the local pimps liked Adam. Whilst they partied in local nightclubs, scouting for talent, and touting for trade, they often trusted him to keep an eye out for the girls on the streets. This simply meant intervening if some punter or passing yob decided to get violent. Adam was not expected to fight, but just to draw their attention, and soak up the blows, while the girl ran round the corner to fetch a cop. Bruised and bloody, getting a 'good kicking', this passed for employment in Adam's brave new world. Good to their word, the bling bedecked pimps would throw a few beer cans his way. Adam's pimp of choice was a tall swarthy Serbian named Dragoslav. Only around on the weekends, Drago always treated Adam like a real man. If Adam received a bad beating, Drago, in his deep gravelly voice, would ask the cops to give the culprit a particularly uncomfortable night in the cells. Drago also gave the best payment.

"Hey Professor, for your many troubles."

Drago handed Adam a litre bottle of Scottish malt whisky. Hiding the bottle under his jacket, Adam said, "Laphroig, my favourite—pricy stuff."

"Da, it is not cheap, but it tastes a whole lot better than the shit you recommend with the calculator."

Leaning forward, Drago whispered in Adam's ear, "If you wait a short while, Natasja needs a bed for the night. Have a feel of the tits my friend, but no fucking. I want Natasja fresh for tomorrow."

Honouring Adam with a manly nod, Drago turned and got into a blood red Maserati Quattroporte that had just drawn up. The offer was really an order, but female companionship was a rare comfort not to be passed over.

All the hookers had better accommodation than Adam, even desperate illegals like Natasja. If she needed a place to crash, then Immigration was probably snooping, or money owed. None of these considerations mattered as they stumbled drunkenly into Adam's bedsit. Natasja was hard-faced; her gaudy makeup failing to restore lost beauty, the young girl long vanished from her steel blue eyes. A long sleeved, red spandex top extenuated her money-making curves, whilst hiding the purple network of tracks on her arms. She lay back on the sofa, unzipped her top, displaying her bruised and greasy breasts. Awkwardly manoeuvring his obesity, Adam got on top. Natasja pulled his lips towards hers:

"Tongue kiss me Mr Prof. Then you enjoy the tits, da?"

She held him at bay a moment, her face serious, "Remember, no touch the pussy. You make with the prick, and I tell Drago."

"I won't. I promise."

"Good, because if you make with the prick, Drago, he cut the … cut off the ballbags."

Smiling again, Natasja pulled Adam forward, lips engaging, tongues deeply entwining. Her ruby red bee-stung lips were soft and warm, sticky with hastily smeared lipstick. Only the faintest taste of jism tainted the moment. He fondled her breasts like an overeager teenager, tweaking and squeezing the nipples with unseemly haste.

"Ah, switch me on, Mr Prof. You go with the mouth and suck the nipples … but no biting, da. The tits have too much biting tonight."

As their lips parted, Natasja let out a putrid belch of cigarettes and alcohol. Adam passed out, or maybe just fell asleep. Belching, booze, and second base, took their toll on his diminished constitution.

Shafts of cold morning sunlight cut through the gaps in the curtains. Lying on the floor, Adam felt gentle kicking. His body stiffly shifted, eyes opening with painful reluctance. Brushing the floor with a hand, he tested the reality. He tried to raise his head, but found it almost impossible, stuck to the floor with vomit. Through blood shot eyes, Adam saw Natasja standing by the door, looking down on him.

"Ah Mr Prof, I wake you at last. I take shower in the hall. Now I must go."

She waved the still half-full bottle of scotch.

"This I take. It pay for the tits you enjoy, da."

Before turning to go, Natasja treated Adam to a genuine smile, saying, "Mr Prof, you are better man than many. You didn't make with the prick or the fists. You not even try. The man like you should not live like this. Why you not make with the wedding and the family? You make a good parent, da?"

"You too," croaked Adam, his throat acid raw.

"Maybe …one time. Some are forced to leave the families behind." With a look of regret she added, "Some can never go back."

Slamming the door behind her, Natasja quickly left.

"I know," thought Adam, his head splitting. "God, do I know."

Publicly foraging for food was a constant activity. Adam was always on the lookout for discarded wrappers, whether in bins or simply lying on the street. Adam's worst food experience were the remnants of an Indian meal discarded in an alley by a group of horny teens, more interested in pleasures below the waist than the culinary treasures of the East. Back at the bedsit, Adam was sickened to find three or four used condoms in the Korma. Eating around them, the chicken was still moist, the sauce cold but creamy.

Suspicious of the taste, he chomped a large mouthful of Nan bread, only to find that one of the filthy bastards had wiped his arse with it. A gallon of water later, the urge to vomit subsided and the hard won calories were retained.

Living up to his nickname, Adam calculated that the highest rate and volume of take-away accidently dropped or intentionally thrown was outside the late night/early morning burger and kebab grills. Tabbas Grill & Chippy seemed the most prolific. When the clubs kicked out, those young men without a girl for the night, headed for a greasy fix to take their mind off their romantic failings.

Only the hardened veterans managed to walk and eat, staggering drunkenly along the littered pavement, often detouring into the road but doggedly holding onto their food. The others should have handed their food straight to Adam, as they fell flat on their pissed faces, or threw away the chips instead of the paper wrapper. The too far-gone were hilarious to watch, determined to pick up the meal they dropped, approaching from different angles and at different speeds. Some managed the pick-up, some head-butted a wall, most meandered off into the night.

One of the owners of Tabbas took pity on Adam, and twice weekly, gave him free burger and fries in the service road behind. He always ate the food immediately, never taking the food back to the bedsit in case the neighbours demanded a share. Tabbas was a definite highlight in Adam's life, but back inside the bedsit, he concealed a treasure that eclipsed all other aspects of his lowly existence.

It was a couple of months after Adam moved in to his bedsit, that a plywood wallboard came loose revealing a locked panelled door. After working away for a few minutes with an Allen key, he picked the lock. The door had no handle so Adam wedged it open with a kitchen spatula. Beyond the door lay a Victorian washroom with an original Thomas Crapper china pedestal and cast iron high-level cistern. Though dusty and grimy, the toilet was functional, after removing a bung blocking the water inlet. Adam thanked the Gods for this discovery, seeing it as some life-transforming omen.

Everyone in the house used the under-stairs communal toilet and bathroom. It may have been well stocked and clean, but was next door to Pete, the violently demented skinhead. If he heard so much as a wet fart, he would bang on the wall, and threaten all sorts of physical abuse on the wilting defecator. Sailor Sam, too scared to use the facility, relieved himself in the neighbour's hedges.

Within a week, the Crapper gleamed as new: scrubbed, polished, and disinfected. The wall received a new lick of paint, and the floor a tasteful vinyl remnant. The tiny washroom became a priority in Adam's life. He always kept a good supply of Wet-wipes in the Crapper—a handy tip from the street hookers when they had only a few minutes to clean up between punters. Adam used them as the last wipe, ensuring good hygiene no matter how drunk or tired he was. 'Aloe Vera Babysoothers' were his favourites, but any cut-price wipe was good. The final job was to disguise the door with the original wallboard, hiding the door from spying neighbours.

Here, on the Crapper, there was serenity. Here, on the Crapper, Adam dreamt about all he had lost:

'Warm summer days walking along the promenade, with the twins in their pushchair. Exchanging cute kisses with Julia, and letting a friendly Labrador lick the twin's fingers, giggles ensued.

Visions of better days, reminding Adam of visiting the seaside as a child with his parents - a faded Kodachrome drive from London to the Dorset Coast. The beach was pure joy: white cliffs, seashells, grey sand, and a Cornetto ice cream if he was lucky. Baby Robert, Adam's brother, always got a sneaky lick of ice cream.

Peering into the eyes of his ever-smiling baby brother, Adam became four again, running into his parent's room, crying from a nightmare. His father lifted him into the bed, placing him between both parents. As his mother gently snored, Adam's father quietly recounted fantastic tales of princes, princesses, scary villains, and magical lands. Somehow, Adam always woke up in his own bed, his mind rich with images of children lost deep in the forest, evil trolls, and mysterious genies who could grant wishes.'

Back in the grotty bedsit, Adam descended further into misery: financially, physically, and mentally. The bedsit was beyond help; infused with piss, sick, stale beer, and rotten food. Spending more time cocooned in the sanitary bubble of the Crapper, aware of the filth on the other side of the door, this tiny cubicle became a haven, a final remnant of civilisation.

With the rent well overdue, it was only a matter of time before Adam lost everything. When faced with a downturn in their lives most people swore there was still light at the end of the darkest tunnel, but for Adam, for now, there was just Aloe Vera.

Now, in the annexe washroom, hundreds of years removed from his despairing past, Adam had the chance of a new life, and a fresh beginning. Except for eating close to midnight, Adam's old self-destructive habits of gluttony and binge drinking were now of no consequence. Reconnecting with his family was now a priority. Starting in this small cubicle, invoking the positive spirit of his beloved Crapper, Adam vowed to make a success of this second chance.

After carefully using two pieces of toilet roll, weak single-ply, he reached up to a small shelf for a wet-wipe. There were none. Adam stood up and searched around the small space, but this only confirmed their absence.

'So much for my profile', thought Adam.

Sitting back down, he employed another few pieces of the fragile tissue, and hoped for the best. Was this was an inauspicious start to Adam's brave new world? Perhaps it was another chance to be like 'normal' people?

VIRO

Staring in shocked disbelief at his new clothes, Adam damned his profile: hot pink hibiscus Hawaiian shirt, slim fit white trousers, and blue canvas deck shoes. More acceptable, yet just as mystifying, was the leather strapped Tommy Bahama hula-girl wristwatch, perfectly accessorising the Aloha clothing ensemble.

Minutes later, lying on the floor, grunting with effort, Adam found the tight trousers impossible to button up. He squirmed and cursed for some time, before reaching a breakthrough moment. Underpants discarded, stomach sucked in, the button was finally fastened.

There was a sharp rap at the front door. Adam recognised a familiar voice, albeit with an overly officious edge, "Adam, are you in there? This is your father."

"Hi Dad, just be a minute." Adam slowly pulled up the zipper, avoiding any painful mishap. Slipping into the deck shoes, he opened the door.

Harry Eden, slim in his original life, was now of solid build. Always clean-shaven, easy going in manner, favouring casual shirts and slacks, he now struck a strikingly contrasting pose. A large waxed handlebar moustache was new, as was his choice of attire: an old-fashioned tweed suit, complete with breeks, an ivory-topped cane, and deerstalker hat. Adam found the new look disturbing.

"I can't say we were expecting you," said Harry offering an overly firm, though brief handshake. He arched an eyebrow:

"Planning a trip to Hawaii?"

"It's my profile. I had no choice. I look like I'm going on a cruise."

"Ten days and you can wear what you want. Hmm, let me guess. You're late twenties, yes?"

"Spot-on, Dad. And you're … mid-thirties?"

"Late forties," Harry corrected, rapping Adam's forehead with his cane.

"Ouch, not so hard. I just thought you looked younger than that. One thing though, have you got hair hiding under that hat? You used to be bald. I have no memories of you with hair."

"Yes," said Harry, stone-faced, feeling no compunction to remove the hat. "I'll get straight to the point. Adam, you're invited to a welcoming dinner at the cottage."

"By the bridge?"

"That's the one. Three o clock this afternoon. We're having curry I believe. You'll get to meet the neighbours, Stern and Kaylee. Nice couple – Americans. They live across the stream, far up on the high meadow. One of those designer houses, single storey, all glass. Can't see their place from here."

Harry turned to leave.

"Wait, Dad. Why don't you come in? I'll make a cup of tea."

"Rather not, if you don't mind. Have a wander round the viro. Get your bearings."

"Viro? Short for environment, yes?"

"Bravo, they obviously cloned you a couple of brain cells. Now, I have to get back to the Manor. Your mother's waiting for her breakfast."

"Manor?"

"Eden Manor. And it's a shame the concierge saw fit to stick this ugly flat-roofed carbuncle on the side." Harry waved his stick angrily at the annexe. "Damn thing's only fit for undesirables."

Before Adam could respond, a loud voice shrieked from the main house, "Why are you still talking to him! Get back here and make my breakfast!" It was Edna Eden, Adam's mother.

"Three o clock, at the cottage, it's a tradition," said Harry hurrying away.

Back in the annexe, Adam checked out a large aluminium wall panel in the lounge area. Laser etched into the cold touch metal were the words 'Computing and Communication'. The panel slid aside with the softest push, revealing a slim-line PC, and large LCD screen. A shelf pulled out with gloss black keyboard and mouse, and Adam nodded approval at the Razer branding. Completing the setup, an ingenious folding ergonomic chair swung out from under the shelf. After booting the computer, Adam found the Windows desktop familiar, except for five circular icons: Products, Media, History, Environments, and Events.

Adam resisted the temptation to investigate all the icons, instead going straight for Environments. Deftly navigating numerous tabs and menus, he found an Arrange Visit utility. Simple to operate, Adam entered the name Emmanuel Beaumont in the space provided, and a list of three names appeared. Adam refined the selection by adding Manny's birth year. One name remained, accompanied by flashing blue text, BLOCKED ACCOUNT. Repeating the procedure changed nothing. Undeterred, he tried another name, this time Scarlett Slaughter. The flashing yellow text, NOT ALIVE, made Adam shudder.

Giving the utility one last try, he entered the name of his son, Charles Eden - BLOCKED ACCOUNT, flashing red. Adam stabbed the Enter key repeatedly in frustration. After a search on his daughter, Emma Eden, produced the same sad result, he tearfully shut down the utility. At least they were alive.

Fetching a cold drink from the nearby product dispenser, Adam sat back at the computer. This time he investigated the Media icon, which called up the most extensive media library he had ever seen. It was complete, impressive, and intuitively searchable. Every piece of audio or visual media imaginable was available, right up until the exact moment of Adam's death. Within a minute he found what he was seeking - CCTV feeds. Breaking a sweat in anticipation of what lay ahead, Adam tracked down the relevant feed outside Horatios Tavern, and rewound five minutes from the end.

The image was grainy, silent, the camera facing the promenade, probably hidden above the tavern's faux regency sign. Adam watched his fat former self casually exit the premises, hands in pockets, looking about for a place to piss. Out of shot, somewhere to the left, were the father and son. Fat Adam casually walked to a dark part of the walkway to the right of the screen and pissed into the harbour. Adam stared hard at the screen, looking for clues. Fat Adam zipped his flies and began walking back to the bar. Something off-camera distracted Fat Adam, perhaps the father and son. Adam futilely willed the camera to turn left as Fat Adam walked out of view towards the distraction. Abruptly, a man ran into view from the right of the picture. The man entered Horatios, and the feed abruptly ended at the exact time of Adam's death.

Switching off the computer, closing the panel, Adam chose to take his father's advice and explore the viro. So far, the first day in this new 'paradise' had proved depressing, no wet-wipes, no questions answered, rebuffed by both family and friends.

34

THREE FEET OF SKY

The trousers were too tight for comfortable walking, and Adam experienced significant chafing. Undoing the button would have helped but Adam decided against the idea, envisioning his trousers falling down, revealing his lack of underwear. Maintaining a very straight-legged short stride minimized the discomfort, as did clenching his buttocks.

Walking alongside the shallow stream that bisected the viro, Adam headed towards the wall. Fatigue quickly set-in due to the energy draining mincing waddle and he began panting and wheezing. Deciding to rest, Adam carefully reclined against a small bush, narrowly avoiding a split in the crack of his trousers,

Concealed by the shrub, Adam noticed a distant flash of bronzed flesh way back down the stream. A man crossed the cobbled bridge, confident and naked. At this distance, Adam could discern long raven black hair, honed musculature, and huge, pendulous, swinging, genitalia. Feeling somewhat self-conscious, Adam slinked lower, realising the man was coming his way. He tried to suppress the panting but it only made it worse, resulting in low volume squeaky wheezes.

Within a few minutes, the bronzed Adonis was standing only a few feet away from Adam's hiding place, pausing a while, purposefully tossing the black mane, swivelling his body from left to right - every position perfectly posed. Casting an unexpected glance at Adam's bush, the imposing stranger struck a muscular side chest pose. Standing side-on, hands clasped tightly together, he turned his chiselled torso slightly frontward. Chest puffed out, the powerful arms tensed against each other, and his muscles gunned into massive ripped magnificence. Peering furtively through the reeds, Adam noticed a striking metallic tattoo on the man's upper arm - 'STERN The Golden Hind'. After relaxing the pose, the man stretched, yawning nonchalantly and then headed towards the woods.

Breathing a sigh of relief, and raising his head slightly, Adam watched as the man slowly disappeared amongst the trees. Far away, across the meadow, Harry and Edna stood at one of the Manor's large bay windows, gawking at the man. Even from this distance, Adam could see his mother lowering a pair of opera glasses, a sly contented grin on her young face.

For now, laying low was an imperative, at least until free of naked men and prying eyes. Gazing up at the greyish blue three feet of sky revealed an absence of clouds. A sky bereft of birds and their song, without the subtlest breeze rustling the foliage. Reaching out, Adam picked a blade of grass, and rubbed it between his fingers. The grass was dry, artificial, with a weak aroma of metallic rubber. He attempted to scratch out some dirt, but the ground remained unscathed. Perhaps the resurrected were the only organic life in the viro. Adam wondered how he would cope for the many centuries, perhaps millennia ahead. Still, he reminded himself, it was better than being dead.

An hour later, after following the edge of the woodland, Adam reached his goal, the viro wall. Though the wall was invisible, Adam recognised a stone-topped earth bank from the concierge's model that he remembered ran alongside. Climbing up onto the stone capping was easy, and once atop the mound, he looked for signs of the wall. Although he knew the view was some kind of artificial projection, all he saw no matter how hard he stared, was a believable landscape of gently rolling countryside: small rural hamlets, and a patchwork of fields surrounded by numerous hedgerows and dense woodland. Taking a risk, unusual for Adam, he reached forward into what looked like empty air. Only a foot away, his hand touched the invisible barrier. Expecting a hard smooth surface, it was instead surprisingly soft, almost foam-like. Adam steeled his resolve, and pushed his hand hard against it. The harder he pushed the more resistance he encountered, the artificial view briefly warping around the contours of his hand. Without warning, the wall popped powerfully back to shape, sending Adam sliding backwards on his smooth soled shoes. Losing his footing, he fell from the earth bank, landing heavily on his back.

Slightly dazed, and aching all over, he lay still for a few seconds, worried about serious injury. After building up the courage to stand, a brief inspection revealed no evidence of broken bones. Adam checked his watch, 2:00pm, one hour until the dinner. Still sore, he slowly made his way to the cottage, a pronounced limp adding to his already incongruous walking style.

A MATTER OF TASTE

Investigating the cottage was a frustrating anti-climax. Although much larger than expected, with numerous doors and windows, Adam could not gain entry nor look inside. Even a flimsy looking plywood door to the back of the building seemed to have the strength of steel, not budging a single inch despite Adam's best efforts. Behind the cottage was a long one-storey windowless building with twelve evenly spaced doors. As he expected, each door was locked.

Walking back to the front of the cottage he spotted a window that he had not yet checked. Rubbing the glass, staring as hard as possible, he could not see a thing:

"Damn frosted glass."

He circled the cottage two more times, before finally giving up. With just ten minutes to go until three o'clock, he waited, sitting uncomfortably on the wall of the cobbled bridge.

Suddenly, a black two-seater hunting buggy appeared in the distance: rapid, midnight black, scarab-like, and dangerous. After recklessly charging down the meadow on large off-road tires, a flash of the wheel and the vehicle skidded into a parking position on the far side of the stream. Two figures disembarked, obscured by the hump of the bridge.

Split thigh, backless and strapless, a flame haired vision appeared first, barely contained in a glossy red dress. One hand waving, Martini glass in the other, she skittered expertly across the cobbles on red high-heels.

"Hi there handsome, I'm Kaylee! It's s'good to see a new face," she squealed.

Following close behind, Adam recognized the man from earlier in the day, though now wearing clothes: tailored pinstripe suit, sharp lines, power shoulders, classic black oxfords. Stopping atop the bridge, striking another perfect pose, the man coolly adjusted the cuff of his jacket, before continuing.

Kaylee ran straight for Adam, kissing him on the cheek with an exaggerated smacking sound. Her scent betrayed a sultry femininity without a trace of fragility: cotton candy and wild tangerine, cut with vanilla musk.

"Love your outfit, Robert. Kinda reminds me of Andre, my old hairdresser in L.A. He was just soooo gay."

Before Adam could correct his mistaken identity, he experienced the perfect handshake.

"The name's Stern. Pleased to meet you, Robert."

Masculinity and sophistication, Stern smelled expensive, in control: juniper, dry cinnamon, with earthy vetiver. His striking blue eyes, almost hypnotic in their intensity, fixed on Adam.

"It's about time we got some new blood around here. Hmm, those pants, they can't be comfortable."

"They're not … but my name's not Robert. I'm Adam … Adam Eden."

Stern rubbed his strong, lightly stubbled chin, "So you're not the Aussie guy, the property developer?"

"That's my younger brother, Robert. I've never been to Oz. Never been out of the UK."

"Strange, your folks never mentioned you."

Putting an arm around Adam's shoulder, Stern drew close:

"You were the guy in the bushes this morning, taking a sneaky peek."

"I was just resting," spluttered Adam, his face blushing a guilty shade of beetroot.

"You must have been busy there. I could hear you heavy breathing."

"No, no … my trousers were tight. I was getting tired."

"I do have that effect on people. Did you like my muscleman pose? That was just for you."

"Err, I guess so, but only in a macho way, not in a … sex way."

"Now, I take a naked stroll most mornings. If you want to watch, then it's fine by me. In a macho way of course."

Stern smiled and winked.

"I'm not gay! I prefer women!" Adam spluttered.

"Ha, so do I. Don't worry I'm only kidding around. You are so easily intimidated, and I like that in a person."

Kaylee pointed excitedly further down the stream, as a white golf cart slowly rolled into view:

"They're here! It's Edna and Harry!"

As the golf cart approached, so did the sound of bickering. Harry steered erratically, almost driving into the stream, as Edna issued loud warnings, berating his driving skills.

The bickering continued as they left the vehicle.

"If you were better organized we'd have got here with time to spare," scolded Edna.

"You wanted to take the scenic route around the wood. I could have timed it better if we'd just come directly across the meadow."

"It's too steep!"

"The bloody thing only goes 15 miles per hour!"

Edna floated up in a voluminous 50's style debutante dress, complete with silk gloves, and diamond-studded tiara – her thick make-up only a taste away from fondant icing. Harry, now moustache-less, wore black Victorian eveningwear, complete with a silver-topped ebony cane. Adam saw his father with hair for the first time, slicked back and short.

Where's the top hat?" asked Stern. "Never seen you come to dinner without the hat."

Edna cast an angry look at Harry:

"It fell in the water, thanks to his 'expert' driving."

Adam walked tentatively over to his mother. Beneath the make-up, he guessed she was younger looking than him, perhaps twenty-four or twenty-five.

"Hello Mum, it's great to see you again."

Without smiling, Edna nodded, "We weren't expecting you. We thought Robert was coming back."

"Sorry to disappoint you," joked Adam.

"No you're not."

"Honestly, things are different now. New life, new me. I'm making a real effort."

"Effort? You don't know the meaning of the word."

Somewhat troubled by the altercation, Stern intervened:

"Wow, Edna, you look ravishing. Kaylee will have to keep me on a leash. And don't worry, I'm gonna keep a close eye on Eden Junior."

Edna sufficiently subdued, Stern turned to Harry:

"You could have given the boy some other clothes. At least some better fitting trousers. Those look painfully tight."

"Ten days and he can wear what he likes," snorted Harry. "Can't break with tradition."

"Tradition, I respect that, Harry. You stick to your guns."

Stern whispered in Adam's ear, "Come over tomorrow. I'll fix you up with something less constricting."

At precisely 3pm a soft bell sounded.

Stern opened the door and ushered the group in:

"Ladies, gentlemen, flavoursome pleasure awaits."

Gentle sitar music piped from unseen speakers, the air smelt of spicy lemon and poppadum. Subdued lighting revealed a large dining area with black heavy velour seating. Paintings of prancing elephants and turbaned Rajahs adorned dark-red flock wallpaper.

A diminutive man in a smart black suit greeted each guest, nodding deferentially. He was not Indian, Adam decided, though perhaps Mediterranean. His accent had a definite Latin flavour.

"I am Frederick, your waiter, and today this is the Royal India. Adam, may I take this opportunity to welcome you to the Environment. As you are the guest of honour you will sit at the head of the table. Please help yourself to dhal, poppadum, chutney, and raita. I will return in a short while to take your orders."

Everyone sat around a large red-clothed table, Adam noting that his nearest dining companions were his mother and Stern. Frederick disappeared through a beaded doorway next to a dark-wood bar, a vista of spirits and liqueurs lining the shelves behind. The décor was pristine: no peeling paper, or beer sticky carpets. Whether a perfect 1970's recreation, or ironic pastiche, Adam approved.

A raven-haired woman appeared through the beads. She looked like Frederick's female twin:

"I am Amelia, and I will be serving drinks. Adam, I would like to welcome you to the Environment."

After taking the drink orders, Amelia also disappeared through the beaded doorway.

"Are they robots?" Adam whispered to Stern. "You know, like the concierge."

Stern, was engrossed in the menu:

"Well, actually they are androids, but fully autonomous. They're not avatars. They have their own minds, so not quite like the concierge."

"One other thing," said Adam. "Is this place always locked until three, or is it variable."

"It's open all day, from eight until midnight. It only locks for about half an hour for interior refitting."

"Refitting?"

"Yeah, if you book an Indian meal, then it refits to reflect the expected style. If you choose something else, such as Mexican for example, then it refits in that particular style. Now, if you don't mind, I'm nearly ready to choose."

Turning his attention to his father, Adam said, "Hey, Dad, you look good without the 'stache. Must have been quite a job shaving that thing off."

Harry reached for his cane and rapped it on Adam's head:

"It's a false moustache, you twit. Can you imagine eating a curry with that thing above your mouth. Mess, total mess."

Rubbing his sore head, Adam looked daggers at his father, but before a row could break out, Amelia returned with the drinks - leaving a large pitcher of vodka martini just for Kaylee. Frederick returned to take the orders, addressing Stern:

"Will Sir be ordering for the group again?"

"If it's OK with everyone. Anyone not like the idea?"

Nobody objected, but Adam crossed his fingers that he would not get a Korma. Stern chose an impeccable selection of breads, rice, and starters, before turning to the main meals.

"Easiest ones first. Well. I know Kay doesn't like curry, so Chicken Maryland for her. And Harry, you never stray from your Lamb Rogan Josh. Choice of a true gentleman."

Harry gave a thumbs up, nodding with sycophantic approval. Turning his attention to Adam, Stern rubbed his hands together:

"Now, let's get down to business. The new arrival. What does our honoured guest prefer?" Stern's face clicked into granite mode as he unleashed his powerful gaze. If this was a staring contest then Stern was the master. Adam froze, unable to resist the piercing blue eyes probing deep into his psyche. An almost imperceptible twitch of Adam's neck jawline, and Stern clapped his hands:

"Chicken Madras. You like the heat, but not the fire."

Adam nodded, relieved to be free of the intense stare, and glad it was not Korma. Without a second thought, Stern chose a King Prawn Korma for Edna. He handed back the menu to Frederick, and ordered an Erachi Olathiyathu for himself.

"Erachi Olathiyathu, Sir, good choice."

"Sorry it's not on the menu, Frederick."

"A true gourmand need never apologise. I shall be pleased to prepare the dish."

Before Frederick could leave, Edna changed her mind:

"I always have the Korma. I fancy a bit of a change. Are there any dishes similar to Korma? I don't like spicy curries, just the creamy ones."

"Mum, try a King Prawn Pasanda," recommended Adam. "It's like a luxury Korma, only more creamy, and nuttier. Trust me, you'll love it."

Edna gave Adam a stony stare:

"No, Stern is right as usual. I'll stick with the King Prawn Korma."

The starters arrived, generously portioned, colourful, and delicious. All conversation subsided, the first tasty mouthfuls savoured.

Finishing his Samosas, Harry was noticeably uncomfortable:

"Stern, I noticed, purely accidently, that you're still doing the early morning nude thing."

"It bothers you?"

"Well … Edna asked me to …"

Edna interrupted, smiling coquettishly at Stern:

"Don't listen to him. It doesn't bother me at all. People should be free to express themselves. For goodness sake, there's no law against it. It's just that Harry gets a little…"

"It doesn't bother me either," spluttered Harry. "I'm usually very busy at that time in the morning, so I never even notice."

"Well, if you're both sure it's Ok. If you've got some hang up about it just let me know."

Finishing his main meal, Stern leant over and nudged Adam:

"Do you wanna hear how me and Kaylee died?"

Adam nodded, carefully piling chicken and sauce onto his Nan bread, before manoeuvring it towards his mouth.

"Well, it was March 2036, about 10pm, total darkness except for the street lamps. Picture a Pontiac Firebird doing over 90 along Interstate 95 just out of New York. We were both in the driving seat, if you catch my drift, enjoying some sweet ass action."

"He means anal sex, Adam," explained Harry, prompting a hard slap round the head by Edna.

Stern continued, gesticulation dramatically, "I reached the point of no return, and shot my load. Kaylee screamed 'Oh Yeah' and jammed her foot on the accelerator. That's all we remember but reports said we lost control of the Firebird, it flipped, caught fire, we were toast. Intense, totally intense."

Stern sat back, noticeably aroused:

"So Adam, tell me, how did you pass on"

Adam took time chewing a chunk of chicken, before answering, "It was November, 2011. I was with some friends in a Portsmouth pub. I went outside for a wee. Then I fell in the sea and drowned."

"And your last memory?"

"Zipping up my trousers."

Stern started chuckling, almost uncontrollably, causing everyone except Edna to break into fits of laughter.

"That's one for the ages," said Stern, finally composing himself. "So, Adam, what did you do in your first life? I can usually guess, but I'm having trouble reading you."

"Well, I worked for a large accountancy firm ..."

"Hah, as a low paid temp," spat Edna.

"But I was trying to get into the IT department. I was on a course ... then ... things went a bit wrong," Adam cleared his throat.

"Wrong?" asked Stern.

"I pretty much lost everything. The wife left me. She took the kids, and the house. I even lost my job. Nearly ended up on the streets, but I managed to keep hold of a bedsit. Things were looking up a bit before I died ..."

"So, how old were you when you passed on?"

"32 ... still young enough to have turned things around. Shouldn't have gone out for a piss."

"Hmm, you're definitely not the type for resurrection. Can't see a guy like you generating any auction action. You were tacked onto the back of a real target, weren't you."

Triumphantly, Stern clicked his fingers and pointed at Adam:

"You're an undesirable!"

Adam wanted to disappear under the table. The smug expression on his mother's face was enough to realise his humiliation was almost complete. Stern, however, seemed more curious than judgemental:

"Look, I also suffered setbacks in my life. Luckily for me, fortune intervened, and changed everything."

"So what did you do?"

"Well, the morning before I died I was given a UN ambassadorship. You know, help feed the starving and all that. I'm sure I could've made a difference."

"So you were a politician."

"Oh no, not even close. You see, Adam, I was a Hind-Reader."

"What the Hell is a …"

"Oh, there were already a few rumpologists plying their trade, but I considered them mere charlatans. You see, whereas they relied on sight and touch, I used a finely honed sense of smell combined with anal empathy. Whereas they falsely claimed to see into a person's future, I was a diagnostic tool, penetrating deep into the personality."

"Are you saying that you smelled peoples' arses for a living?"

Edna shouted angrily at Adam, "Don't be disrespectful. The man's a genius. You're lucky he's even talking to you."

"Adam, my gift was real. I became a household name across the globe. You see, I am Stern Lovass, the greatest Hind-Reader in history.

RISE OF A HIND-READER

All Adam wanted was for the humiliation to end, and to get back to the annexe. So, when Stern offered to explain his rise to fame, Adam eagerly agreed, hoping this would waste some time, and shift the spotlight away from him. Though Harry and Edna had obviously heard the story many times, they positively gushed with excitement, sitting forward, wide eyed, waiting for Stern to begin. Conversely, Kaylee drained her Martini glass, and sat back in her chair, eyes closed.

"I won't lie to you," Stern began. "I was born with a silver spoon in my mouth, and it was one mother of a silver spoon. I'm talkin' billions here. My family were the Saghausens of Virginia. Shipping and finance was just the tip of the iceberg. I couldn't tell you everything we owned … basically because I never gave a shit, and I was sole heir to the lot."

"I guessed Stern Lovass wasn't your real name," said Adam.

"Lucius Saghausen, named after my great grandfather who put us on the road to riches. Ironic really, considering I turned my back on the whole enterprise. I think my father always knew I was bad for business. You can't blame him for not trying though. When I turned 18, he sent me England to study finance at the LSE. He sweetened the deal with a mansion flat in Kensington, a maid, cook, and chauffer, and best of all … 5 Ks Sterling a week to spend on whatever the hell I wanted."

"I'm guessing there's a 'but'."

"Of course there's a 'but'. One that led to a life filled with butts. As soon as I hit London, I ignored my father and enrolled at the London College of Fashion. Not for the study, I didn't give a shit about that. It was for the sex. I figured the chicks would be many, and the few guys probably gay. Trouble is, before I even started the course, father found out and took quick and ruthless

45

revenge—he could always turn emotion into decision in the blink of an eye. Ok, I kept the flat, and the maid, but lost the cook, chauffer … and the Merc. Worst of all, I had my allowance cut to a lousy 500 quid a week. So you see, Adam, I know what it is to suffer."

"500 quid a week! I was lucky if I …"

Harry's cane swooped across the table, this time missing its intended target:

"Don't be an idiot, Stern's talking about relative poverty not absolute. Relative poverty!"

Adam protested, "Oh, it's just that my poverty was pretty much absolute."

"Why don't you just shut up," shrieked Edna. "You're ruining the story."

Stern, smiling, raised his hands, calming the situation:

"My friends, my friends, simmer down. Adam is right. Remember, I always had whatever I wanted. I couldn't imagine being down and out on the street, even though I made a few purchases there. But now we get to the important bit. The incident that changed my life.

"Money meant everything to me, but I wasn't gonna give in. I was low on the disposables, but girls still didn't stand a chance. Killin' above and below the waist, you've seen what I got. So, I was walking across Hyde Park, the weather fine, unusually hot for September. As I got near Oxford Street, I noticed some hipster chick filming me with her phone. Now, understand this, I was drunk, not totally wasted, but not quite in control. Like some douche, I stripped of my top and started dancing as I walked."

"Wow, that's so lame."

"Yeah, I said I was douche-like. My music player was partly to blame. It meant I was moving to a beat nobody else could hear. I remember waving, and shouting out ,'yeah baby, just zoom in' and 'get in close there'. Once I reached the edge of the park, I put my top on and went shopping. It was only an hour later I got a text from one of my friends in the States. It just said, 'Yo who dat bitch'. A few minutes later, another came through, 'Way to get your ass smelled Lou'. Then some guy from college phoned. He was killing himself laughing. Told me to get on the net as soon as possible, something about a Butt-reek video."

"Butt-reek?"

"Trust me, it took me by surprise. I logged on and searched. Only took a couple of minutes to find the video. It was going viral - the hits ticked up hundreds every second. It was me in the park, acting like a fool. Thing was, there was a bloody dog, a Labrador, sniffing my butt all the way. Every stupid move I made, it just pranced in step, nose up my crack. You know, I never felt a thing. 'Butt-reek and his Bitch' they called it. Hmm, I suppose I can't complain about the accuracy of the title. By that evening, people were adding versions with voiceovers and funny captions. By the next morning, there was even a Sparta remix, and I knew I had an internet meme on my hands."

"Wait, what's an internet meme?"

Stern looked incredulously at Adam, "I thought you were an IT guy. That's like a basic lack of knowledge. There were plenty of memes out there before you died: double rainbow guy, lol cats, the Trollollo man. Charlie bit my finger, surely you've heard of that?"

Adam shook his head, "I have absolutely no idea what you're talking about."

Edna leant forward, "That's because you spent five years lying in your own vomit."

"An internet meme is something, in this case my video, which spreads via the web and evolves along the way. Within a few days, there were so many versions out there. Herschel Pick, an old college buddy from the US, begged me to be my agent. He said he could get me on TV. I said yes, and a week later I was on Breakfast News, along with the Hazel the Labrador, and the girl who took the video. To save my father further disappointment, I didn't use my real name, but instead called myself Mr Butt-reek. Herschel said the new name would get me more appearances, and he was right. Over the next month, I appeared on kid's TV, radio spots, a couple of news items for American TV, and opened a number of high profile events. I had a great time.

"Then Herschel gave me the bad news. My 15 minutes were almost over. He only had one more job for me, and that was some sleazy late night chat show. You know the type: flaming presenter, sex talk, stupid games, and Z-list celebrities …"

"Like you," said Adam.

Yeah, like me. At least they had a well-stocked green room, and I drank far too much. I was first up, and made a complete fool of myself. I was irritable, disinterested, and kept insulting the presenter. Blame it on the drink, but I made a few gay jokes, and ended up getting booed.

"Next up was Letty Petunia, some minor reality star. She was cute, amazing legs. Again, blame it on the drink, but I decided to leap off the guest sofa, go on all fours like a dog, and start sniffing her arse. That got a few laughs, but she didn't look very impressed. We both sat down, but I didn't stop there. Waving my arms about like some Las Vegas magician, I stared into her eyes, and announced, 'Poor Letty, your arse speaks to me. You have suffered great heartache today. Abandoned and betrayed when the future seemed so full of love and contentment. But, you have a sting in the tail. Wreak your vengeance girl … you'll feel so much better.' I stopped making stuff up after that, mainly because I was feeling a bit sick."

"How did Letty take it?"

"She burst into tears, and I thought I was gonna get lynched. People were standing up, waving their fists, swearing. If it got any worse I was gonna make a run for it. Even the security looked pissed off, and I'm sure the presenter was about to give me a slap. Then, Letty saved me. She stood up and told everyone that I was right. Turned out, only an hour before the show, her Premiere League fiancée ditched her for some lingerie model. Letty explained that the church was already booked, and that top designer, Hugo Capel, had shown her the most wonderful dress. She vowed revenge, saying she'd already talked to her agent, and everyone should expect some saucy secrets to come out. Then after praising my 'gift', she planted the biggest kiss on my cheek. The audience went wild with applause. At that moment, my 15 minutes became a lifetime.

"The offers came rolling in, and I ditched Herschel. He was a nice guy, but he was so out of his depth. My new team suggested a more transatlantic name, Stern Lovass, and within a week I was signed up to present my own show, 'Back-Hatch Matchmaker'. It was a dating show, where each week, five guys and five girls would get their arses read by me, and I decided who would pair off with who for a weekend together. I was introduced as the Hind-Reader, and I predicted how the date would go. Oh, it was such fun, and was a massive massive hit.

"After two successful seasons in the UK, it transferred to the US with me as the host. I had to be careful with the language, seeing as I spent so much time in the UK: ass not arse, pants not trousers, and fanny … well the less said about that the better. The ratings were phenomenal, and the show ran for twelve seasons. By now I was married, and had a beautiful daughter, Sofia. By the age of 35, I was the richest and most influential person in the business. I even co-wrote a screenplay about a Hind-Reader, called 'The Golden Hind', loosely based on my own experiences."

"So that's what the tattoo's about. I was wondering."

"That's right. Glad you noticed."

Stern winked at Adam and continued:

"After releasing my autobiography, 'The Assman Cometh', on my 40th birthday, I went into semi-retirement. I still made the odd TV appearance, and conducted private readings for the rich and powerful, but my efforts were now focused at highlighting food poverty in parts of Africa. That's when the UN approached me about the Ambassadorship. I accepted the position, died in the car crash, and ended up here.

RUMP STAKES

Conversation continued over delicious dessert. Whatever the subject, every twist and turn led back to Stern. Though rarely the instigator of the thread, he was more than willing to voice an opinion, tell a tale, or make a decision. Harry and Edna eagerly lapped up every word, revelling in the slightest attention. Despite Stern's fondness for self-promotion, using every opportunity to sell his superiority over 'normal' immortals, Adam found it difficult to dislike the man. A virtual walking pheromone, Stern trod a high testosterone path between virile masculinity and ironic macho exaggeration – the type of guy all other guys pushed forward as their flag bearer. Despite this, Adam had misgivings. Could he really spend an eternity basking in the theatrical glow of Stern's overbearing ego?

As Frederick collected the dishes, Adam took his chance. Standing up, he tapped a spoon on the table, declaring, "Well, I'd better get back to my new place. Haven't had a good chance to check it out yet. Thank you all for a memorable dinner. Best Indian food I've ever tasted. Although I never expected death would lead to a place like this, I'm sure I'll get used to it. The viro is so beautiful, the food's great, the company's ..."

"Nooo," complained Kaylee. "Don't go yet, honey. Stern can give you a reading. It'll be sooo cool."

She clapped her hands with glee, as Stern agreed - albeit feigning reluctance. Though only an inch tall, Adam now wished he could shrink into oblivion. This could only lead to further embarrassment. However, remembering his promise to himself to make an effort, Adam sucked in his pride, entrusting his vanishing dignity to the mercy of Stern's talent.

Stern stripped down to a black leather micro kilt, once more exposing his impressive manly physique. An anxious Adam received a sliver of hope from an unexpected source, Edna.

"Surely, you don't need to do this now. Can't you see the poor boy's tired? We could do this another day when his new bottom has matured a bit. I bet it doesn't have any smell yet."

His mother's concerned expression convinced Adam that this timely intervention was not due to motherly love, but something deeper. However, if the reading was cancelled then he did not care about her motives. Stern immediately dashed his hopes, positioning Adam in an open space away from the table. A click of Stern's fingers and the lighting dimmed, except for a small spotlight centred on Adam. Effortlessly sliding into his Host persona, Stern addressed his audience:

"Ladies and gentlemen, the Hind-Reading is an ancient and sacred ritual: a ritual not to taken lightly, a ritual of serious skill and observance. Many are those who profess the gift, but only one individual truly possesses the ability, and the power.

"Here, today, you will witness the extent of my gift, as I sniff out the hidden truths. I, Stern Lovass, the original and the best, welcome you to the Hind-Reading of Adam Eden. Let his essence be known!"

The audience, including Frederick and Amelia, burst into spontaneous applause. As the noise subsided, Stern announced, "There are two rules that all should be aware of. Rule one!"

"No anal clenching!" shouted the audience.

"Rule Two!"

"No anal acoustics!"

Leaning over, Stern whispered in Adam's ear, "That's right; you do not cheek-squeeze my nose or fart in my face."

Stern began writhing and flexing suggestively, as sensual pulsating music filled the room. He circled Adam, groaning almost sexually, making light bodily contact. Adam stood, stiff as a board, longing for the ordeal to end. Again, Stern addressed the audience:

"I shall now strip the subject to his underwear!"

Adam was horrified:

"No! You can't do that. Why on Earth do you want to do that?"

"It is difficult to hind-read through layers of clothing. I'm happy to let you remove your own trousers … if my doing it makes you uncomfortable."

Aware that all eyes were focused on him, Adam said meekly, "I … I'm not wearing any underpants. My trousers were too tight."

The audience let out a collective gasp, bordering on disgust. Stern shook his head in disappointment. Edna saw her chance:

"You may as well stop the reading. We'll all get together another time. I'm sure Adam will be wearing underpants then."

"He didn't get this habit from me," added Harry waving his cane. "I wear underpants every day. Every day."

After considering the matter for a moment, Stern decided to carry on, citing the fact that the trousers only constituted a single layer, and therefore would not affect the reading. Then, with a theatrical flourish,, Stern knelt down, and firmly gripped both sides of Adam's buttocks.

"I am now going in for a preliminary evaluation of the area."

Stern's nose edged towards the crack of the trousers.

"I'm getting a gay sex vibe from this," joked Adam nervously.

"Please be quiet, my nose isn't that long."

Pressing his nose softly against the target, Stern inhaled deeply and purposefully. A moment of silence, then Stern leapt to his feet. He directed a look of pure loathing at Adam:

"That is just not on. That is revolting, unnecessary, and in the world of Hind-Reading, totally taboo."

Solemnly, Stern turned to his audience:

"Ladies and gentlemen, it is only on rare occasions that the Hind-Reader mentions Rule Three, but this is, I am sad to say, one of those occasions. And what is Rule Three!"

The audience reacted immediately, well acquainted with the rule:

"Good anal hygiene!"

"That's right, 'good anal hygiene'. So, Mr Eden, why don't you explain to us why your hind smells so bad?"

"I couldn't find any wet-wipes. I looked but …"

"Was there toilet tissue?"

"Well, er …I …"

"Mr Eden, answer the question! Was there toilet tissue?"

"Yes, but … you see … only one ply. And … I don't always use toilet tissue."

"Oh dear, that is truly disgusting, even for an undesirable?"

"He always used toilet tissue as a boy," cried Edna. "He never went without. We taught him to wipe properly. Please, stop the reading, Stern. You shouldn't have to go through this. He's not worth it. He's an undesirable."

"Ah, yes, an undesirable, and as such we should perhaps allow a degree of latitude. Tell me, Adam, what have wet-wipes to do with this? I thought they were for babies."

"Well, no matter what condition you're in, a wet-wipe will always do the trick. Oh, and they make you smell nice. I had a friend who could pick me up a job-lot of my favourites for cheap money."

"And your favourites are?"

"Aloe Vera Babysoother Wet-Wipes."

"Good choice. Ok, ok, given your unconventional lifestyle, I guess that makes a bit of sense. I'm guessing that Adam here indulged in some late night eating. The concierge must have warned you of the consequences."

"She did. I just didn't realise it would be so ... prolific."

"Well we all learn by experience – most people don't eat after 11:00 pm. Now, even though the reading cannot now continue, I'm sure the audience would love to hear where you got the ingenious wet-wipe idea."

"Natasja and Sonja. If they were pushed for time after a client they used wet-wipes to clean up."

"What ... are you talking about hookers?"

"... yes."

"So, you were either a pimp or a john. Hell, latitude or not, I can't get with that. I've always been one for romancing the ladies, but they were never objects to be bought or sold."

Edna rose from her chair, seething through her teeth, "He wasn't a pimp or a john, and I'm sorry that he is my son. But, do you know what he really is? Do you want me to tell you?"

Harry grabbed her arm:

"Edna, remember our little conversation. You promised to let me handle this."

Shrugging of her husband, Edna launched into a fearsome tirade:

"He's a damned murderer! The drunken sod killed a father and son. That's right, he's a child killer!"

"Edna, you promised," muttered Harry, head in his hands.

For a moment, the shock was palpable, everyone unsure where to look or what to say. Stern stealthily returned to his chair, and Kaylee actually put down her glass.

Adam broke the silence:

"But … but I didn't kill anyone."

"Tell that to little Einstein Kennen, or his father, Derek" said Edna. "Out for an evening stroll, watching the ships, and then you walk up all drunk and threatening. You pushed them in. You drowned them. You took away a young boy's future, and a father's pride and joy."

"I don't remember this, and no way was I drunk. I only had a couple of lagers, and they were halves. I just went out for a wee."

"Just because you don't remember it, doesn't mean it didn't happen, and doesn't mean you're any less guilty. Oh yes, you died and escaped all the consequences, but we all suffered. Why did they have to resurrect you rather than my dear little Robert?"

"Adam, there were witnesses," Harry quietly mumbled, "The official report indicated you had drunk over four times the recommended allowance. The tests don't lie. You attacked them, pushed them into the harbour, and then you tripped and fell in as well. I was planning to tell you about this later."

"I honestly didn't drink that amount. I was almost sober when I went out. There's no way this can be true."

Edna collapsed into her chair, sobbing:

"They threw stones through our windows, and swore at us in the street. They said we were bad parents. We needed police protection at your funeral."

Adam had never seen his mother so distraught. Her tears were genuine, her anguish profound.

"It was in the local paper," choked Harry, holding back tears. "I remember the headline 'Binge drinking bastard! Binge drinking bastard! ' With that picture … I was so ashamed. Your name, our name …"

"What picture?"

"You, starkers except for your underpants, grinning and covered in sick, waving a beer can. It was all over the internet as well."

Adam groaned. Manny had placed that photo on the 'Friends Again' website.

"I know we are partly to blame," said Harry. "We shouldn't have let you have that glass of wine on holiday in Portugal when you were seventeen. It probably gave you a taste for alcohol."

Edna looked at Adam, her make-up a smeared impressionist confusion:

"We had to leave the Bridge Club, and we never got any more party invites. Nobody wanted to know us. And … Robert … never came back. We never heard from him again, not even a call. But at least you got your beer. I guess that's all that matters to you."

"What about Manny and Scarlett, they knew I wasn't drinking? Did anyone think to ask them?"

"I don't know about this Scarlett," said Harry, rising from his chair, tenderly comforting Edna, "but that Manny fellow committed suicide a few months after the murders. Apparently, he blamed himself for not watching you more closely. He told police you'd probably spiked your own drinks. You let him down, Adam. You let us all down."

Harry gently manoeuvred his wife to the door, his cane now a support rather than a weapon:

"Come on Edna, let's go home."

Adam ran to the door, pleading as his parents set off in the golf-cart:

"Mum, Dad, it can't be true. There is no way I would have murdered anyone. It must be a mistake. Please believe me. I'm trying to make an effort. I made a promise to lead a better life this time around."

STERN ADVICE

Adam watched his parents head back to Eden Manor in the golf cart. They took the direct route, up the meadow, this time without bickering. Returning despondently to the restaurant, Adam fell into his seat.

"I owe you both an apology. I didn't mean to spoil the dinner."

"Are you kidding?" said Stern. "Nothing usually happens here, so anything out the ordinary is interesting. And the murderer thing, I certainly didn't see that coming. Never pegged you for a murderer."

"But doesn't that make me desirable in this weirdo world?"

"No, not at all, you're still an undesirable. I'm guessing there was no intent, or forward planning. You were just some drunken bum taking a piss, and took offense at something. Maybe you thought they were watching you, so you 'taught them a lesson'. What you did wasn't memorable, dramatic, or thought provoking, just plain squalid - especially drowning that kid."

"Yet, if I was some psycho, and planned the whole thing, I would be desirable?"

"That's market forces for you. We don't make the rules. At least you're not a danger to anyone. Otherwise they wouldn't have put you in a viro with normal folks like us."

"But killing that kid," said Kaylee, lowering her glass, "that really sucks. He coulda gone to college, got married, had kids of his own. You took that away. It's kinda nasty, and I don't think I like you anymore."

"I still can't believe it," said Adam. "I don't think I'm a murderer. Is there any way to find out what really happened? Some proof perhaps."

"Don't sweat it. There is a chance your folks are exaggerating. You know how family can make a big deal outta things. I'll take a good look tomorrow, and let you know what I find."

"But I really wanted to make a change. Be the person I always should have been."

"Hmm, I doubt that's gonna happen. You are who you were. Your status in your first-life is how people will always see you. With everything served up on a plate, there's not much opportunity for proving otherwise I'm afraid. Time will take the edge off of the situation, and we have plenty of that."

Stern clicked his fingers to summon the coffee menu, and then slapped the table:

"Your folks, wow, what a secret they've been keeping."

"But they seem so strange," said Adam. "Their personalities are nothing like I remember. They're almost like cartoon characters."

"I've seen this in many of the resurrected," said Stern. "They're old, not physically, but mentally. You and I died relatively young, but they lived long enough to experience serious deterioration. Some take years to shake off their geriatric habits and views. Did you notice that your mother drools when she eats?"

"And Dad's 'Lord of the Manor' routine."

"Oh yeah, I just love that. You know, they probably spent their final years scared and vulnerable, waving their fists at the world, blaming everything on the government, welfare cheats, immigrants, and those damn kids. Give them a few years, and they'll lighten up. It could be this murderer thing is the breakthrough. First time I've seen them ever express anything close to real emotion. I mean, your mother. She was really spitting fire. That look in her eyes, then the tears, those wonderful tears. I have never seen her like that."

Stern licked his lips, and smiled wickedly:

"You know, I'm turned on. Oh yeah, I can feel it."

Frederick came to the table with the coffee menu. Stern declined.

"The French Coffee is particularly excellent, Sir," said Frederick.

With an unexpected urgency, Stern waved him away. "Thank you Frederick, but now I have something else in mind. Kaylee, I have the urge. I gotta have sex, and soon."

"Oh hon', at last," shrieked Kaylee.

"Will you be requiring the table for your intercourse?" asked Frederick. "If so, I will supply fresh linen."

Stern nodded:

"Don't want any stray chilli in my crack, so yes, a clean cloth would be a good idea."

Adam sat shocked as Stern already naked began sexually manipulating himself.

"What on earth do you think you're doing?"

"Well, I don't wanna go into the details, but at some point," Stern waggled his penis, "this is going into Kaylee. Didn't your folks teach you anything?"

"You know what I mean. Is it normal here to just start having sex in your local restaurant, and in front of anyone?"

"It's the libido. Surely the concierge told you about the libido."

Adam shook his head.

"Our new bodies are engineered differently. No one knows exactly what they've done to us, but basically we all have significantly lower libido than normal, and there's no damn sex pills to compensate. Supposed to keep us calmer and less violent, so I guess it helps us get along a little better. I always had a mega sex drive before, so even with the reduction I can get it up occasionally. When you get the urge … you gotta go for it."

Frederick retrieved a clean tablecloth from behind the bar, precisely dressed the table, and then turned to Adam:

"Will Sir be requiring coffee?"

"No thank you. I really should be going." Adam left his seat. "Got a lot to think about."

"Stay if you want," suggested Stern, a mischievous glint in his eyes. "I'm sure we can squeeze you in somewhere. We can all get to know each other a little better."

"I thought you preferred women."

"Oh I do, and don't worry; you'll definitely be the woman."

Adam backed away, smiling affably. "I don't think so."

"We've plenty of ghee."

Adam headed for the door.

"Wait up Adam, I'm only kidding around. Don't worry, I'm not gonna start screwin' just yet. I've got some advice for you."

"Go on."

"You need cheering up. Hell, you've been resurrected, and found out that you're a good for nothing stink-ass murderer. Just remember, you have an eternity to get through this. My advice is simple: visit a party viro, and have a good time with people you don't know. There are always thousands to choose from. You can arrange it on your computer. Are you familiar with the system?"

"Yeah, I had a good look at it this morning. It all seemed quite straightforward."

"Just look in the Events section, find something you like, and press ENTER. If it says PENDING or ACCEPTED, go to bed; wake up in the morning, voila, good times."

"And if it says BLOCKED?"

"Just try another. Now, if you don't want to stay for the show, you had better leave."

GLAM ROCKS

A sharp knock at the door and a man's soft voice: English, educated, faintly northern accent, "Hey, you in there get a move on, the party's already started. We're having a Seventies buffet by the fountain, and I don't want to be standing out here all day."

Loud clopping footsteps faded into the distance.

Adam cursed his trousers, struggling as before to fasten the zip without any painful injury. No longer in the annexe, this room was compact and utilitarian, like some cheap motel. Although there was a functioning ensuite bathroom, washing was unnecessary, as Adam woke up clean and fresh – obviously, far more than just sleeping took place at night.

Breaking with character, Adam had taken Stern's advice from the previous evening, arranging a party visit. There were thousands available, and unable to filter the list, Adam resorted to fast scrolling and jabbing his finger at random, hoping fate would provide an interesting destination. The method chose 'Groover's 1970s Glam Rock Theme Party', a strange choice but worth investigating.

Born too late to experience the real thing, Adam looked forward to a day of stomping tribal beats, cheeky lads and androgynous sophisticates decked out in flamboyant costumes: space age makeup, platform heels and glitter satin chic. Travelling to this new viro was simply a matter of going to sleep at midnight and waking up in the chosen destination. This was a new day, and another chance to change his negative ways.

Emerging from the ground floor cubicle onto a wide asphalt pathway, Adam took in the new viro. The building he had exited was a huge concrete five-storey block, with rows of white doors but no windows. Concrete walkways crossed each level, connected at either end to industrial steel stairs.

Adam followed the path to the end of the building, then turning the corner, gasped at the sight before him.

This Environment was strikingly different to his own, and appeared to be highly populated. Up ahead, crossed by a bridge, ran a steep sided urban canal, fronted by a huge grey bunker-like amenity buildings with tiny glass windows. Tarmac roads and pavements snaked around ten slab-sided apartment blocks that encircled the urban core – the design reminiscent of brutalist 1960's housing estates. Yet, everything seemed new, pristine. Unlike the original shabby eyesores that Adam remembered from his previous life, the architecture here had not deteriorated beyond the architect's vision. On the far side of this stark grey urban landscape, beyond a row of warehouses and a road, lay green meadows and some woodland—a striking contrast.

"Hey there, hang on a minute; I'm the reception committee."

It was the same voice as before, accompanied a cloudy reek of cheap aftershave: animalistic musk swathed in amber and cedar-wood. Adam looked round. Perched precariously on silver platform boots, the man staggered over and shook Adam's hand. Flared silver lamé jumpsuit, large ankh medallion, and a long straight blonde wig, he introduced himself as Rampage.

Rampage balked at the sight of Adam's clothes:

"Good grief, did you pick the wrong party? You look ready for a sea cruise or a beach barbecue. This isn't Copacabana, mate."

"I'm new, the profile chose this stuff."

"I know that. You're still on your first ten days."

Rampage smiled broadly, accentuated by the glitter-star transfers on his cheeks:

"Oh, and before you ask, we will not lend you a change of clothes. Sticklers for tradition around here, you see. Don't let it bother you though, because this happens to most of our guests. You could be dressed as a dirty hippy and you would still be welcome."

Adam and Rampage crossed the concrete and steel footbridge, beyond which lay a large paved square filled with colourfully dressed people. An abstract fountain stood at its centre, a confusion of stainless steel pipes, and cubes. There were hundreds present, all kitted out in garish glam-rock fashion, noisily milling around trestle tables laden with early 1970's snacks and treats. Rampage handed Adam a paper party-plate.

"Help yourself to food. If you want beer, I recommend the Watney's Party Seven, or Carling Black Label. If wine's your bag, we have Mateus Rose, Blue Nun, and a nice Piesporter.

Adam piled his plate with sausage rolls, egg sandwiches, cheese and pineapple on sticks, crisps, and quiche. Sadly, no chilli burgers, but salad was thankfully not on the menu. He was dismayed not to hear the tribal stomp of glam rock music accompanying the buffet, but Rampage promised they were saving the 'sacred sounds' for the main event.

"Besides me, how many other guests are here?" asked Adam

"Well, let me work it out. About 400 of us live here, so we can invite and accommodate approximately 800 visitors. Now, by my estimation, today we have attracted … five. "

"Five hundred, that's good going."

"Nah, not 500, only five. Five's quite normal."

"Why so few?"

"We don't get the repeat custom. Who knows why? Perhaps they object to pink custard and sherry trifle. And, who said the early Seventies weren't popular."

On the other side of the fountain, near the entrance to one of the tower blocks, a man sat majestically on an elaborate gold cushioned mirror-glass throne: arched eyebrows, rocker styled bouffant of raven hair, silver jumpsuit with giant stuck-up collar. Around him, an honour guard of four glam rockers made sure others kept their distance.

"That guy on the throne, he looks familiar. Who is he?"

"He's in charge, and he goes by the name 'Groover'. None of us uses our first-life names. For now, we have these glam nicknames."

"So you're not real glam rock stars?"

"No, but most of us achieved a certain level of notoriety in our previous lives."

"Oh I see," said Adam, still wondering where he had seen Groover before. "These theme days, do you hold them often, or is it a one off?"

"All the time, we live it. We've been trying out the 70's glam scene for about a month now, and I must say it is a gas. We tried Goth for a couple of years. Loved it at first, then like an overused bad joke, we grew to hate it: sad poetry, permanent frowns, red wine or absinthe, here taste my blood. We even dressed up the towers and amenities in stone cladding. Victorian streetlamps everywhere, fog machines. Oh, the misery and pretention … pathetic. Groover got fed up with it and went for something bright and cheerful this time."

"So you like this better?"

"No way, this is just as bad, only different. These ruddy heels play havoc with my ankles, and the wig makes my scalp sweat. But, the worst is that

Groover will not allow beards. I was so proud of mine, and now my chin feels all nude."

"Maybe they should put you in charge."

"Oh no, no," whispered Rampage, "we don't talk about that sort of thing. You can get in all sorts of trouble. He may be a bit of an oaf, but he does have what it takes. But, I'll be honest and say that I do find it a little disconcerting when I have a medical degree. I was a Doctor before ending up here."

"No need for your skills now."

"On the contrary, my skills are very much in demand."

Adam had no idea what Rampage meant, since everybody healed at night, and there was no illness or disease. Changing the subject, Adam complemented Rampage on the attention to 1970's detail.

"Glad you like it. Groover adjusted the dispensers to perfection, with my help I might add. Only products widely available in Great Britain from 1972 to 1975 are dispensed."

"How can you alter the dispensers? My concierge told me you could get anything available during your own lifetime. Could I alter my dispenser?"

"Nah, not a chance, but some viros are special. Our Groover controls most of the output."

"I thought the concierge's were in charge?"

Rampage grinned:

"Usually, but as I said, this place is special."

Adam spent the next couple of hours chatting with various locals, finding their attitude friendly though somewhat vague and evasive. He noticed that if he got near Groover, a crowd would form, blocking any potential contact.

As the picnic wound down, Adam sat with one of the other guests, Joshua Daniels, a 40-something burly black Texan. Joshua seemed very bewildered at the gathering – having also used the 'point and choose' method of selecting a viro to visit. The superiority of Texas over everything was his preferred conversation, and after enduring a ten-minute fevered lecture on barbecue, and the breakfast burrito, Adam attempted to turn the conversation:

"Tell me Joshua, how did you die: barbecue accident, mesquite poisoning perhaps? I fell off a harbour wall into the sea. Hit my head on a mooring ring on the way down. Split my skull and drowned."

Shifting uncomfortably in his chair, tears welled up in Joshua's eyes. His face screwed up pathetically, voice broken, reflecting a deep sadness:

"My Pa shot me when I got back from ball practise. He already killed my ma and baby sister. They put me in a viro with my grandparents, but they won't tell me much. I don't know why Pa did it."

It was Adam's turn to shift uncomfortably in his chair, deciding not to mention his brush with alleged child murder.

"Do you think Pa hated me? Must have been something to do with me, 'cause it was the day after my 13th birthday, and he never showed up for the party. I didn't do nothing wrong."

Adam did not know what to say. He never anticipated that some of the resurrected were children in adult bodies. Joshua looked in his forties, yet this was a pleading child. Hesitantly, Adam advised:

"Joshua, perhaps it would better if you discussed this with … your own kind."

"My own kind? My own kind? Shit, you mean I just opened my heart to some motherfuckin' racist?"

"No … no … I meant people like you who died when they were kids. There must be loads of them out there facing the same problems. It's hard for me to relate to a child in an adult body."

"I ain't a child, I'm a teenager. I died when I was 13, remember. But I take your point, and I'm sorry for the swearing. Pa would've grounded me for that. Strange, when you think he killed me for nothin'"

Alleviating the tension, Rampage made a timely return, and pulled up a chair. He seemed happy, excited.

"Enjoy the picnic?" he asked. "You look upset Joshua."

Joshua composed himself, "No, I'm fine thanks. Just remembering the dark place, but I'm fine now."

"Great, really great."

"So where's the prawn cocktail and Black Forest Gateau?" asked Adam, reaching for another chocolate finger.

"Oh that's for later, at the grand feast. I placed my order first thing this morning. I'm having avocado stuffed with prawns, Steak Diane with chips, and of course The Gateau."

"Not sure about the avocado, but the rest sounds great. I like my steak rare, but not 'kissed the pan' type rare."

"Just the way I like my steak," said Rampage, "bloody but bruised. Shame you won't be having any. Ha, you will be dead by then."

Adam sensed the sincerity in Rampage's voice, and shuddered. "Oh no…please no."

Joshua clapped his hands:

"Oh yeah, that's British sarcasm. You say one thing and mean the opposite. I heard o' that. You guys are so weird."

"Joshua, I don't think he's joking."

Waving away Adam's warning, Joshua stood, exaggerating his height, "Well then I better warn ya, don't mess with Texa … aah … aah …"

A stain of crimson spread out over Joshua's shirt, a blade nimbly slipped between his ribs. Rampage withdrew the blade, and in a flash held it against Adam's throat. Adam raised his hands in submission, and Rampage nodded, pulled the knife away, and scolded Joshua:

"I'll mess with whoever I damn well choose! Don't you worry, the wound won't kill you."

Rampage cleaned the blade with a paper tissue, and skilfully palmed it into a wrist sheath.

"Speed, anticipation, and accuracy, that's what it takes to win a knife fight. I use the dagger for quick close up blade-work. My main weapon's a gladius short sword, like the Romans used."

Adam listened in silence as Rampage continued.

"Now, my colleague Stardust over there, the bloke dressed in black with the white fright-wig, he loves using a rapier. Ziggy, the giant in the red metallic jacket and mirrored top hat, he's all muscles and violence, so he uses a cricket bat. Oh yes, the girls in the flouncy yellow trouser-suits and gold bandanas, they're Roxy and Quatro, our foxy long-range archery twins. However, let me warn you, everybody's well-trained in the use of a blade, and if it comes down to unarmed hand to hand fighting, you won't stand a chance."

"Why do you want to kill us?" gasped Joshua, shaking with fear, using a clown party-plate to stem the bleeding.

"It's what we love doing, and we are very very good at it. When Groover gives the signal, you will get a ten-minute head start. After that, we will hunt you down. I told you my skills were in demand, just not my medical ones."

"I suppose you're going to torture us?" said Adam.

"Nah, been there, done that. We tried torturing in our Goth phase but we quickly ran out of ideas. We got so efficient that in the end it was more like a brisk early morning at the butchers. Now we go on the hunt and it feels more like a real competition. You only have to face the five deputies, including yours truly. Roxy and Quatro might wing you a couple of times with their arrows, you know, to slow you down. After that, the rest of the gang will finish you off. When you're dead, we chuck your bodies in the canal. During the hunt, the locals watch from the towers, and cheer you on. Don't worry, they're not allowed to give away your location if you're hiding, but Groover can if he wants to"

"Any other rules to your sick game?"

"Hmm, let me see. Oh yes, you mustn't harm a person's … err … genitals. It's something we most certainly don't approve of. Real men don't do groin stuff."

"So what if I just kill myself now? Pretty much ruins your little game doesn't it. I'll get resurrected anyway."

"Good point. However, I don't think you will do that. You see, if you die you have to go through that dark place again, and I am sure you'll want to avoid that. We guarantee that if you are still alive at five pm, we will spare your life, and sort out any injuries you might have. Then you can join us for the grand feast. And tell you what, if either of you survive till five, I'll cook your steak myself."

Rampage was right. Any chance of avoiding the dark limbo and the painful burning strands was worth taking, and Adam doubted that any previous victims of this sick game ever took their own life. It was time to get rational.

"Do we get weapons?" asked Adam.

"Oh come on, we are British; fair play and all that. Of course you get a weapon. Take your pick."

"Shotgun then."

"I also choose a shotgun," shivered Joshua, "It was good enough for Pa."

Rampage's tone hardened:

"Don't be stupid, even here you can't get firearms or explosives from dispensers. There's nothing combustible in the Viroverse. Any type of spear, blade, bat, or bow will do. We start in about twenty minutes so you better think quickly."

"But Joshua's just a kid!" protested Adam. "He's only 13 for God's sake!"

"Who cares? In my world, there are just the living and the soon to be slain. Everyone gets equal treatment. No exceptions!"

The locals began leaving the square, filing into the towers in a well-practised manner. Many waved and wished the visitors good luck, eagerly looking forward to the main event of the day. Adam saw the other three guests sitting on the other side of the square with Stardust, their hollow expressions mirroring his own. When asked, Adam chose a baseball bat as his weapon, for no other reason than the other weapons required skills that he did not possess. Joshua chose the same, copying his new father figure.

Once the tower doors closed and locked, the locals securely ensconced inside, a troop of android waiters streamed out of the multi-amenity buildings, marching in perfect unison across the bridge. Bow ties, and white aprons, French style paradigms, with slick brilliantine hair, and curled waxed moustaches. The waiters cleared the tables with swift silent efficiency, dumping the debris into garbage skips by the nearest tower. Adam and the other guests were forced to stand as the waiters folded the tables and chairs, stacking them in nearby storage units. A couple of the guests tried pleading with the waiters for help but received no response. Once satisfied with their efforts, the android army headed back across the bridge, the square now stark and uninviting.

Suddenly, one of the guests, a fair-haired girl, dashed to the bridge. Joshua tensed, ready to follow but Adam warned him to wait. Adam wondered if the girl's plan was to follow the waiters into the amenity buildings. Sensing the girl's approach, the waiters halted, and with military precision, wheeled around, blocking the bridge. The girl stood helplessly exposed, as Roxy, bow in hand, assumed a shooting stance. With expert fluidity, she nocked an arrow, raised, drew, and released. The fair-haired girl fell to the ground screaming, the arrow embedded in her upper arm. After politely applauding, the waiters continued on to the amenities. Adam watched the waiters leave. Looking up at the towers, the array of windows a gallery of eager, menacingly expectant faces, Adam remembered the last moments of his original life - the Cherbourg ferry leaving Portsmouth. Closing his eyes for a moment, Adam wished he were aboard that ferry, with just the gentle throb of the engines for company, heading to France in the peaceful night - France or death, and he had the wrong ticket.

Ziggy swaggered over to the injured girl, and roughly dragged her over to where Adam and Joshua sat. Rampage viciously pulled out the arrow, then inspected, cleaned, and bound the wound.

"She'll live," he informed Groover.

"I see your medical skills are in demand." spat Adam, with cold disdain.

"Yes, the power to save life and the desire to take it."

"Kill any patients in your old life, or have you only recently given up the Hippocratic Oath?"

"Oh my friend, I killed many many patients. The old dears trusted me with their feeble flickers of life, and I snuffed them out. I altered Wills, took money, but I would have done it anyway. It took them years to shut me down. They say I killed hundreds. I lost count over the years but it sounds about right."

Quatro appeared with a microphone and stood by Groover. Roxy wheeled out a large suspended brass gong and Groover rose from the glittering throne, wobbling unsteadily on the tallest platform boots Adam had ever seen. He picked up a two handed stick and banged the gong with such force that he tripped back a couple of steps. Discarding the stick, Groover grabbed the microphone. His voice, an abrasive West Country burr, boomed across the viro from powerful speakers on the tower block roofs:

"Alright me lovelies … Get … It … On!"

STEPHEN AYRES

GLAM SAFARI

Not needing any encouragement, the unfortunate guests set off in a number of directions. Adam raced across the bridge with Joshua following close behind. They crossed a road, and crept through a couple of fields, before reaching the relative cover of some woodland. Once hidden by the undergrowth, they saw Rampage and the gang in the distance, heading off behind the farthest tower, tracking the fair-haired girl. Adam spent a few seconds concocting a plan, and then they cautiously doubled back to the canal.

The concrete sides of the canal were steep and smooth with ladders every few yards. Adam and Joshua climbed down to the water's edge. There was no towpath, just a precarious one-foot concrete lip running the canal's length. Adam slipped into the water twice before reaching the bridge, his clothes sodden and clinging. Climbing some pipework, they managed to squeeze onto a girder ledge under the roadway. Whilst getting into the structure was easy, staying there was numbing and confining. As time passed, lying on the cold hard metal became increasingly painful. Loud glam rock classics accompanied every aching moment, a constant tribal stomp, masking any distant sounds of fighting, desperate screams for mercy, or the crack of breaking bones.

"Damn, my watch is broken," groaned Adam. "What's the time, Joshua? This is getting uncomfortable."

"Time is 3:25," said Joshua, pressing the light on his G-Shock. "We've been hidin' here for over an hour. Only got one hour and 35 minutes to go, then those Glam dudes will let us live. That's if they can be trusted. Why are they doin' this to us."

"They're serial killers."

"Huh?"

68

"I thought some of them looked familiar, especially Groover. I think they're all notorious British serial-killers, psychopathic murderers, and general sickos. They must have stuck them all in one viro together."

"Well, let's hope those psychos don't find us here. We should be safe here, huh? We're pretty well hidden."

"Look Joshua, I don't think staying here's a good idea. If they find us, we're sitting ducks … dead ducks. If I stay here much longer, my legs will be so numb I won't be able to move. These damn trousers were tight to begin with, and the water's made them worse."

"Just take off the pants. Maybe you'll feel better."

Adam contemplated running around half-naked, but quickly banished the unsettling image from his mind. It was then he heard footsteps on the bridge above. Delaying the decision was no longer an option:

"Joshua, you stay here," ordered Adam, just a touch too loudly, "and I'll try to lure them away. If I can make it to the countryside beyond the warehouses, you might have a chance. Just stay put and I'll try to run out the clock."

"Don't leave me here alone. Maybe they won't find us."

Adam leant over and whispered some final words in Joshua's ear, before shuffling sideways, and dropping into the canal. He hit the water awkwardly, creating a large noisy splash. Leaving the baseball bat behind floating in the murky water, he swam to the canal-side bordering the square. Arms aching, he hauled himself up a nearby ladder.

"Look, it's the hottest thing north of Havana!" taunted a familiar voice. "Going somewhere, Copacabana?"

Turning quickly, Adam saw Rampage and his glam friends leering and pointing from the other side of the canal. The three men were blood spattered, particularly Ziggy's heavily stained cricket bat, which dripped with the sticky red liquid. Roxy and Quatro, spotlessly clean, had already raised their bows, eager to inflict deadly wounds. Rampage made them stand down:

"Looks like the young American and your good-self are the only ones left. Kudos to you, it is always the smart ones double back. We will hunt you next and then look for the man-child. I think he has gone to ground somewhere but give us a few minutes and we will find him. You see, if we're at a loose end, then Groover points out roughly where to look. He can see pretty much the entire Environment from up on the towers. Now, by my watch, we have well over an hour remaining, so plenty of time for some sport. Come on

Copacabana; show us what you can do. We will give you 30 extra seconds head start. Go on … run!

Without need for further encouragement, and not wanting to give away Joshua's hiding place, Adam headed across the square. Despite strenuous efforts, his gait was a sluggish sopping lope, the soaking wet clothes weighing far more heavily than anticipated. He caught sight of Groover standing on one of the tower block roofs. The head psycho waved at Adam, before demonstrating an 'up yours' sign with his arm. Ignoring the gesture, Adam ran through the narrow alley between the warehouses. Once out the other end, he stopped, leaned against the concrete wall, and rested a moment to catch his breath. Whilst physically able to keep running—his new body healthy and fit—Adam mentally retained the physical caution of a sedentary fat man.

The party pulsing beat and sharp gravelly vocals of Slade's 'Merry Xmas Everybody' resonated across the viro. Obviously a favourite with the locals, Adam could hear a multitude of voices enthusiastically singing along to the Christmas hit, and saw their distant silhouettes dancing behind the tower block windows.

'Look to the future now," Adam sang to himself, summoning the resolve to continue. Leaving the warehouses, and crossing a small tarmacked area—nearly tripping over a final lip of pavement kerbing—Adam was now in open countryside.

If Adam had thought to outrun the glam gang across the rural terrain, he had made a major miscalculation. The grass and soil in this viro were real and very muddy, and Adam's smooth soled deck shoes lacked grip. Only quarter of the way across the big field, already in earshot of his pursuer's smart jibes and lewd insults, he was fast losing ground. Despite their incongruous heels, the well-practised glittery hunters made short work of the distance.

"Shit! Shit! Shit!" swore Adam, in an uncharacteristic display of expletives. Despite increased exertion and a keen will to live, the slippery soles, and ever-tightening trousers slowed him to a short-stride mincing waddle.

An arrow sailed past, grazing Adam's side, tearing the fabric of his shirt. Staggering forward, he tumbled to the ground with ungainly momentum. Mid-fall, another arrow sheared the left side of his head, taking away his ear, a spray of blood issuing from the wound.

Rolling awkwardly to a stop, Adam covered the wound with his hand, his face a contorted expression of agony and fear. Never the hero, he started crying, howling in pain, tears and blood streaming down his mud-scuffed cheeks. The predators approached.

"Oh please, that's not going to kill you," laughed Rampage.

"It hurts, God it hurts," screamed Adam. "Don't kill me, please don't kill me. Kill Joshua first. I know where he is."

"So do we" said Rampage. "Roxy saw you both sneaking along the canal. You were both hiding under the bridge. She even heard your plan to lure us away. Well, in honour of your noble act, we thought we would indulge you, and leave your friend until last. Once we've finished with you, Roxy and Quatro are going to shoot him from his perch, and then we'll just drown him. I doubt he'll put up much of a fight. But back to the business at hand ... your death."

"No, please, it's these trousers," cried Adam. "They're too tight. I can't run in them."

Ziggy stepped forward, wielding his bat, and grunted, "Let me ... smash ... his ... head in!"

Rampage brushed him aside:

"No, not yet, my eloquent friend. This is the first time anyone's used ill-fitting trousers as an excuse to beg for their lives, and originality's always worth rewarding. Copacabana deserves one last chance. He just needs to loosen up a little."

Rampage knelt down next to Adam, and deftly ran a blade down the side of the tight trousers.

"Whoa, no!" gasped Adam, imagining the sharp edge licking against his skin.

"Relax, and keep still, or I will cut you badly. The blade is pure obsidian—razor sharp."

Scared, and stressed, Adam complied, successfully willing his body to stop shaking. Rampage sliced open the trouser legs to the bottom.

"There you go, just a few small nicks, and not much bleeding. Look how flappy your trousers are. You just can't beat a good pair of flares. Now if you would like to use those 'tiger feet', we will allow you a few more seconds' head-start."

Picking himself up, finding his balance, Adam gestured to Roxy and Quatro. "What about them? I can't outrun their arrows."

"Ooo, isn't he just darling." sighed the twins in unison.

71

"Roxy and Quatro only get one shot each per guest," explained Rampage. "After that, they use their blades. Quatro nearly ruined the game with that last arrow. She was only supposed to wing you in the arm or the side. She very nearly got a fatal headshot. They'll be with us for back up, but it's all down to us three boys now. Well, what are you waiting for? G-g-g-g-go!"

Legs released from the confining trousers, Adam achieved a new level of acceleration, racing across the field with renewed vigour. He cleanly jumped a hedgerow, and charged through a field of ripened wheat - the abrasive crop thrashing his body - the chase now deadly serious. Adam never achieved such speed in his previous life, nor displayed such stamina, yet now felt he could easily run-out the clock.

Approaching a much larger hedgerow, feeling supremely confident and liberated from mental obesity, Adam leapt like a champion hurdler, soaring, stretching for those extra inches. He was over the hedge, and …

Slaaap!

Straight into the viro wall. Adam froze mid-flight sinking slightly into an invisible barrier of firm foam.

Pop!

The wall sprung back into shape, the force thrusting Adam violently backwards through the spiky hedgerow, and slamming him hard against the ground.

Unable to speak, dribbling a mouthful of blood and teeth, Adam did not move. Unlike his last encounter with a viro wall, this time there were significant injuries. The glam gang closed around him - sparkling towering figures, as if viewed through a fish eye lens.

"Copacabana, you are so full of surprises," said Rampage. "Sure, there have been others we've caught at the wall, but none that made such an impression. You were right about the trousers slowing you down, and I suspect that if you knew the viro layout, we would have struggled to catch you. Loose trousers and good local knowledge, the perfect combination, who'd have thought."

Adam heaved his broken body into a semi-sitting position, the hedgerow providing a thorny backrest. Trying to talk only coughed up sticky gurgles of blood and phlegm, and one of his legs appeared to be at an impossible angle, a splintered bone protruding sharply through the lower calf.

"Now me … smash … him up!" shouted Ziggy, his cricket bat raised, ready to strike.

Once again, Rampage intervened, and Ziggy, glowering fiercely, lowered the weapon.

"You gave us some good sport there, Copacabana. It's all recorded, even the parts before you hid under the bridge. We will watch the chases on the big screens at the Grand Feast. Unless your Texan friend does something amazing, your wall-smack has got to be the highlight of the day."

Another gurgle of crimson bubbles flopped from Adam's mouth, as he attempted to plead for his life - his vocal chords a punctured mess of twigs and thorns.

"I am going to let you choose the manner of your death," said Rampage. "I know it's a bit of an empty gesture since you won't remember it tomorrow, but you've earned it. Now you have three options. Firstly myself."

Rampage waved his obsidian blade in front of Adam:

"I work fast. I simply cut your throat, and as you bleed out, I might stab you a few times just for fun. No variety, just quick and efficient. Now let me introduce Stardust, the quiet one."

Stardust, pallid and gaunt, unsheathed a slender steel rapier, the hilt an ornate 17th century affair.

"I look forward to using this on you," he said softly, his expression cold, unkind.

Rampage continued, "What Stardust will do is basically flourish his sword and run you through; straight through the heart. Then he'll swish his sword across your chest, making an 'S' - carving his signature. Ziggy here, will 'smash you up'. There is not much more to it than that. Could be a slower death, because Ziggy's not so precise when he's in his 'smashing' rage, unless he starts on your skull of course. If you're unlucky, you might live to hear the crepitus of your broken bones, much like a sharp scratchy bass line. If it goes on too long, say a couple of minutes, then I'll force Ziggy to smash in your skull."

Rampage rubbed his hands together in eager anticipation. The whole gang leaned in, waiting for Adam's answer. Not being able to talk, Adam used his fingers. He intended to pick option one, the blade. Unfortunately, in his reduced state, some fingers stiff and twisted, he inadvertently gave the group the 'screw you' single finger.

Rampage frowned, "That's unfortunate. That is very unfortunate. I thought we had a little unspoken understanding here, a bit of mutual respect."

Realising his mistake, Adam tried to shout an apology, but instead just launched a spray of sticky red globs that coated his assailant's legs and boots. Rampage, now enraged, motioned for Ziggy and Stardust to step forward.

"You disrespectful little shit. We are now going to make you suffer. Remember I told you about our torturing period, how efficient we became. Well, we work best as a team, so get ready for some painful synchronicity. Shame you won't remember this tomorrow."

Rampage flicked his wrist, bringing forth the blade:

"Come on boys, let's get to work!"

The world went black. Everything became almost nothing, with an enveloping liquid darkness, and the burning strands fast approaching. Adam Eden was dead … again.

RESURRECT AND REPEAT

Adam shuddered awake, gulped a lungful of air, and howled with fear and anguish. Alive again, back in the annexe, the burning strands of the dark place still tormented his mind. He ran his fingers across the bed sheet, seeking texture, sensation, corporeal affirmation. This time there was no welcoming committee, and no orange jumpsuit with black boots. Despite feeling sluggish and stiff, the pain was less intense this time, and he had little trouble keeping his eyes open. It seemed that, like most things in life, resurrection was easier the second time around.

Sitting up in bed, Adam struggled out of a transparent polythene-like coverall, feeling uncomfortably like a delivery from a dry cleaner. Discarding the coverall on the floor, he noticed a red band around his wrist. Closer inspection revealed it to be elastic, perhaps silicon or neoprene, with tiny white symbols all the way round. It reminded Adam of the charity bands that people found so popular in his previous life. He put the band in the top drawer of his bedside cabinet, wearily got to his feet, and stretched.

Adam drank down the small bottle of revitalizing blue liquid left thoughtfully by the bed, which brought instant energy and suppleness. He ignored the protective eyeshades, since his eyes were only slightly sore. Next to the eyeshades, folded neatly was yet another set of the Hawaiian clothes. Adam groaned.

There was change, hardly noticeable, but the clothes had subtly altered. The trousers seemed looser in the crotch, still very tight, though no longer painfully so. The deck shoes, once smooth, had gained an almost imperceptible weave pattern on the soles. Though grateful for the small differences, Adam still thought the clothes far too colourful for his tastes.

Downstairs in the lounge area, hazily unsure of his priorities, Adam retrieved a bottle of Belgium beer from the dispenser, and slumped into a leather chair by the front window. He desperately wanted to talk to someone about his violent experience. Due to the time channelling rules on memories of death, his last memory from the previous day was running through a field of wheat. Anything beyond that was gone.

The clock read 9:21am, and Adam caught a glimpse of a figure in the distance. Peering furtively through the vertical window blinds, he saw Stern striding naked alongside the stream.

Adam had no idea what took place under the cover of the trees every morning, but he needed answers. It was time to pay Stern a visit. Before Adam could finish his thought there were three sharp knocks at the side door only a few feet away. Adam, startled and still shaky from his recent resurrection, dropped the beer bottle on the floor. It did not sound like a cane, but whoever was out there had chosen to knock, thrice, hard, and insistent.

Opening the door, he half expected his father to be standing there. Instead, it was a woman in a full-length figure hugging dress that seemed entirely made of hoops of gold brocade. Elegant and mysterious, Adam caught a waft of her perfume: metallised leather and anise. Possessing perfect alabaster skin, and stylishly coiffured auburn hair, her eyes burned with a piercing blue intensity that easily matched Stern's. Before Adam could speak, a small plastic package was thrust in front of his face, accompanied by a well-mannered voice:

"Aloe Vera Babysoother Wet-Wipes for the man who cannot wipe properly!"

Taking a couple of steps back, Adam's foot rolled on the dropped beer bottle, causing him to lose his balance. Toppling backwards, wildly flaying out with his arms, he narrowly avoided cracking his head on the wooden windowsill. Instead, he fell against the leather designer chair, his neck sliding heavily along the sharp edge of the stainless steel arm.

Adam blacked out for a few moments before opening his eyes. Feeling strangely serene, he found himself lying face up on the floor, the unknown woman kneeling over him, frantically ripping open the wet-wipes packet. She held a number of wipes firmly against Adam's neck, and through her sobs he could hear her speaking:

"What happened? Why did you fall over like that? It will not stop. I cannot get it to stop."

Her sobbing increased and she clasped Adam's face, one hand wet with warm blood. Moving closer, lips almost touching, she whispered softly, "I cannot stop the blood. The cut is too long and too deep. I am so sorry I cannot do more for you. Please forgive my damned ineptitude."

A single tear fell on Adam's cheek, and he closed his eyes once more. Soon the shadows of unconsciousness got menacingly darker. Adam was yet again, dead again.

STERN ACCOUNT

Alive once more, bawling his eyes out, the painful darkness still overwhelmed his thoughts. Adam thumped the sheets, screaming for the mental torture to end. Slowly, mercifully, the reality of the annexe took precedence, allowing a modicum of physical control.

The transparent coverall was discarded, and the wristband thrown in the top drawer of the bedside cabinet, joining the one from the day before. Despite the extreme mental anguish, Adam did not experience real physical pain this time, though he still drank the blue liquid left by the bed for the instant energy it provided. Puzzlingly, lying alongside the now redundant eyeshades was a blue plastic packet of Aloe Vera Babysoother Wet-Wipes. Either the AI was feeling sympathy for him, or someone had been in the annexe. Adam shuddered. Perhaps they were still here. His last memory from the previous day was watching Stern walk into the woods. How had he died? Was it murder?

After changing into his clothes, Adam just sat on the edge of the bed, unsure about going downstairs. Shivering with fear, he attempted to clear his mind of his recent harrowing ordeals.

Suddenly, Adam heard the door downstairs unlocking, and the sound of someone hurrying up the spiral staircase. Adam rose to confront the intruder. It was Stern, panting heavily, naked except for boxer shorts and trainers, and glistening with sweat.

"Oh my God," cried Adam in fear. "What do you want? Why are you here?"

Stern raised an arm, imploring Adam to let him catch his breath.

"Don't get any nearer," warned Adam. "I'm not dying again this week. Have you come to kill me? Are you carrying any weapons?"

Stern made an 'are you kidding me' gesture, and slowly managed to control his breathing:

"I promise I'm not here to kill you. I know what happened. It was an accident, nothing more."

"So I wasn't murdered?"

"It didn't go down like that. Look, I knew you'd be stressing out so I got here as fast as I could, without your folks knowing. I jumped straight outta bed at eight, and floored it here in the Satan Bug. I didn't even stop to dress. The buggy's hidden a couple of hundred yards away behind some trees. I sprinted the rest of the way."

"Hidden? Why the secrecy?"

"Your folks are great guys but they're still riled up from the dinner. They think we should all give you the cold-shoulder for a few months. Kaylee has no problem with that, but this is my viro, and I obey nobody's rules but my own. That said, I thought it best to keep this between just you and me."

"Your viro?"

"Long story, another time, muchacho. Come downstairs. You look like you need a strong drink."

Settling in the lounge, Adam sat uncomfortably in the designer chair by the front window. Stern handed him a brandy, Calvados Pays D'Auge, and drew up a chair for himself. Knocking back the warming red mahogany liquid, Adam tried to relax. Running a hand down the arm of the chair, he shuddered, the dark place momentarily seeping into his consciousness.

"I can't stay here," said Adam. "I've gotta get out. Anywhere but here. What about your house, can we talk there?"

"I don't think Kaylee would approve of that. You're a child-killer, remember. Look, there's a place in the woods. Very peaceful, I spend a lot of time there."

"Sounds good to me."

After a brisk walk, they reached the buggy, and were soon speeding across the meadow. They raced into the woods, bumping dangerously along a narrow rutted track. Stern did not slow down, grinning maniacally, enjoying the rush, purposefully driving close to the trees. About halfway into the woods, close to a ford where the stream passed, Stern slammed on the brakes.

Relieved that the ride was over, Adam disembarked. Stern grabbed a holdall from the trunk, and led Adam a few metres back down the track. A large gap in the trees revealed a small path winding through the artificial undergrowth. They followed the path to a circular grassy clearing, where a couple of fallen tree trunks provided seating. Between the trunks was a flat-topped storage chest, which also served as a low table.

Whilst Stern got dressed in a simple jeans and t-shirt combo, Adam nonchalantly opened the chest. It was full of paperback books. Closer inspection revealed them as dime store romance novels – the covers adorned with attractive couples in passionate embrace, heaving chests, and swathes of blue silk and red velvet.

"Whoa, how did you open that?" demanded Stern, obviously alarmed.

"Easy, I just lifted the lid. The key's still in the lock."

"Damn, I thought I locked it. All that trouble with you yesterday, and I must have forgotten. Damn."

"They're only books. What's the big deal?"

"They may only be books, but it's my reputation at stake."

Stern slapped his own forehead:

"The first time I bring someone here, I leave the damned storage box unlocked. After all these years, why now?"

Adam closed the lid:

"I still don't get what's the big deal."

"People can't know I read romance novels. You know my story. You know how I am with the ladies. It took huge amounts of marketing to convince people that Hind-Reading was sexy and manly. Women read these novels so that they can fantasize about guys like me. I'm supposed to be the guy in the novel, not the guy reading them."

"I'm sure some guys …"

"Gay guys, effeminate guys, over-emotional guys, but not me. Not Stern Lovass."

"And what's this got to do with your naked walks?"

"Oh that," he sighed. "Ok, seeing as you know about the books I may as well tell you. It's to do with your parents, that's what. Kaylee's no threat. She lies in bed drinking and watching soaps all morning. I take the buggy so she'd have to walk here if she wanted to know what's going on, and that's never gonna happen. However, your parents, no offense, are both nosey, and Edna's a natural born gossip."

"And how does walking into the woods naked make them less nosey. For goodness sake, my Mum had her binoculars out."

"Do you seriously think Harry is gonna follow a naked man into the woods? He probably thinks I get up to all sorts of depraved acts in here, and that's how I want it. There's no way he wants a piece of that. And, as for Edna, there's no way Harry will let her follow a naked man into the woods. The routine has worked for years. You're the worry now."

Adam promised to keep the books a secret, although he still considered the entire matter trivial. He locked the chest and handed over the key. Stern, unconvinced, exposed an unexpected malevolence, and grabbed Adam roughly by the collar:

"Don't mess with me, Adam! None of this gets out, understand? Otherwise, you'll have another appointment with the dark place. You have my guarantee on that."

Other men, greater men, would have taken offense, and retaliated against such an unnecessary threat. Adam, burdened by the habits of his former life and subdued by recent events, simply nodded, mumbling that Stern had nothing to worry about.

Sensing he had gone too far, Stern slapped Adam on the arm:

"Thanks buddy, I respect that. Just got my reputation to think of, that's all. I shouldn't be so hard on you, considering what you've been through. Now, I expect you'd like to know how you died."

Adam was surprised at how quickly the events leading to his death were explained. He had no recollection of Sofia, Stern's daughter, paying a visit, or of slipping up on a bottle. The designer chair throat-cutting incident made him wince, as did Sofia's inability to staunch the gush of blood. At least he now knew where the wet-wipes came from.

"So, the chair did it. I thought someone had murdered me because of the child murderer accusation. I went through all that pain because of a stupid designer chair."

"Don't forget the bottle," laughed Stern. "The bottle's gotta take some of the blame. Now, talking of bottles ..."

Rummaging through the holdall, Stern produced a couple of beer bottles—Export Lovass Lager—and tossed one to Adam. Pale gold in colour, full-bodied and aromatic, with a dry bitterness produced by extended cold lagering, it went down easy.

"So Adam, now for the main reason for our little powwow. When Sofia realised she couldn't do any more for you, she called me ... we have walkie-talkies for emergencies. I was here at the time, reading, and ran straight over. By the time I got to the annexe you were dead, but Sofia wanted me to look upstairs."

"I know where this is going."

"It was obvious you'd just been resurrected. I mean, there was a protective coverall on the floor, and eyeshades next to the bed. What happened? I called

81

round the day after the dinner but nobody answered. I figured you took my advice and went on a trip. You didn't commit suicide, did you?"

"No, I took your advice. I visited a 1970's Glam-Rock Party Viro."

"And?"

"Well, at first they were fabulous hosts. I felt out of place with these clothes, seeing as everyone was dressed in glam costume, but they made me feel welcome. They even laid on a 70's buffet, which was very impressive. It was all going great until they announced that all the guests would be hunted and killed. Obviously, I have no memory of my death, but I'm sure it was pretty gruesome and extremely painful. So, thanks for the advice."

Much to Adam's surprise, Stern showed no remorse or sympathy, instead clapping his hands together, and whooping with delight:

"Yes, yes, that's a story right there! Oh wow, sounds like you dropped-in on a psychoviro. That's where they dump all the lunatics. Rare, so rare. Tell me, do they hunt people regularly or was it a one off event?"

"They killed me! I went through that bloody dark place with the burning lines. A warning would've been nice."

Stern raised his hands as if owning up to guilt, yet remained unnervingly upbeat:

"You're right. I apologise. I should have said something about those kinds of places, but I had the sex urge and wasn't thinking straight. Blame this one on the glorious gonads. It's just that psychoviros are so rare. Now if you don't mind, I want you to tell me everything you remember, and don't spare me the details."

Stern sat wide-eyed, enraptured by Adam's lurid account of the fatal visit. Whether it was the buffet, the local's colourful attire, or the choice of weaponry, he thirstily drank in the information. Out of fear of being implicated in another child-murder, Adam decided to keep Joshua out of the story. When Adam mentioned the 1970's dispensers Stern called an abrupt halt:

"Hold on there, what do you mean the dispensers were altered? Dispensers adapt themselves to the user, they can't be set to a specific place or period. Even a concierge can't do that. Are you sure of this?"

"Well, I guess Rampage could have been lying."

Stern waved the matter away, and told Adam to carry on the story. Listening intently, he did not interrupt again until Adam described the chase across the slippery field:

"Whoa, hold on a minute. Do you mean the field was wet?"

"Yes, I kept slipping."

"Was it muddy, or just wet?"

"Muddy, definitely muddy, like real wet soil. They had much higher quality trees, grass, and everything. It looked, felt, even smelt like the real thing. I admit it had me fooled."

"That's odd; I've never seen a viro with real flora, and definitely not mud. The quality here is pretty low, and we don't have any audio and olfactory effects, but what you've just described is mega high-end. You know, I'm getting a delicious vibe about this. It might just be that you visited one of the rarest viros of all. Tell me more about this leader."

"They call him Groover, but there's not much to tell. If I got near him, I got blocked by some of the locals, but he was definitely in charge."

"Did anyone call the guy by any other name? Think very carefully, because this is really important."

"Well, I already told you I recognised some of them as famous serial killers. I'm sure in his original life, Groover was really ..."

"No, no, no, I'm not interested in his first life name. Try to remember if anyone used another name or title in reference to this guy. Anything, no matter how stupid you think it sounds."

One incident came to mind, which Adam previously thought too trifling to mention:

"Now don't get mad if this is a load of nonsense, but there's something I remember at the buffet. I was already pretty stuffed, but fancied trying the fondue. There were these two locals next to me, whingeing about the luncheon meat sandwiches. They were obviously blaming the leader for the low quality of the meat, but they weren't calling him Groover. They were whispering so it was hard for me to hear, and you must realise that I was deep in thought at the time. I couldn't decide whether to have cheese fondue or chocolate fondue."

"And so ..."

"Oh, I chose the chocolate."

"No, you idiot, the name!"

"Oh yes, the name. I think they were calling him, and don't laugh at this, 'Gino', or maybe 'Gina'."

Stern looked deadly serious. Trembling with anticipation, he asked in a calm measured manner:

"Now, are you sure it was one of those names, or was it something very slightly different?"

"To be honest, and again don't laugh, it sounded more like 'Genie'. You know, like the fat bloke in the lamp who grants three wishes."

Before the sentence was even finished, Stern was ecstatically leaping about the clearing, cheering wildly, waving his arms in the air like the Grand Prize winner on a game show. Troubled by this callous display, Adam considered leaving. Stern, failing to hide his obvious pleasure, sat down and explained himself:

"Adam, my friend, you hit the jackpot. Of all the viros in all the Viroverse, you visit one with a Genie. I know you suffered, and nobody wants to go to the dark place again, but seeing a Genie has gotta count as a silver lining."

"I certainly don't feel privileged. What the hell is a Genie?"

Stern explained how Genie was Viroverse slang for Original, the first humans selected for resurrection. In the beginning, the researchers brought back inanimate material from the past, then as the process became more reliable, channelled animal memory and brain tissue.

When it came to humans, they needed subjects who were despised, and who would not be missed if the experimental procedures failed. Historical figures, such as infamous dictators, were excluded, since the authorities already knew they had strong market value.

A handful of irredeemable serial killers were chosen. Resurrected into a world before the construction of the viros, and before miniaturisation, it was rumoured that these originals were given full size bodies, and had access to the real world. They apparently struck up close relationships with the research scientists, saw the draft plans of the extensive viro system, and even witnessed the first commercial resurrections. When the time came, they too were miniaturised, but not before gaining a vast knowledge of the both the real world and the Viroverse. Given special privileges, and viros of their own design, the Originals lived like feudal barons, albeit confined to their own despotic square mile.

Bound by a loose code of honour, it was said that any deal struck with a Genie was golden, but that only the foolish would dare enter their lair. Luckily, Genies and other inhabitants of psychoviros were prohibited from requesting visits to other viros – like pseudo-vampires they could only be invited in. Although intrigued by the story, Adam was far from happy:

"Ok, it might be a silver lining but not worth suffering the dark place, not even close."

"Can't disagree with that, but at least you've given me some kickass stories to tell. There's usually nothing going on in this new world, apart from mindless gossip, so any scrap of real news is highly prized. So far, you've supplied me with the dinner episode, death by chair, hunted by psychos, and now topping all that, a close encounter with a Genie. Not bad for an undesirable."

"I'm glad my suffering has proved useful to you."

"Ha, sarcasm won't make you happy. Try to look at the upside of things for once. Look, I owe you big for the stories you've given me. Name your price, and I'll see what I can do. Come on, what do you want?"

"A way out of his madhouse."

"Ha, not a chance. There's no way out. You could click your heels all day long, but you ain't Dorothy, and you ain't going home. Now, think again, what do you want?"

"Ok, I want to get in contact with Emmanuel Beaumont and Scarlett Slaughter. I was with them the night I died. Trouble is, Manny has blocked me and Scarlett hasn't been resurrected."

"Do you know if Scarlett's status is yellow or red?"

"Yellow, I think. The text was flashing yellow."

"You're in luck. Yellow means she is on the resurrection shortlist. Should only be a few years. Not long in the scheme of things, but you'll have to wait. Now, what about Manny, what colour was the text."

"Blue, although my children flashed red. What's the difference?"

"Red, I'm sorry to say, means a personal block, and I think we know what that's about. Blue means a global block, so it's probably not personal. Could be your friend has some issues with this new world."

Realising that contacting Scarlett was an unavoidable waiting game, Adam gave Stern more details about Manny. Stern promised to look into the matter, promising to convince Manny to contact Adam. With an extensive network of contacts, and many favours owed, Stern guessed it would only take a couple of weeks. After shaking hands on the deal, Stern made to leave:

"Should be getting back before Kaylee starts missing me. I'll drop you off first."

"I think I'll sit here a while longer if you don't mind. Not really ready to go back yet."

"Suit yourself, friend," said Stern turning to leave.

Before disappearing down the path, Stern paused a moment:

"Hey Adam, if my daughter comes calling, please don't die on her again."

SURPRISING SIREN

Eight a.m. two days after the meeting in the woods, and it took only seconds to realise the annexe had changed. The bed, previously a super king, was now a standard double, and the room itself appeared smaller. Throwing on his gown, Adam glanced out of the rear window, only to find the bedroom was now on the ground floor. Opening the new bedroom door led straight into the lounge, and he immediately noticed that the staircase was gone, the ceiling smooth plastered. Compounding the shock and disbelief, the beloved Crapper-style toilet was also gone, replaced with a bland push-button compact unit—a sterile utilitarian mockery of Adam's contemplative sanctuary.

About three in the afternoon, wearing the usual attire, Adam sat slumped in the now infamous designer chair by the front window. There was absolutely no access to the upstairs, the spacious two-floor annexe now a 'cosy' two room affair. Finishing a bottle of dark Belgium beer, his third, Adam wondered if this was a punishment for some unnamed misdemeanour. Asking his parents was not an option, and Stern had not visited since their woodland meeting.

Someone gently knocked at the side door. Placing the empty bottle on the windowsill, Adam opened the door to greet his visitor. It was a woman in full-length figure hugging dress that seemed entirely made of hoops of red brocade. She had flawless alabaster skin, and stylishly coiffured auburn hair. Before Adam could speak, she proffered a mesh-gloved hand, accompanied by a well-mannered voice:

"Sofia Saghausen, pleased to meet you."

Taking a step back, Adam accidently knocked the beer bottle onto the floor. Sofia reacted instantly, grabbing him by the collar and drawing him into a close embrace. Cheek to cheek, Adam savoured the heady fragrance of metallised leather and anise. She spoke softly into his ear:

"Call me old-fashioned, but a gentleman should at least offer a lady a seat and a drink before dying."

Hurriedly breaking the embrace, Adam apologised, awkwardly teasing that Sofia would be the death of him.

"Dear boy, I was just an innocent bystander. Rather blame your innate clumsiness. And, as for the neck wound, that was down to Ludwig Mies van der Rohe."

"So there was someone else involved. I thought as much. I guess Stern lied to me."

"Stupid boy, Mies designed the chair you fell on. The Brno chair, gorgeous 20th century modernist cantilever design, though evidently unsuitable for the innately clumsy and death prone."

Too bewildered to react, Adam politely offered his guest a seat, and sat down on the sofa. Sofia simply stood, emitting a single polite cough.

"What now?" asked Adam

"It is customary for the host to stand until the guest is seated."

"Ha, but when in Rome."

"I assure you, we are a long way from Rome. Now, if you don't mind."

Grudgingly, Adam stood up, gesturing politely for Sofia to sit. Infuriatingly, she choose to sit in the place he had just vacated. Adam sat at the other end of the large sofa, allowing two cushions of separation.

"Hmm, you seem to be missing a staircase," noted Sofia.

"It was like this when I woke up this morning. I have no idea what's going on."

"Don't worry yourself, dear boy. Probably just a two-night remodel. You will know when you wake up tomorrow. Now, where's that drink you offered?"

"I didn't offer one."

"I know. You have the worst manners."

Persuaded by her beauty rather than her demanding pomposity, Adam went over to the dispenser:

"What'll it be, tea?"

"Jasmin thé vert, s'il vous plait."

"Ok … err … one jasmine green tea, coming right up."

"And make sure it is fresh diffused loose leaf, served in a bone china cup, with a saucer of course. And don't you dare add milk or sugar."

"I've only got mugs. I'm still on the limited dispenser access. You're welcome to get one yourself if you wish."

"A mug will suffice."

Not wanting to arouse further scorn, Adam also had a mug of green tea, which he did not enjoy. Asking if Sofia knew why Stern had not called prompted laughter and further insults:

"You are so naïve. Father only spent time with you to get some good gossip. I'm sure he doesn't really like you. You see, he believes that this is his viro, and that you are one of the little people he must watch over. He sees you more as a Subject than a friend."

"This place just keeps getting better and better. So why are you here? Don't you know I'm the local leper."

"Well dear boy, don't let this flatter you, but I need someone to talk to. Father invites me here every Thursday. It is an open invitation, but he is often away visiting some other viro and forgets to inform me. Even when he is here, I have time on my hands."

"Your mum seems the lively sort. Don't you get on with her?"

"You mean Kaylee, don't you?"

Adam nodded slowly, cautiously, prompting a fierce response from his guest.

"How dare you! You think that bubble-headed lush is my mother? Do I look like I have even a smidgen of her trailer park DNA? Sheesh, it is no wonder everyone's avoiding you."

"No, no, it's just nobody told me. I wouldn't have thought it otherwise ... honestly."

"Kaylee was a trainee make-up girl on the set of The Golden Hind. She and my father were having an affair. My mother lives in a viro with her devoted second husband. Kaylee's still with my father because the dim-witted AI thinks they are right for one another."

Working hard to find common ground for conversation, Adam showed Sofia the computer. She marvelled at the device, amused at its large size and low processing power, attracted by its antique charm.

Eventually, the subject of movies and television came up. Sofia was an aficionado of the 'classics', meaning late 20th century entertainment. An in-depth discussion ensued about zombies, killer cyborgs, early CGI, and the convergence of media. Sofia's revelations on cerebral interaction and retinal projection were expected developments, but still stunning. She went on to describe the virtual corporate worlds of the 22nd century, and the all-encompassing 24-hour mind monitoring, which made good on science fiction's dark promise. Adam was at first surprised how indifferently Sofia accepted such a mentally invasive commerciality, but soon realised that every generation took society's constructs, good and evil, for granted.

"So Adam, what movie, television series, or video game does this remind you of? I'm talking about the whole set-up: resurrection, the viros, everything. Just give the title and I will tell you what I think."

"What about books? Do they count?"

"You read, splendid. I always forget that reading was still popular in your day. Now, take your best shot."

"The Matrix?"

"So many people choose that, but it is such a lazy choice. No resurrection, or eternal life, and we are not batteries."

"Immortality Inc?"

"Oh my, I have never heard of that. Tell me more."

"People are resurrected in the future into new bodies. No viros though, and they have proved there's an afterlife. I think they made a film about it called Freejack."

"Oh, I have heard of that. Nothing like this. Anymore?"

"Cockaigne?"

Sofia eyed Adam suspiciously. "Again, I have never heard of that. Sounds a bit rude, you're not making it up I hope?"

"No, it's a mythical medieval land of plenty. You live forever, and can have anything you want. An old bloke from the streets told me about it. He called it the hobo's paradise."

"If that's true then well done. Still not quite there though."

"Riverworld?"

"Oh my, you are more knowledgeable than I thought. You've got resurrection, and you're brought back if you die again. Even free food is provided. Very close, but not quite."

"Ok, I give in," said Adam. "What's the answer, if there is one?"

"Three Feet of Sky."

"Never heard of it."

"Very popular in its day. A classic of the late 21st century."

"Hey, I died in 2010, how the Hell am I supposed to know about that?"

"Oh stop your whining; it is just a bit of fun."

"Ok, So what's 'Three Feet of Sky'? Is it a movie?"

Well, so you won't get confused, I will call it a movie, although it was far more interactive and emotionally socketed. It came out in 2099. The plot was nothing special, just some pithy romance, but the background details fitted this world like a glove: technological resurrection, Caretakers, Environments, falling asleep at 12 pm, even decreased libido. Some say the movie was the original inspiration for this entire project - a prime example of life copying art. You don't have the technology to view the movie, so I'll describe it to you."

Only initially interested, for the next hour Adam endured a long laboriously detailed deconstructive review of the movie. Only after the strategic placement of fondant—fancies and iced buns did the conversation move to other matters. Licking sticky icing off his fingers, Adam told Sofia about Stern's sexual urges at the Indian dinner. Without a hint of shame, she readily accepted it was a family trait, and that she had been without a partner since resurrection. Adam joked that he was currently available, and received a blunt belittling response:

"Oh Adam poor misguided baby, I'm not interested in becoming your new Eve. Even if I liked your personality, you do not have what it takes … physically."

"Oh, I see … err, hang on, how do you know that?"

Lost for words, Sofia slightly lowered her gaze, hiding a guilty expression.

Adam furrowed his brow, "When I died, did you …"

"Well, father was conducting a hind-reading round the back, so I took a peek round the front."

"Oh … my … god, I was dead! What kind of family are you?"

Sofia regained her composure and waved away Adam's indignation:

"Oh get over yourself. Neither of us found what we were looking for. At least you get the benefit of my sparkling conversation once a week. Now, why don't we discuss French cuisine? How do you feel about Poulet de Bresse?"

The mostly one-sided conversation carried on for another hour, before a loud siren wailed across the viro, interrupting any further tedium.

"Oh this is so exciting," exclaimed Sofia, already out of her seat. "That's the resurrection siren. My dear Adam, you are about to have a new addition to the viro."

OH BROTHER, WHAT ART THOU?

Only fifty yards from the annexe, all present stood waiting, gazing at a small circular area of grass ringed with red lights. Nearby, the ovoid pod with the red reclining cushion hovered silently, ready to transport the newly resurrected to the concierge. Harry and Edna stood close to the ring of lights, ready with a bottle of the blue liquid and a pair of the eyeshades. Though seemingly eager to greet the new arrival, their body language and nervous tone conveyed a subtle sense of trepidation – they knew something and they were worried.

Adam and Sofia stood a few feet away, watching quietly as the resurrection time loomed. Stern and Kaylee were not present, Sofia blaming their absence on her father's aversion to the resurrection process. Realising his parents were still giving him the cold shoulder, Adam decided to keep his distance. He was sure that Robert, his younger brother, was about to appear – not only was he an obvious candidate, but Harry and Edna kept muttering the name.

A faint trace of smugness betrayed Sofia's otherwise serene countenance. She evidently relished the notoriety of standing alongside the viro pariah, aware of the gossip it would generate:

"My dear Adam, please forgive my forgetfulness, but I looked into that murder you allegedly committed. It was the main reason I came to see you today, but with all the interesting conversation, it completely slipped my mind."

"You said 'allegedly'. Does that mean you don't think I did it?"

Sofia tittered in an affected patronising fashion:

"No, no, no, I think you did it. All the evidence points to you as the murderer: witness statements, forensics, psychological reports, and the autopsy. I only used the word 'allegedly' because I do not claim to have professional detective skills, nor any innate talent in this area."

"But, Stern said you were the one for the job."

"Silly boy, father died when I was only twelve, and I will always be his little Princess. He thinks I can do anything."

"Oh great, now I don't know what to think."

"Well, if it's any consolation, there was one piece of evidence that did not sit straight with me."

"Go on."

"CCTV footage from a hidden camera behind the bar. You cannot see much because the bar is so crowded, but every now and then a gap opens up, and there you are."

"Are you sure it's me? I was much larger then."

"Hah, please don't remind me, or I will start laughing again. There was a drunken blonde woman who I gather was your legal representative, and some skinny balding fellow who had his back to the camera. You were sitting between them."

"Yeah, that was me. So what didn't sit straight?"

"You did not appear to be drunk. In fact, you looked quite cheerful, calm, and sober. Even in the CCTV footage from outside the bar, you appeared sober. However, the autopsy found excessive alcohol in your bloodstream so I guess you are just practised at hiding your inebriation. As I said, I do not possess any professional detective skills."

"I was not drunk!"

"Oh Adam, don't you see, if you were sober, then it means you were fully in control when you murdered the poor father and his son. At least being drunk, you can blame the alcohol."

Adam sighed, and shook his head. With the resurrection time fast approaching, he asked Sofia to leave the murder discussion for another day. Sofia, always in eager conversation mode, switched subjects without a break in breath:

"So, what is Robert like? All I know is that he dabbled in property and lived in Australia."

"Let's see, he's shorter than me and has never been fat: hair a bit lighter than mine, perfect teeth. You know, I hate to say this but he was always the better looking one."

"What about personality? Intelligent, likeable or is he like you?"

Adam ignored the insult:

"Robert's the type who's outwardly friendly and cheeky, but underneath he's extremely sensitive. Never took much to upset him, and he could never admit when things went wrong. I'm sure that's why he never came back from Oz. In 2006, he decided to leverage all he had to get into property speculation. I believe he raised nearly three million dollars using the ... err ...Yen Carry Trade. I remember it because the phrase always made me think of Chinese Takeaway."

"No wonder you got so fat. Hmm, 2006, just as the bubble burst. Poor boy should have done his homework; the signs were already there. I studied the crash at University. So much borrowed by so many with so little knowledge. Do you know where he wasted the money?"

"Bought into developments in Florida, and a couple of apartment complexes in Bulgaria, maybe more. Certainly lost a fortune when the crash came. To be honest, I never heard from him again."

"Well let's hope he is over it after all these centuries. I just adore an emotional family reunion."

All conversation ceased as the ring of lights turned amber for a few seconds, then green. With unexpected speed, a silvery metallic cylinder, the size of a large phone box, thrust up through the grass. A doorway slid silently open, and the jump-suited occupant was smoothly ejected. Once clear of its human cargo, the cylinder slipped back down, and the grass returned to its previous state - the lights flashing red three more times.

It was not only Edna's scream that signalled something was wrong. The figure standing before them was nearly seven feet tall, and grotesquely muscular, the orange jumpsuit stretched over every bulge. Though vaguely reminiscent of Robert, only a close friend or family member would have recognised him. Sitting atop a disturbingly thin sinewy neck was a huge misshapen moonfaced head, with large cartoonish eyes and a small patch of sticky up hair.

Robert cried huge teardrops and stomped his booted feet, clearly suffering the pain of resurrection. Though clearly shocked, Harry acted with fatherly stoicism, and attempted to administer the rejuvenating blue liquid. Robert drank only half the bottle before letting the rest dribble down his front. Edna, armed with the eyeshades, approached her son, a determined smile on her face:

"Robert, it's your mother. Do not be afraid, my dear, I am here to help. Let me put these on you, and the nasty pain in your eyes will go away."

At the sound of his mother's voice, Robert emitted a cheerful squeal, and lifted her off her feet. He clumsily danced around with guttural howls of pleasure, Edna swinging wildly about. Displaying an uncharacteristic presence of mind, boosted by motherly determination, she climbed a few inches, and fixed the eyeshades in place. However, free of eye pain, Robert danced with increased enthusiasm.

"Robert, put me down! Put me down at once, you're scaring me!" wailed Edna, clinging desperately to her hulking son.

Robert immediately obeyed, placing his mother gently on the ground, and patting the top of her head in an act of apology. Harry edged forward, and cautiously shook his son's fat hand:

"Welcome home Robert. It's good to have you back, son. You need to see a very nice person called the concierge, but first your mother and I are going to take you to the house, where you can relax. Do you understand?"

After a few wide-eyed nods, and a sharp gurgling sound that may have been the word 'yes', they began the slow walk back to Eden Manor. As Robert passed Adam and Sofia, he stopped and pointed. Adam waved at his mutated brother:

"Hey, Robert, It's me Adam, your brother. We'll get together sometime for Cornettos."

Robert's eyes bulged like golf balls, and he continued pointing excitedly at Adam, screaming with strained maniacal laughter, his huge slobbering mouth contorted into a mocking sneer. Without a word, Harry and Edna continued on, arm in arm with their son. Adam turned to Sofia, shaking his head:

"I just don't know what to say. Monstrous, absolutely monstrous. He's like a big orange Hulk with the head of a Cabbage Patch Doll. What the Hell's gone wrong?"

"Degraded DNA, I've seen it before. Do not worry yourself, your brother is not a danger to anyone, otherwise he would not be here. Everyone is thoroughly vetted by the A.I. You were right about one thing though."

"What's that?"

"He is the better looking one."

Projecting a tone of disinterest, Sofia nonchalantly made an excuse to leave, perhaps anxious to tell Stern about Robert's arrival. Before leaving, she promised to visit the same time the following week. As a parting shot, she asked, "Did you know I was married eleven times?"

"No."

"Splendid, that's what we will talk about next Thursday over tea and cakes. You can hear all about my husbands, and I will not spare you the juicy details. Au revoir, Adam."

Once Sofia was a fair distance away, Adam ran after his parents, catching them only a few yards from the house. Edna kept her back turned, but Harry was prepared to talk:

"What do you want, Adam? Can't you see we're busy? Remember, you're still persona non grata around here."

"You knew something was wrong before Robert came back. How did you know?"

"The concierge told us Robert was due for resurrection, and she hinted that there was a problem. Still a bit of a shock though."

"I thought the concierge didn't talk about anyone else. She told me it wasn't allowed."

Edna faced Adam, fuming at the delay:

"Don't be such an idiot. It depends how you phrase the questions. You don't have to be a genius to get the right information."

Harry explained, "Sometimes, making the question about oneself can get round the rules. Now, if you don't mind, we have promised Robert a strawberry ice-cream and a nice mug of hot chocolate before he goes to see the concierge."

Adam began walking back to the annexe when a shocking thought occurred to him. He called over to his father, who was manoeuvring a resistant Robert through the Manor doorway:

"Dad, just one question."

"Make it quick, this is wearing me out. Better still, give me a hand, he's a stubborn one."

Returning, Adam lent his weight to the big push:

"Robert, is he going to live with you?"

Harry hesitated, feigning a moment of breathlessness, before sheepishly replying, "Yes, well sort of. He's got the upstairs of the annexe. There's a new door adjoining the Manor ... noticed it this morning. Your mother and I agreed to keep an eye on him until he finds his feet. Concierge's idea."

"So I lose half of my house. I've only been here a few days."

Edna narrowed her eyes, eagerly interrupting the exchange, "What did you expect? You never could hold on to anything important for long. Why break the habit of a lifetime?"

A final concerted heave and the baby-like giant was safely in the house, With Adam still outside, Edna slammed the door shut without a word of gratitude. Abandoning viro protocol, Adam marched to the ovoid pod. Angrily determined, teeth gritted, fists clenched, he needed to pay the concierge a visit. Robert would have to wait.

DOES BO PEEP DREAM OF ELECTRIC SHEEP?

Gingerbread bricks and vanilla cream mortar, fruit flavoured pictures with candy cane frames, Adam closed his eyes a moment to savour the sweet smell of rich confectionary. A hard toffee trestle table, adorned with bowls of gummies, marshmallows, and other sugary treats sat alongside a chocolate fountain. Beyond the fountain, a beautiful shepherdess, swathed in summer pink silk, slumbered on an ornate sugar-spun filigree chaise lounge, a frilly bonnet obscuring her golden ringlets. By her side lay a white shepherds crook, festooned with pink ribbons.

Grabbing a handful of jelly babies, Adam approached the sleeping woman. He called softly, "Hello, can you hear me. I know it's early but I need to talk to you."

Apart from a comfortable sleeping sigh, the woman lay still. Taking the shepherds crook, Adam prodded the sleeping figure, gently at first but more forcefully after receiving no response.

"Hey, Bo Peep, wake up! It's me, Adam Eden!"

This time he got a reply, but not from Bo Peep. Trotting out from behind the chaise lounge, a sheep, wearing a pink collar, addressed Adam. The voice was human, female, and less than friendly:

"Save your breath, Adam, Bo Peep is just window dressing. Shout as loud as you like, she won't wake up. And yes, it is early, but more importantly, you are not meant to be here."

Resisting his first instinct, to hit the sheep with the crook, Adam instead stood dumbfounded.

"Yes, I'm the concierge," said the sheep. "Remember, this is not for you. Luckily, in situations such as this, appointments are automatically rescheduled and relevant parties informed. Please, sit at the toffee table, and tell me why you are here. Don't worry, it won't break."

Adam put down the crook and sat at the table. Jumping up onto the bench opposite, the sheep stood facing Adam, front hooves on the tabletop.

"I've come about a few things, but I guess the first is what on earth has happened to my brother, Robert. He looks like some inbred hillbilly steroid abuser."

"I cannot talk about anyone else with you. Surely you remember that?"

Remembering his father's advice about making the questions about himself, Adam tried again:

"OK, what if I had resurrected looking like some inbred hillbilly steroid abuser? What would have caused that?"

"Almost certainly the cause would be degradation of your extracted DNA. It is an extremely rare event, and unfortunately cannot be corrected."

"Couldn't you get another sample of my DNA?"

"No, your DNA is extracted from the channelled brain fragments that make up 'the self'. To avoid creating a paradox, channelling these fragments from the past is a one-time only process. Whilst there are a number of procedures that can be performed to enhance your life experience, the law strictly prohibits anything that would further damage your sense of self. As long as you can sustain a measure of independence, and have the potential for happiness, no further action is taken."

"So that's it? Robert's stuck like this?"

"I cannot talk about anyone else with you."

"You can't do anything for him?"

"I cannot talk about anyone else with you."

Helping himself to another handful of jelly babies, Adam decided to reveal the real reason for his visit:

"So, why have I lost half of my house? There are two other much larger houses in the viro, so why take mine?"

"You were not a planned purchase, and therefore you have the lowest priority. There are many rules and protocols, and in my financial situation, I am in no position to bend them. In time, you will get back the whole annexe."

"How long?"

"Three years. I cannot afford another dwelling until then. You may not be a priority, but I still care about you."

"Hey, does that mean Robert gets the new house even though I was first in line."

"I cannot talk about anyone else with you."

Unable to contain his fury, Adam slammed his hand down on the table, encountering an unwelcome syrupy stickiness. With his other hand, he pointed at the concierge, venting his pent up anger:

"I did not ask to be brought back! Since arriving here, I've been hunted by psychopaths, cut my throat on a chair, and now lost half of my house. On top of that, I've been accused of murder, and nobody in my family will talk to me, including my own parents and children."

"I cannot talk about anyone else with you, but remember that you were not a planned resurrection. For you, this Environment is a best match: not a perfect match, not even a good match, but a best match."

"And you just let this happen? What kind of life is this?"

Thumping a hoof on the table, the concierge replied:

"It is life! It is your life! What happens in an Environment is dictated by its inhabitants. No concierge is permitted to enter an Environment, nor observe the activities therein. Adam, apart from these visits, which I cherish, you are no more to me than a stream of invoices."

"But I died!"

"That is unfortunate, and I have nothing but sympathy. If you wish to discuss these tragic events in detail, then please arrange an appointment. Other than that, I can only advise you to take greater care in the future."

Defeated, finding it impossible to maintain a sufficient level of anger against a sheep, Adam sat back and ate a couple more jelly babies. Unexpectedly, an idea came to mind, a scheme so diabolical that he cast it immediately aside. Shaken by his own thoughts, Adam felt it was time to go. As he left the table, the concierge protested:

"Adam, must you go so soon? Midnight is less than five hours away. Why don't you stay? You could have a chilli burger?"

"A lamb chop might nice, but I think I'll pass. Now, if you don't mind, I want to get back to my shoebox."

"Remember I was so disappointed that I couldn't pole dance for you?"

"I somehow don't think that'll work."

Adam looked the concierge up and down, somewhat fascinated at the prospect of a pole-dancing sheep.

The sheep shook its head:

"No, this time I've memorised a number of nursery rhymes. Please let me share them with you. I could have used instant recall, but instead they reside in my own memory. That's almost unheard of these days. I promise the pod will be operational as soon as I have finished."

"Do I have a choice?"

"No, you don't. Now, sit back down, and I will sing to you."

Adam grudgingly returned to the table, hands clenched, toffee tight under his fingernails. The concierge gave a bleat of delight, and leapt onto the tabletop. She sang with a pronounced sheep-like bah bah vibrato, her hooves kicking in time to the rhythm. Thirty nursery rhymes later, and Adam, disgruntled and still seething, travelled back to the viro.

Trying to calm his anger, Adam settled down on the sofa for an evening eating and drinking in front of the TV. One of the high spots of this new world was access to any television media that existed before one's death. Created from people's memories, even once lost episodes were now available, with many black and white series now in colour. An added bonus was the creation of new episodes - the AI accidently basing these on people's plans, dreams, and desires rather than real life experience. These new additions were indistinguishable from the real thing, and fascinating to watch.

Subconsciously influenced by Sofia's pretentiousness, Adam had chosen an upmarket version of his second favourite food, kebab. Served on an oval stainless-steel platter, two rapier style skewers held generous cubes of lightly charred lamb on a bed of fragrant rice pilaf, a small pot of yoghurt dip on the side. Impeccably grilled, the meat was tender and juicy, flavoured with aromatic Sicilian lemon, white garlic de Lomagne, and Egyptian cumin. Dipping another chunk in the fresh, cooling, coriander and mint dip, Adam felt a pang of disappointment.

Whilst the food was deliciously impressive, and of the highest quality, it failed to satisfy. He yearned for a Tabbas chilli burger: the comforting stomach lining greasiness of the meat, the sharp tang of the chilli sauce, and the limp salad, all contained within a warm soggy bun. Perhaps what he really yearned for, despite the filth and misery, was his original life, and a cheap Tabbas burger was simply a taste of home.

A loud thudding above caused Adam to jump. From the general commotion, and muffled voices he deduced that his parents were introducing Robert to his new apartment. Unable to concentrate, Adam switched off the TV and waited for the noise to die down. In this world of futuristic smart materials, he wished for better soundproofing, but it seemed authenticity came first.

It was only a few minutes before Harry and Edna left, and with them the noise. Adam put on some music, mainly Motown dance tunes, and resumed eating his dinner. Only seconds later a rhythmic stomping, keeping uneasy time with the music, pounded overhead. Adam turned off the music and the stomping stopped. When he put the music back on the stomping started. Decreasing the volume only altered the balance in favour of the stomping.

Vainly hoping that Robert would grow tired of his primal dance stomp, Adam endured the noise. Three songs later, Adam could stand it no longer. He shouted up at the ceiling for his brother to stop, only to receive a barely comprehensible guttural mimicry of his words. Angry and frustrated he shouted again, and received the same response. Enraged, Adam threw his dinner platter across the room, and covered his face with his hands. Yet again, the extreme scheme came to mind, this time receiving contemplation before rejection.

It was the next act that finally put Adam over the edge. Robert began relentlessly thumping the floor with his large fists, and laughing loudly - Adam imagined the slobbering mocking sneer, and the crazy bulging eyes. Adam covered his ears with his hands, but the incessant noise just echoed in his head. One night of this behaviour was unbearable, and the three years promised by the concierge unimaginable.

The diabolical scheme was now at the forefront of his thoughts, to be enacted without question or delay. Provoked into action, Adam slid open the PC wall panel - the thumping now a persistent motivation. He booted up the computer, and selected the Visits icon. Fully aware of the scheme's guaranteed pain and potential for humiliation, Adam filtered the results of his search. Finding the intended target, 'Groover's 1970s Glam Rock Theme Party', he hesitated only a moment before pressing Enter.

RUBBING THE LAMP

Rampage ambushed Adam the moment he opened the wake-up cubicle door. In the dark shadow of the huge concrete visitor building, the silver clad psychopath wrapped an arm tightly around his victim's neck, and roughly hauled him out onto the asphalt pavement. As Adam's face reddened, eyes bulging, Rampage snarled angrily:

"You stupid little shit, I'm going to kill you right here, right now!"

Unable to alleviate the pressure, Adam choked, his windpipe dangerously compressed. Fortunately, before he died, along with his grand plan, Ziggy intervened, effortlessly prying loose his teammate's arm. Adam wheezed a grateful lungful of breath, and checked his neck for damage. Rampage, squirming in Ziggy's powerful arms, was unrepentant:

"You think you can mock me by coming back here, Copacabana? First chance I get, you're dead!"

Ziggy, almost losing his prized mirrored top hat in the struggle, threatened Rampage:

"Calm down … or you get …hurt! You … know I … do it. Can kill … Copa … later."

Obviously not wanting to anger his dim-witted, yet muscular friend, Rampage reluctantly obeyed. Once released, he stood back, arms crossed, his glowering face betraying the evil thoughts racing through his mind.

Adam regained his composure, and saw that the entire gang was present. Roxy and Quatro, colourful and breezy in their yellow trouser suits and gold bandanas, seemed genuinely pleased to see Adam, whilst Stardust, menacing in black silk and leather, lurked almost invisibly in the shadows some distance away. With Rampage and Ziggy leading the way, Roxy and Quatro linked arms with Adam, and merrily escorted him along the path. Stardust ran on ahead, taking a shortcut between the buildings, and within moments was out of sight.

"Oh darling, you'll have to forgive Rampage," said Roxy. "His dislike for you is purely personal. The poor man's been like this ever since the man-child beat the clock."

"You mean Joshua wasn't killed?"

"No," said Quatro, "your clever little ruse succeeded. You naughty man, making us think he stayed under the bridge. Groover usually points out where our guests are hiding, but this time chose not to. I think he wanted to teach someone a lesson."

Adam smiled broadly. His plan to save Joshua had succeeded. Realising that someone was on the bridge, obviously listening, he had told Joshua to stay put, knowing that they would hear. His final whispered words to Joshua, before leading the gang away, were to make for the hedgerows, using the buildings as cover, and then lay low.

The girls laughed as they described Rampage's frustration at finding Joshua gone, and the clock ticking. As the time finally ran out, Rampage was furious, and totally humiliated in front of the entire viro population. When they eventually found Joshua, he was understandably scared and suspicious, but after many assurances that the hunt was over, he took his place as guest of honour at the Grand Feast. Joshua apparently had a wonderful time, especially enjoying the steak cooked, as promised, by Rampage. That evening, at the public screening of Adam's bloody and brutal demise, Joshua broke down in tears.

While the girls talked, Adam noticed how alike they were. Facially he could not tell them apart, every feature a perfect match. The choice and application of make-up was also identical: smoky eyeliner, long lashes, glitter stars on their cheeks, large hooped earrings, and cherry-red lipstick. Their conversation seemed effortlessly synchronised, their voices indistinguishable. Adam found the experience unsettling:

"You know, I've never met identical twins before. You seem to have that mental bond thing going on."

"Oh darling, common mistake, but we're not really twins," said Quatro.

"We're actually the same person," said Roxy

"The same person? What … what do you mean?"

Roxy continued, "We were one person in our previous life, but there was obviously some cock-up in the resurrection process."

"Yes," said Quatro, "they made two of us, one genuine, and one copy."

"Which of you is the real one?"

"We don't know," laughed Roxy. "We both think we're the original, but only one of us has the channelled brain matter. Groover told us he could find out if we wanted, but we prefer not to know. You see darling, we are the best of friends."

Turning to Adam, they said in unison, "The only friend we ever had."

Passing the first of the tower blocks, they approached the bridge. The square beyond was packed with happy revellers. Without warning, Ziggy blocked the way, and Rampage walked over to Adam, demanding:

"I'm not letting you any further until you tell us why you're here. And don't say it's because you enjoyed yourself so much last time, because I'm not in the mood for jokes."

"Ok, fair enough, I want to talk to Groover—in private."

"That's not going to happen. Groover never engages in unsolicited meetings. As his deputy, you may talk to me, and I will decide if he needs to know."

"Aw, come on Rampage," said Roxy. "I'm sure Groover would like to meet the man who helped Joshua to victory."

Stardust broke the impasse, swaggering smugly across the bridge from the square, a slit of a grin across his ashen face. He announced in his usual hushed whispered tone that Groover wanted a meeting. Rampage was livid:

"Who the hell gave you permission to inform Groover? That's my job. I'm the educated one around here. I'm the deputy."

"Stuff your education," hissed Stardust. "I don't need anyone's permission, and you're only in charge during the hunt. Groover wants me to escort him, so out of my way."

Rampage huffed petulantly, crossing his arms, and sauntered back behind the girls, nose in the air. Ziggy stood a moment, perplexed, scratching his head, and then followed. Stardust beckoned to Adam:

"You come with me, Copa, and no funny business. As for the rest of you, Groover wants you mingling with the crowd, so you'd better lighten up. We don't want to worry the other guests."

As they reached the square, the group split up. Adam reflected on the tall concrete structures around him. His previous reaction, before facing the horror of the hunt, had been one of delight, relishing the 1970's retro ambience of the stark urban landscape. Now the architecture seemed hard, unyielding, and bereft of hope – a blank canvas on which the cold-hearted psychopaths spattered their crimson visions.

Pushing through the crowd, many of the locals dropped their false smiles as Adam passed. Recognising him, they eyed him suspiciously, wary of his intent. Groover stood waiting in the entrance hall of his tower block, the frosted glass of the doors distorting his image. Stardust ushered Adam inside, then casually stood guard on the tower block steps.

Inside, the temperature was unnaturally cold, at odds with Adam's Aloha summer-wear. Bland, grey, and brutally utilitarian, the hallway had few features, save for a communal stairwell, lifts, and a number of featureless doors. The smell of disinfectant was all pervasive and quite unpleasant.

Towering on platform heels, Groover was a daunting, ruggedly primitive looking figure, a dark curly mat of chest hair escaping from the V of his silver jumpsuit. Not offering to shake hands, he gave a contorted gap-toothed smile, and introduced himself. The rough timbre of his west-country voice matched his coarse, vaguely ape-like face:

"I 'ear ee wants to talk to me. Now, normally I would turn ee down, but I had a right larf when Rampage couldn't find yee pal the other day. Needed takin' down a peg or two if ee ask me. Snobby bugger was gettin' too cocky with the timin', cuttin' it a bit fine. So, what's it ee want from me?"

"I want to make a deal."

"A deal! What makes ee think I'm one for makin' deals?"

"Well, you're a Genie aren't you?"

"Don't ee be usin' that word on me! I aint be livin' in no soddin' lamp! We's called Originals, but ee aint important enough to call me that. So, before ee do any more insultin', I won't be answerin' to anything else other than Groover. Ee got that?"

Adam nodded nervously.

"Now, what's this deal? Ee don't look like ee 'ave anythin' I want."

"I'm told that Gen ... people like yourself have vast amounts of knowledge about the viros, and the outside."

"Ye're right there, and plenty more than Rampage with his precious medical degree. I tell you, it really pisses 'im off that I knows so much about this world. Now, what do ee want to know?"

"How do I get out of my viro? I ... want to leave."

"When ee say 'out', do ee mean like visiting other Environments on the midnight special, or do ee mean like outside the walls?"

"Outside the walls."

Groover started to shake and laugh, a piggish nasally snigger at first, which quickly developed into loud uncontrollable rasping bellows. Tears streamed from his tiny blue eyes as he sought to steady his balance, using the wall for support. Adam stood silently as Groover laughed and laughed, not regaining his composure for some time:

"Ye're a funny bloke, what with ee poof clothes. I can't tell ee 'ow to get out. That be the most secret knowledge of all. Ee must 'ave somethin' bloody special for me to tell ee that. Just for a larf, tell us what ee be offerin'."

"Well, I've come here to be hunted in exchange for the information."

"But, we're goin' to kill ee anyways, even if I tell ee nothin'. What kind of deal is that?"

Adam realised he had not thought the plan through, and hastily tried to rectify his mistake:

"Ok, and I promise to come back next week as well. Will that do?"

Groover nearly started laughing again:

"No deal. Ee're never gettin' that information outta me. I gets to watch people croak almost every day. What's so special about watchin' you?"

Adam thanked Groover, and made to leave. Before he had taken even a couple of steps, Groover pulled him back:

"Hey, where's ee be goin'? Ye're supposed to come back with a better offer, not walk off. Don't ee know 'ow to make a deal? Now, seein' as ee obviously don't know what ee're doin', I'm goin' to make ee a deal, and ee can take it or leave it.

"I want ee to fight the gang every Friday, dressed in them poof clothes. If you kill all five of the gang by yerself then I'll tell ee how to get out of the Environment. If ee miss a week of fightin' then the deal's off. Now, ee mustn't get direct 'elp from the other guests, or tip 'em off about the hunt before it starts. Ye're not even to tell the gang about the deal. This is strictly between ee and me."

Adam interrupted, noting a problem with the proposal, "If I come here every week, and die, then I'll never get past the 10 day dispenser limit. I'll only be able to get food and drink. Oh, and I'll have to wear these same damn clothes every day."

"I aint be caring 'bout any of that. I only be givin' ee this chance for two reasons. One, 'cause I don't think ye're ever goin' to kill all five of the gang, so I get a free show every week for nothin'. Two, 'cause it'll really piss off Rampage. And, one last thing, I 'ear the gang 'ave given you the name Copacabana, on account of yer poofy clothes. I thinks ee should always go by that name when ee come 'ere to fight. Keep yer real name a secret. And, don't tell anyone outside this Environment that ee come 'ere every Friday. Not even yer friends and family. To sweeten the deal, I'll make today count. So, take the deal or walk away."

GREAT DEAL OF PAIN

Adam sat quietly with Stardust as the terror began. At the announcement of the hunt, the two other guests, a man and a woman, began pleading with their uncaring hosts. The man made a run for it, dodging past a number of the locals, only to be intercepted, and aggressively body-slammed by Ziggy. Dragging the dazed man back, Ziggy held him fast until the ten-minute head start.

Adam was already regretting accepting Groover's gruesome deal. He knew that today he had no choice but to fight, and would almost certainly die. Tomorrow, after recovering from the traumatic experience of resurrection, Adam would reconsider his decision. His fear rising, he attempted to block out the sobs and pathetic begging of the other guests by misguidedly engaging Stardust in small talk:

"Must say, I like the 'man in black' image. Did you choose it yourself?"

Stardust gasped, fixing Adam with the disturbed eager expression of a crazy outsider starved of company and conversation:

"Yes, yes I did. Well, all except this hideous white wig. I love leather, the smell, the feel, the strength. I enjoy being wrapped in another creature's skin. The sequined silk shirt is a little chintzy for my tastes, and the platform boots are a glossy black nightmare, but they do have a certain avant-garde charm. Your choice of clothing is not something I would wear but you certainly stand out from the crowd. Am I right in thinking that you are not wearing underpants?"

"Err, yes."

Stardust smiled, raised his eyebrows, and nodded slowly in some twisted display of kinship:

"Good choice. I don't wear any either. I enjoy the sensation of the leather against my skin, the constant rubbing. Do you like the rubbing?"

"No, you don't understand, my trousers are very tight."

Stardust winked, still smiling and nodding. Adam, feeling fairly tainted by the exchange, learnt an important lesson – never chat with psychopaths. Stardust leant up against Adam, believing himself part of a new pant-less brotherhood, and asked, "Don't you just adore my scent? Smell my neck, along the warm jugular, and tell me what you think."

Adam reluctantly took a quick sniff, and received a powerful burst of rose. Exuding an atmosphere of Victorian gothic, the fragrance was engagingly attractive, and suited Stardust perfectly.

"So, what did you think? Did you get the dark rose? I just love the dark rose."

"Yeah, smelt it straight away. The aftershave suits you perfectly. What is it?"

"Ah, it is a glorious English cologne from the early 1980s, No 88 by …"

"Hey, wait a minute, early 80s? I thought you were only allowed products from 1972 to 1975."

Stardust shuddered and whispered covertly to Adam:

"Keep this to yourself, my brother, but I managed to hold back a couple of bottles from our gothic phase. I decanted the cologne into empty bottles of Jovan Musk, which I cleaned and sterilized in anticipation of the restrictions. Nobody suspected a thing, bloody plebs. Thank goodness they lack my class and sophistication."

"What will you do when it runs out?"

"Hopefully by then this vulgar lowbrow sojourn will be over. You may find it hard to believe, but in the 1970s, I was a small-minded commoner, only interested in rape and murder. Life imprisonment, and then awakening in this wonderful eternity, opened my eyes to a new world of possibilities. I have sought and obtained an education, am now both literate and numerate, and whilst I still enjoy the regular taking of life, I have successfully exchanged my love of sexual violation for elegant refinement with a substantial dash of panache."

"Well, I guess giving up the rape's a step in the right direction. So if you can only use early 70s products, how come you have that old fashioned sword? And, I'm pretty sure the twins' bows and arrows are 21st century types."

"Groover makes up the rules around here. My rapier is a reproduction of a 17th century design. Rampage thinks it's ineffective for the hunt, and wants me to switch to a cutlass, like the pirates used. But I won't change, not unless Groover orders me to."

"So you think the rapier's better?"

"You see, the cutlass is for slashing, whereas the rapier is a long thrusting weapon. You must choose it, Copacabana. I keep mine well oiled, and it feels sooo good sliding it out of the leather scabbard. Then it's grasp the hilt, and thrust and penetrate! Thrust and penetrate! Thrust and penetrate! Thrust and penetrate! Thrust and penetrate! ... "

Through increasingly laboured breaths, Stardust kept chanting the words, his face reddening.

"Ok, stop it," demanded Adam, "I'll go for the rapier!"

Stardust sat back, rubbing his hands slowly along the thighs of his leather trousers:

"Hmmm, you see the rapier is long with a very sharp tip. You can usually put it in someone before they get too close. It's a wonderful feeling. Once the rapier is in your hand, you'll know what to do. Just grasp the hilt, and thrust and ... "

"Thrust and penetrate! Gotcha, I won't forget."

Roxy and Quatro took the weapon requests from the guests, and swiftly returned with the closest acceptable matches. As Adam inspected his rapier, he noticed Rampage scowling at him from across the square, perhaps viewing the weapon choice as another insult to his wounded pride. Not having a belt, Adam had nowhere to fix the scabbard, forcing him to carry the sword unsheathed.

When Groover announced the start of the hunt, Adam ran straight for the alley between the flat-roofed warehouses. Taking up position halfway down the alley, he practiced a few lunging movements with the rapier, only to find the words 'thrust and penetrate' disturbingly etched into his brain.

Waiting for the gang in the alley was part of a plan he had concocted the night before. Since the alley could barely accommodate two abreast, and was further constricted by various storage bins and exterior pipework, he intended to make a stand, benefitting from the gang's inability to fight as a group in the confined space. One end of the warehouses jutted out into the square, the other end obscured by the furthest tower block. Adam hoped the gang would be unprepared for his one-man stand, thinking he had run straight through the alley and headed out across the fields—much like on his previous outing to the psychoviro.

Once off the leash, the gang found Adam in less than two minutes. Groover, already on the roof of his tower block, had pointed out his location. Adam trembled as Stardust, followed by Ziggy, appeared at the far end of the alley by the square. Wolf whistles from behind made him turn, only to see Roxy and Quatro smiling and waving, taking up position behind boxes some distance away. Anticipating this scenario, Adam moved against the sidewall, in front of a ventilation duct, cutting off their line of sight.

He anxiously raised the rapier, beads of sweat forming on his forehead, as Stardust and Ziggy strode brazenly towards him. They stopped about ten feet away, and Stardust circled his sword in an elaborate flourish, before pointing the tip at his prey:

"Oh Copa, your stance is all wrong, and the blade should not be shaking like that. Your thrusts must be bold and precise. Remember, thrust and penetrate."

"Come any closer, and I will run you through," warbled Adam, unable to contain his fear.

Stardust took one deliberate step, and flourished the sword again. Before Adam could react, an arm wrapped tightly around his neck from behind, and a sharp paralysing pain shot up his spine. He felt another sharp pain, then another. Unnoticed by Adam, Rampage had stealthily climbed down a drainpipe from the warehouse roof, a surprising feat giving the incongruousness of his platform boots, and was now stabbing him repeatedly in the back. Whether through true paralysis or just sheer pain, movement was impossible. Stardust sauntered up, carefully pushing his blade through Adam's ribs and into the heart:

"No need to thrust now, Copa. Ease it gently in, and then slide it gently out ... and you're dead."

Rampage shoved Adam roughly to the ground, and stood over him, one boot planted firmly in his back:

"Why the hell did you come back? You add absolutely nothing to these proceedings!"

Already unconscious and fast approaching brain death, Adam heard none of this. The painful darkness was only minutes away.

The next morning it took nearly an hour to fully recover from resurrection. It did not help that in the room above, Robert mimicked every cry and scream, eventually forcing Adam to suffer in silence. His last memory from the day before was Stardust's swaggering appearance in the alley, everything after that moment now lost. Being unable to recall his death was a definite relief, but unfortunately it also meant that Adam could not learn from the experience. Had he put up a decent fight? Had he killed any of the gang? All he knew was that his one-man stand in the alley had resulted in his death, but he would never remember why.

As before, after his last resurrection, the clothes fitted a little better. The trousers slipped on nicely, though still not loose enough for underwear, and the shirt fabric was subtly stronger. Sitting by the lounge window, drinking a cold beer, Adam fantasised that this evolution would eventually lead to armoured Hawaiian clothing.

THE NORMAL DAYS

As the weeks turned to months, Friday's violent events increasingly dominated Adam's thoughts. Still shunned by his family and neighbours, he spent most of his days simply catching up on old TV series, drinking beer, eating burgers, and watching the artificial world go by. He also began to notice the dysfunctional nature of Stern's influence in the viro.

Two of Stern's activities greatly troubled Adam: the naked walk, and the buggy racing. Both were physical displays of Stern's larger than life character, and on the surface might be forgiven as macho bravado, but Adam began to see the flip side of this behaviour: a selfish hedonism with no regard for other people's feelings or physical well-being.

The buggy racing was the most deplorable example of Stern's lack of care. Whenever the urge took him, he raced recklessly around the viro in his hunting buggy, unconcerned about the danger to others. Running on a silent electric motor, the Satan Bug loomed unheard by those unfortunate enough to be in its path. Stern, totally stoked, listened to thunderous death metal through his headset, oblivious to any injury caused by his automotive rampage.

On two occasions Adam witnessed his own mother become the victim of the 'bug'. The first time, she was on her way to see Kaylee. As she crossed the humpback bridge, the buggy appeared in front of her, menacingly leaping the brow. Edna, demonstrating extraordinary agility, jumped over the side, but landed awkwardly on some rocks in the stream. Wet and wounded, she pulled herself up and waded to the bank. She lay still on the grass for a few minutes before trudging back to the manor, blood oozing from a gash on her forehead. Adam ran across the meadow to assist his mother, only to be waved away. Denying what Adam had clearly seen, Edna claimed her wounds were from an accidental fall.

The second incident occurred as Harry and Edna were enjoying a romantic picnic by the edge of the woods. Lounging in the grass, blissfully unaware of the impending flypast of the black scarab of doom, Harry popped a fresh strawberry in Edna's mouth. She giggled coquettishly before the Satan Bug ran over her upper legs, shattering both femurs. A sharp shriek saw her spit out the semi-masticated fruit, the red pulp hitting Harry in the forehead creating a gunshot-like stain. Adam ran out of the annexe to help, only to be indignantly shushed away by his parents, both doggedly in denial. Powerless to intervene, Adam watched as Harry slowly dragged a screaming Edna by the shoulders all the way back to the manor, some 200 yards away.

Whilst not so directly damaging, Stern's naked walks were also a cause for concern. After almost every dick swinging swagger-by, Adam heard raised emotions in the manor. On one such occasion, he listened at the wall with a glass, not feeling a sliver of guilt—after all he was his mother's son—and heard an altercation that distressed him enormously.

Harry suggested that he and Edna not watch Stern's walk-by, reminding her that in their first life such an act would have prompted a swift call to the police. Even the briefest glimpse of male genitalia on TV and Edna would switch channels in disgust, grumbling about the decline in moral standards.

Edna's bellowed response was mockingly emasculating, accusing Harry of jealousy with regard to Stern's impressive physique, and magnificent manhood. The longer Harry resisted, the more personal the insults became, reducing him to tears. Day after day, the argument was repeated, and every time he listened, Adam found his parent's volatile though loving relationship deteriorating further. In truth, Adam knew his parents had the same views on public nudity, but both avoided confronting Stern, fearing the loss of his friendship, and the ability to bask in his golden light. For Adam, this in turn explained Harry's strange 'Lord of the Manor' persona as a comically tragic attempt to reinforce his flagging self-esteem, and win back the respect of his wife.

However, Harry and Edna were not always the victims, as attested by their over protective treatment of Robert. Rather than teach him the necessary skills for living in his own house, they cosseted him like a pampered pet. The hulking colossus only appeared outside the manor on a wrist leash, accompanied by both parents, often dressed in a ridiculous blue and white frilly sailor suit that one might find on a toddler. Every now and then, Edna pulled out a hairbrush to tame Robert's spiky mop. He screamed and struggled as the brush tugged and pulled at his hair, only to receive a hard rap around the legs from Harry's cane. The ritual was pointless since Robert's mutant hair always sprang upright after a few minutes. Never fighting back, he was much like a loving and loyal pet dog, remaining docile and obedient no matter how harsh the treatment from its bullying owners.

At other times, Adam overheard shouting in the manor, and the familiar crack of the cane, accompanied by Robert crying. From what Adam was able to deduce, the punishment was mostly in response to trivial misdemeanours, such as lapses in table etiquette, or for simply being too noisy. On many evenings, along with the continual stomping and mimicry, Adam was haunted by the pitiful sounds of his brother's sobs. To maintain his sanity, and feeling guilty at not intervening, Adam resorted to wearing noise-cancelling headphones when listening to music or watching TV.

All attempts to intervene, to put things right, were summarily rebuffed by his parents, his deep concern treated with distain. Rather than becoming a force for good, Adam was now the master of the twitching curtain, that half-seen face at the window. A man of reluctant inaction, he might soon depose Edna as the chief voyeur, the resident peeping tom.

Luckily, not everything in the viro was negative. Sofia's weekly Thursday visit was an unexpected revelation. Despite her pretentious self-centeredness, her constant chatter brought about a calm before the horrors of Friday. It took the edge off Adam's fear.

The first Thursday, Adam gave Sofia a long list of every conceivable item he needed from the dispenser. The deal with Groover meant Adam would never come off the ten day limited access. Since he did not want to arouse suspicions in the coming weeks and months by wearing the same clothes, he needed to trick someone else into getting him the things he needed. Flattering Sofia worked a charm, saying he greatly respected her superior knowledge of brands and products and that he only wanted the best of everything. She eagerly obliged, filling Adam's meagre living space with a virtual Aladdin's cave of high-end electronics, bespoke fashion, and other luxury items.

Thursdays were rarely spent in the annexe, due to the incessant noise from above. Instead, Adam and Sofia, armed with cushions and a hamper of fine fare, headed for the ruined medieval style chapel that lay a few hundred yards behind the manor. Tucked away in a secluded corner of the viro, at the furthest extremity of the woodland, the ruins were the perfect place to enjoy a day's conversation.

Of course, there was never an intact chapel on the site, the ruins were only generic viro ornamentation—much like the clichéd plastic diver and treasure chest in a domestic fish-tank. Adam and Sofia always sat in the same position; on a faded wooden pew facing the crumbling apex wall, using the cracked alter as a table. From here, bathed in the soft sunlight shimmering through a circular stained glass window of the Madonna and child, Adam cast away all thoughts of the impending hunt, enjoying a few hours of welcome tranquillity.

Comfortably settled, he listened to Sofia's lectures about any subject that caught her fancy. Typical topics were haute couture, fine dining, or A-list celebrity friends – all of whom were unknown to Adam. There were a few subjects that were of mutual interest, but only two that gave Adam any insight into Sofia's true personality.

Having lost her father at the age of 12, she was expected to live the life of a pampered princess forever in Stern's shadow. Instead, she turned her back on his legacy, and took up the mantle he declined. Reverting to the Saghausen name, and highly educated in business and finance, Sofia took over the family business from her Grandfather at the relatively young age of 36, bringing a sharp mind and predatory hunger to the enterprise. Mindful of her privileged upbringing and well trained in its rituals she fully understood the implications of her status. In life, many were dealt potentially winning hands, but only the chosen few knew what game they were playing. Sofia Saghausen was among the very best, swimming with the sharks for over a century before finally relinquishing control on the eve of her 130th birthday, the business more successful than ever.

These facts dispelled Adam's previous take on Sofia as a precocious educated indolent. Now she was a figure of respect, someone not to cross or to toy with. Deep down this hurt Adam, as it seemed Sofia was yet another person to outrank him on every level.

Stranger than Sofia's business acumen were her views on relationships. Married 11 times, she loved courtship, and all it entailed, eking out each romantic moment in the journey to matrimonial bonding. She adored the ceremony of marriage, and the honeymoon passion of the ensuing days. Then it fell flat. Despising her new financial, social, and conjugal expectancies, secret detailed plans for divorce were often conducted on the journey back from the honeymoon - the adoring, unwitting spouse still dazed from the physical exertions of the previous few days. Money, power, and a cast iron pre-nuptial agreement assured the amicably swift departure of the bewildered man, whilst also ensuring the rock-solid uninterrupted perpetuation of the family business. Some pleaded for a second chance, but love's flimsy arrows had no effect on the gilt-edged fortress of the Saghausen Estates. As far as children were concerned, Sofia could not conceive, and did not want to conceive. The irony of her business success was that at the peak of its power, with no living relatives, Sofia relinquished control to a financial conglomerate of strangers—like all great empires, the finest hour came just before the fall.

Sofia made it clear she had no romantic interest in Adam. She wanted her next romantic conquest to fulfil three criteria. In keeping with her family obsession, the man must be well endowed, and secondly, willing to abstain from sex until after marriage. Her third criteria was a break from her usual choice of man, high powered business types, since she was looking for a challenge—someone without sophistication who she could nurture and mould. Even if he had measured up to the first criteria, Adam would never push for a closer relationship with Sofia, fearing the inevitable comparison between himself and 11 rejected alpha males.

Always, at around 8pm they made their way back from the ruins - Sofia to her father's house, and Adam to the annexe. The remaining hours before midnight always seemed to flash by. Keeping to a fixed routine, Adam accessed the computer and set up the Friday psychoviro visit. Then, seeking a last minute refuge from the hunt, relaxed on the sofa, eyes closed, listening to a meticulously picked playlist of classic Motown through his headphones. As the midnight hour approached, Adam remained on the sofa, the soothing music a smooth slide into Friday Hell.

FIGHTING FRIDAYS

The first five months of Adam's battle against the psychos was a total disaster. Rampage always singled out Adam for the first kill of the day, dispatching him with ruthless speed. Unaware of Groover's deal, Rampage was frustrated and furious with Adam's persistent appearances, and took it personally. Week after week, Adam died a gruesome death, never inflicting any significant damage on his glittering opponents.

Confronted with such overwhelming failure, most people would have retreated from the enterprise, but then most people had not experienced lives of overwhelming failure, and crushing disappointment. Used to defeat, Adam faced the fight with pained indifference. In his first-life, he had been a man with only his life to lose, but now there was nothing.

Good or bad, exciting or boring, Adam remembered none of his final moments. Denied the memories by the rules of resurrection, he relied on the word of the psychos to rate his previous week's performance. Every Friday, one of the gang was waiting outside the wake-up cubicle to escort him to the square, and berate his efforts. It always embarrassed Adam to learn how quickly he died, but the barbarity described was often the stuff of nightmares.

VISIT 7: Friday 8th October: The Walkway Incident

This day was memorable for a number of reasons. As he exited a ground floor wake-up cubicle, Adam, smiled contentedly, and clenched his buttocks. This would be his first hunt wearing underpants, and it felt good. Stardust, this Friday's escort, looked distraught when Adam broke the news, their pant-less brotherhood now officially ended.

When the hunt began, Adam headed straight back to the wake-up building, having chosen an excessively long rapier as his weapon. Quickly, he climbed the metal stairs to the top level, and from this high vantage point peered around the side of the building to view the impending onslaught. It was then that Adam observed the second memorable event of the day.

Standing side by side on the bridge leading from the square were the three other guests: all siblings, one woman and two men armed with cricket bats. The stoic trio stared out their adversaries only a few yards away. Powerfully built, cold expressions, they showed not a trace of fear as they stood waiting for the gang to attack.

When the 10 minute head-start was over, Groover unleashed the gang, who charged forward issuing frightening battle cries – all meticulously rehearsed no doubt. The three valiant guests braced themselves as Rampage, Ziggy, and Stardust raced towards them. With less than ten feet to go, Roxy and Quatro worked their deadly magic from the far canal bank, simultaneously letting loose their arrows. Both arrows hit their targets with deadly precision, one in the knee of each of the brothers, who fell away in pain, leaving their sister vulnerably exposed.

Roaring with infernal fury, Rampage and his men engaged the now weakened wall of defiance. The brothers, reeling from the arrow wounds, were easy meat. Stardust deftly ran his sword through the heart of one, whilst Rampage made short work of the other with a lightning fast slash to the throat.

In typically primitive fashion, Ziggy ploughed headlong into the woman, bulldozing her a few stumbling feet backwards. She desperately tried to maintain her footing, dropping her bat in the process. As the woman tried to turn and run, Ziggy swung his cricket bat hard against the back of her head, a large portion of scalp brutally sheared away. She fell flat on her face on the concrete path, and lay motionless. Adam hoped she was unconscious, as Ziggy moved in for the kill. With cries of animalistic rage, Ziggy repeatedly brought his bat cracking down on the poor woman's head, pulping it into a misshapen sodden sack.

Adam froze, shocked by the bloody spectacle. Up until now, the gang always killed Adam first, so he had never actually witnessed any of the deaths. Now, their sickening lust for blood was laid bare, dispelling any notions of honour or fair competition - this was calculated ritualised slaughter. Truly psychopaths, they laughed and congratulated each other on a job well done, revelling in their superior savagery. Nobody stepped in as Ziggy pulverized the brother's heads. Quite the contrary, this seemed to raise their spirits, and they proceeded to ridicule the brave trio, spitting on and kicking the bodies with obvious delight, before Stardust sliced his initial in their chests.

Ziggy raised his bat, now dripping with blood, and pointed it towards the wake-up building. Although just a distant face peaking around a high corner, Adam was now in their sights. Feeling vulnerable and on the edge of panic, he withdrew along the walkway, as if what he could not see would not hurt him, but he knew the truth, that they were already on their way.

Only a couple of minutes later, Ziggy appeared, rounding the corner of the neighbouring building. After catching his breath and wiping sweat off his wide brow, the lumbering beast started up the stairwell, the hard soles of his platform boots clanging against the metal treads. Five floors up, Adam instinctively moved further along the walkway, putting distance between himself and the bat-wielding maniac.

Before Ziggy reached the top floor, Rampage appeared along the path with Roxy and Quatro. The two women took up positions on the ground, their aim pointed upwards, tracking Adam like human ground-to-air missile launchers. Fortunately, all the walkways were concrete floored and sided, offering strong protection from their arrows. Rampage quickly followed Ziggy up the stairs, his gladius already unsheathed. Stardust was nowhere to be seen.

Cricket bat swinging by his side, Ziggy walked towards Adam. As he neared, he tipped his mirrored top hat in an ironic gesture of greeting:

"So…we meet…again, Mr Copa. I…kill you…just…like before."

From this distance, Adam got a good look at Ziggy. With his grotesquely wide head, and lumpy muscular body, he was reminded of his brother, Robert. Could it be that this psychopathic killer was the product of a tragic mistake of degraded DNA? If so, then perhaps in his first life, Ziggy had been of sound mind, maybe a family man, warm and loving to his wife and children.

Adam wondered whether these thoughts had crossed his mind on a previous encounter, now lost due to the rules of resurrection. In turn, perhaps this questioning was also a repeat from an earlier encounter, an empty matryoshka doll of lost thoughts. For Adam, the missing memories' were like moments of real death in an artificial oasis of immortality, representing permanent unconscious nothingness. Suffering a sudden flash of mortal fear, Adam chuckled to himself. If these were the final few minutes before his death, then tomorrow, all these morbid thoughts, no matter how disturbing or profound, would be forgotten. Ignorance was truly bliss.

Adam lifted the rapier, readying himself for the impending attack. Ziggy, swinging the bat around menacingly, lumbered forward, seemingly unconcerned about any danger posed by his opponent. Letting out a half-hearted battle cry, Adam lunged blindly, and the blade pierced clean through Ziggy's upper left arm. Pulling back the blade, he readied himself again. Both men stood silent and still for a moment, knowing that this was the first time Adam had actually injured one of the gang. Unluckily for Adam, Ziggy's weapon arm was unharmed and he swung his bat against the rapier, slamming the slim blade against the walkway siding. The powerful impact sent a painful vibration up Adam's arm, causing him to drop the weapon. Narrowly avoiding the bloodied bat as it swooped past his head, he turned and ran.

With Ziggy following in hot pursuit, Adam came up with a desperate plan. He climbed over the siding, and carefully lowered himself until he was hanging precariously by his hands. His intention was to drop down, grab onto the siding below, and pull himself onto the walkway. Once there, he would sprint to the stairs, race back up to the top floor, and hopefully retrieve his rapier before Ziggy could get to him.

The plan failed at the first step. As Adam dropped to the next level, his chin made pulverising contact with the concrete siding, shattering his entire lower jaw. The impact clamped his teeth straight through his tongue, impaling the mandibular incisors into his upper palette. Somehow, his hands still did their job, grabbing hold of the siding, with only the dislocation of a little finger for their troubles.

Without the strength to pull himself up onto the walkway, Adam just hung pathetically. Rampage appeared wearing an expression of false sympathy. Leaning over the siding, he looked down at Adam:

"Oh my dear Copacabana, glad you could drop by, that was truly jaw dropping. Now I would usually expect a groan for such bad jokes, but you're obviously in no condition to complain, are you?"

Reaching down, Rampage slapped back and forth the hanging bag of skin, which used to contain Adam's lower jaw. The bony fragments rattled inside, and a low moan issued from the baggy stretched mouth. Rampage chuckled gleefully:

"Just checking the damage, dear boy. Remember, I was a doctor before I came here. Now, in my professional opinion, you need a couple of injections for the pain."

Rampage stood back, and then shouted, "Roxy, Quatro, let him have it, and make it interesting!"

Down below, two arrows let loose, each hitting its intended target, Adam's buttocks. The stainless steel heads buried themselves deep in his pelvic bone, and blood oozed freely down the shafts, staining his white trousers. Adam moaned in agony, and nearly lost his grip, barely holding on with one hand. Rampage stepped forward again:

"I see the injections had the desired effect … pain and more pain! Now, I don't know why you keep coming back here, but it's time for you to go now."

With those words, Rampage raised his gladius and bought the blade down hard on Adam's fingers, chopping them off at the base. Unable to grip with short bloody stumps, Adam dropped the four storeys to the concrete pathway below—Roxy and Quatro already well out of the way. Landing butt first, the impact forced the arrows through the bone, the metal points thrusting up through Adam's waist. Despite shattered bones and major blood loss, he was still alive. Hardly able to perceive his surroundings, a hazy blur obscured his failing vision. It was Stardust.

"You know why I stayed away, don't you? I thought we had a connection, you and I. We were like brothers. I was always proud to slice my initial in your chest after a battle, but not now. You don't deserve it. Was it worth it? Did your underwear save you? No, of course it didn't. Today you chose underpants over our bond of brotherhood, and I can never forgive you."

Unsheathing his rapier, Stardust kissed the blade, and then stabbed Adam through the heart.

Though Adam's memory of this particular day mercifully ended with Ziggy's appearance on the walkway, the following week Rampage relished filling in the details of the grisly finale.

VISIT 18: Friday 25th December: The First Christmas

Adam was unconcerned that Christmas Day fell on a Friday this year, Edna having arranged a party in the utility building to which he was not invited, and Stern promising a special seasonal hind-reading for everyone. Not wanting to appear lacking in festive cheer, Adam allowed Sofia to adorn the annexe with various decorations, including an artificial tree with lights and baubles, although he felt he had little to celebrate.

The next morning in the psychoviro, Adam felt a chill blast as he left the wake-up cubicle, and immediately slipped over on the icy path outside. The whole area was covered in snow, with spiky icicles hanging from the undersides of the walkways, and crisp cold weather to match. A hand reached down and helped Adam to his feet. It was Rampage, though dressed very differently than usual:

"Ho, ho, ho, do you like the outfit Copacabana?"

In keeping with the spirit of a glam Christmas, Rampage wore a glittery red jumpsuit with a fur lined gloves and Santa hood. A bushy silver beard and glossy black platform boots completed the look. He handed over a pair of metal spiked straps, and instructed Adam to attach them to his shoes. Once fitted, it was much easier to maintain his footing.

"It's bloody freezing," Adam complained, crossing his arms and stomping his feet to keep warm. "A coat would be nice, or even a jumper."

"Well, if you insist on wearing light summery Hawaiian clothes in the depths of winter, what do you expect?"

"My viro is always warm; I didn't know you could turn the thermostat down. You could have warned me."

"I know," said Rampage, "but then it wouldn't be so funny. Changing the weather is one of our special privileges. I'm disappointed you haven't complemented me on the outfit. It was my idea to go for the Father Christmas get-up."

"Great, it looks just great, but seriously, I need to get out of this cold."

"The square's clear of snow, and we've installed outdoor heaters. You'll love it. We've got a huge tree this year …"

Rampage suddenly grabbed Adam and threw him to one side, a large sharp stiletto of ice falling treacherously where he was just standing. After being helped to his feet a second time, Adam brushed off the snow, and offered reluctant thanks. Rampage shook Adam's hand, saying:

"Things are different here on Christmas Day. Like in World War 1 when the opposing sides came out of their trenches to play football. We also want this day to be special, a break from the usual."

"Sounds fine by me, now, can we please get to the square, before I freeze my knackers off."

A few hours later, after a wonderful buffet of festive fare, Adam learned that this 'break from the usual' was not what he imagined.

The four other guests screamed as robotic waiters held them down in their chairs, whilst one of the gang clumsily shaved their heads with electric clippers. Adam sat silently through his part of the ordeal, knowing that the little nicks and grazes were only the start of today's horror. Once bald, fancy dress reindeer antler headbands were stuck to the guests' heads with fast acting superglue, and bright red plastic clown noses stuck to their faces. One unfortunate guest had wide flared nostrils, making it difficult to stick the nose in place, but a quick trim of the offending flesh with scissors achieved a nice snug fit.

As traditional Christmas carols piped out from the rooftop loudspeakers, Groover made one more change to the winter scene. With a mere click of his fingers, the sun blanked out, replaced by an ink black sky filled with stars and a large full moon, its light lending the snowy landscape an ominous shadowy iridescence. Strings of multi-coloured fairy lights came to life, illuminating even the darkest corners of the viro with a fanciful beauty that belied the coming slaughter. Stardust seemed emotionally charged by the spectacle, raising his rapier to the sky:

"Do you see that? Do you see that? La Luna, our wicked mistress! May we prove ourselves worthy in her presence. Oh how we shall play in the moonlight, and then return for feasting, wine, and gifts."

Almost unable to contain his laughter, Rampage slapped his black-clad colleague on the back, and called over to Adam:

"My apologies Copacabana if this all seems a bit crass, but you know how commercial Christmas has gotten these days."

With only 10 minutes to find a reasonable place to fight, Adam's original intention was to reach the large woodland near the viro's edge, but he underestimated the difficulty of running in the snow and the freezing cold. Christmas glam favourites now replaced the carols, and the locals enthusiastically sang along from their high towers.

With time running out, sword heavy in hand, Adam diverted across a large field, heading for a low hedgerow. Still far short of his target, sharp headlights beamed past him and he heard the sound of an approaching engine. A sleek red snowmobile shot past some yards to his left, driven by Stardust, with Roxy riding pillion. As Adam changed direction, they circled back for a second pass, but this time Roxy had her bow raised. With skill evocative of an experienced horse archer, she let fly an arrow. Adam threw himself sideways, the arrow narrowly missing his head.

Picking himself up before the snowmobile returned for another attempt, Adam decided to make a stand in the open. More snowmobiles approached from the direction of the tower blocks—the rest of the gang riding in to join the 'sport'. Shielding his eyes from the intense beams of the headlights, Adam almost forgot about Stardust and Roxy, a shrill whoop alerting him to imminent danger. He spun round to see the red snowmobile headed for a close pass-by, Stardust driving one handed, rapier ready to strike. Instinctively, Adam ducked, the flashing blade slicing off one of his antlers. Then, in a lightning move more appropriate for the movies, Adam leapt at the passing vehicle, successfully dislodging a startled Roxy from her seat, who suddenly found herself rolling painfully across the snow.

Adam settled himself in the seat before attempting to strangle Stardust with his own wig. Choking, Stardust let go of the handlebars to defend himself, and the vehicle powered ahead, the two men struggling for dominance. Stardust produced a small dagger, and frantically stabbed at his attackers' hands until the neck-hold was broken. Once free, the psychopath unexpectedly threw himself from the snowmobile and Adam only had time to shudder as the vehicle smashed headlong into a low stone wall. The impact sent him hurtling over the handlebars and the wall, somersaulting and cart-wheeling with bone-breaking speed across a snowy field.

Unable to move, every limb broken and his back horribly twisted, Adam showed no reaction to the arrival of the gang. Stardust and Roxy, bruised, dishevelled, and looking understandably angry, stood back as Rampage sat down in the snow next to Adam.

"Ho, ho, ho, you put on quite a show there. No point really, since we're all fine. You just don't have what it takes, do you? Why you keep coming back, I just don't know, but because it's Christmas Day we all think you deserve a couple of presents. Merry Christmas Copacabana."

With a reassuring smile, Rampage produced a couple of small glittery baubles, one white and one blue.

"Oops, I forgot to wrap them. Let me box them up for you."

Adam screamed, as his eyes were cut out, and the baubles pushed into the empty sockets—his broken body quivering, bones rasping with grating crepitus. With a maniacal Santa laugh, Rampage drew his gladius and decapitated his sightless victim.

Later, in the square, the psychos sang carols and danced merrily around the huge Christmas tree, now macabrely decorated with their guests' antlered bauble-eyed heads.

STERN APOLOGY

A typical Thursday morning, and Adam paced around the lounge waiting for Sofia's arrival. Always edgy the day before the killing, he needed conversation and casual companionship to cope as the hours slipped away. Around 9:30 a.m. a figure crossed the bridge, heading for the annexe ... but it was not Sofia. Within a few minutes, Stern, thankfully fully dressed, was sitting comfortably on the sofa, apologising for not visiting more regularly. Since he usually had breakfast around this time, Adam invited his guest to join him, and Stern eagerly, perhaps too eagerly, agreed. Whilst wondering if this was an opportunity to confront his neighbour about the nudity and reckless driving, Adam instead played the perfect host:

"So, what'll you have?" he asked, already by the dispenser.

"You know, I gotta try one of those Tabbas Burgers that Sofia's told me about. Sounds like quite an experience, my friend."

"But she hates them. She says the meat probably comes from the bits that even the animal was glad to get rid of. I can't even eat them in front of her without her fake vomiting every few minutes."

"But you like them, and that's good enough for me. We'll be two men chowing down on manly food."

"Ok, do you want a posh one, or one of the take-away ones that I like?"

"Adam, I've spent more than a lifetime eating fancy food, so I'll have what you're having."

Despite detecting a subtle hint of reluctance and insincerity in Stern's voice, Adam nodded:

"One Tabbas, quarter pounder chilli burger coming up. Oh, do you want fries with that?"

"Mmm, thin greasy sticks of potato. How can I refuse? Bring 'em on."

As Adam ordered the food from the dispenser, he sensed faint movement near his backside. Looking around, he noticed Stern was no longer on the sofa, but sitting close-by in the armchair, suspiciously rubbing the end of his nose. Slapping his hands on the arms of the chair, Stern stood up and announced:

"Not comfortable enough. I think I'll go back to the sofa."

Practised at ordering his favourite food, Adam had the food on the table within moments. Sitting in the armchair vacated by Stern, he asked bluntly:

"Did you just smell my arse?"

"Oh Adam my man, it is my job … my calling. Yeah, I know it's unprofessional not to ask permission first, but I simply can't resist. Anyway, as usual it was a complete waste of my skills, because you just don't have a smell."

"I must smell of something."

"Only the generic human scent, nothing more. Seriously, you are an olfactory non-entity. You're clean-shaven, but I don't get the slightest hint of cologne. I can usually pick up even the non-scented stuff, so what are you using?"

"Water … cold water. I've never bothered with aftershave or balms. Never found one I liked."

"Ah, that explains it. Well, I suggest you ask Sofia for fragrance advice. She's quite the perfumista."

Adam nodded, not revealing that Sofia had already picked out a potential 'signature scent'—now permanently residing at the back of the wardrobe, virtually unused and definitely unwanted.

The fragrance, apparently hugely popular in the mid-21st century, Adam disliked intensely: 'Chalut Pour Homme' by Henri Filet. Described as a masculine seafood aquatic, the opening of lightly lemoned North Atlantic prawn braced with iced vodka swiftly gave way to pungent heartnotes of briny aged seaweed bedecked in refined pressing of Whitby smoked haddock, before settling on a long-lasting murky base of Cornish huile de sardine, and galley char of intertidal mussel beard.

The container disturbed Adam far more than the scent itself. Called a bio-bag, the small synthetic living pouch shimmered with soft fishlike scales, the word 'CHALUT' hovering in crystal holographic text close to the subtly trembling surface. Two mysteriously dark artificial fish eyes were set either side of the bag, near a tiny wrinkly pink hole. Gently rubbing the eyes caused the bag to 'spit' fragrance from the labial orifice.

For now, Adam would continue using his own aquatic aftershave splash - cold tap water.

Hungrily biting into his burger, Adam noticed Stern eating just the lettuce and onion, purposefully avoiding the meat.

"Is everything alright? I promise you it's harmless."

Stern broke off a small piece of the grey meat, eyed it suspiciously, and then placed his food on the coffee table, making the excuse of needing a drink to aid digestion. Adam dutifully returned to the dispenser:

"So what do you want, beer, wine, or something stronger? What about some Laphroig?"

"Hmm, that might make this ... excellent burger even more appetising. It's a little early for alcohol, unless you're Kaylee of course, but I wouldn't say no to an Islay malt."

"So that's two votes for my favourite whisky," said Adam.

Suddenly seething, Stern clenched his fists and punched the arm of the sofa:

"Don't talk to me about fucking votes! That word is strictly taboo!"

Reigning in his anger, Stern immediately raised his hands in apology:

"Sorry about that, I'm just a bit on edge today. I've been like this all morning since coming back from the Mama Fiesta hub. Now this is strictly on the down-low, but yesterday that bitch Stinkerella tried to oust me as Chairman of the Hind-Readers Guild."

"Before you carry on," said Adam, "three questions. Mama Fiesta hub? Stinkerella? And, you actually have a guild for ... that thing you do?"

"A hub is a place where the locals just love visitors, and they go all out to please. Some people call it a party viro. Mama Fiesta's my favourite hub - Mexican style, and extremely popular - you have to book weeks in advance. My guild always meets there for business, gossip, and hard partying. As for Stinkerella, she's a no good low-rent hind-reader who's been gunning for top spot ever since we let her join. She's amateur trash out of an online reality show, but she's hot as hell and has quite a following."

"So, are you still Chairman, or did she ..."

"Yeah, I'm still Chairman but it was a close run thing. I only held on thanks to last minute support from Booty Ranger and Sir Arser Colon Soil. They're enigmatic mysterioso types, and usually stay out of the politics. But ... when the guild's reputation was at stake they stepped up."

Stern gave Adam a sly grin before unexpectedly asking, "Just where do you go every Friday?"

Adam, caught unawares, was lost for words. He thought for a moment, unable to gauge whether Stern knew about the psychoviro or was innocently fishing for information. Carefully, he replied, "How do you know about Fridays?"

"You're never in on a Friday, that's how. I've stopped by a few times to see how you got on with Sofia the day before, but I never get an answer. Now, I guess you could be hiding behind the curtains, pretending to be out, but I can't see that, especially since it's loveable me. No muchacho, you're definitely out visiting on Fridays, and I want to know where."

"It's personal … my business," Adam meekly mumbled.

"Oh no my secretive friend, I told you about my guild problems, so it's only fair you tell me everything. Come on, I want to know what's going on …"

"I … I go to a self-help group. You know, to deal with all the mental problems."

"Ah, you mean coming to terms with those murders, and being ignored by your family. What are the rest of the group like? Are they normal, or are they undesirables like you?"

"Hmm, you could call them undesirables, but they're nothing like me."

Adam was desperate to chance the subject:

"Is there anything else? You didn't come here for breakfast and a chat, did you?"

"No, but I'm finding it difficult to find the words. You see, I'm not the type of guy who usually says this type of thing, but … I've come to apologise. Yes, it's true, Stern Lovass saying sorry. I have let you down, and you need to know that I feel so bad about it."

"Sorry for what?"

"Your friend, Emmanuel Beaumont, I promised to get him to contact you. You remember the promise I made in the woods, don't you?"

In truth, Adam forgot about Sterns promise in the woods many months ago, other matters being of more painful and immediate importance. He had on occasion attempted to contact Manny, but the connection was always blocked.

"Must have slipped my mind. I remember you saying it would take a couple of weeks, so I just let it go … months ago. Look, I'm not bothered about seeing Manny again. He has his God to see him through, so he probably doesn't want to see me. Most of the people I knew from my past life either don't want to see me or aren't resurrected. To be honest, I've resigned myself to a life of solitude."

Stern took a swig of whiskey:

"You should know that your friend is in a bad way. After the first day of resurrection, he shut himself in his apartment and hasn't been seen since. The locals have tried to contact him, ringing the doorbell and knocking at the windows, but only get a 'piss off' for their concern."

"He actually used those words, 'piss off'? You could have tortured Manny for days and he wouldn't have used language like that. Are you sure there's no way of contacting him?"

Stern explained in detail the supreme efforts he had made. Manny was in a viro of followers, a close-knit Christian community dedicated to their particular creed. Like all inhabitants of such viros, Manny was too absorbed with his faith to live with non-believers—even family or friends—such people serving only as an unwelcome distraction.

Stern tried to contact other members of the follower viro, in the hope they would allow a visit, but the hind-reader's career and hedonistic lifestyle were anathema to their pious ways. For months, they resisted his attempts at communication, but in the end reluctantly granted an audience with their official spokesperson, the fierce and fervent Sister Josephine Maguire. Since she regarded Stern as a demonic vessel, it was a prerequisite of the meeting that they spoke through a mutually acceptable intermediary, the internet evangelist, Louis Fatherson.

Fatherson and his wife were the only human inhabitants of a luxurious Vipo—environments for historical VIPs—landscaped with fragrant pine forests, and affording spectacular vistas of cloud topped mountains. Perched on a craggy outcrop next to a thundering waterfall, surrounded by mist-laden woods, Fatherson's grey gothic mansion was a truly imposing sight. Inside, the spacious rooms were clad and furnished with the rarest polished hard woods, the walls hung with an ungodly plethora of grandiose oil paintings, all featuring Fatherson in various histrionic poses. Meanwhile, a small army of medieval costumed android servants catered for every need. Stern described Fatherson's Vipo with a note of restrained bitterness, and Adam realised that the celebrated hind-reader felt cheated of such a destiny. Adam was intrigued:

"You make it sound like Fatherson's got a Dracula thing going on. I imagine him as Bela Lugosi, or maybe Christopher Lee."

"You couldn't be further from the truth. The old fraud is a Western nut. Wears cowboy gear - more Eastwood than Wayne. Even has a silver cross on his Stetson. God's Gunslinger was his nickname in his evangelist days, although I would say God's money-spinner is nearer the truth. Still, he was the only person acceptable to both parties, so I guess he bridges the gap between true believers and the rest of us."

"So Sister Josephine, she didn't talk to you directly?"

"Not a word. We sat around a small table in Fatherson's study. In turn, we had to talk to Fatherson, and he'd relate the message to the other - and back and forth, back and forth. I felt stupid listening to the same thing twice. Especially when the damn nun was sitting only a few feet away. You know, I was polite as a debutante's fart, but she crossed herself every time I said a word, and every idea I came up with she just thumped the table and said 'no'."

"Did she explain why?"

"No. Maybe she saw my ideas as the work of the Devil. I even offered to attend prayers at their viro for a couple of months. Huge, huge mistake."

"Didn't work then?"

"Hell no. She stood up, and looked straight up at the ceiling. Then she clutched this huge gold cross to her chest, and started chanting in this creepy low voice. It was Latin, and I believe she was invoking the angels or saints. Sounded to me like an exorcism. Scared the shit out of me. Fatherson should've cut in, but the asshole stayed out of it by pretending to pray."

"So, was the Devil in you exorcized?"

"Roused is the word, roused. I couldn't contain my true character any longer. I stood up, struck a dramatic pose, and roared, 'What a showgirl, Sister! You gotta send a copy of this to my agent, 'cause I believe you'd be the hottest butt-nosing hind-reader ever to hold a mass – and you can hold mine right now if that cross gets too cold for you."

"That can't have gone well?"

"Nope, not at all, but sometimes you have to go for the fun factor. She went totally nutso. Her face went baboon-ass red, and her eyes nearly popped outta their sockets. And, you should've heard her voice. Screaming and cursing me with all sorts of pain and fiery torture - even some I haven't tried with Kaylee." Stern winked, grinningly devilishly. "That idiot Fatherson still pretended to pray, until Sister Joe cracked him round the head with a hefty great bible. She ordered him to remove the irredeemable demon from her sight, and so Fatherson had me escorted back to the wake-up cubicle. He even posted a couple of android guards at the door. I think it was then, my friend, when I finally gave up the quest."

"So I don't get to help Manny?"

"Not a chance."

Draining his whiskey, and suffering a small token bite of the burger, Stern slapped his thighs, and got up to leave, apologising once more. Adam decided it was time for a confrontation:

"Hey, Stern, I want to talk to you about your behaviour. I don't like the effect it's having on my parents."

Without turning, Stern halted in the doorway:

"Think carefully Adam, are you sure this is a conversation you really want to happen? I could just walk home, send Sofia over, and we all have a good day. Or, we stand face-to-face, man-to-man, and you try to explain yourself without ending up unconscious, bruised, and humiliated."

Taking the initial silence as a sign of capitulation, Stern took a step forward, a smug smile wormed across his face.

"It's you who needs to explain himself," ventured Adam, in a steady confident tone. "So, maybe you should get back here and discuss it like a man."

Without another word, Stern strode back, and squared up to Adam. Staring unblinkingly, and standing well within Adam's personal space, he simply said, "Start talking."

"You walking about in the nude every day is destroying my parent's relationship. My mother's not really a bad person, but you've given her a stick to beat my dad with. Any time he won't do as he's told, she just insults his manliness … and you know what I mean by that. She never did that before. They always bickered but these arguments are one step away from physical violence."

"Ah, the concerned son, how touching. You're wrong though. Your parents are mature adults. Not only did they live much longer than you, but were far more successful. You have no idea how their relationship evolved in the years after your death, do you? For all you know, they were already drifting apart, and you're just witnessing the final throes."

"But the nude …"

"Ok, tell me if this is acceptable. I go to your parents and tell them I can't go naked anymore because their meddling son is listening at the walls every time they raise their voices."

"No, that's not what I …"

"Adam, what gives you the right to interfere in other people's relationships, when your own are such disasters. Now, what else was it? Oh yes, my buggy racing, what the fuck's wrong with that!"

131

Wishing he had never called Stern back, Adam's wavering voice slightly increased in pitch:

"You forced mum … my mother off the bridge. She was hurt … badly … rocks in the stream."

"Hmmm, I had no idea. I agree, that is very bad, go on."

"They were picnicking by the woods, and you ran over my mummy's … shit … my mother's legs. She was in real pain, but you didn't even notice."

Stern put his hand on Adam's shoulder in a patronising fatherly manner. Adam frowned, and gave Stern a 'what the fuck do you think you are doing' look. Surprisingly, Stern removed his hand and said:

"Thank you for telling me about this. Sometimes it's good to have a neighbourhood snoop spying through a crack in the curtains. Again, I'll tell your parents what you told me, and see what they recommend."

"They'll say it doesn't matter. They'll probably deny it ever happened."

"You're not their keeper, Adam. They are capable of making their own decisions."

"But they're obsessed with you, with your celebrity. They will never, and I mean never, say anything to upset you."

Stern rubbed his chin, contemplating his royal verdict:

"Well muchacho, here's what's going to happen. Regarding the buggy racing, I will not change a thing. I keep to a pretty regular circuit so if people want to impersonate road-kill that's their problem. We all heal in the night so at worst there's nothing but a few hours of discomfort. Let me tell you Adam, I know real physical pain. Twice, while racing, I've stuck my hand out in the rush of air, and caught it on a branch. One time, I had a gash in my palm almost two inches long. I just sucked up the pain, bandaged it, and got on with the day. Anyway, once the viro fills up over the next few centuries, it'll be too crowded to race around. So I'll have fun while I can."

"What about the nude thing … my parent's marriage?" asked Adam, resigned to failure.

"Again, I'm not going to change a thing, and you promised to keep your mouth shut … remember?"

Grudgingly, Adam nodded.

But don't feel so bad about it. We're here for eternity, or at least a big chunk of it. In that time, relationships will come and go, and change in all sorts of ways. Whether we want to believe it, there will come a time when you and I will get it on."

"No way … never …"

"I don't like the sound of it either, but there's an ocean of time ready to make it happen. Hey, one day you'll even have a hot threesome with Edna and Harry."

"No, not ... why don't you shut up ..."

Stern shuddered dramatically, "Nightmare vision, my friend, but stamped with a rock solid guarantee courtesy of immortality."

Again, Stern turned to leave, his adversary now thoroughly beaten. As the triumphant hind-reader passed through the doorway, Adam bleated defiantly, "Never happen! Just shows what a sick, sick, perverted mind you have! Never happen!"

As he left the house, Stern called back, "Listening at walls and leering through the curtains? Only a few small steps, only a few small steps. Have a nice day now, y'all.

An hour later, Sofia arrived, oblivious to the earlier encounter. Whilst she spent the day filling the silence with her usual vacuous tales of money and haute couture, Adam kept thinking about Manny. Adam owed his friend an enormous debt for getting him off the streets, and now circumstances required a similar act of courage and selfless loyalty. If Adam was to contact Manny, then it was perhaps time to strike another deal with the Genie.

GOING UNDERGROUND

Without question or complaint, Stardust agreed to take Adam to meet Groover. The psycho-in-black seemed unusually awkward this Friday, shuffling along the path without a hint of his former cavalier swagger - as if suffering a bout of tense self-consciousness. Before they reached the canal bridge, Stardust halted, and turned to Adam:

"Wait a moment, Copa. You're the only one I trust. You must help me."

"Are you sure? I'm not usually considered helpful to anybody, or anything. This isn't about underwear, is it?" Adam hoped to avoid another weird, perverted conversation with the unwholesome killer.

"I … I've run out of my fragrance. It happened yesterday."

"You've got something on; I can smell it from here."

"Ah, at least it has good projection, but there's really nothing from 1972 to 75 that meets my specific needs. I'm wearing Aramis 900, and I cannot deny its worth, but is it me? Please, come closer and smell me."

"Why? I told you I can smell you from here. You're wearing quite a lot."

"There is one note, one scent, which feeds and reinforces the sensual romantic aspect of my personality. I need to know if you can detect it. Please smell me."

Warily, Adam stepped forward and sniffed:

"I've never been great with aftershaves and perfumes, so tell me what I'm looking for."

"No, I didn't tell you last time, and I won't now. If it's there, then you can tell me. Trust your nose, Copa."

Sniffing again, Adam racked his brains trying to recall the smells that Stardust described all those months ago. Something … floral? Then he remembered, and sniffed one last time to make sure:

"Hmm, I'm getting some rose here, yep definitely rose. Can't place any of the other smells but I'm certain you've got rose in there."

"Spot-on, the rose, lady of both darkness and romance … so relieved … splendid day after all. And, you like it? You see, it was either this or Timeless by Avon, and that's a tad too feminine for me."

"The Aramis is fine. Look, I'm not a perfume kind of guy, but if you want something more your style, couldn't you mix it up yourself? My Mum used to make soap for Christmas, and she used to buy all sorts of smelly oils. I'll bet they had the stuff in the early 70's, what with all the hippies about, and you won't be breaking Groover's rules."

Stardust leapt forward and hugged Adam tightly, the scent overpowering:

"Thank you, thank, you, that is genius. I could even attempt my own version of   Voleur de Roses. Copacabana, for a gentleman who wears underpants and beach party attire, you truly think outside the box. Though our special bond is still broken, I will once again proudly carve my initial in your chest."

As they walked across the bridge and through the crowded square, Stardust had a marked spring in his platform booted step, dancing as if half of a waltzing duo - even Groover raised an eyebrow at the uncharacteristic mood joyeux. Leaving Stardust on guard outside the tower block reception hall, Groover invited Adam inside.

The silver clad Genie, leant against a plastic coated bannister rail, and got straight to the point:

"Ee look like ee mean business. So, what might ee be after?"

"Is it possible to visit a viro without invitation, say if someone is blocking you but you still want to see them?"

"Thar is a way, but I don't see why I should tell ee. What are ee offerin'?"

"I thought you could tell me as a bonus for all the times I've been here."

"That's no offer. I see ee die every Friday, and ee are bloody borin'. Ee 'aven't killed anyone in all these months, and I'm beginnin' to think I got the raw end of the deal. Just ee get back out there and die like ee always do, and forget any … bonus."

"But I'm reliable. I haven't missed a week, have I?"

"Hah, hah, haven't missed a bloody week. Let me show ee what that means to old Groover. Come with me."

Adam followed Groover to the far end of the hall, beyond the stairwell, to a door marked 'Supplies'. After, making sure nobody was watching, Groover opened the door, and the two men went inside. Little bigger than a walk-in closet, the janitorial room reeked of disinfectant, an assortment of cleaning equipment neatly stacked against the sidewalls, and chemicals lining the shelves. Adam held his nose, the caustic smell bringing tears to his eyes:

"Oh God, it stinks! Why do you need all these chemicals? All this stuff is redundant. Everything gets cleaned while we sleep."

"Realism, and I don't like people comin' in 'ere," said Groover, apparently unaffected by the smell.

To Adam's horror, Groover shut the door behind them, and pulled a latch across, locking them in with the stench. Before Adam could complain, the Genie spun round and slapped the back wall, which immediately vanished.

"Through 'ere," he ordered.

Once through the gap, Groover put out his hand and the wall reappeared behind them. This side of the wall was smooth, glossy-white, with a glassy quality, reminding Adam of the transport tube walls leading to the concierge. They were in a short hallway with a door either side. In front, connecting to a lower level, were a set of whisper quiet steel and chrome escalators: one up, one down.

Groover sat on the floor, fiddling with his boots, quickly clipping off the high platforms. Standing up, looking relieved, he said:

"That's more comfortable, but I still look like a ruddy spaceman in this silver get-up."

His broad West Country burr had gone, replaced with a standard Home Counties accent:

"The one thing I cannot stand about this Glam theme is the platform boots. Broke my ankle twice before I got these clip-ons and hidden ankle braces. Only for me though. I have no idea how the gang run about the way they do, but then again I was always a bit unbalanced, ha ha."

"Your accent ... why are you speaking like that? And, what is this place? Are we outside?"

"Surely you can still pick up a bit of the West Country?"

"A little perhaps, nothing more than a hint."

"I've been resurrected for over forty years now, and in that time I have never come into contact with anybody who has even the slightest West Country accent. I spent the first ten years in a research station on the outside, and everyone there spoke through translators in this perfect posh English. Now that, combined with that ponce Rampage being my number two, has pretty much wiped out me old way o' speakin'."

"And you put on the accent in the viro because ...?"

"Because it makes them obey me. I put on a pirate act. It's nothing like the way I used to talk, but they seem to like it. Rampage knows about it, and now so do you. Come on, time's wasting and you aint seen nothing yet."

Together, they descended the escalator to a wide corridor below. Tucked either side of the escalators were sleek white golf carts, each bearing a blue pop-art logo of Groover's apelike face. After learning that this was not the outside, but a complex maze of tunnels and rooms under the psychoviro, Adam climbed into the passenger seat of one of the vehicles. Groover already seated, was eager to drive.

As they slowly travelled along the series of interconnecting tunnels, Adam asked:

"Where are you taking me? This place is something out of a Bond movie, with you as the super-villain."

"We're nearly there, and you're right about the Bond connection. When they designed this place, I persuaded them to add an underground lair, complete with guardrooms, video walls, and all manner of surveillance equipment. At first, I thought I could cause trouble all over the Viroverse with my army of killers, but then they imposed the damned restricted travel rules on us, just because of our ... special needs. Still, I like it down here when I need a break from them upstairs, and only I have direct access."

"No shark tank though."

"Ha, this whole Environment is a ruddy shark tank; I thought you knew that by now. Perhaps you need some education. After all these months, you still don't really get what we're about here do you? Let me enlighten you with a quick detour. I wasn't originally planning on showing you this, but we've got time."

Groover stopped the golf cart, pressed a button, and the vehicle spun 180°. They drove back the way they came for a few yards, and then turned down a side tunnel. Up ahead, the tunnel narrowed to a round tube, just wide enough for the cart. Adam felt uneasy, especially with the way Groover was mumbling and chuckling to himself. As they entered the tubular tunnel the cart halted, and as in an automatic carwash, the wheels clicked into a conveyor. Dark shutters sealed each end; the tube suddenly plunged into pitch darkness and icy coldness. Adam could faintly discern his tormenters silhouette, sitting back, relaxed, hands clasped behind his head. The cart glided silently forward, and in the darkness, Groover's head slowly turned:

"Now you will see, hear, and smell my experiences. Don't bother to look away, because the images will follow you."

Starting deceptively gently, like a virtual theme park ride with a first person view, the experience soon revealed its unrelenting horror. Through the eyes of a serial killer, a quick-fire montage of images assaulted Adam's eyes: sickening sexual depravity turned to violent rape, to torture, to death, to cutting, ending in pitiless unlamented burial. Adam closed his eyes to block out the brutal sights and clasped his hands to his ears, desperate to stop the sounds of crying, screaming, and the repetitive thudding chunk of the garden spade. The nightmare continued unabated. The accompanying odours were potent in their portrayal of the grisly narrative, from the heady pheromone-rich stench of carnality, the salty rust aroma of blood, and perhaps most chilling, the rooty smell of the dirt. From the shadows, Groover aggressively thrust an elbow in Adam's side:

"Open your soddin' eyes, boy! Don't you dare try to block this out. This is my ride, and these are my memories."

Adam conceded defeat, sinking back into his seat, soaking up the sensory punches as a bruised and beaten boxer caught on the ropes. Though the visceral imagery gradually blurred into a single nauseous stream, the last living moments of the victims burned into Adam's memory. These were discarded 'undesirables' rendered helpless, fragile, their eyes deadened pools of resignation in the face of heartless psychotic ferocity. Such memories were trophies to Groover but Adam would bear them as permanent scars. Abruptly the scene changed, and leering euphorically at Adam from a large mirror was the naked, quivering killer, soaked in sweat mixed with spatters of blood. Breathing heavily, the face brimmed with demonic satisfaction, and Adam avoided looking into the eyes, for fear they held his own reflection.

The images suddenly disappeared, and the ordeal was over. Emerging into the light at the end of the tunnel, Groover regained control of the vehicle, and drove into the wide corridor beyond. Halting the cart once more, he asked:

"So what did you think? Are you a convert? Do you understand now?"

"No, never," said Adam firmly. "I could … never be like that. And, as for understanding, all I know is you're insane.

"Ah, too bad, too bad. Now, we'd better get moving. You haven't seen what we came here for. Oh, and as a special bonus, to reach our destination, we have to go back the way we came, through my memory tunnel … and it works both ways. Ha, ha, maybe you'll enjoy it more the second time around."

Laughing hysterically, Groover spun the cart around, and headed back into the ghoulish tunnel.

NOBODY'S HOME

Finally, they reached their destination, though Adam was still dizzy from the return ride through the tunnel. His relief after exiting the first time had stripped him of his defensive reserve, making the second run an unbearable ordeal. Getting out of the cart, he detected a strange odour, strongly redolent of olive oil, which seemed present only in this particular area. It was also colder here, giving Adam a refreshing boost on his unsteady feet. Groover, already out of the vehicle, slapped his hand against a nearby wall bearing the words 'Nobody's Home'. As before, a section of the wall vanished, and Groover walked through, beckoning Adam to follow.

The room on the other side was bitterly cold, and the olive oil accord far more pervasive, making Adam quite dizzy. Narrower than the corridor outside, and sparsely furnished except for a few white Panton chairs, the room stretched for about fifty feet. One side was dominated by two large shelves, one about two feet above the other, which stretched the entire length of the wall. The bottom shelf was empty, the top shelf filled over half its length with a neat line of head-size objects. As Adam stepped closer, he realised that the reason the objects were head-size because they were in fact severed heads, nested in simple metal stands. Groover smiled, and gestured to the gruesome line-up in the manner of a perfect host introducing a new guest:

"Adam, meet your deadhead selves, the Adamses, your very personal guide to twenty three weeks of failure."

"Me … they're me …? Oh no … oh …"

"Take a good look because," Groover stepped forward and clasped either side of Adam's head, "this is certainly joining them tonight."

Pushing the grinning Genie away, Adam looked along the grisly line-up, and felt nauseous:

"You psychopath, why are they here? Why are you collecting them?"

"Not too aggressive there if ee don't mind. The reason they're here is because I was hoping for a bit of competition, and that you'd get some payback occasionally. The other shelf, the empty one, is for the gang's heads. I wasn't expecting their shelf to fill up too quickly, but I thought that gradually you'd get into the swing of things and start evening the odds. At this rate I'm going to need both shelves just for you, you bloody failure."

Groover picked one of the heads from its cradle, and carried it over to Adam. It was the bauble-eyed Christmas head:

"It's a shame I don't have the head from your first visit, before we made the deal, because that one really caused Rampage a shed-load of embarrassment. This one's my favourite from the shelf, and not 'cause of the pretty decorations. This one at least tried to put on a show, and you need a bit of entertainment on Christmas Day. It was like at the movies. You knocked Roxy off the snowmobile, and had a tussle on-board with that weirdo, Stardust. Had me thinking a kill was on the cards, until ee crashed into a bloody wall and ruined it all."

"And what's all this got to do with my request for a bonus?"

"It has everything to do with it," said Groover, kissing the Christmas head's forehead before carefully placing it back on the shelf. "We already have a deal, and I don't see why you deserve any ruddy bonus. What you are really askin' for is a favour, and I don't do those. Same goes for most of us in this place. If we weren't all busy with the hunt and the stupid fancy dress, we'd probably be cuttin' each other's throats every day. I don't care about other people's needs and feelings, and I thought your little trip down my memory lane would've shown ee that."

"So you brought me all the way down here, and showed me all this, just to say no? May as well go back then, unless you have any more surprises. Anyway, that smell's getting to me, making me a bit dizzy, and I wouldn't want anything to ruin your entertainment."

"Don't get smart with me, boy. You're down here 'cause I'm going to offer you a deal. And, ignore the smell. It's only some preservative that keeps your shelf mates nice and fresh. Get used to it, 'cause that head's joining them later."

"OK, I get it," said Adam sharply, uneasy with the gruesome image.

Groover exploded with spitting aggression, "No ee don't, ee don't get it at all, boy! Don't you see, I'm bound by a ruddy code? I can't join in the killin'! I can only watch. You've seen what I'm capable of, the things I used to do, but now I can only watch like some shitty couch potato."

Prodding Adam in the chest, Groover demanded, "Give me something worth watchin' you lazy bastard!"

The shouting and anger increased Adam's dizziness, and he sat down in one of the plastic chairs, which was surprisingly comfortable given the austere single piece moulded design. Groover stood over him, rubbing his hands together, visibly relishing his dominance.

"So, here's the deal. Today, I want one of the gang's heads on that bottom shelf. Any one of them will do, but you have to make the kill yourself. In return, you'll get a message tomorrow telling you how to visit someone even if they're blockin' you. If you fail, then don't be botherin' to ask for any more bonuses in the future."

"What if I badly wound one of them, would that do?"

"Not a bloody chance. You need to up your game, get some revenge, and I know twenty-three of your mates would be noddin' in agreement … if they had any ruddy shoulders. Now, you listen to me, there are four reasons why you fail. Two of them are your fault and two aren't. I'll start with the ones that are.

"First, you are a naturally lazy sod. It's true, I looked into your background, and you're one of those 'undesirables' who gives up on everything in life. You should never have been bought back, you don't deserve it. I see it every bloody time you turn up, with your half-arsed plans, and total lack of fightin' spirit.

"And then there's the second reason. You have absolutely no training. Rampage and the gang train almost every day. As ee can imagine, in a place like this we have some martial art masters, and weapons blokes around the place, and they're always helping out and giving advice. You're seriously lacking in fightin' skills, and it shows."

Groover nodded in agreement with himself, and pointed to the head laden shelf for emphasis:

"You already know the third reason, and that's the memory loss. You don't remember anything leading up to your death, and that's when most of the important fighting takes place. No matter how many times you come here, you have sod all experience. It used to be funny seeing ee use the same losing moves each week 'cause you forgot you used them before, but now it's just bloody boring. This is your twenty-fourth week, and I bet you go out there again as if you never fought before. That's why ee need trainin', boy."

"And the last reason?"

"Now, even though I don't like you, I do trust you with secrets. You're gonna get a freebie bit of knowledge that only us Originals know about, plus a few trusted commoners. You've heard about the low sex drive, eh?"

"Yeah, everyone knows about the lower libido. Our new bodies are engineered differently. It's supposed to be a secret but everyone knows."

"Engineered differently, my arse. That libido stuff's nothing but a lie. Them concierges put those rumours about to fool you all, and it bloody well worked. What's really going on is that everyone is sedated. It's nothing powerful, but just enough to take the edge off. Remember when you were first brought back, you felt calmer than you should?"

"Yes, the concierge said it was some chemical which would wear off after a few days, once I settled in."

"Well, that's the same stuff, only a stronger dose to get you started. Once that's run out, they apply a sedative at night, once every five days. Now, thanks to my special privileges we don't have that muck here, so we've still got our edge. Puts you at a disadvantage, 'cause the stuff's still in your system."

"So, you're saying there's no hope for me? You're saying there's no way I can beat the gang?"

"Bloody Hell, doesn't anything other than loser talk come out of ee're bloody mouth. What I'm sayin' is you need to get some training, serious training, but most of all you need to grow a massive pair o' bollocks, meta ... metaph ... metapho ..."

"Metaphorically speaking?"

"That's the word. Yes, ee need to grow a pair of metabollocks, and start putting some heads on that bottom shelf. Do it today, and I promise you'll get the information you want. Now come on, it's time we got back to the party before Rampage gets all panicky."

Groover grabbed Adam's shirt to pull him out of the chair. The Genie frowned at the feel of the clothing:

"Hey, this looks like your normal Hawaiian party gear, but the material feels really tough. It's nothin' like when we first made the deal. I thought I said ee gotta turn up in the same clothes every week, not some sneaky body armour."

"Blame the AI and my profile. I just wear what I'm given. I'm still on my ten-day restriction, food and drink only. Thanks to our deal, I haven't been alive more than seven days in a row so I don't qualify for full dispenser access, and it's not easy keeping it secret from the neighbours."

"So ee're clothes are … evolving," said Groover, clearly intrigued. "That's weird, never heard of that before. Pity ee're not evolving as well; might make your fights less boring. Now, come on, Copa, it's time to put one 'o the gang's heads on that shelf."

A FIGHTING CHANCE

Ignoring the pain from a long laceration across his left pectoral, Adam quickly climbed up the drainpipe and heaved himself onto the flat roof of the warehouse. Minutes earlier, Rampage had ambushed him by the canal bridge, and during the brief ensuing fight, Adam received a flashing blade across the chest, causing him to drop his sword. Fortunately, his overly confident opponent lost his footing, slipping clumsily into the murky waters. The first thought was to drown the evil gang leader, but the sudden appearance of Ziggy and Stardust sent Adam sprinting away from the scene.

Unarmed and outnumbered, Adam lay low on the gravelly asphalt, waiting for the gang to follow him, vainly hoping to push one off the roof, perhaps to their death. He groaned in disappointment as Roxy and Quatro appeared on the roof of the other warehouse, across the alley, leisurely taking up position, gleefully laughing and waving as usual.

Huffing and puffing with effort, clothes heavy from his canal soaking, Rampage managed to haul himself up the drainpipe. He stopped short of fully climbing onto the roof, instead choosing to hang cross-armed on the edge, facing Adam, and wearing a mocking sneer:

"So, Copacabana, how shall we kill you this week? Shall I join you up there for some swift knife play, or should I let our two lovely ladies wound you a bit first? You never know, you might be able to dodge the arrows, but I doubt it given our previous encounters. Stardust tells me you're both friends again so maybe I should let him have a go. Hmm, what difficult decisions a leader has to make."

Adam kept his gaze on the two archers, well aware of their speed and accuracy. Then, taking his chance, sprung to his feet, intending to run over and kick the grinning psycho full in the face. Before he took even a step, powerful arms grabbed him from behind, holding him fast. It was Ziggy:

"Too ... slow ... Mr Copa. Too busy ... watching ... the girls. Me ... thinks you ... fancy ... them."

Rampage shook his head:

"You would never think someone so large could be so stealthy, but then again he's caught you out before with his tiptoeing. You never learn do you? Well, I've made my decision, and I think my smelly colleague, Stardust, should finish you off. See you next Friday, you stupid fucker."

With that final remark, Rampage disappeared from view, carefully climbing back down the drainpipe. Seconds later, Stardust appeared at the edge of the gutter, and dramatically leapt onto the roof with catlike grace, but then began fussily adjusting his wig and pulling at the fabric of his black sequined shirt:

"Damn it, damn it, snagged some sequins on something No matter, it won't interfere with the execution, and at least I still smell good."

Time was running out, and with it Adam's chance of seeing Manny. Stardust flourished his blade, and pointed it at Adam's heart:

"My friend, my brother, I will make it quick and clean, straight through the heart, and when you come again, you shall smell my new fragrance."

A spark of thought, the merest hint of an idea, and Adam acted without delay. Clasping Ziggy's arms tight around him, he lurched forwards, heading heart-first for the outstretched sword. The lumbering giant followed, wrong-footed, not expecting the move, adding bulk to the momentum. Stardust, horrified, forgetting he was at the roof's edge, stepped backwards as Adam impaled himself upon the sword. Adrenalin partially masked the pain as the blade passed easily through, and drove into Ziggy, both men skewered like meaty chunks on a shish kebab. Embedded up to the hilt in the onrush of human flesh, the force rammed Stardust off the roof, and all three fell to the concrete path some thirty feet below.

There was no time to contemplate the possible outcome of the situation since death came swiftly to Adam. There was no time to wonder whether Stardust would break his neck in the fall or whether Ziggy had suffered a fatal wound. Was it two chances of a kill, or perhaps none, since Groover might credit Ziggy's bloody demise to Stardust's swordsmanship, or Stardust's crushing death to Ziggy's considerable weight? The only certainty was that

Adam would face the truth with a brand new head, since the current one was destined for the Genie's shelf.

Saturday morning, back home, a new day, and new body. It took over an hour before Adam, wearing only a silk robe, wearily ventured from his bedroom, fearing the truth waiting for him on the computer. His last memory from the hunt was of the sneering Rampage appearing at the roof edge, anything after that now lost. With reluctance and trepidation he booted up the computer and stared intently at the screen. The operating system loaded, and a message flashed on the desktop:

"Congratulations. My trophy room now contains a hint of Stardust. You kept your end of the deal and now I will keep mine. Follow the instructions carefully, and carry out every part. This is one-time only, and if you get even one part wrong then it won't work. You won't get another chance!"

The instructions came in two parts. The first part was a ninety nine character code which Adam typed into a text box—annoyingly, cut and pasting was disabled for this tedious task. Once completed, a simple green tick appeared, and he turned his attention to the second, far more disturbing task. Using the product dispenser, Adam was required to order a mug of boiling hot Earl Grey tea, without milk or sugar, and drink it down within ten seconds without crying or screaming. After that, he was to return to the computer, search for Emmanuel Beaumont, request a visit, whilst all the time attempting to sing Manilow's 'Copacabana'. An evil smiley icon accompanied the request, testament to the Genie's warped intent.

The mug of tea was much larger than expected and almost full to the brim - in a bitterly ironic twist, the mug size was based on Adam's own greedy profile. In a show of stoical courage, he gulped down the scalding hot liquid without uttering a sound. The pain in his mouth and throat was horrifying and intense as he sat back at the computer, and began searching for Manny. Remembering the song request, a croaky tortured rendition of 'Copacabana' slurred awkwardly from his swollen purple lips.

Pressing the VISIT button brought an instant ACCEPTED response, and the Genie's message promptly disappeared. Another message immediately appeared in its place:

"Surprise, you really only had to enter the code and press the visit button. Ha, ha, the drink and the song were just for fun! Don't suppose your singing now. As those American folks say, 'have a nice day!'"

After checking the Viro's version of the internet for information on the formidable Sister Josephine Maguire, Adam spent the day quietly sipping ice-cold water, grateful that his airway had not swelled significantly. Death by suffocation would bring about the automatic cancelation of the visit, making a mockery of all he had suffered. Adam decided it was best not to take chances and just sipped the water. Tomorrow, the injuries would be gone.

MAN TO MANNY

A small leather bound bible by the bed, and an illuminated icon of Christ on the wall powerfully indicated that this was the correct viro. Resinous grains, heated in a small copper dish filled the small room with the fresh sharp balsamic aroma of frankincense and myrrh—a heady Catholic ambiance, complete with complementary communion wafers on an ornate silver tray and a small goblet of Clare Valley sacramental wine. Adam was reticent to leave the meditative serenity of the wake-up cubicle, imagining an irate Sister Josephine and a crowd of enraged cross-wielding believers waiting outside in a daunting stone and marble Environment of ecclesiastical late-renaissance grandeur.

Stepping outside dispelled these fears, as there was no angry mob, nor the expected colonnades and basilicas. Instead, the scenery was a paradisiacal masterpiece. Immaculately mowed meadows of lushly luminous green rolled up to majestic snow-capped mountains, the air sparklingly crisp and fresh. Adam found the architecture a fascinating fusion of traditional Swiss chalet and Oriental pagoda: vast apartment blocks with sweeping red-tiled gabled roofs, intricate wooden balconies and pastel coloured louvered window shutters. The majority of the buildings stood on the far side of a huge reflective lake that dominated the centre of the landscape, their stately facades cleanly mirrored in the calm waters.

The wake-up building was a stark contrast to the concrete and steel brutality of the psychoviro - five storeys in the same sino-helvetic style with black lacquered cladding and pastel painted doors. Elaborately carved staircases wound their way up to polished wooden balconies, which bore various religious symbols.

Not knowing where to find Manny, Adam made his way along a yellow gravel path towards the apartment blocks some half a mile away. The crushed stone was surprisingly comfortable underfoot, and Adam enjoyed the gently scented air from the Yoshino cherry trees that gracefully lined the path, their delicate branches blooming with beautifully fragrant light-pink blossom. In the distance, behind the lakeside buildings, some way up the grassy slope, was a very large but simple church: black roof and spire, small windows, and white weatherboard clad walls, reminiscent of Scandinavian design.

As Adam reached the first of the apartment buildings, he encountered his first Nun. Taking the direct approach, he walked up to the black habited figure and politely asked, "Good morning, Sister, could you help me. My name is Mr Eden, and I need to know the whereabouts of my friend, Ma … Emmanuel Beaumont. He supposedly lives here somewhere, but I don't know the exact address."

The Nun replied softly, her voice gentle, innocent, "And good morning to you, Mr Eden. So pleased to meet a fellow Catholic."

"Well … I …"

Don't worry, I'm not a mind reader, I can smell the holy incense on you. For sure, you came out of one of our cubicles. About your question, I'm afraid I have not heard of this Emmanuel Beaumont. Are you sure he lives here? Did he invite you?"

"Ah … yes he did," lied Adam. "He wasn't able to meet me … I guess. You see, I've heard that he never leaves his apartment."

The gentle voice hardened dramatically to a shocked shrillness, "Saints preserve us, you mean Manny the foul mouthed hermit! Why would anyone want to visit that filthy minded man? And, why don't you have an escort, Mr Eden? All visitors are assigned an escort—it's the rules. Wait here, and I shall fetch Sister Josephine right away. Oh, and I would tuck your shirt in if I were you. Sister Josephine will not approve of your dishevelled appearance."

"No, wait," panicked Adam. "We don't have to bother Sister Josephine, do we? I'm sure she has more important things to do."

As the Nun stopped to reconsider, Adam began tucking in his shirt, and in doing so, accidently popped open his trouser button, the white jeans falling unceremoniously to his ankles. The Nun gasped and covered her eyes, rooted to the spot with shock. Apologizing profusely, and glad he was wearing underpants, Adam tried to pull up his trousers, but tripped and lay writhing for a moment at the feet of the now distraught bride of God. Once back on his feet, he jumped about, eventually getting his trousers back up. Before the

Nun could run for help, Adam pleaded for her to divulge Manny's whereabouts. Still covering her eyes, she crossed herself then gestured to one of the apartment buildings:

"Third house … top floor … far end. Now go … now … please."

Offering a final apology for his clothing mishap, and noticing other Nuns peering down from the balconies above, Adam quickly headed for Manny's apartment. It took only a few minutes to reach the building, but already a large group of Nuns was following along the path. At the head of the dark cluster, Adam recognized Sister Josephine, striding purposefully, a severe expression on her face.

Hurrying up the stairwell to the top floor, Adam sprinted along the balcony to the furthest apartment, hoping Manny would open the door before the Nuns caught up with him. He frantically pulled the iron bell chain, and heard loud chiming inside. A bald man in Monk's robes opened the door, exhibiting a look of surprise at his visitor's colourful clothes:

"Yes, how may I help you?"

"You're not Manny? I thought my friend Man … Emmanuel Beaumont lived here. Is he here?"

"Ah, the hermit, he lives next door, I am Brother Matthias. Strange one, your friend, I saw him at his rebirth, but he has not left his rooms since. Careful though, if you knock at his door, as he has quite an obscene tongue on him."

At the other end of the walkway, the Nuns emerged, and advanced slowly. Matthias edged back into his apartment, looking fearful:

"Oh dear, what trouble is this? Sister Josephine looks angry … very angry."

Before slamming the door shut, Matthias put a comforting hand on Adam's shoulder:

"God bless you, and good luck with your friend, but I have to go … right now."

Adam ran to Manny's door and repeatedly pulled the bell chain. After a few seconds, a voice screamed:

"Please leave me alone, and engage in copulation with yourself!"

"Quick, just open up; the Nuns are coming!"

"Please piss off, whoever you are, you deluded degenerate."

"Manny, it's me, Adam! For God's sake let me in!"

"Adam? Adam Eden? How did you …?"

"No time to explain. Let me in, I bloody suffered for this …"

150

The door opened, and there stood Manny: naked, sweaty, and extending a welcoming hand:

"Nice to see you again, Adam. You look so slim, I hardly recognise you."

They firmly shook hands.

"Err, Manny, why is your hand so warm?"

"My sincerest apologies," Manny dryly replied. "I have been masturbating. Please come in."

Once inside the spacious apartment, the Nuns a problem for later, Adam appreciated Manny's luxurious living conditions. Though simple in style, everything was of the highest quality: cool ivory Quaker cabinets, plush glacial-silver jacquard seating, and soft beau blue carpeting. Only the awkwardly fidgety Manny seemed out of place, with his flushed pink nudity, long dark beard, and thick mop of tousled bed-hair.

"Adam, sit, please sit," said Manny, gesturing to a wide, comfortable armchair.

Adam sat, sinking into the generous cushioning, whilst Manny disappeared into another room. He promptly returned with a hard backed kitchen chair, which he placed on the floor facing Adam, and sat, still naked, legs slightly splayed, genitals on full display. Adam pretended at first not to notice, but within seconds felt compelled to object:

"I know they say 'when in Rome', and you're the 'master of your own domain', but don't you have any underwear … or even a towel … you know … to cover up."

"Oh I am so sorry, where are my manners. I was planning to masturbate again, but that can wait. I'll be back in a jiffy."

Manny left the room again, and returned with a small red and white stripe hand towel, which he neatly placed over the offending appendages:

"There, that's better. Now, you must tell me why you are here?"

Adam wondered whether he should complain again, since the small towel was scant coverage for Manny's obviously erect organ, creating a disturbing image of a little circus tent on his lap. Increasingly concerned about his friend's state of mind, for now Adam let the matter lie.

"I can't tell you how I got here, that's a secret, but I can tell you why. I wanted to contact you when I first got resurrected …"

"Only the Lord can resurrect the dead!" roared Manny.

"Ok, calm down, I respect that. Well, because you blocked everyone, I asked a neighbour for help. He found out that you … that you …"

"Had fallen from Grace?"

"No … that you …"

"Were waylaid by the demons of science on my way to God's Kingdom?"

"He said you'd gone nuts, and never left your apartment."

"Oh…I see," muttered Manny softly, noticeably embarrassed.

"Well whether he's right, or those things you just said, it's irrelevant to me. I'm here because I heard you were suffering, and I want to help. I mean, what's with all this nakedness and … masturbating."

"I masturbate all day, no matter how intense the pain. It gets so raw, sometimes bloody, but it is a necessary penance."

"Oh no … no… that's horrible. God, that's horrible. Penance for what?"

"For being here and not in Heaven. The concierge explained the rebirth process to me. My body, my original body, is out there somewhere … just a pile of bones."

"You were cremated."

Manny shuddered:

"Oh, I see. Then at best, soil or dust in the wind. Who's to say that the tiny fragment of brain transported through the centuries, the only original flesh, contains the soul? Most likely, my soul has gone to Heaven, and this manmade heresy is a barren husk, a hollow shell doomed to nothingness. Adam, imagine a train chugging along the tracks towards its intended destination, and then someone maliciously separates the engine from the carriages. The engine proceeds to the station, whilst the carriages are rerouted down a dark siding to … oblivion. That is where I am. That is what this life is … oblivion … nothingness."

"Does that mean you're an atheist now?"

"No, it means I'm an empty shell, nothing more. I am a hollow man."

"And the wanking? How will wanking sort this out?"

"I do it in the hope that God will one day acknowledge my pain, and take pity on me, and reunite the soul with the self. Every day I sit on the sofa over there and masturbate. Yes, I admit that I am what you call … a filthy wanker. It is the sordid burden I must bear."

Adam looked over to the sofa, and was shocked that it faced a large portrait of Christ. Seeing this reaction, Manny hurriedly explained:

"No Adam, there is a large flat screen TV in the sideboard below the picture. You press a button on the remote and it automatically slides up into place. It completely hides Jesus. I watch porn while I …"

"No way! Emmanuel Beaumont watch porn, no way! You used to think it was indecent if a woman didn't wear a coat on a chilly day."

"Things are different now. I watch porn. I watch filthy porn. Eager young things, their sweaty bodies writhe and I respond with my masturbatory self-flagellation."

Manny reached under the 'circus tent' prompting a swift response from Adam, "Stop that right now! There'll be no playing with your 'hollow man' whilst I'm here."

Once sure that the deed was averted, Adam left his seat and went over to the sofa. Spotting the remote on the sideboard, he inspected the buttons:

"How do you switch this on? The green button at the top's not doing anything."

"Think carefully, Adam. Do you seriously want to expose yourself to such depravity?"

"Of course."

"Press the U button and the screen comes up. Then you press the green button. Be warned, the porn will appear immediately. I have it programmed in a continuous loop."

Adam pressed the button and the large screen slid smoothly into place. Once the show started, he stood silently for nearly three minutes watching the nubile female bodies display their energetic talents:

"Manny, does it go on like this all the way through?"

"Yes it does, except for a few other positions. You can't say I didn't warn you."

"Manny, this isn't porn. It's a cheesy 1980's aerobics video. There's no nudity at all. They're all wearing short pants and cut-off t-shirts. You can't even see the shape of their nipples, so they must be wearing sports bras. Must say, I feel a little cheated here."

"But the way they stretch and pose is obscene. Can't you see the degenerate I have become?"

"Jerking off to pink and blue Day-Glo Lycra is at worst a little kinky, but not degenerate. To be honest, it's the all-day wanking that worries me. And, whilst I totally get your explanation about the empty shell, and dark sidings leading to oblivion, I think it's me that must take the blame for all this."

"Truthfully, you think that? Why are you to blame? I most certainly do not blame you."

"Your suicide. You killed yourself because of … the murders they say I committed, even though I'm sure there's some mistake."

"The murders? Why do you think that?"

153

"I was told it was in all the papers and on the TV news. They said you killed yourself because of the shame of the murders. You know … my drinking, and you wish you'd kept on eye on me."

"You always told me, quite forcefully, and on numerous occasions, that the papers lie and exaggerate, and that they were only good for wiping one's backside."

"Hmm, that's true, I did used to say that," chuckled Adam, remembering the many drunken rants that Manny endured during their time together. Not sharing the humour, Manny continued in a more serious tone:

"Adam, I absolutely did not kill myself because of you. I felt immense sadness at your passing, and much regret over the murders. In addition, yes, I will admit I experienced some self-doubt, and wished I had been stricter about keeping alcohol away from you, but my faith saw me through those dark days."

"But you did kill yourself over something."

Manny clasped his hands together, and tightly closed his eyes, in deep anguish rather than prayer. Breathing in deeply, composing himself, he finally admitted, "I was spurned."

"Spurned?"

"Yes, spurned. Rebuffed, rejected … by Scarlett."

"Scarlett? You mean Scarlett Slaughter? You can't mean Scarlett Slaughter."

Manny simply nodded, too choked to speak, his eyes still tightly closed. In his first life, this news would have floored Adam, or at least struck him dumb with surprise, but frequent violent visits to the psychoviro had rendered him impervious to such minor shocks.

"But she hated you. She spent the whole time insulting you."

Regaining a measure of emotion, Manny looked at Adam with mild disdain:

"Is that so? You're the one who told me that a little teasing between men and women is often a sign of attraction."

"I said a little teasing? She spent the whole evening insulting you, and your beliefs. I'm sure at one point she called God a serial killer."

"Remember, she was a little tipsy that evening, and you told me people can be a bit wicked in that state."

"She was way beyond tipsy, and people often speak their mind when they're in that state. I should know; I was an expert on piss-talking."

"If she hated me so much then why did she … err …?"

154

"Why did she what?"

"That night, when we first heard about the incident outside the pub, Scarlett took control. She was amazing ... sobered up in an instant. A couple of off-duty police officers by the bar started organizing people, and Scarlett went straight over to talk to them. I do not know to this day what was said, but she managed to get us both out of there before the police arrived to cordon off the place. We took a taxi to a local hotel: luxury room, sea-view, very expensive."

"Scarlett paid, I'm guessing?"

"She handled everything. She said we needed to lie low for a day or two until she knew what we were dealing with. Then she ... or rather we ..."

"What, got arrested?"

"No, thankfully that never happened. No, that night we ... engaged in intimate relations."

Adam, struck dumb for a moment, fought against the disturbing mental imagery of any carnal encounter between Manny and Scarlett:

"By 'intimate relations' you do mean ..."

"Yes, I mean penetrative intimate relations."

"Manny, I just want to get things clear. By 'penetrative intimate relations' you mean that your ... tent-pole," Adam pointed at the stripy lap cloth, "went inside Scarlett's ... err ... vagina?"

"Yes, amongst other orifices, and on multiple occasions. Scarlett had an insatiable appetite. I was quite giddy by the time I went home. Some of the positions were quite exerting ... even painful. There was one where she used a ..."

Adam waved his hand to stop Manny from continuing:

"Whoa, no more details, please. You're saying you killed yourself because you had sex with Scarlett outside of marriage. I know it's a sin, but ..."

Shaking his head, sighing, Manny continued, "She arranged for us to give statements to the police, and after wrapping up the legal side of things, she went back to France. Over the next couple of weeks I realised I could not live without her. I desperately wanted her ... no, needed her. I tried calling and texting but she never replied - playing hard to get I suspected. In the end, I decided to go to France, and declare my undying love for her, and ask her to be my wife."

"Oh dear, I bet that didn't end well."

"No it did not. It most certainly did not."

"I guess you found out she's a lesbian ..."

Manny, looked horrified:

"But I am male and we … many times … many many times. I lost my virginity!"

"Calm down, Manny … um … it was probably the heightened emotions with all that happened earlier. And, when I say 'lesbian', I don't mean totally exclusively. Scarlett loves sex, especially when she's had a few drinks and is all hyped up. Didn't you see her eyeing up the barman? She's got a bit of the sexual predator thing going on."

"You mean she raped me?"

"No, no, no, don't be daft. I'm just saying she goes for any old port in a storm. It wasn't you she wanted, it was the sex. Anyway, you obviously enjoyed yourself by the sound of it. I'm guessing you weren't forced."

"Yes, I cannot lie; it was most enjoyable, but later … heart-breaking."

The doorbell suddenly chimed, causing both men to jump. A commanding voice shouted outside:

"Mr Beaumont, this is Sister Josephine, please open this door. You have an unauthorised visitor in there, which is against the rules. All visits must be countersigned by either Reverend Stevens or myself. Now come on, open up!"

When the doorbell chimed again, Manny left his seat, and quietly walked to the door – the little tent towel precariously hanging on.

Angrily shaking his fist he screamed, "I strongly suggest you piss-off, you black garbed harpy of the Devil! Bother me again and I shall masturbate, whilst imagining you naked and riding a billy goat across Vatican Square!"

After receiving a muffled disharmony of shrill gasps and Hail Marys, Manny returned calmly to his seat:

"Sorry about that, Adam. That should take care of them for a few hours."

Stunned at the shameful outburst, Adam began to wonder whether he could really help Manny. Still feeling partially guilty for the suicide, he persevered, fumbling along like an incompetent psychiatrist:

"So Manny, tell me about France."

THE LOVE OF MANNY WILL NOT GROW COLD

Manny's constant shuffling about on his chair was distracting, each squirm heralding the potential dislodging of the lap towel. Before any further discussion about the trip to France, Adam politely told his naked host to put on some clothes. Manny agreed, apologising profusely for his lack of manners, but after a hasty trip to the bedroom, he returned wearing only a small pair of plaid boxer shorts. For a moment, as Manny sat back down on the hard-seated chair, Adam wearily accepted the slightly improved situation, but the sudden sight of a squashed testicle peeping out from the left leg of the underwear changed his mind.

Adam pointed to the offending genital, "You're popping out."

Apologising again, Manny tucked the testicle back into the shorts and shuffled in his seat, only for his other testicle to make an appearance on the other side. Adam could take no more and angrily demanded:

"Put on some bloody clothes, Manny! And, real clothes: not a towel, or a thong, or a sash, or a robe …! Proper men's clothes with underwear, trousers, a top … and socks!"

"Adam, I'm trying to lead the simple life … only the basics. All that clothing is a distraction, a barrier between me and my God."

"That may be, but right now I really need a barrier between myself and your genitals. Now put some clothes on!"

With a quiet acquiescent huff, Manny went back to the bedroom. Taking much longer than before, he returned transformed: clean-shaven, wearing cheap blue jeans, a Christian Volunteer sweatshirt, grey socks, and sandals. Adam recognised the clothes as exactly what Manny wore that fateful evening in Horatio's Tavern all those centuries ago. Nodding approvingly as Manny once more took his seat, Adam remarked:

"Thanks, Manny. You almost look your old self again … apart from the full head of hair of course."

"Would you like me to shave that off for you? Leave some round the edges for that touch of authenticity?"

"No, no, there's no need for sarcasm. Just, you look normal now, and your boys are under control."

Manny smiled, displaying the faintest whisper of mirth, his bitter seriousness perhaps tempered by the comfortable familiarity of his old clothes. The subtle change in mood cheered Adam, and he restarted the discussion with renewed confidence:

"So, where were we? Ah yes, I remember. So what happened in France?"

"I travelled on the early morning Eurostar, straight to Paris. The early train was half the price of the later one … saved nearly £40. That evening I surprised Scarlett with my proposal of marriage and she rejected me."

"That evening? What did you do the rest of the day?"

"Took in the sites. It was quite a walk from the station to Scarlett's apartment …"

"You walked? Isn't the Metro really cheap?"

"Then I would have got there too quickly, and had to stand around in the cold all day. Saved a couple of pounds into the bargain."

"Ok, go on," said Adam, now recalling Manny's infamous penny-pinching behaviour.

"Well, the traffic was heavy and the streets were far more crowded than I expected, so it was slow going. I stopped to eat at Marcel Pagnol Square."

"Some cheap bistro I expect, or did you splash out on fine French cuisine."

"I sat on a park bench and ate the fish paste sandwiches in my hat. Lovely setting with a beautiful view of the church … inspiring. Little bit chilly, but luckily I was wearing my thermal socks and underwear."

"You had sandwiches in your hat?"

"It's alright, I wasn't wearing it. I just didn't want the sandwiches stinking out the Harrods bag and ruining the roses and chocolates."

"So you bought Scarlett gifts from Harrods. Very posh, and there was me thinking you're a cheapskate."

"Mrs Kenning, the church organist, lent me the bag. She also told me they were doing artificial roses half-price at Lidl … bargain. I sprayed them with loads of air freshener before I left."

"Rose, I hope."

"No, the rose one was too expensive for me, but luckily Lidl had ex-Christmas stock on a buy one get one free deal – spiced apple and winter berries."

"I'm guessing the chocolates weren't from Harrods either."

"Of course not; I used that box of Ferrero Rocher you won in the church raffle. Since you were dead, I didn't think you'd mind. You don't mind do you? I wasn't expecting you to find out."

"I was on a diet anyway. So no, I don't mind. If you were intending to propose, I guess you had a ring."

"Of course, and before you mock me, I paid for it, and it wasn't a cheap one. I bought it off one of the shopping channels, Bid-Down TV: 9ct gold plate with over 1ct of genuine Wagovski crystals. Cost me £68 delivered, so there'll be no more calling me a cheapskate."

Not wanting to hurt Manny's already fragile ego, Adam kept his views on the ring to himself.

"So, after eating your sandwiches, where did you go next? Did you put your hat on?"

"Don't be daft, Adam, I'd look pretty stupid wearing a top hat around during the day. Next I headed to …"

"Top hat? Why did you have a top hat? Please don't say you were carrying a top hat just to keep your sandwiches in?"

"Remember, I was surprising Scarlett in the evening, so I wanted to look debonair. I wore a tuxedo with a cane and a cape - very dapper if I do say so myself. I thought the hat would look great when it got dark … Monsieur Emmanuel Beaumont, every inch la romantic Parisian gentleman."

"Incredible, why didn't you just wear a black beret, stripy top, hang onions round your neck, and carry a baguette?"

"Oh Adam, that's daytime wear. Although strangely, the only person I saw dressed like that was a mime artist by the Eiffel Tower, so it might be more of a provincial thing. It was by the Eiffel Tower that a group of Chinese tourists harassed me. They mistook me for one of the street performers and wanted to take photos of me with the hat on. I refused, even after they offered me money. They got quite abusive. Anyway, the hat still stunk of fish paste, and if I'm honest, was a little too large for my head. The whole outfit was left over from the church's production of 'My Fair Lady', and was a couple of sizes too big. I turned up the trouser legs, and the jacket cuffs—they were fine—but the hat kept slowly slipping over my eyes even after I padded the lining with cotton wool."

Every step, every new detail of Manny's trip across Paris, signalled and compounded the distressing certainty of rejection and failure. Adam imagined Manny as the tragic clown, shabbily innocent, bumbling along to a comically sad death. Though enjoying the guilty pleasure of this ominous preamble, the scene was now vividly set. Therefore, Adam suggested, "Look, let's skip to later, when you proposed to Scarlett."

"About 9 o clock I left Trocadero Park and headed down Raymond Poincare Avenue to Scarlett's building: classy neighbourhood, extremely expensive. Thank goodness, I was wearing the tuxedo and top hat, or I might have felt out of place."

"So, now you're wearing the hat. Did it slip?"

"Ah, prepare to be amazed. I came up with an ingenious idea to keep the hat in place. Earlier, in the park I found a couple of newspapers in a bin. I rummaged around some other bins until I found a plastic carrier bag. Then I scrunched up the paper, filled the bag, and pushed it into the hat so that it rested perfectly on my head. Voila."

"So now you have garbage on your head. Very debonair."

"Apart from a little wobble, and a quiet scrunchy noise, you would not suspect a thing. It should have been fine," Manny's voice dropped to a feeble murmur, "… should have … should have."

As Manny sank into sad silence, Adam clapped his hands sharply together:

"Come on, Manny, don't stop now. This is all good. You're finally getting this off your chest. We're making excellent progress here."

"You're right … I need to go through this," Manny agreed. "Well, when I got to the building it was locked, and there was a security guard in the foyer. He looked rather brutish, and I thought I had made a big mistake. I nearly gave up there and then. But, miracle of miracles, he opened the door and ushered me in. He seemed very friendly, perhaps a bit too friendly, because he put an arm round my shoulder and whispered in my ear, "L'Ambassade?" I didn't know what it meant but I nodded, and he winked and let me go through."

"It means 'The Embassy'. He probably thought you were some kind of diplomat. Though what kind I don't know."

"That explains it. There were a few foreign embassies in the area. Therefore, my suit got me through the door. I'm tempted then to say God smiled on me with my choice of attire, except for what happened next."

"The proposal?"

Manny nodded:

"I took the lift up to the top floor and found Scarlett's apartment. The hallway was so luxurious that I began feeling a bit intimidated and … a bit sick. I knocked at the door …"

"Wasn't there a buzzer?"

"Yes, but I was so nervous that I didn't notice it at first. I left the Harrods bag to one side, and clutched the ring in my hand. It seemed absolutely ages before the door opened, and I was considering whether to knock again or just run away. But then, there she was, my beloved Scarlett. She was beautiful in a golden silk robe, radiant facial glow, straight from the shower, her hair still wet. Before she could speak, I went down on one knee and held out the ring. I was so nervous that I could hardly speak, but I managed to say the words."

"And she said?"

"Something like, 'What the Hell is this? Who the eff are you?' Except she used the real eff word. I realised she probably didn't recognise me with the hat on, so I took it off and gazed up into her eyes."

"Did she recognise you without the hat?"

"Yes, but my head was so sweaty that the stuffing bag had stuck to my scalp."

Adam found the situation hilarious, but sensitive to Manny's pain made a supreme effort to avoid a gleeful expression. Manny continued:

"I pulled and pulled, but the bag was stuck fast. I ended up putting the hat back on. I tried to propose again, but she started insulting me. She said I was demented, and needed psychiatric help. Even insulted my beliefs, and made explicitly lewd references to Christ. Then she threatened to call security if I did not leave immediately."

"What did you do?"

"I left. I obviously wasn't wanted."

Instead of sadness and longing, Manny projected damaged pride, giving Adam hope that a successful conclusion was within reach. Recognising that this may be the critical moment of the day, he gambled that Manny was ready for a dose of harsh reality, and proceeded with firmness:

"Sounds like our Scarlett alright. What did you expect from her? She's ruthless, intelligent, irreligious, successful, materialistic … and a lesbian?

That's the wonderfully powerful woman who got me access to my children, and who got you out of the firing line that night at Horatio's. Not the deluded fantasy you've created in your mind. Were you on some missionary kick, hoping to change her? She's definitely no Eliza Doolittle, and as for you being Henry Higgins … the clothes just don't fit."

Manny looked shocked for a moment, but then started quietly chuckling. Soon, the chuckling gave way to a broad smile, and he exhibited the unmistakeable air of a man relieved of a heavy mental burden. Adam let out a long thankful sigh, and decided that sweet milky tea was required.

Drinking the comforting hot beverage, Manny expressed regret for his behaviour:

"Adam, what on earth have I done? The foul language I've used … insulting those dear nuns. How could I let my standards fall so low?"

"I'm surprised you didn't ask Jesus for guidance. In the past, he was your go-to guy for absolutely anything."

"Being in this place, with my soul already ascended to heaven, I didn't feel I had the right."

"But you're fine now, aren't you? I'm sure he's still listening."

Manny nodded, his smile returning.

"One thing I don't get, Manny. You killed yourself by jumping in front of a train … in Portsmouth. There must have been a Metro station close to Scarlett's apartment. Did it take you all that time to decide to commit suicide?"

"No, I made up my mind as I left Scarlett's building. I chose Portsmouth because I didn't want my church to pay for the repatriation of my corpse."

"Hmm, you know that actually makes a lot of sense, very thoughtful. Now that's the Manny I understand."

"Also, I had return tickets, and it would have been such a terrible waste not to have used them. Plus, I saved another pound by not using the Metro."

Adam laughed, "That's definitely the Manny I understand. To be honest, it was Sofia who couldn't understand your choice of location. She came up with all sorts of fanciful ideas."

"Who's Sofia, your girlfriend?"

"No, she's the daughter of one of my neighbours. A good friend. She comes round for a chat when she's nothing better to do. Loves to talk, and talk … and talk."

"I like the name Sofia. It means wisdom."

"Let me tell you Manny, she's definitely … "

Adam nearly said 'not your type', but then reconsidered. Manny and Sofia, could it work? Superficially, Manny met all three of Sofia's criteria for a new partner, but Adam did not want his friend hurt once more by a strong woman, and Sofia most certainly belonged in that category. However, whilst Scarlett rarely hesitated to kick savagely below the belt, Sofia never ventured beyond dry wit and mildly insulting sarcasm.

"Definitely what?" asked Manny, his interest piqued.

"Err … definitely worth considering if you … are still looking for someone. I could put in a good word for you if you want. That's if you're not blocking everyone from now on."

"I won't block anyone anymore. As for your offer, I'm not sure …"

"Given I haven't much time, I'll take your 'not sure' as a yes, and I'll try to set something up. Just remember to take things slowly this time. Proposing on the second date is not necessary or expected. And it's no big deal if it doesn't work out. You can always find someone else, or take up a hobby. Just promise me you won't do the all-day wanking thing again."

"I promise. You know, line dancing has always intrigued me."

"Hmm, you and a bunch of monks and nuns line dancing; sounds … interesting. Now, I believe it's time we went outside to meet your neighbours."

Manny reacted with alarm:

"But the nuns are probably still out there! Sister Josephine will be with them!"

"Oh come now, Manny," said Adam. "What about Christian love and forgiveness? Where's your faith?"

"Your right, and though I suspect you have little faith yourself, thank you for your help and concern. You've changed, Adam, and for the better. The Adam Eden I knew, the old Adam, would have moaned all day about his own problems, and not cared a jot about anyone else."

"And, obsessed about beer and burgers. You can't forget the beer and burgers."

"Oh yes," Manny grimaced, "I can't ever forget them. Well, you are right; it is time I returned to my faith."

Motioning to the front door handle, he asked, "Adam, if you would do the honours."

STEPHEN AYRES

CRUISEWEAR CRUSADER

Somewhat apprehensively, Adam opened the door, and walked outside. The nuns immediately swarmed into position, blocking either side of the walkway, leaving a clear area in front of Manny's apartment where Sister Josephine stood alone. Instead of the fantastical vampiric attack that Adam had foolishly built up in his head, the Sister gracefully stepped forward and gently took Manny's hands, smiling with obvious delight:

"Welcome Mr Beaumont. I truly hope this means you have returned to the flock, for it is with sorrowful hearts that we have passed your locked door these many many months. Know that every day you were in our thoughts and prayers."

"Thank you, Sister," said Manny, "and may I apologise for my abusive and hurtful words. There can be no excuse for my bad behaviour, and I accept whatever punishment is due."

"There is no punishment. We are simply overjoyed that you are with us again. This place, this new life, is a special challenge for those expecting the Kingdom of God. Oh, your colourful language brought a blush to many a face, and gave my authority a prickly slap, but I never punish to satisfy pride or petty vengeance. Besides, you are a Methodist, and come under Reverend Stevens' jurisdiction not mine. He ministers to the Protestants in the viro."

Turning to Adam, Sister Josephine's expression changed to one of simmering anger and loathing:

"Lucky for you that unwanted guests also come under the Reverend's jurisdiction, because I would have tanned your backside … and that's just for starters."

"I'm sorry for breaking your rules, Sister Josephine, but I had to help Manny. I owed him from my first life. If Stern offended you, then I apologise for that also. He meant well, but he can't help being ... err ... um ... rude. I didn't actually ask him to speak on my behalf ..."

"Save your breath, Mr Eden. Your Devil words will find no purchase with me. Sneaking into our home with your clown clothes ..."

Clutching the fabric of Adam's shirt, Sister Josephine went silent for a moment, then asked, "What kind of material is this? Would you believe, it looks like flimsy cotton but feels as strong as leather?"

Letting go of the shirt, the surprised nun gave Adam a curious stare, and looked ready to ask another question, when a short statured black man, wearing an Anglican black cassock with white tab-collar, pushed through the crowd. Panting heavily, he took a moment to catch his breath, and after wiping some sweat from his brow with a white cotton handkerchief, introduced himself as Reverend Calvin Stevens:

"Joy of joys, what a splendid day!" he merrily proclaimed, enveloping Manny in a hearty hug, almost lifting him off his feet. "I jumped on my bike and rushed over here as soon as I heard the news. Oh Emmanuel, how we have worried about you, and prayed that you might return to the fold. And here you are at last!"

"Glad to be back," said Manny. "My rehabilitation was all down to my friend here ... with God's undoubted guidance."

The Reverend turned his attention to Adam, his smile now polite rather than warm:

"Ah yes, Mr Eden. Now just how did you slip under our radar? Sister Josephine or myself are required to countersign any visit requests, and I strongly suspect that Emmanuel here was not involved."

"No he wasn't. He knew nothing about my visit until I knocked at his door this morning."

"Our rules are important, Mr Eden. They ensure that outsiders do not threaten our way of life. They are not there to be broken, no matter how important an issue might seem. Now, I have no idea how you got in here, but I want your word this will not happen again."

"I'll gladly give you my word, but you won't need it. This was a one-time only deal. I won't get another chance."

"Good, then the matter is settled. I suggest you say your goodbyes to Mr Beaumont here, because you will be spending the remainder of the day in a wake-up cubicle. I will take you there myself on my bike."

Adam and the Reverend made their way downstairs, leaving a bewildered Manny surrounded by excited nuns, all eager to meet and question the former foulmouthed hermit.

The bike, a white pearlescent electric moped bearing a silver cross emblem, had a long leather seat designed for two people. Not bothering with helmets or any other safety measures, the men were soon speeding along the gravel path back to the wake-up building, Adam enjoying the cool stream of blossom-scented air.

Once at their destination, the Reverend parked up the moped, and walked with Adam to the designated cubicle only a few feet away. Before entering the room, Adam asked:

"If I arrange an open invitation for Manny to visit my viro, say every Thursday, will you countersign it?"

"If he also wishes it, then I see no problem with that. I see myself as a simple gatekeeper not a prison governor. My role in this is merely to allow time for reflection."

"Then, thank you."

"Mr Eden, I notice this is the Catholic side of the building. Do you lean that way in your beliefs?"

"I don't think so. Just a coincidence. Does it matter?"

"Not at all, just an observation. You may be surprised to learn that we all get on really well here. We even hope some Popes will visit this summer. I'm not sure which ones yet, but a couple have already expressed an interest. We're expecting a full house on that day. Perhaps you might like to visit … unless it falls on a Friday, I presume."

Calmly, the Reverend reached out and felt Adam's shirt, carefully evaluating the evolved fabric. Then, in a measured, almost sombre tone, he said:

"Mr Eden, I am a man of God, and I am also a man of peace. For me, all violence is an expression of evil, and I pray for both its victims and perpetrators. I believe you can only truly defeat evil by starving it of its needs, by promoting love and understanding … by turning a cheek. However, there are those who fight evil more … directly, more physically. They seek to use the evil of violence against a greater evil. Do you get my meaning, Mr Eden?"

"Go on," Adam replied.

"But, whilst I believe all evil is bad, even I would not wish to see a greater evil prevail. Outside this viro of tranquillity, I know there are places of black darkness and despair, where the dice are loaded against the righteous. Perhaps some assistance is required to even the odds ... some expert help. Confidential of course."

Reverend Stevens took out a notebook and pen, and jotted down a few words, then silently handed Adam the message, which read:

"Born 1962: Elliot Stevens: AKA: 'Sarge', Special Forces Combat Training."

"You can trust this person," the Reverend assured. "You have my word on it. He's my older brother, visits once a month for my Sunday sermon. Last time he was here, he spoke of a rumour, of a man who fights evil."

"I can't talk about ..."

The Reverend shook his head:

"Save your words, Mr Eden. My brother is the one you need to talk to. Memorise the note before midnight because it won't return with you."

Without elaborating further, the Reverend shook Adam's hand, and turned to leave. Closing the cubicle door, his nostrils reunited with the heady smell of incense, Adam thought he heard the Reverend murmur:

"May God protect you, our dark crusader."

SOFA, SO GOOD

Tuesday morning, and before dressing, breakfast or the first beer of the day, Adam scheduled a visit to the Sarge's viro for the following week. Also, making good on his promise, he invited Manny to visit on Thursday – the request accepted within mere minutes.

Eschewing the profile-provided beach party attire, Adam selected a pair of faded slim-fit black jeans, a smoke grey wide collared shirt, and aged leather Cuban heeled Chelsea boots – three of Sofia's better choices, given Adam's preference for more neutral styled clothing. Then, after hungrily scoffing a hearty breakfast of garlic buttered rye toast, heaped with creamy scrambled eggs and flakes of hot-smoked salmon, he relaxed by the front window in his favourite chair, sucking slowly on an amber bottle of ice-cold Belgian beer.

Mulling over the events of the previous day, it was not Manny's return to civilisation that worried him, but that someone outside the psychoviro knew about his Friday exploits – a reality fervently illustrated by the Reverend's 'dark crusader' comment. Adam previously believed that Stern, the world famous ass detective, would nose out the truth, or that Sofia with her constant wearying chatter might catch him off guard. Since neither displayed the slightest suspicion, this incident might be a one-off, some convoluted connection between the psychoviro and Manny's spiritual paradise. Even with less cheerful clothing, Adam could never imagine himself as a dark crusader, or a crusader of any kind - the only red cross he might likely bear would come from Stardust carving his initial incorrectly.

Deciding a little background information on the Sarge might be useful, or at least pass the time, Adam walked over to the PC cabinet, nonchalantly brushing his hand along the black leather Corbusier sofa in passing. An unexpected female chuckle alerted him to another presence in the room. A voice immediately followed:

"You're there aren't you, Adam? Do not be alarmed, it is me, the concierge. I'm afraid I could not afford the ability of sight, so I cannot see you. I was waiting for the perfect moment to announce myself, but then you tickled me."

"What the …? Tickled you? Where are you?"

"The sofa. I am the sofa. Only temporary though. For the duration of my visit the sofa has avatar status."

"The sofa's an android? "

"Bio-infusion, not an android - androids are permanent durable utilities. Temporary avatars are the original object, in this case your sofa, plus various bio-engineered sensory attributes, which are all removed by the next morning."

Adam let his hand stray along the leather again, and another chuckle ensued. Barely pausing for thought, he kicked the back of the sentient seating, and heard a sharp cry of pain.

"Ouch! Please don't do that, Adam. I may not have sight, but along with speech and hearing, I purchased the sense of touch for this avatar. It's a little more sensitive than I expected, so please be careful."

"What are you doing here? I thought you weren't allowed in the viro."

"Please sit down on me, carefully, and I'll explain everything."

"Sit … on you?"

The concierge purred sensually, "Oh, I'll make you very very comfortable, but only if you promise to be gentle."

Ignoring the offer, Adam sat in the armchair next to the dispenser. Though it felt strange talking to a piece of lounge furniture, he asked:

"So, straight to the point, tell me what you're doing here."

"You die every week. As your sponsor, I am quite concerned about this."

"So, it's the cost."

"Oh no, Adam, the cost of resurrection is negligible. Time channelling is the expensive part of the procedure, and only then if years or centuries are involved, not hours as in your case. A colleague confidentially informed me that you died every week in his Environment. I found this news alarming, because I care about you."

Adam caustically replied, "I'm so touched by your concern. Now you've told me, I guess you can go."

169

"Please stop dying, Adam. I know it's humiliating being an undesirable, and that you're upset living in such cramped conditions, but dying every week is not the answer."

"And what is?"

"If you stop, I can make it worth your while. I have made some big changes in my life, and new revenue streams are now available to me. If you stop dying, I promise you a house of your own, large or small, any popular design from your first lifetime. Your choice, Adam, and you could move in tomorrow if you want."

"Sounds tempting and you obviously went to a lot of trouble on my behalf. You're here illegally, aren't you?"

"Yes I am. No one must know of my visit. You see, bypassing the security systems, and arranging an Environment avatar is expensive and risky, and the shadows who arranged all this are of low status. If the authorities find out, then I am in serious trouble, but I just couldn't let you suffer any longer."

"What if I want other things as well? Maybe the house isn't enough."

"The house will take all my resources! I simply cannot afford anything else."

"Ok, screw the house. I have a better idea. There are two things I want from you. Firstly, I know about the night-time sedation, and I want it stopped."

"There is no sedative. Your testosterone is …"

"Shut up and listen. You will stop my sedation. I know you can do it, and this is non-negotiable. Otherwise people will hear about this visit."

"But that's blackmail! Why would you do that? You may be an undesirable, but your profile does not suggest you would resort to such measures."

"Maybe it's time you updated that damned profile."

"Your threats are without weight, Adam. No one will believe you. You are an undesirable. You have no status."

"But they'll believe a Genie … an Original, and I know one who trusts me. You probably know that too."

After a long silence from the sofa, the concierge finally replied, her voice broken, defeated:

"The sedation will stop. What else did you want?"

It took only five minutes of almost completely one-sided negotiation to agree the second demand. Both demands would be ready by the following morning. It was obvious the concierge did not understand Adam's new focus and selfless opportunism, and she muttered with surprise at his indifference to the offer of a new house. However, Adam was not finished:

"Just so you know, I'll be dying as much as I bloody well like. Probably this week, and many many more after,"

"But I thought we had a deal?"

"I never said I'd stop dying."

"I thought it was understood."

"Understand this, leather-face; I just gave you a set of demands for me keeping quiet about your illegal activities. You don't get anything else."

With an almost pitiable sadness, the sofa whimpered, "But why do you do it? Why do you want to die every week?"

"I said you don't get anything else! Now, it's time you left. You can do that can't you? You're not here until midnight I hope."

"No, I can leave, but I need a few minutes to ease out of the connection. Otherwise it can be fatal."

Adam waited only a minute before retrieving his wireless headphones from a nearby drawer. He quickly scrolled through his music playlists on the digital music server, and selected a Motown favourite: R. Dean Taylor's 'There's a Ghost in My House'. Unable to see what was happening, the concierge asked:

"Why is the music so quiet? I don't mind hearing this type of sound pattern."

"It's not quiet, I'm using headphones. That way I don't have to listen to you."

"Don't worry, I won't make any noise."

Turning up the volume on the headphones, Adam coldly predicted, "Oh yes you will."

Singing along with vengeful enthusiasm, he bounded onto the Corbusier, viciously stamping up and down on the cushions, digging his heels into the smooth skin of black leather. The shrill screams and sharp tortured cries of the concierge were a muffled background accompaniment to the music, and Adam stepped up the aggression, punching and kicking with wanton abandon. Seconds before the song finished the sofa fell silent, and Adam, laughing breathlessly, shaking with nervous adrenalin, jumped back onto the floor.

STEPHEN AYRES

MY BIG BROTHER

Dwarfed under Eden Manor's grand Georgian portico, Adam rang the antique brass and white porcelain doorbell, and waited apprehensively. For the first time in almost a year he chose to wear the Hawaiian party clothes in his own viro – forsaking the drab and the neutral, he believed that on this day, bright sunny clothing was particularly appropriate. Without much delay, the door opened, followed by a soft, almost feminine fragrant billow of carnation and clove. It was Harry Eden, luxuriously decadent in a quilted gold satin robe, black velvet tasselled lounging cap, and lavender embroidered felt slippers. Displaying a faint, slightly embarrassed smile, Harry seemed a little surprised to see his son.

"Hi Dad," said Adam, offering a handshake.

Ignoring the outstretched hand, Harry asked, "Adam, what can I do for you? I do believe this is the first time you've ever called round. And damned early as well. It's only twenty past eight. I haven't had time to dress yet."

"I like an early start," Adam lied, really hoping to avoid a hostile encounter with his mother.

"Best make it quick then, before Edna finds out you're here. She's still putting on her face."

"Dad, I would like to take Robert out for the morning. Is that OK?"

"Take Robert out! Are you mad? You know how strong he is, and how dangerous. You'll be lucky not to get hurt. Only your mother and I know how to control him."

"Please Dad, it's important. I've got a surprise for him. Just for a few hours."

"Well, I think you're making a big mistake, but you are his brother. I'll have to square it with your mother first."

172

"Aw, come on Dad, does she really need to know? You know what she thinks of me. There's no way she'll say yes."

Harry spoke quietly, "Of course she'll say yes. We haven't had a break from Robert since he was resurrected. Be nice to let someone else take the knocks for a change. Just don't blame me when he breaks your arm or," Harry gently rubbed his head, "pulls a great big clump of your hair out."

"I take full responsibility. Who knows, if it goes well, maybe it could be a regular thing?"

"Well, on your head be it. And, I must say, I didn't think I'd see you in those clothes again; most peculiar."

"Thought I'd wear something cheerful for Robert. You're looking particularly … sumptuous yourself. What's your excuse?"

Unable to hide a blossoming blush of embarrassment, Harry said, "Your mother invited her Great Great Aunt Pearl over last month. Quite the fashion expert in her day apparently. Bit like Sofia, only Victorian."

"Oh dear."

"Spent the entire day giving your mother all kinds of ideas and tips. Worst of all, Pearl was born in 1882, so your mother had a field day with the dispenser. Now, I'm Monsieur Ponce McFop, the dandy clotheshorse. Pearl's coming back soon, so don't be surprised if next time you see me, I'm wearing a ruddy ball gown and tiara."

"Well, if it means anything, Dad, I think you'll look fabulously gorgeous in diamonds and a frock. Mum will be so jealous."

After sharing a rare moment of laughter, Harry hurried to tell Edna about the request. He returned only ten minutes later, accompanied by his grumpy sour-faced mutant son. Robert's huge misshapen body was squeezed into an elasticated blue and white sailor suit, and his gross swollen head sported a childishly cute white beret complete with a red pompom. Harry handed over a heavy red and white carrier bag containing a large cardboard bucket:

"Robert loves the Colonel's southern fried chicken. He prefers the drumsticks, but he eats the bones and they get stuck in his throat. You have about 40 boneless fillets in there, so if you think he's getting out of hand then chuck him a couple – usually works. There are a few cold cans of Coke in there as well - Robert's favourite. I think that's it, so good luck."

Without another word, Harry went back inside and shut the door, eager to enjoy a Robert-free morning.

Quietly and obediently, Robert followed Adam to the far side of the annexe, then squealed with delight at the surprise parked there—a bright red two-seater pedal car, with Ferrari styling, and scaled to accommodate even the bulkiest adult frame. Placing the bag of chicken in the small boot, Adam manoeuvred his gleefully agitated brother into the passenger seat, and then got in beside him. Bursting with energy, Robert began furiously pedalling, and they sped off down the meadow, careering towards the stream. Regaining control took a supreme effort, as Adam frantically fought with the steering wheel, eventually turning sharply back up the hill. The vehicle almost tipped over with the sudden change in direction, but Robert simply clapped his hands, shrieking with delirious excitement.

At no time did Adam need to help with the pedalling, since Robert exhibited almost superhuman strength and stamina. Rolling along smoothly on its large pneumatic tyres, they headed towards a screen of new trees close to the ruined chapel. Upon reaching their destination, Adam ordered his brother to stop pedalling. To his surprise, the order was immediately obeyed without complaint.

Of Adam's two demands, the pedal car was only a small part of the second. Whether the first demand had been met, the cessation of sedation, would only become apparent after a few days, as the levels in his system gradually ran down. For now, he was ready to reveal the full extent of the second demand, for which he had forgone the chance of his own house. This was for Robert.

Retrieving the chicken bag and a small cool-box from the boot, Adam led his brother through the light thicket and into a brand new playground, equipped with a classic selection of high quality apparatus: swings, a tall slide, seesaw, roundabout, and twisty framed monkey bars. The robust construction looked tough enough to withstand the roughest abuse.

Whooping and howling with joy, Robert clumsily scooped Adam under one arm, and charged straight over to the slide. Dropping the bag and box, Adam flopped and flailed helplessly as his brother carried him up the ladder. Once at the top, Robert gave a loud hoot, and then threw his terrified brother headfirst down the steep slippery slope. After a rapid descent, Adam shot off the end, and rolled for a couple of yards – the ground mercifully covered with soft matting, and a generous layer of spongy green-rubber chippings. Chuckling in his usual raspy manner, Robert launched himself down the slide, headfirst on his belly, and ended up happily chewing a mouthful of chippings.

Jumping to his feet, Adam ran over to the discarded chicken bag and took out a couple of fillets. He waved them enticingly in the air, luring Robert over to the seesaw rather than face another nightmarish slide dive. Thankfully, the seesaw had an automatic sliding counterweight, compensating for any weight disparity, ensuring that even the most unevenly matched couples could enjoy the experience. Once comfortably seated, and finding a mutually acceptable rhythm, the brothers merrily seesawed for nearly half an hour, pausing only for swigs of Coke and bites of the Colonel's tasty chicken.

Before leaving the seesaw for the swings, Adam fetched two ice creams from the cool box. Robert's face beamed as he saw the 1980s era Cornettos: the creamy sweet promise of his childhood seaside memories. Without seesawing, they sat quietly, eating away with sibling synchronicity, both biting off the chocolate-filled point before devouring the ice cream top, and then picking apart the remaining cone. Once finished, they simply faced each other in a fleeting moment of contentment and unspoken camaraderie.

Suddenly, Robert began pointing at his brother and laughing maniacally, his face a contorted drooling grimace. The unexpected mood-swing was a disturbing repeat of their first encounter in the viro. Adam remained silent. He hoped that by projecting an air of calmness, the demented episode would swiftly pass. Yet, as the strange behaviour continued, the laughter took on an odd staccato quality, the warped facial features relating a touch of sad frustration. As tears welled in Robert's huge eyes, Adam realised the slow-witted giant meant no malice, but was trying desperately to form words. A nod of brotherly encouragement seemed to give him strength, and so with strained emotion, tears streaming down his face, Robert made one final effort:

"Ha … ah … Ahdam. Adam, m-my b-big brudda!"

EDEN RISING

Monday, 20th April, early afternoon in the Krulak Memorial Sports Hall. Negotiating the narrow wooden beam was a hard enough balancing act without the tirade of verbal threats from the Sarge, or the random impact of a hard leather baseball. Repeatedly, Adam lost his footing, clumsily falling to the rubber matting some seven feet below. Standing at five feet ten, khaki t-shirt and shorts hugging his taut muscular body, Sergeant Stevens' combat hardened countenance was never less than serious, his tough training techniques brutally effective. Like many of the resurrected, he carried over his personality intact from his first life – abruptly ended by a roadside bomb whilst on routine patrol in Southern Afghanistan.

As Adam wearily picked himself up for another attempt, the Sarge barked:

"Get up there, Eden, and just run across the fuckin' beam! I don't wanna see any more of that tippy toe shit from you! You ain't training for no faggot ballet!"

"I'm only trying to avoid the balls," huffed Adam, hoisting himself up the rope ladder for another attempt. "If one hits me then I'm going to fall."

"Damn right you're gonna fall! That's why you gotta ignore the fuckin' balls and just get across. If you stop or slow down, then it's like shootin' fish in a barrel; you're definitely coming down. Focus on the objective. Block out the shit around you. You might still be hittin' the mat, but at least you stand a chance."

There was an unspoken understanding between Adam and the Sarge. The psychoviro hunt, its players and rules, were never explicitly mentioned, and no details given or requested. All training proceeded on the simple basis that Adam faced a gang of experienced killers every week, and that direct assistance on the field of combat was strictly forbidden. Since Adam regularly got a new body, any strength or stamina training was pointless. Instead, the Sarge concentrated on various close quarter combat skills, such as stealth, blade, and mixed martial arts. Mental agility and physical confidence were also important, allowing Adam to act quickly and decisively, whilst gaining an intrinsic understanding of his body's capabilities.

The Sarge's viro was an almost featureless dry grassy flatland, with the faint outline of low hills in the simulated far distance, shimmering in a sunny haze. A small village of side-gabled ranch bungalows, all with neat white picket fences, nestled around a meandering narrow creek. Three utility buildings stood nearby, all colonial style mansions – one incorporating the large sports hall and gymnasium. As far as Adam could tell, most of the eighty inhabitants were ex-service personnel. Predominantly US Special Forces, plus a few partners and other family members, their number included the softly spoken Helen Stevens, former medical officer, and the Sarge's devoted wife.

Adam trained twice weekly, Mondays and Wednesdays. The lessons were punishing and often painful: grazes, sprains and broken bones regular testament to the ruthless intensity of the Sarge's methods. Despite this, night-time cured all ills, and Adam always awoke refreshed the following morning back in his own bed.

Always upfront in his opinion, the Sarge never hesitated to criticise or advise. Adam learnt this on their very first meeting, when he was asked to select a blade. The Sarge's reaction to his choice was scathing:

"What the fuck … a rapier? You compensating for something, Eden? This ain't no fancy French fencing class! No, I'm issuing you with a Benchmark 9101, 3.6 inch folding blade with part serrated edge and quick release button. You need to travel fast and light if you're gonna get in close. If you're caught in the open, and must go bigger, then a Special Forces machete is the way to go. Fuckin' rapier."

Or, his reaction the following week to Adam's comments about blade handling:

"Don't give me that street shit. The blade is not, I repeat not, an extension of your hand. You will be using a variety of weapons, of which the blade is just one. They are not part of your body. They are tools. Tools for killin'. You ain't Eden Scissorhands."

However, most of the time, week after week, the Sarge just gave good solid advice:

"Remember, you are not there to fight, you are there to kill. Take your enemy by surprise, deal a killer blow, and then get the fuck outta there. And, don't stand there watchin' the asshole die, because time and delay is what gets you killed."

"How will I know if it's a killer blow?"

"Trainin' and practise. Even if you miss your mark, you might cause enough damage to take them outta the game. Then you go back later and finish the job."

As the months passed, Adam experienced increasing confidence and skill – a new lease of life in his ability to deal death. Upon asking whether he would ever be capable of 'taking out' all five of his adversaries, the Sarge's reply was depressingly blunt:

"Eden, I could train you for decades. You could become my all-time star pupil - a stone-cold assassin. However, you face a highly organised squad of proficient killers … and on their own turf. Sure, you might take out one or two, three if you're lucky. The truth is, that barring a miracle, you're always gonna wind up dead. Maybe, you should put more faith in the Lord God Almighty. Could give you the edge you need."

"Faith? That won't help. Believe me, where I go is a Godless place."

"There is no place unknown to God."

"Well, Sarge, if God ever dares show his face there, I promise you'll be the first to know."

Back in the comparative tranquillity of his own viro, Adam kept his promise, and took Robert to the park every free morning. Although his brother's strength was always a threat, injuries were rare and easily avoided with understanding and judicious use of chicken. Both brothers learnt to unload their anger and frustrations at the park, and completed each circuit of the apparatus in an unchanging, almost business-like fashion – ritually pausing for Cornetto's on the seesaw. Sadly, Edna and Harry still stubbornly maintained their distance; the alleged Portsmouth murders the same tired excuse.

Often, after dropping Robert back home, Adam headed back to the park for an intense training session. The lack of sedative in his system, and the constant preoccupation with combat gave him heightened levels of aggression that he put to effective use. Treating the playground as an obstacle course, he would throw himself down the slide headfirst, run along the top of the monkey bars, and even practice commando rolls by launching himself from the swings. Though his injuries were many and sometimes severe, Adam never hesitated in 'hitting' the apparatus hard.

Sofia and Manny were very much in love, and already engaged. Manny, true to form, proposed on their second date, ignoring his experience in Paris, and Adam's advice. Sofia willingly accepted. They spent Thursdays promenading around the viro, enjoying romantic candle-lit dinners in the utility building, and serenading one another in the woods. By mutual consent, they abstained from extramarital sex, preserving their new-life virginity as a most sacred gift for their wedding night. However, this did not stop constant amorous public displays of affection, hugging, kissing, and cutesy pet names that left Adam somewhat jealous, and sadly aware of his loneliness.

Adam missed Sofia's company on Thursdays, and now spent the day watching action movies, especially those with martial arts content. The Sarge's attempts to dissuade him from indulging in such artificial depictions of combat were totally ignored. Whether Stallone or Schwarzenegger, Jet li or Bruce Lee, these were the inspirational celluloid Gods punching and kicking their way through Adam's pre-match nerves.

At first, the training had a detrimental effect on Adam's Friday performances. He brimmed with undeserved confidence in the first few weeks – like some long-term obese dieter, embarrassingly squeezing into a tight t-shirt after losing only a few pounds. During this time, the glam gang's kills were quick and brutal, along with their mocking comments about the new blades. However, as the weeks turned to months, the tide began to turn, and more often than not, a psycho's head ended up gracing Groover's bottom shelf. In response, the gang closed ranks, adopting a noticeably more disciplined and cautious approach, treating Adam's abilities with greater respect and increasingly a hint of fear.

For now, with the Sarge's threats and insults ringing loudly in his ears, and hard leather balls whizzing close past his head, Adam gritted his teeth, and ran determinedly across the narrow beam.

GIRLS NIGHT OUT

dam sprinted between the second and third tower blocks, and into the square. He knew the gang were some way behind, though not yet in the alley, and still out of sight. Usually, he took this route when heading for a final showdown at the warehouses – consciously or unconsciously his favourite destination. This time, breaking with habit, the plan was to quickly double back around the buildings, allowing for a surprise rear attack on his pursuers. The timing was critical, and Adam had practised the run repeatedly, both at home and with the Sarge.

Catching his breath a moment at the rear side of the second tower block, Adam peered cautiously around the corner. He allowed himself a brief smile of satisfaction as Rampage, Stardust, and Ziggy disappeared down the alley. Roxy and Quatro, following a safe distance behind, stopped to sheath their blades, readying their bows for long-range support. Skirting close to a row of storage bins as light cover, Adam moved stealthily towards the girls. Accelerating the final few yards, fixed on his target, he grabbed Roxy from behind, cupping his hand firmly across her mouth, whilst ripping through her throat with his blade. Leaving the fatally wounded twin helplessly floundering against the wall in a wash of her own blood, he moved straight onto Quatro, without hesitation, without emotion.

Quatro screamed, hopelessly lashing out with her bow to fend off the clinically precise attack. With one hand, Adam deftly took control of the cumbersome weapon, and used it to restrain his panicked prey. He struck hard with his blade, straight into Quatro's heart, then, disregarding the Sarge's sage advice, he paused for a few seconds, watching as his victim slumped to the ground. Whether it was a momentary lapse in training, a sudden pang of sympathy, or just morbid fascination, the hesitation would prove a costly mistake. As Adam turned to leave, Roxy, in a final act of near death defiance, fell forward with an arrow outstretched in her hand. The sharp point dug deeply into Adam's ankle, and painfully hobbled, he lost his footing, slamming face first onto the concrete slab paving.

Face down, dazed and bloody, Adam regained consciousness after a couple of minutes, and began crawling slowly along the alley. Perhaps there was still hope. Slowly, his mind returned to hazy focus, and ignoring the pain in his ankle, he slowly heaved himself up into a standing position. A sudden sharp cranial impact sent Adam spinning to the ground. Lying on his back, almost stunned back to unconsciousness, he saw Ziggy raising his bat for another swing. The top-hatted giant spat with fury:

"You killed the … girls! Now you … die … you piece of shit!"

With barbarous force, the well-oiled willow cracked against Adam's skull, and for another week, the mission was over.

REVELATION POSTPONED

Leaving her beloved Manny alone to suffer a morning with Stern and Kaylee, Sofia strolled down from the high meadow, and made her way across the cobbled stone bridge. It was time Adam learned the truth about her past, and her plans for the future. She wondered how he would react knowing that she was a murderess, a serial killer … a black widow. Not only did she financially destroy her husbands in the divorce courts, but she also took their lives. Though she endeavoured to kill them herself, in some hard to reach cases, she hired the most cold-blooded assassins.

The problem stemmed from Sofia's crazed infatuation with courtship and the wedding day. Whilst she simply adored the early foolish romance and the meticulous preparations for the special day, the marriage once consummated left her feeling ice cold, and totally numb to the prospect of lifelong commitment. The unfortunate spouse always became the personification of the despised marital hereafter, and Sofia made her plans accordingly. Though never caught, or even suspected in her first life—all the deaths officially unfortunate accidents—the all-knowing AI had placed her in a female only psychoviro.

Only her parents, and now Manny, knew about Sofia's murderous past. At first, she loathed Adam for introducing her to Manny, since she knew their blossoming affection was doomed once the wedding night was over. Not wanting her adoring beau to suffer a post-marital demise, Sofia confided in Manny, expecting him to make a hasty exit. His reaction was unexpectedly sympathetic, and bizarrely he agreed to stay. Their new marriage arrangement was that after a courtship of not less than three years, and a lavish wedding day, Sofia would murder Manny: conditional on the act being quick, painless, and unexpected. The next step, avoiding one another for a year, was a precursor to rekindling their relationship, and re-embarking upon the long amorous path to another murder-most-marital.

Finding the door to Adam's apartment open, and nobody home, Sofia decided to wait inside. Distant sounds from the direction of the ruined chapel suggested that Adam was at the park with Robert, and she knew from experience not to disturb them. A few weeks previously, she and Manny had unwisely interrupted the brothers in their hallowed playground. Robert, obviously incensed by the intrusion, screeched loudly, and waved his fists. With violence in mind, the lumbering giant chased them across two fields. The disturbing incident was surreally ended only when Adam repeatedly shouted out the words, 'chicken fillet'.

Passing the time, whilst waiting for Adam to return, Sofia switched on the TV, and scrolled through the list of recently watched shows. They were all action movies, predominantly from the late 20th century. The classic genre was a known favourite of hers, so she naturally assumed this was her influence at work. One item in particular caught her interest, a three-hour compilation of bookmarked scenes. To her surprise, the compilation consisted solely of hand-to-hand fighting from the various action movies: no cheesy one-liners, no build up, just fighting. She could only watch for a few minutes before she became dizzy and disorientated from the non-stop kinetic aggression. From her knowledge of late 20th century culture, Sofia recalled that it was often customary for males to watch late night sex and violence, whilst consuming copious amounts of pizza, beer, and various bagged carbohydrate snacks. Nodding in smug agreement with her theory, Sofia switched off the TV and decided to take a furtive snoop around the apartment.

A detailed trawl through Adam's wardrobes revealed only the clothing that Sofia had picked many months ago. Flattered at first that her choices were so revered – her superior sense of style and fashion so visibly validated – a further search in the lounge cupboards and kitchen drawers brought on a growing feeling of unease. Apart from the original profile sourced items, everything was something that she had produced from the dispenser. Whether socks or shoes, books or magazines, pictures or ornaments; everything was her own selection. There was nothing new. One item in the wardrobe further piqued her suspicions – a luxury Pansardo cashmere cardigan. A close inspection of the garment revealed fraying on the arm and a large hole. Sofia wondered why Adam had not thrown the cardigan away, and simply got a new one from the dispenser.

For a moment, Sofia toyed with the notion that Adam, naturally smitten by her beauty and sparkling wit, was the victim of some deep romantic obsession. Maybe he saw the worn out items as treasured relics of their time together before Manny. Shaking off such foolish thoughts, the shrewd Saghausen brain kicked in. After all, it was Adam who set her up in her new relationship. In addition, at no time during her many visits did Adam seem romantically interested, and Sofia was an expert at detecting such vibes. Weighing up the possibilities, it crossed her mind that Adam might still be on limited dispenser access. A cursory glance at the lounge table supported the theory. An empty carton of orange juice and a half-finished bowl of cereal showed Adam could access food and drink. Nearby, a badly chipped Lalique glass, and an almost illegible coffee stained magazine, both of which should have been replaced long ago, perhaps evidenced that access was indeed restricted.

Aware of the implications of her theory, Sofia went back into the bedroom, and headed straight for the bedside cabinet. She remembered their first encounter, when Adam had sliced his neck on a designer chair. On that occasion, scouting around the annexe after his death, she had found a body bag on the bedroom floor, and a resurrection wristband in the bedside drawer. Could it be Adam never lived long enough to enjoy full dispenser access? It only took ten contiguous days of life to qualify, and once achieved was permanent.

She slowly pulled open the drawer, and peered inside at the contents. Despite already aroused suspicions, she could not contain a loud gasp of astonishment. The drawer was full of wristbands. Sofia rummaged through the drawer, attempting to gauge how many there were. She stopped abruptly, experiencing a sudden pang of guilt, and worried that Adam might return at any moment. Silently sliding shut the drawer – but not before estimating the number of wristbands at around 100 – she hastily covered her tracks, and left the apartment.

Revelations about her murderous past put aside for another day, Sofia hurried back up the high meadow. She knew what the wristbands represented, and their link to Adam's Friday excursions, but decided that this was not the time for confrontation. For now, she would tell no one, not even her father, and keep the shocking secret to herself. Confirming her suspicions would require some information from one of Manny's recent associates: Joshua Daniels, founder of the 'Hidden Innocence' volunteers group.

PSYCHO SUPERSTAR

A week after his encounter with the twins, little did Adam realise when he emerged from the wake-up cubicle that this was his final Friday visit to the psychoviro – at least as part of Groover's deal. Stardust was waiting outside, grinning yet markedly anxious. The man in black seemed decidedly dapper this day, sporting a new shoulder-length wig of fine ash blonde hair and a black leather belt encrusted with blood red gems. After a firm enthusiastic handshake, and a narrowly avoided hug, Adam offered:

"Nice hair."

"Copa, I just knew you'd notice. I decided against the usual nylon vulgarity, and went for nun's hair—genuine Irish nun's hair. A weave of the finest quality and craftsmanship. So lustrous yet light; I feel like the girl with the sun in her hair."

"You mean artificial genuine Irish nun's hair. Nothing's actually genuine in this place. And, the belt?"

"Rubies! Genuine ... I mean perfectly replicated Burmese rubies. Pigeon blood no less."

Unexpectedly, Stardust whipped out a small glass spray vial from his trouser pocket, and held it forward ready to spray. Adam acted instinctively, and grabbed his arm.

"Keep your finger off the trigger, Stardust, or I'll rip open your throat, and spray the juice straight down your fucking neck hole!"

"No ... it's only fragrance, nothing harmful. I made it in your honour, for this special day. Please try it, Copa. You have no idea how long and hard I've worked designing this for you."

"Hah, and then I'll be easier to track. I've sniffed you out a few times because of that homebrewed rose shit you're always wearing. That's why you die more than the others do. At least the twins go easy with the Charlie Blue."

Desperation crept into Stardust's voice, "Please, it's just an eau de toilette … not much stronger than cologne."

"If it smells of concrete and tarmac with a hint of blood then maybe I'll give it a go. Otherwise, keep it well away from me."

Stardust fell to his knees, and nestled his face against Adam's hand:

"Oh please try it. I went with the Copacabana theme. It has a wonderful cocoa banana accord, with bitter coffee, bourbon vanilla, and the finest dark rum. Only the very best for you. Only the very best."

"What the Hell? What the Hell is this all about?"

After choking back a couple of muffled sobs, Stardust meekly explained:

"I never meant to offend you. I am trying to please you, so that you might … spare me this time."

"Spare you? You mean not kill you?"

Trembling, Stardust nodded. Adam laughed:

"Killing you bastards is the reason I'm here, you stupid lunatic. What did you think, that I come for the fondue? Anyway, what's the big problem? If you die, then you're back with your pals the next morning."

"But the dark place is so insufferably painful. The burning and the cutting … I … I can't stand it."

"Then perhaps you should leave the gang. Give someone else a shot."

"No … no, that's no good. You see, I must indulge my murderous inclinations. I must murder. I just don't want to be the victim. Can't we come to some arrangement?"

Adam hauled the quaking psycho to his feet, and looked him straight in the eye:

"Listen up, Rosebud. The dark place with the burning and the cutting, get used to it, because it's nothing less than scum like you deserve. Don't worry; I won't single you out. To quote that piece of shit, Rampage, 'In my world, there are just the living and the soon to be slain. Everyone gets equal treatment. No exceptions!' You see, I despise you all equally. The twins found that out last week."

Seizing hold of the vial, Adam spritzed some fragrance into the air, and took a deep sniff. Releasing Stardust from his grip, he nodded appreciatively:

"Hmm, you know that's actually pretty good. What with all that raping and murdering, it smells like you missed your vocation. I still won't wear it, but it's made me a bit hungry so I think we'd better get to the party. Oh, and you said this was a special day. What's so special about it? Nothing like that Christmas or Halloween lunacy I hope."

"Not at all, Copa, and thank you for your kind comments about the fragrance."

Regaining his composure, Stardust wiped away the tears with the back of his black silk glove:

"You're our only guest today. Never happened before in all my time in this infernal prison. We usually get at least twenty visit requests, and Groover whittles down the number to what he considers suitable for that particular day. Five is the maximum for a real challenge, but he goes as low as two if he thinks we need a breather from the bloodlust. Today there were no other requests, so Groover proclaimed it Copacabana Day in your honour. Appears you're getting the psychostar treatment. I'll admit I'm a tad jealous."

Adam did not like the sound of the special day. If he was the sole focus of the hunt then his chances of success were slim to nothing, especially if Roxy and Quatro sought revenge for their previous week's demise. As they headed towards the corner of the wake-up building, Stardust advised:

"I should warn you that since you're the only guest, Groover's told everyone that they don't have to pretend they don't know you."

Without breaking stride, Adam replied, "Probably get the same creepy looks though, I ..."

As they rounded the corner of the building onto the main pathway, an explosion of enthusiastic applause greeted Adam. He halted a moment in stunned surprise. Hundreds of joyful glam clad locals lined the route to the square, waving and cheering at Adam's much anticipated arrival. Some thrust their fists into the air chanting the name 'Copa', whilst others simply smiled and clapped in respectful admiration.

At once emboldened and bemused by the impassioned response, Adam conferred a single appreciative nod to his admirers, and then continued towards the square. Walking along the asphalt path of fervent adulation, Adam gave no further sign of acknowledgement. although Stardust, swaggering proudly alongside, was happy to soak up the slightest residue of praise – casually tossing and flicking his new hair as if starring in his very own shampoo commercial.

Nearing the canal bridge, the jubilant throng trailing in his wake, Adam recognised a familiar face in the crowd up ahead. It was Roxy or Quatro, but wearing a flamboyant turquoise outfit instead of the usual yellow and gold. Impassive and distant, a haunted intensity in her mascara veiled deep-blue eyes, the glitzy killer turned her back on the proceedings.

"I see Roxy's still smarting from last week," Adam joked to Stardust. "Or is it Quatro?"

"She's both."

"Both? What do you mean?"

"Such a tragically bizarre affair. You killed them both, but only one was resurrected. Well … both minds in one. That braggart Rampage thinks he understands it. He believes the AI has interwoven their memories to create a single entity, and without any serious overlapping. He also says it's for the best, but I'm not so sure."

Crossing the bridge, Adam tried to ignore the loud persistent applause:

"That's … just crazy. So what do I call her now, Roxy or Quatro?"

"Well, to avoid any confusion, Groover decided to give her another name—Rhapsody. Unsurprisingly, she's not as bubbly as before, but her archery skills have greatly improved. Her aim is perfection. She's almost inhumanly precise."

"And she's probably out for revenge."

"Guard your testicles well, Copa. Guard your testicles well."

Across the bridge, in the main square, the mood was less celebratory. As usual, the trestle tables surrounding the modernist fountain were generously laden with an impressive assortment of 1970's party food, but the enthusiastic welcome was absent here. The smattering of locals gathered on this side of the bridge neither smiled nor clapped. Most refused to even acknowledge Adam's presence. These were the true psychopaths, self-obsessed sociopathic monsters, so egotistically persuaded of their superiority that no one else mattered. To them, the idea of a day in someone else's honour was pure anathema.

On his glittering throne at the far side of the square, Groover sat impassively, attempting to project a regal bearing. Rampage stood nearby, his face barely repressing a harsh scowl, whilst Ziggy nonchalantly leant against a wall, thoroughly engrossed in a session of two-fingered nose picking.

The gleeful crowd poured across the bridge, and soon filled the square, their glittering attire an oasis of sparkling jewels amidst the drab concrete of the tower blocks. Stardust led Adam through the throng to meet Groover, and after a cursory exchange of feigned pleasantries, the Genie stood up high on his platform boots, microphone in hand, and addressed the gathering.

"Listen up people! Today be a special day for two reasons. Today be special because we only 'ave one visitor, but it also be special because that visitor be none other than our regular guest, and kick-arse killer, Copacabana!"

At this, many burst into spontaneous chanting of the name 'Copa'. Groover, satisfied with the ecstatic reaction, took a moment to calm the rowdy crowd, before continuing:

"As ee are no doubt aware, I 'ave declared this to be Copacabana Day. This bloke, with 'is poofy arse clothes has come 'ere every week for nigh on two years. I think we can all agree that for quite some time 'e was nothing but a load of boring bollocks."

Groover faked a load drawn out yawn, and a light wave of laughter rumbled around the square.

"But lately, my people ... but lately, I think the bloke's grown some bloody big balls. With some serious trainin' and a ruthless attitude, Copacabana's given us some nail biting thrills and kills over the last few months. I even think the gang's got a bit scared of 'im. Maybe gettin' a taste of their own medicine for a change. I be likin' that. We all be likin' that. Keeps the buggers on their toes. So, before we be getting' down to some serious partying, I thinks we should be 'earin' from the man 'imself."

Reluctantly accepting the microphone, Adam climbed the entrance steps, and then looked out over the glittering sea of expectant faces. In his first life, the nearest Adam got to public speaking was an alcohol fuelled, expletive spattered, blathering rant at anyone within earshot – a mixed audience of piss buddies, random passing strangers - and a policeman or bouncer to close the show. Now he felt calm, focused, and ready to tell the psychoviro inhabitants just what he thought of them:

"Since you are all cruel depraved scum, and I don't want to waste my breath on you, I'll keep this short. I've been coming here, to this godforsaken abattoir, every week for nearly two years. In fact, I believe that next week is the 100th anniversary of my first visit. The disgust and hatred I feel for you, for the evil you have perpetrated, gives me strength, and keeps me coming back. And, though my efforts are focused on taking out 'the gang', be in no doubt that if it were possible I would come here every week and slaughter every last one of you. You are nothing but unrepentant revenant filth, undeserving of resurrection. If our misguided keepers had any sense of justice then all of you would spend an eternity of torture in the dark place." After a short pause, Adam simply smiled and said, "Thank you for listening."

Handing back the microphone, Adam was unprepared for the reaction of the crowd. A stunned silence turned to light applause, before swiftly progressing to passionate cheering and chanting. Within moments, the crowd was delirious with praise. Some screamed oaths of fanatical undying love, whilst creepy grinning perverts tore open their clothing to display their aroused extremities. Even the hard-core sociopaths slinking in the shadows overcame their egos just enough to offer up a clap or two. I took Groover nearly ten minutes of jokes and threats to quieten the crowd enough to announce the start of the party.

Rampage walked over and slapped Adam heartily on the back. In keeping with the special day, his silver jumpsuit sparkled more brightly than usual, with diamonds set amongst the sequins, and like Stardust, his long blonde wig seemed finer and less synthetic.

"Well Copacabana, it seems you have quite a following. You know, you might have fooled most of the inmates in here, but not me. I can see through your lies."

"What lies? I was ready for a bloodthirsty mass assault, not applause. What on Earth did I say to make them so happy?"

"As if you didn't know already. You sounded just like one of us. All that talk about depravity, slaughter, and torture, is music to our ears."

"But I meant every word."

"Yeah, sure you did. No one knows why you come here every week. I suspect you have some secret deal with Groover that involves killing the entire gang, and if that's true then good luck to you because it's never going to happen. Most of the locals think you come here purely out of bloodlust. They like that, and therefore they like you. Give it another year or two and then maybe you'll be one of us, but at the moment I can still detect the faint reek of goodness and compassion."

"I'm going to make a special effort to kill you today, Rampage."

"Not going to happen. Despite your training, I am faster and more skilful than you'll ever be. I'm the only gang member you haven't been able to kill, and it's going to stay that way. You know, I'm probably the one that's going to kill you today, but I doubt it'll take a special effort."

"Made a special effort with your outfit though. And for my special day … I'm flattered. Is that nun's hair you're wearing?"

190

"Fuck off, Copa," Rampage snarled. "Groover ordered us to make an effort. You should be more concerned about today's fighting arrangements. It's my job to fill you in."

Rampage explained that instead of the traditional hunt, the fighting would take place in just one place. Adam was to choose the location – subject to the condition that the battle be visible from the tower blocks. Rampage added that Groover wanted a fair fight to ensure the entertainment lasted more than a few seconds. To achieve this, the gang were only allowed to engage Adam two at a time – fairness being a relative concept in the insane world of the psychoviro.

Adam chose to fight on the flat roof of the huge warehouse bordering the north side of the square. It provided a perfect viewing spectacle for the locals, and with only two opponents on the roof at any one time, he just might stand a chance.

After loading a paper plate with tossed salad and a few almond stuffed dates, Adam said:

"So, I hear there's only four of you now. Does Rhapsody count as two or do you have a replacement?"

"Rhapsody is far more deadly than either of the twins. You did us a favour there. But yes, we have a new member. Her name's Dynamite. She's the tall one with the curly brown hair talking to Stardust."

"You mean the woman with the big sunglasses and grey fur jacket?"

"That's the one. She often stands in for one of us on a Monday if we need a break. Don't underestimate her though, she's a natural born killer. Her chosen weapon is the tomahawk axe, and she's got such a vicious way with it."

"Whoa, sounds nasty."

"You'll find out soon enough. Enjoy your salad."

Up on the Roof

Watching impatiently from the many apartments facing the warehouse, eager for Groover to start the fight, the locals cheered and chanted, pounding their windows with enthusiastic expectation—a riotous cacophony almost drowning out the thumping glam rock backbeat. Groover, microphone in hand, standing tall on the roof his tower block, boomed across the psychoviro:

"Ladies and gentlemen, it be the main event of the year! I give ee our very own glam gang versus the mighty Copacabana! Ee don't want to wait! I don't want to wait! So let's get this started! I want to see some action!"

Adam, alone on the vast featureless warehouse roof, paced around vigilantly, attempting to guess where the first attack would come from. There were seven possible ways onto the roof, all exterior via ladders and various pipework. He knew the gang were somewhere down below, but so far they had remained silent and unseen.

Forgoing the Benchmade knife, Adam carried a straight bladed Special Forces machete—eighteen inches of razor sharp high-carbon steel with a deadly hammer handle. Out here in the open, without the element of surprise, facing swords, tomahawks and cricket bats, a short blade would be suicide, or as the Sarge liked to put it:

"It's only when you expose yourself that size matters."

A loud 'thunk' in the gravelly tarmacked decking alerted Adam to his first challenge. He swivelled around to face the alley and saw Dynamite hauling herself up onto the roof using her tomahawk for support. Only twenty feet away from her quarry, the new recruit nonchalantly dusted off her fur jacket, before retrieving the embedded weapon.

Sashaying in knee-high ivory-leather platform boots, Dynamite approached as if casually meeting a friend for lunch. Gaunt and expressionless, she seemed cool as midnight behind her large black lenses and thick chrome frames. Only the deadly steel tomahawk swinging by her side revealed her true intent.

A strong waft of roses warned Adam that Stardust was about to surface. Glancing behind, he glimpsed a black gloved hand reaching onto the roof. With a sharp cry, the hand disappeared, followed by a heavy thud. Stardust had lost his footing and slipped back down to the pavement below. However, any hopes that he was dead or at least incapacitated were quickly quashed by the sound of loud foppish cursing and a screamed promise that he would get back up as quickly as possible.

Realising that for the moment it was one-on-one, Adam took the initiative and charged towards Dynamite, machete raised. Unflustered and stylishly aloof, the fur-lined ice-queen paused and moved into a defensive stance.

Adam attacked with unflinching force, the curved blade sweeping down in an angled disembowelling movement. Despite Rampage's earlier warning, Adam was unprepared for Dynamite's speed and agility. She sidestepped the machete with an easy dexterity, and swerved to Adam's left. Her tomahawk struck, its razor sharp edge biting straight through Adam's Hawaiian shirt and into the flesh beneath. Since Adam was already backing away, the wound was bloody, but mercifully superficial.

Seizing the momentum, Dynamite struck again, sending Adam stumbling awkwardly to avoid the attack. He felt the cold rush of air as the arcing blade narrowly missed his head, and had only a split-second to steady himself before the deadly weapon lashed out once more.

The third swipe was an unexpected bluff. Dynamite skilfully reversed her thrust, hammering the butt of the tomahawk's handle against the side of Adam's head. The impact sent him staggering sideways, and he weaved erratically, failing to avoid a second handle blow, which struck him squarely on the forehead.

With an expression of dazed confusion, Adam fell backwards onto the hard gravel. Dynamite immediately leapt forward, sensing victory over the celebrated Copacabana, and raised the tomahawk high above her head for a mighty strike. She brought the weapon down with tremendous force, aiming to split open her hapless victim's skull. However, now Adam was bluffing. Taking the blow to the forehead was an intentional desperate attempt at turning the tide —the impact lessened by falling backwards at just the right moment. Before the axe reached its target, he shifted sideways, losing only a few hairs in the process.

Dynamite frantically attempted to retrieve the tomahawk from the roof, but the deeply embedded blade was stuck fast - a fatal mistake. Adam swung around, slicing open her thigh with his machete. With blood spurting from the wound, she screamed, and hobbled towards the edge of the roof in the vain hope of escaping. Unable to make it, Dynamite fell to her knees, and turned to face her attacker. Adam noticed that Stardust was back on the roof, albeit a fair distance away, so hurried to finish the job. He kicked Dynamite hard in the face – his canvas deck shoes were by now so evolved that the toecaps were like steel. The brutal impact shattered Dynamite's sunglasses into her eyes and sent her plummeting over the side of the warehouse to the path below. Dead or not, she was out of the game.

Delirious with excitement, the locals shouted out football-style chants accompanied by clapping in honour of Copa. Stardust swaggered over, thrashing his rapier from side to side with dramatic bravado. Bringing up support, Ziggy appeared at the far end of the warehouse, and began lumbering over. Stopping about fifteen feet away, Stardust called over to Adam:

"How rude of you, Copa, killing a girl on a first date. Ah, but that brings back such sweet memories."

"Just get over here and fight! Today, I'm sending you all to Hell!"

"Perhaps I shall wait for my colleague. Then we shall see who is going to Hell."

Adam estimated he had less than a minute before Ziggy arrived. Adopting a mocking tone, he said:

"You know, I don't think you're the best swordsman anymore. I've been having fencing lessons lately. My instructor insisted upon it. He reckons I'm a natural."

"Pah, that's absolute nonsense!"

"Then let's see. Modern rules or classical?"

"Whatever you desire. It makes no difference, because I can beat you either way."

"Modern then."

Adam strolled forward, his machete held at the ready.

Stardust laughed rambunctiously, and waved his sword in the air. In a real fencing match, Adam knew he did not stand a chance against his enemy's exemplary swordsmanship. The key to success was to break the rules and get in close, rendering the rapier almost useless and forcing Stardust to rely on his unsatisfactory hand-to-hand combat skills.

Standing a few feet apart, both men raised their swords in salute. Stardust shouted, "En-garde!" and they adopted the fencing posture. "Prêt! Allez!" and the bout began.

With surprising speed, Stardust lunged forward, rapier aimed straight at the heart. Adam clumsily parried the attack, knocking away the blade with his machete. He knew Stardust would toy with him for a while before stepping up to more lethal thrusting. Stardust lunged again, this time piercing Adam's left shoulder.

"What are you waiting for? hissed Stardust. "Show me your moves ... if you have any."

After a few inconsequential parries and feints, Adam took his chance and rushed forward with screaming aggression, using his machete to whack the rapier out of his path. Terrified, Stardust shrieked as Adam ploughed into him, knocking him off his feet. Close combat was unnecessary, as the fragrant black-clad psycho smacked his head hard on the gravelly roof, rendering him unconscious. Kneeling down beside Stardust's motionless body, amid a perfumed veil of darkest rose, Adam clutched his machete with two hands and, as if despatching a sleeping vampire, drove the blade into his fallen adversary's heart.

As Adam withdrew the blade, he heard the unmistakable sound of footsteps on gravel just behind him. Springing to his feet, he spun around, the bloody machete whipping through the air with lethal velocity. With no time to change expression, Ziggy just grinned as the flashing blade sliced cleanly through his neck, and his decapitated head dropped to the floor – smashing some of the hat mirrors in the process. Before buckling at the knees and slumping over his own head, the giant stood for a few seconds, blood brimming and pluming from the gaping neck stump.

A deep collective gasp, and the locals were stunned into silence. Adam stood alone again on the warehouse roof, save for the bloody corpses of Stardust and Ziggy. From his high vantage point, Groover announced with perceptible unease:

"Two more 'ave fallen: the swashbuckling Stardust and the mighty Ziggy! So, it be three down and only two to go! Copacabana, ee may be on fire today, but watch out because Rampage and Rhapsody are comin' to douse those flames!"

Rampage climbed onto the roof nearby, wielding both a combat knife and his gladius short sword. With a strained expression, he could barely contain his fury:

"Copacabana, come over here and fight toe to toe. We'll soon see who's the better fighter. Or are you afraid that everyone's going see that you are just a lucky sod, because be in no doubt, your luck has just run out."

Ignoring the pain in his bleeding shoulder, Adam took up the challenge, and strode over. As he neared Rampage, the locals began banging the windows, and shouting out warnings. Adam stopped, and looked behind him. Some fifty feet away, Rhapsody had stealthily crept onto the roof. Bow raised, arrow knocked, she was poised to attack. Rampage shook his head, and waved for the former twin to stand down. Dutifully, Rhapsody lowered the weapon. Turning his attention back to Adam, Rampage said:

"This is between just you and me."

Taking up position, weapons at the ready, both men watched each other intently, looking for the slightest tell of an impending attack. Cautiously sidestepping and tactically altering their stances, each waited for the other to make the first move or display a lapse in attention.

Adam cried out in agony as an arrow suddenly lodged itself in his upper leg. Before he could react, another arrow hit him in the knee. While Adam reeled from the pain, Rampage attacked using a skilful two-blade combo, chopping off Adam's weapon arm with the gladius, whilst simultaneously slicing open his stomach with the combat knife.

Collapsing to the floor, guts spilling out, Adam knew the fight was over. His best chance in two years at defeating the gang had ended in failure. Without pity or remorse, Rampage grabbed the collar of Adam's shirt and roughly dragged him across the roof, leaving a bloody trail behind.

"Copa, you fucking stupid fool," he laughed. "What kind of amateur instructor do you have? Didn't he tell you never to trust your enemy in the middle of a battle."

Reaching the edge of the roof, adjacent the square, Rampage heaved Adam to his feet. Staring squarely into his vanquished enemy's eyes, he said:

"You won't remember this tomorrow, you piece of shit, but I'll say it anyway. Fucking stay away from my viro!"

Without another word, Rampage threw Adam off the roof. Landing headfirst on a concrete paving slab, Adam cracked his skull and snapped his neck. He died instantly.

ADAM VS. STERN

After a simple breakfast of dry toast, and a small bowl of chopped fruit, Adam sat in his favourite chair by the front window drinking a large mug of rich black coffee. Dressed in neutral greys, he looking out over the verdant gently rolling downland, and mulled over the previous day's defeat. His last memory of 'Copacabana Day' was squaring up to the hated Rampage. Obviously, the evil psycho had prevailed, making good on his boast of being the better fighter. Adam wondered if it was worth continuing with the Fighting Fridays.

It was not the humiliation that concerned Adam, but the realisation that he was at the limits of his abilities, with very little hope of further improvement. The problem was simple. To stand a chance against the gang he needed to improve his physical strength and fitness – facing the fast and agile Dynamite starkly revealed this. However, dying every week put Adam back in a brand new body, and six days of exercise was nowhere near enough time to make a difference. Avoiding the psychoviro for a few months would enable him to exercise his body into perfect shape, but that would mean the end of the deal and losing all hope of escaping the Viroverse.

Loud shouting next-door jogged Adam from his dilemma. Through the wall, he could hear his parents arguing, and as usual, Stern's behaviour was the root cause—specifically, another painful encounter with the Satan Bug. For a moment, Adam considered listening to some music through his headphones to block out the noise. Instead, with his anger still fuelled from the day before, he threw on a light jacket, put on his boots, and then headed out for a showdown with Stern.

197

Choosing to stay for eternity in the viro was an option worth considering. Although still faced with the permanent stigma of being an undesirable and a murderer, life had gradually improved. Apart from having some influence over the concierge, Adam now enjoyed subtly better relations with his father and mother, and now looked forward to his mornings with Robert – even though his relationship with his brother was much like taking a pet dog for a walk. It seemed that only Stern's excesses stood between Adam and a life of comfortable insignificance.

Adam chose to go the long way to Stern's house, along the woodland path. Taking the shorter route across the cobblestone bridge might catch his parent's attention, and he definitely wanted them well out of the way. Though Adam did not want to use violence to convince Stern to alter his behaviour, he was well aware of the hind-reader's short temper and willingness to make threats.

Once through the woods, with Stern's house nearly two hundred yards away across a large sloping meadow, Adam found himself directly in the path of the infamous Satan Bug. The speeding vehicle showed no sign of slowing, with Stern at the wheel callously disdainful of any unforeseen obstacle. Instead of leaping out of the way, Adam sprinted towards the oncoming menace. Jumping with precise timing before the impact, he intended to hurdle the vehicle. As the Satan Bug passed perilously underneath, Adam caught his foot on the top of the roll cage, which sent him somersaulting dangerously through the air. Before hitting the ground, his training kicked in and he executed a perfect triple commando roll, with a sore ankle as the only negative consequence.

Stunned at what had just occurred, Stern slammed on the brakes, and brought the buggy to a skidding halt. Adam sat on the grass, rubbing his ankle. The wound, though seemingly insignificant, vividly illustrated his lack of physical training. With a fraction more speed, and a better strength to weight ratio, he would have cleared the vehicle with ease. Here, as in the psychoviro, his training and skills were throttled by deficient physicality.

"Adam, are you alright, buddy? said Stern, helping Adam to his feet. "I was just coming over to speak to you. Wow, that was mucho spectacular! Please say it wasn't some punk-ass fluke, 'cause I'd kill to see that stunt again. When you didn't get outta the way, I tagged you for road-kill."

"I was on my way to see you," said Adam coolly. "I'll get straight to the point. I want you to stop driving around like a maniac and walking naked past my parent's house."

With a scornful smirk, Stern said, "Oh ho, not this again. Look, better you shut-up right now or that ankle will be the least of your worries. I am not going to discuss this crap again."

"I had no intention of discussing it. I'm simply suggesting that you choose to do the right thing rather than having me force you."

"Force me? You think an undesirable nobody like you can force me? I'm not threatened by a little guy like you."

"You've only got a few inches on me."

Hitting below the belt, Stern said, "I got quite a few more inches … where it counts … little guy."

"Real men don't do groin stuff, but then again you're not a real man … with your fake name and fake skills. What was your original name again … Lou … Loser?"

"It's Lucien," seethed Stern, "but you don't get to call me that."

"Ah yes, Loser Shitschnauzer. Now I remember."

"It's Saghausen," shouted Stern, "and one more insult about my family and your toast!"

"I'm not insulting your family. Sofia is proof that the Saghausen name commands respect. But, you don't qualify for that respect. You couldn't cut it as a Saghausen. You were the useless runt, only good for sniffing people's arses … Loser Shitschnauzer."

Eyes wild with rage, Stern charged, and Adam steadied himself for the impact—feigning surprise and vulnerability with the real aim of gauging his opponent's ability. Stern clumsily piled into Adam, landing a hard punch to the face in the process. Falling back onto the grass, Adam tucked his chin into his chest, and put one hand behind his head, breaking his fall. He could have executed a perfect backward roll, but that would have looked suspiciously skilful. Springing back to his feet without a trace of discomfort, Adam coldly warned:

"Stern, this is your first and final warning. Agree to my demands or face the consequences. You're very strong, and quite fast, but believe me, you don't have what it takes to win."

Shaking his head in in arrogant disbelief, Stern warned:

"Oh, you're gonna learn what it takes, because I'm taking it to you right now!"

Stern charged again, in an amateurish repeat of the previous attack. Adam countered with an effortless sidestepping manoeuvre, tripping up Stern, and firmly grabbing his right arm. Before the shocked hind-reader had even hit the ground, Adam proficiently twisted and pulled the limb out of its socket, and then broke one of Stern's legs with a body weighted elbow slam.

199

Bewildered and in a state of shock, Stern attempted to sit up, but immediately fell back down, screaming in pain. He shook with fear as Adam knelt down beside him, understandably terrified of further injury.

"Try not to move," Adam advised. "Moving only makes the pain worse."

"What the …? What was that? You fucking psychopath! You've had fucking training, haven't you? Self-help group my ass. You've been training just so you can take me out!"

"Stern, please listen to me," said Adam softly. "There'll be no more nude walks. I want you to talk to my father, and tell him about your book-reading secret. I promise he won't mock you, or tell anyone else … and that includes my mother. He's an honourable man, and he'll make sure you're not disturbed in the woods. Will you do that?"

"Ok … ok, I agree to give it a go, but only because I'm in damn fucking agony."

"Nobody put a gun to your head, but I would've if I had one. Might have saved you the pain you're in now. Now, the buggy racing. That's also got to stop."

"Oh no, wait a minute, please. What if I let people know beforehand? Give them a heads-up."

"No, not good enough."

Stern began blubbing pathetically. Experiencing a sudden pang of guilt at bringing such a colossal ego down so low, Adam felt compelled to seek a compromise. After a moment's deliberation, he suggested:

"What about this? You warn people beforehand, and you fit some kind of noise generator to the buggy. Not too loud, but just enough to let people hear you coming. Also, no driving near my parent's house. Do we have a deal?"

"Whatever you say. You're obviously the boss now."

"To be honest, I'm more comfortable with you being the big man around here. This was for my parents."

"The dutiful son, eh. Can't say I can identify with that; what with me being a no good Shitschnauzer."

"Yeah, sorry about that. Never been good at witty insults."

"Hah, don't apologise. Excellent name for a hind-reader."

With a sudden unannounced reach and shove, Adam popped the dislocated arm back into the socket. Stern yelled out in stunned surprise, and lashed out with his other arm. Ignoring the feeble slap, Adam said:

"That got it. It'll still hurt like Hell for the rest of the day, and need a bit of support, but you should be able to manage now. As for the leg, I'll drive you back to the house and rig up a splint."

Kaylee appeared from the house, remarkably without a martini glass in hand. Wearing a shimmering pink cocktail dress and spiky high heels, she stumbled awkwardly across the meadow. As she approached, Stern groaned:

"Oh crap, now my reputation's officially ruined."

Thinking fast, Adam replied, "Not necessarily. Look, just act like you're in real pain, and let me do the talking."

"But I am in fucking real pain."

Kaylee arrived, gasping from the exertion, and only one step away from hysterical. Before Adam could stop her, she knelt down and gave Stern a tight hug. Face red and eyes bulging, Stern sucked up the pain through gritted teeth. Adam pulled her off, and Stern sighed with relief.

"Calm down Kaylee," said Adam. "Stern's going to be just fine. Guy's an absolute hero. I wasn't paying attention and stupidly walked in front of the buggy. Thank God, Stern saw me and swerved out of the way. He braked hard and got thrown onto the grass. His leg's broken, and his shoulder's extremely sore, but he'll wake up right as rain tomorrow."

With Kaylee tending to her brave hero, showering him with cherry sweet kisses, Adam fetched the Satan Bug. Then, with great care, they both helped Stern into the passenger seat. Kaylee warned Adam to be more careful in future, and declined his offer to rig a splint, saying:

"Oh don't worry hon', I can take it from here. I got a sexy PVC nurses outfit in the closet that I've been just dyin' to wear. I kind of like the idea of fixing him up without his pants on."

"Mmm, nice," slurred Stern seductively. "I like the sound of that too."

Kicking off her heels, Kaylee engaged the engine, and kissed Stern one more time. Adam, remembering Stern's earlier words, called out:

"Hey Stern, you said you needed to speak to me!"

"Oh yeah, completely slipped my mind. Probably because I was preoccupied with avoiding smashing into your dumb jaywalking ass. I was coming over to invite you to the Mama Fiesta hub next Thursday. Just you and me, pal. They're holding a couple of reservations for me, but we have to confirm by tonight or we lose them."

Adam knew that visiting Mama Fiesta's on Thursday would rule out visiting the psychoviro the following day. Whilst he still intended to give up on Groover's deal at some point, he felt it too soon to make the final decision. Reluctantly he declined:

"Mmm, but I've got the self-help group on Friday, and if I'm not here Thursday night I'll miss it."

"Your loss, my friend. I'll tell Scarlett you can't make it."

"Scarlett? Scarlett Slaughter?"

"That's the gal, living and breathing."

"I'll be there," said Adam eagerly. The decision was made.

A DATE WITH SLAUGHTER

After waking up in a cubicle at Mama Fiesta's Party Hub, Adam sat on the bed for nearly half an hour, concerned that his AI chosen aloha clothing might arouse Stern's suspicions - or at the very least look odd and out of place. Finally, deciding there was nothing he could do about the situation; he opened the door and stepped outside. It took only a second to know his fears were misplaced.

Colourfully attired party goers, many wearing shirts similar to Adam's, streamed from the stunning pueblo styled buildings. Set into the side of a huge gouged sandstone cliff, a thousand adobe-daubed visitor cubicles dazzled with a rainbow of pastel hues. The walkways shimmered in gold and Maya blue. Unlike the narrow walkways and stairwells that Adam had previously encountered, these were wide comfortable rubberized affairs, with gently curving ramps winding down to a decorated plaza.

The expansive plaza, obviously the vibrant heart of the viro, boasted a rich and festive profusion of colourful banners, food-laden stalls, and lively street performers. High up on the walkway, Adam marvelled at the impressively detailed yet clichéd Mexican-style village below. With a single simple chapel, and many raucous bodegas, the village spread out into a tantalizing maze of alleyways, sheltered between a jumbled mosaic of sun-baked terracotta roofs. A large expanse of savannah surrounded the village, beyond which, to the north, Adam noticed a small tranquil lagoon with a wooden wharf and numerous rowing boats.

Before Adam had a chance to move, a tall, imposing gaucho moustachioed man stepped forward from the crowd. Pompously flamboyant, he wore a back mariachi-style braided jacket with large gold tasselled epaulettes, and sported a huge sombrero. The man smiled broadly and shook Adam's hand.

"Buenos dias, muchacho! Welcome to Mama Fiesta's!" he announced with a brash Mexican accent. "My name is Marcelino Capitan, and I am your guide for the day."

"That's Ok; I'm supposed to be meeting someone."

"Ah yes, you are part of Mr Lovass's group. He is waiting over there by the ramp. However, all first timers are assigned a guide, so I am at your disposal. Here take this pager ring." Marcelino handed over an elaborate bronze ring with an Aztec face motif. "If you need me, just tweak the little nose twice, and I will come straight over."

"Thank you, Mr Capitan," said Adam, somewhat bemused, slipping on the ring – surprised at the perfect fit.

"Call me Marcelino. I lead one of the local Mariachi bands, so you will probably see me around."

"Marcelino Capitan's not your real name is it?" said Adam dryly. "I know it's a fun theme thing, but I've had enough of aliases. I mean, I don't mind the fake moustache and the cheesy accent, but please no more aliases. Makes me uneasy."

"But, Mr Eden, this is Mama Fiesta's! We live this extravaganza, four days a week, every week. Who's to say we are not who we say we are?"

Taking a moment to look his host seriously and squarely in the eye, Adam said slowly, "My real name is Adam Preston Eden, but you can call me Adam."

Marcelino sighed:

"The name's Herbert. Herbert Leach. You know Adam, with those bright festive clothes you're wearing, anyone would think you were in a party mood."

"I guess they would. In that case, can I call you Herby?"

"Marcelino, if you please. Now, if you need me just press the nose."

Negotiating the milling crowds, Adam and Stern crossed the busy plaza. Adam was not surprised that the hind-reader was dressed for the Tex-Mex theme, with riveted-stirrup black cowboy boots and faded blue denim jeans tightened with a brass eagle belt. Showing off his bronzed muscled physique, Stern was naked from the waist up, save for a button-less black leather waistcoat and a silver cross medallion accentuating his rock hard pecs. Noticing Adam's interest, Stern whipped his long raven black hair for effect:

"Hmm, you're looking good, yourself, Adam. I never thought you'd get with the spirit of Mama Fiestas, but I must say you look pretty … festive. Not perfect though. You're giving off a strong 'Nut' vibe, and I never figured you for one of those."

Before Adam could ask what Stern meant by the 'Nut' remark, they left the relatively spacious plaza, and made their way along a narrow winding alley. After a few minutes of twists and turns, squeezing past early morning drunks, they reached a large bustling cantina, 'Platos Carnosos'. Ignoring the main entrance, Stern led Adam to a side-door marked 'Residents Only', and knocked three times.

"Stern, I'm sorry about breaking your limbs the other day," said Adam. "I know I went a bit too far. However, I respect that you've stopped walking naked past the house."

"Forget it. Turns out your Dad learned my secret years ago. He followed me one morning, hid behind some bushes, and saw what I was doing. Never told a soul. Means I've been swinging free every morning for nothing."

Just then, the door opened, and there stood Scarlett, rustically attractive in a white lacy fiesta blouse and an embroidered peasant-style knee length skirt, her long blonde hair tightly plaited, Eying Adam coolly for a moment, she said:

"So this is what you look like without all the blubber. From porky pig to presentable, and all it took was a gruesome death."

"Err, you're looking good yourself."

Stern patted Adam on the shoulder, "You go in and get reacquainted; I've got some important guild business to attend to. I should be back by the time you're done. I'll be waiting in the cantina. With a furtive nod and a wink at Scarlett, Stern headed off to his meeting.

Adam followed Scarlett along a corridor and up some stairs leading to an iron studded mesquite-wood door. The spacious lounge area beyond was high-tech minimalist white and chrome, a sharp contrast to the warm toned Latino vibe outside. Whilst Adam comfortably sat back in one of the generously cushioned armchairs, Scarlett fetched a couple of ice-cold tequila Mojitos from the adjoining kitchen.

Enjoying the refreshing minted drink, Adam asked:

"Is this your apartment?"

"No, I'm just borrowing it for a few hours. Stern arranged it for me. The owners are looking after the cantina downstairs."

"So, how long have you been back?"

"Oh, about four months now. Stern contacted me in the first week, and arranged a meeting. I couldn't believe my luck. Stern Lovass the famous hind-reader, wanted to meet me. I caught his farewell act in New York a few years before his death. Guy's like a pheromone on steroids. I'd let him read my naked ass any day. How the hell do you cope, living in the same viro as a sex god?"

"I guess he's just not my type."

"Well, you don't know what you're missing. It's thanks to him that I'm back. I wasn't supposed to be resurrected for a few more years, but Stern pulled some strings and here I am. Apparently, he owed you. Something to do with that sanctimonious little prick, Manny."

"Really? Stern said nothing about this. If I'd known you were back, I would've got in touch straight away."

"Don't blame Stern. I told him to keep stum. You see, the official explanation of what happened the night you died never sat well with me. There was so much crap that just didn't tally with my own experience."

"Such as?"

"Well, for a start, there was no way you were as pissed as they said. You only had a couple of beers. Manny convinced everyone you sneaked some alcohol earlier in the evening, but that's bullshit. I can tell if someone's drunk or not, and you were definitely not. Without going into any more detail, I never believed you murdered those people."

"Hah, good luck convincing anyone else of that. Haven't you heard I'm the viro leper?"

"Given a little time and effort, I'm sure I could have cleared your name. Trouble was, I didn't fancy jeopardising my career digging up evidence for a dead guy. I just put the whole damned mess behind me and didn't look back. Maybe it was a little late to develop a guilty conscience, but there I was, 122 years old, lying on my deathbed in St Marie Hospice, and all I could think about was how I let you down."

"I'm flattered."

"And that brings me to why I told Stern to keep stum, and why I wanted to see you today. Once I discovered that you had been resurrected and were still being persecuted for the murders, I decided to ease my conscience and clear your name. I made use of my contacts, interviewed a number of those involved—except that shit Manny—and carefully sifted through the evidence. At first, nobody wanted to talk, but then I noticed something odd."

Scarlett picked up a remote control and switched on the flat screen. She pressed a button and a grainy yet familiar image appeared.

"Recognise this?" asked Scarlett.

"Yeah, it's the surveillance video from outside Horatio's. Believe me, I've watched it a hundred times, but never seen anything that proves me innocent."

"That's because this isn't the original CCTV footage. Notice that the video isn't in widescreen, rather the old squarish fullscreen standard, and in black and white. Horatio's was just one of a chain of theme pubs opened by Pitlogan Taverns along the South Coast just after the property boom. Acting on a hunch, I accessed some of the CCTV feeds from the other pubs. All of them used colour widescreen systems—digital high definition, and with sound."

"But surely the police would have checked the camera."

"They did. The camera at Horatio's was a much older model—fullscreen, silent, and monochrome."

"But you just said …"

"I got an accountant friend of mine to go through Pitlogan's financial records. It didn't take him long to find an invoice for the cameras, and the name of the company that supplied and installed them. Unfortunately, the invoice gave no details of the actual models purchased, but I managed to track down and speak with the installer, and he was very helpful … and very much involved."

Knocking back her drink, Scarlett continued:

"The installer, a Mr Andrews, received a call less than hour after you … fell into the sea. On arriving at the scene, he was told about the deaths, and instructed to damage the outside camera and wipe the disks—make it look like the equipment was faulty. After checking the recording, Mr Andrews came up with another idea. He switched both cameras for older models that had been previously used on the Victory Mall construction site, and then ran the weeks' security recordings through some video manipulation software on his laptop. After taking out the sound and colour, he carefully cropped out the far left of the image—creating a standard fullscreen format and removing all trace of the deaths. For added realism, he added a low-light grain, and saved the files back to the security disks in a lower resolution appropriate to the replacement cameras."

"So, thanks to that bastard nerd everyone thinks I'm a murderer."

"Don't blame the nerd, Adam. He was smart enough to realise he was dealing with people you don't cross. Luckily for you, the nerd secretly encrypted the original file and saved it onto a key-drive … for insurance."

"I've tried all sorts of searches, but never come across another version of the security feed."

"That's because the file was secret and encrypted. You know you can only access information that was easily available."

Frowning at her empty glass, Scarlett claimed to need another drink, and left the room. A short while later she returned, Mojito in hand, and a dark haired man in tow.

"Adam, meet Mr Jonathon Andrews, your friendly neighbourhood CCTV installer and the only person who can show you the original video. Now you'll see what really happened."

Without a word, Jonathon sat down, and started the video. What struck Adam instantly was the width and clarity of the picture, filling the high definition widescreen panel perfectly, and pixel-matching dot for dot. The stereo sound, partially marred by the driving wind, nonetheless provided an important new layer of information.

To the right of the screen, Adam recognised his former fat self pissing into the harbour, whilst to the extreme left, the Kennans stood nonchalantly chatting to a sharp suited grey haired man. As fat Adam zipped up his fly and headed back to the pub, the young boy—Einstein Kennan—called out that he had something to show him. Foolishly, fat Adam went over to investigate.

Adam sat transfixed at the nightmare unfolding before him, gripping the arms of the chair with an uneasy tension. He knew that this was a memory lost to him, and hoped dearly that fat Adam would not let him down.

The Kennans leaned in close and whispered to fat Adam. By their body language, it was clear that they were offering something illicit, but the audio was too low and over-washed with the elements to hear the exact nature of the proposition. Drugs were the most likely choice, but fearing that perhaps the boy was for rent, Adam dreaded the response from his former low-life degenerate self.

Adam relaxed a little and breathed a quiet sigh of relief as fat Adam rejected the offer, giving the middle finger as a gesture of disgust. However, as fat Adam turned back towards the pub, Einstein lunged suddenly, going for his wallet. Unbalanced by the unexpected assault, fat Adam staggered backwards, his huge weight pushing Einstein towards the edge of the promenade. The father— Derek Kennan—sensing the danger, instinctively grabbed them both, only to become part of the terrible momentum. With only a lower set of railings in place, the rest yet to be constructed, all three tripped and plummeted over the edge and out of sight—their terrified cries abruptly ended with ominous thuds and splashes.

Now only the grey haired man remained, peering down into the dark water, his face stricken with horror and disbelief. After a few seconds, he turned and looked straight at the camera. His expression quickly changed from surprise to alarm, and finally to purposeful resignation. Without another moment's hesitation, the man walked out of shot.

"That's enough," said Scarlett, and Jonathon immediately stopped the video. After a reassuring nod from Scarlett, Jonathon got up from his seat and silently left the apartment.

"Man of few words," noted Adam.

"Complicated guy. Overthinks everything. Probably banging his head against a wall right now."

"So, the video. What the hell happened?"

"I'll keep it simple for now. You noticed the guy in the Armani suit, yes?"

Adam nodded.

"His name is Gerald Pitlogan, owner of the Pitlogan chain of taverns. You must understand that this was just after the great financial crash. Pitlogan was massively in debt, and all of his properties were in unfinished mall developments. He stood to lose millions. Looking to salvage the situation, Pitlogan turned to some shady contacts amongst local Eastern European gangs that he had made during his years as a customs official. This gave him access to a number of corrupt local politicians, who steamrollered the planning process, allowing the completion and opening of the taverns."

"The Kennans, how do they fit into all this?"

"Well, you've got to admit; Horatio's was not in a prime location. Except for a Chinese restaurant and a couple of short lease charity shops, the whole development was a ghost town. To boost income and attract custom, Pitlogan allowed his new 'friends and benefactors' to conduct their nefarious business on the premises. A few crooked cops on the payroll made sure nobody got disturbed."

"Oh my god, I never knew. I thought it was some new tourist theme pub. So, the Kennans …"

"They were just a couple of new guys selling drugs for one of the local gangs. Pitlogan dropped in to collect some cash from the bar, on his way to a dinner engagement, and just stopped to chat with Derek Kennan while he finished off a cigarette. You came over, and Einstein Kennan grabbed you. You all fell into the sea, and Pitlogan realised he was on a crime scene candid camera that could unravel his entire sleazy little empire. A cover-up ensued with you literally as the fall guy."

"But the Kennans were drug dealers. Surely, that would've come up in the investigation."

"It was their first time. Neither had any previous convictions. As far as the investigation was concerned, it was a doting father taking his son to watch the ships in the harbour, set upon by a lousy drunk. The press were on a binge-drinking crusade at the time, and that, coupled with the fact that Mr Kennan's wife had been killed by a drunk driver the year before, meant you were perfect douchebag for the deed. Given your previous history as an alcoholic, nobody wanted or bothered to look too closely."

"But surely the autopsy …"

Scarlett casually interrupted, "Any other questions you have can be answered with the words: money, threats, or favours. The bottom line is that you are not a murderer. A bit unsteady on your feet perhaps, but not a murderer. If you want all the sordid details, I'll come over to your viro sometime and print them out. If I were you, I'd spend the rest of the day celebrating."

Finishing his drink, Adam thanked Scarlett for her kindness and diligence, and after a heartfelt yet decidedly awkward hug, prepared to leave. Offering a wry smile Scarlett said:

"Not so fast aloha-boy! Sit down. Before you go, I have one last surprise."

Opening the kitchen door, she ushered in two men. Adam recognised them immediately as Derek and Einstein Kennan. Obviously, Einstein no longer had the body of a child, and in fact looked slightly older than his father. They sat side by side on the sofa, wringing their hands nervously. With short spiky hair, beady eyes and long incisors, their gaunt rodent-like features made Adam wonder if the AI purposefully made them look as shifty and untrustworthy as possible. A few seconds of uncomfortable silence ensued until Adam broke the ice:

"You know, this is getting like an episode of 'This is Your Life'. Or, more like 'This was Your Death'."

The hunched Kennans sniggered immaturely through the gaps in their ratty teeth. Prompted by a sharp elbow nudge from his father, Einstein looked over at Adam, and said, "Sorry for fuckin' killin' you."

Fuming, Derek punched his son in the arm, and scolded, "Where's yer bloody manners, boy? I told you to be polite."

Einstein scowled, rubbing his sore arm, and then tried again:

"Sorry for fuckin' killin' you, Mr Eden."

"That's betta," said Derek proudly. "Tryin' to bring the lad up right, Mr Eden. Not easy when the greedy bugger can 'ave anythin' 'e likes. And may I also fuckin' apologise for my part in yer killin'. We aint murderers by trade."

"Err, apologies accepted."

THREE FEET OF SKY

"You see, I was always a bit of a villain, but nuffin' 'eavy. Just some part-time thievin' after me shift at Tescos. When the wife died, I kinda lost it. Turned to the bottle and started missin' work. Kept Einstein out of school 'cause I was too lazy to take him in. Lived off fuckin' crisps and sweets. I know it's hard for a gentleman like yerself to understand, but I ended up losing everythin'. I was nothin' but a useless fuckin' dosser."

"Believe me, I understand."

"Got talking to this Croatian bloke who used to work the same shift as me at Tescos when I first started. Drago put me in touch with some of his mates who needed to shift drugs down by the harbour. Shit money, but I was desperate, and the Welfare just keeps you poor."

Adam wondered if Drago was the generous pimp he used to know on the streets, but decided to keep it to himself.

"I'll tell you, if we hadn't died when we did, I 'ate to think what kinda life Einstein would 'ave 'ad. Drugs, violence, maybe even … even … fuckin' pedo-bait. And all my bloody fault."

Scrunching his hamster-like features, Derek began snivelling pathetically - his long nose bubbling and whistling with un-blown mucus. Einstein, only a sob away from joining in, consoled his father with a supportive side punch. Wiping away the tears, Derek thanked his son, and then continued:

"You helpin' us die was the best thing that could've ever 'appened, Mr Eden. Me, the wife, and Einstein are back together as a family in our own place, and with no fuckin' mortgage round our necks. Yeah, we 'ave a few problems. Einstein 'aving the body of a 30 year old when he's only 14 is a right bastard, especially when I 'ave to give him a slap. We got those 'Hidden Innocence' people helpin' out now, and things are lookin' up. Me and the wife reckon he'll turn out just fine. You 'elped us become a family again."

"Well I'm glad everything's turned out right for you. And thanks for coming here to apologise. Very big of you. I appreciate it."

The Kennans began sniggering again. Derek clapped his hands together and pointed at Adam as if catching him out on a joke:

"We're not apologising for nothin'. We don't do nothin' for free. You always gotta get somethin' out of it or it's not worth the bother. In return for us comin' to see you and apologising, old lezzer here got this arse-smelling bloke to do a show in our viro. I never 'eard of 'im, but some of the others said 'e was off the telly. When 'e got on stage all oiled up and writhin', I thought we'd been tricked into watchin' a fuckin' gay show. Some of the Fratton lads were gonna kick his head in, but once 'e started smelling those

211

arses and tellin' people about their worries and stuff, it was fuckin' awesome. The fucker was right ... every ... fuckin' ... time. Made it look so easy too. Me and me mate Charlie 'ad a go at it the next day. Filthy bugger kept farting in me face—shitty wet ones an all. Never trying that again. I reckon that just like brain surgery or clearing landmines, smelling arses is best left to the experts."

"So you're not sorry?"

"Yeah, we are. Really we are. We just don't do stuff for free."

Scarlett sat silent and cross-armed, perhaps somewhat numbed by the inane conversation of the Kennans. For Adam, their words evoked fond memories of his drunken nights on the street – a meandering chatter, instantly transferring from brain to mouth, without the veils and deceit of those mindful of their status in life. However, like late-night chilli burgers from Tabbas, discarded cans of half-drunk lager, and the Aloe fresh promise of wet-wipes in the Crapper, they belonged to a world fading into a nostalgic distant memory.

As the Kennans prepared to leave, Adam sincerely thanked them again for coming and shook their hands. However shallow their motives, their visit gave him some form of closure regarding the tragic incident that night outside Horatios. Relentlessly sniggering and snorting, as if continually sharing some unspoken joke, the father and son left the apartment.

"That's it I'm afraid," said Scarlett. "I'm all out of surprises."

"Are you sure? No one else hiding in the kitchen? Elvis perhaps? Surely he was involved somehow."

After another round of Mojitos and a promise to meet later for dinner, Adam and Scarlett said their goodbyes once more – albeit minus the awkward hug.

MI COPA REBOSA

Despite Adam's protestations, borne of hunger and the smell of grilled meat, Stern insisted that they leave the cantina immediately. The hind-reader seemed uncharacteristically cheerless compared to earlier, and strode towards the plaza without uttering a word. However, upon reaching the teeming heart of the viro, their progress slowed. The festivities were in full swing, with the well-practised locals providing all manner of entertainment for the enthusiastic crowds. Under a vibrant bustling canopy of colourful wide-brimmed sombreros and cowboy hats, the ubiquitous moustachioed mariachi bands accompanied elegant renditions of the Mexican hat dance, whilst bumbling paint-face clowns performed childish pranks and magic tricks. Outside the largest bodega, muscular masked luchadores wrestled in a hard-hitting high-flying exhibition of Lucha Libre - the raucous spectators, fervent fans of Mexican wrestling, whistled, cheered, and jeered at the thrilling display of violent machismo. Those not watching the entertainment sat at large rough-wood tables, talking loudly, knocking back bottles of ice-cold beer and stuffing themselves with all manner of Mexican street food.

Stopping a moment to absorb the lively atmosphere, Adam became overwhelmed by the rich smell of tempting fare available from the many stalls and kiosks—a mouth-watering aromatic melange of spicy pork, Tex-Mex chilli beef, light creamy coffee, and the darkest chocolate.

"Hey Stern, wait up," said Adam, patting his impatient companion on the shoulder. "I don't know why you're in such a hurry, but I have to get some food."

"Just grab a bowl of tortilla chips, and eat them on the way," replied Stern irritably, pausing a moment.

"That won't do it. I've got the munchies. Scarlett was very generous with the tequila Mojitos, but there was nothing to eat. I thought we were going to eat in the cantina."

Stern rubbed his chin and quickly scanned the food on offer.

"You like burgers, yeah?"

"Hmm, not the cheap greasy ones. I've got quite fussy about quality lately."

"It's always top quality at Mama Fiestas. Grab a couple of shredded-beef burritos from the stall over there. They've got the meaty taste you're after."

"Oh yes, sounds good."

Before assembling the meat-filled wraps, the smiling vendor asked Adam, "How hot do you want them? We've got mild, medium, hot, or the extra-special Culo Infierno."

"What's the Culo Infierno?"

The vendor dropped his smile and arched an eyebrow, evoking an air of ominous danger:

"That Señor, is the dreaded Ass Inferno—a true test of bravery and endurance. Just one taste and you shall later face the painful ring of fire."

"Normally, after a few drinks, I'd so go for that, whatever the consequences. But, in respect to my esteemed friend's noble profession, and sensitive nostrils, I'd better have mild."

With a hearty laugh, the vendor expertly filled and wrapped the burritos. Adam turned to Stern:

"Look, I don't know why you're in such a hurry, but I'm going to stay here, sit down, and eat my food. If it helps, please accept my total gratitude for that show you put on for the Kennans. Having them apologise, and even thank me for what happened, really put a lid on the whole affair."

"Man, that was some tough gig. Never experienced such a hostile crowd. Had to cut short the sexy intro before I got lynched. First time I ever missed my blood-sucking agent; she always shielded me from the psychos. But, you needed to hear the truth, and I never really figured you for a child killer. I told your parents about Scarlett's findings a few days ago, so you should be well and truly back in the Eden fold."

"So what's up with you? Why the hurry?"

"That bitch, Stinkerella has organised another vote for the guild leadership. First heard about it at the meeting this morning, and I do not like surprises."

"What about the mysterious ones? The ones you said step-up when the reputation of the guild is at stake. Can't they save you?"

"Not a chance. Stinkerella's worked her skank magic. She was exchanging smiles and glances with Sir Arser Colon Soil at the meeting, and you don't have to be Sherlock Holmes to know what that means. It'll be close, but I know I've lost it. No disrespect Adam, but it sure seems like everyone's putting me in my place these days."

"I'm sorry. I'll get the food to go."

"Nah, don't worry. You're right, I shouldn't be acting like this. The vote's not for another hour. Just thought I'd get there early, and try to call in a few favours—perhaps twist a few arms. That's why I wanted you there. To twist some arms ... and break some legs."

"No way, I'm not ..."

"Whoa, take it easy my man," said Stern, raising his hands in an exaggerated defensive gesture. "Just kiddin'. Thought you'd like to witness my final hour as Chairman of the Hind-Readers Guild. Plus, when I lose, I'm really gonna need a solid drinking buddy for the day."

Adam placed the warm burritos on a small paper plate, and sat down at one of the tables. Stern joined him after grabbing a bowl of tortilla chips and a couple of bottles of Bohemia beer. Before eating his food, Adam inspected the selection of condiments on the table. As well as the expected salt, pepper, vinegar, and ketchup there were bottles of barbecue sauce, Worcestershire sauce, squeezy honey mustard, olive oil, and Cholula hot sauce. He frowned:

"Do you put extra sauce on the burritos, or just eat them as they come? I've never had them before."

"Whatever you want. It's your food, buddy."

"But what's the traditional way?"

"Well, the Mexicans are totally passionate about their condiments," Stern explained, liberally spattering his tortilla chips with hot sauce before reaching for the honey mustard. "Whatever turns-on your taste-buds. You could chug the Cholula with your beer and it wouldn't be wrong."

Deciding to set a burrito taste benchmark for future reference, Adam left off the condiments. As he prepared to enjoy the first bite, he felt a firm hand on his shoulder, and heard a half-remembered voice—deep, masculine, and markedly Texan:

"Those bad-boys better be thick with the finest shredded steak, 'cause a hero like yo'self deserves nothin' less."

Without taking a bite, Adam put down the burrito and turned around. Behind him stood a tall broad-shouldered black man—well kempt in an immaculate grey suit, white shirt and blue silk tie. Adam recognised the man immediately, and stood up to greet him. A proffered handshake quickly turned into a manly hug. Standing back, both men looked at each other with the wide-eyed smiling expressions of long lost friends. Adam spoke first:

"Joshua Daniels, it's so so good to see you again. Is this just a coincidence, or did you seek me out?"

"A mutual friend, Emmanuel Beaumont said you'd be here," said Joshua. "He wrangled a reservation for me. I been looking for you all morning. Took some searching, what with all the crowds and sideshows, but I had to know if was really you."

"In the flesh. Come, sit down, and I'll get you a beer. This is my friend, Stern Lovass."

"Pleased to meet you Stern," said Joshua sombrely, shaking hands. "You're Sofia's Dad, the ass-dude."

"The best ass-dude!" exclaimed Stern.

Adam drew up another chair, and the three men sat together with Adam in the middle. Stern sat quietly, eating his chips, nonchalantly listening in.

"You're looking pretty smart," said Adam. "Never figured you for a suit though."

"You know, inside I'm still only 15, and in my line of work, I gotta look smart or people won't take me seriously. I know I kinda look outta place here, but I just can't get with the fancy dress. Not after my run in with those glam dudes."

"Your line of work?"

"I set up 'The Hidden Innocence' volunteers group. We track down kids resurrected in adult bodies, and provide help and advice for them and their families. Got nearly twenty thousand on our books so far. Some religious viros are involved and some friendly concierges who don't mind bending the inter-viro communication rules, so things are lookin' up. It's still a long road, but we're gettin' there."

"So, you get older?"

"No, physically we stay the same. Just we don't have adult memories or ways. My job is to help people cope with the transition. With the right assistance, the process takes only half the time it did in the old world, especially since there's no rebellious hormonal stage to get through."

"I tell you Joshua, you've come a long way from that scared teenager hiding under the bridge."

"Well, it's all thanks to you, Copacabana."

At the mention of the name, Copacabana, Stern gasped and nearly choked on a tortilla. Taking a large swig of beer to stifle the coughing, he said hoarsely:

"Whoa Adam, either someone spiked my drink with peyote, or the big guy dressed like an insurance salesman just called you Copacabana?"

Joshua leaned over, and spoke slowly to Stern:

"It's true, this man, this brave man, is the one they call Copacabana. I was just a scared kid facing certain death, hiding under a bridge from the crazies. Then this guy sacrifices himself so I could get away. I'll never forget the screams when they killed him. But you know, even with all that pain, he never told them where I was hiding. Then, badass that he is, he went back, week after week, to give them Hell. Trouble was, I never knew his real name, until now that is. This guy, Adam Eden, is my hero, and my inspiration."

Staring at Adam in wide-eyed disbelief, Stern spluttered:

"Nobody knows who Copacabana is! Nobody knows his real name. You're not Copacabana. You can't be Copacabana. Anyone can be Copacabana, but not you. You're Adam Eden, the undesirable weird guy who peeks through the curtains, and breaks … his neighbour's legs. Oh shit!"

Adam and Joshua looked bemused as a shocked Stern double face palmed, and then slammed the table with his fist.

"How could I not see it? That's where you've been going every Friday. I've been telling everyone you go to some self-help group for undesirables, but really you're fighting those fucking psychos, aren't you?"

Adam nodded as Stern continued:

"That's how you've got those fighting skills. I thought you were training just to take me on. Bloody ego blinded me. And that's why I can't get any readings off your ass. You wake up with a new one every Saturday morning, don't you?"

"Fresh as the new-born," said Adam.

"Oh man, this is totally awesome. Do you have any idea how famous you are? For months now, no matter where I go, I hear people talking about Copacabana, and his fight against the psychos. I was never sure if the stories were true or just fiction, but here you are, true to life, a goddamn living legend."

"But I end up dead every week. What am I, the famous loser?"

"Are you kidding me, Adam? What you do is incredible. Almost nothing new ever happens in this boring snooze-fest of a world, and then Copacabana swaggers up with his blades and attitude, sticking it to the bad guys, carving his name right across history."

"The ass-dude speaks the truth," said Joshua. "So many generations have heard the stories. There's rumours that even medieval viros are verily rockin' the Sonnets of Copa."

"Adam, if you were wearing a ring right now," gushed Stern, "then I'd be on my knees kissing it like you're the sexiest Pope ever."

"But I am wearing one," said Adam, holding out his finger with the bronze Aztec ring.

"Figure of speech, my friend. Just emphasising a point. No matter how awesome you might be, I'm not going down on your finger."

Taking another swig of beer, Stern observed:

"What I can't get my head around is how you can face the dark place every week. I would do anything to avoid going through that painful shit again. You truly have titanium balls."

"I don't like to talk about that place. It's total agony, but somehow I kept going back. And, many thanks for the balls comment. First time anyone's complemented my genitals."

My pleasure. Anything to please the mighty Copabana. One thing though, it's Thursday today. Tomorrow morning you're gonna wake up back in your own bed, so there's no way you'll be fighting the psychos."

"I know. I have my reasons. Maybe it's just time I settled down. Also, I really needed to hear what Scarlett had to say. I guess, from today, Copacabana is officially retired."

"So you don't mind your secret coming out?"

"Sofia, Joshua, yourself, and certainly Manny know the truth, so it's probably time to let people know. I'll let my parents in on the secret tomorrow."

Stern just nodded, offering the faintest of sly smiles. Rising from his seat, he unexpectedly cleared the table, but kept the bottle of olive oil. Pouring a generous amount into the palm of his hand, he began rubbing the slippery liquid all over his toned body.

Joshua and Adam stood up, and watched in uncomfortable bafflement. Stern offered a vague explanation:

"I'm oiling myself up for the public. Not too much. Glistening skin makes my muscles really pop. It's time I gave my fans a show. Not long until the vote now, so if any of the guild members are around, it might just remind them why I deserve their support. However, I'm gonna need some musical accompaniment. That's a Mama Fiesta noob ring you're wearing, isn't it? I saw the mariachi guy give it to you this morning outside the cubicles."

"I'm not sure if …"

"Aw come on, mi amigo, I need this. Just call the guy. God, but you owe me for getting Scarlett back early."

Dutifully, Adam tweaked the nose of the Aztec face twice, and waited. Within a minute, Marcelino emerged from the crowd, carrying his guitar, two other mariachis in tow. Stern immediately stepped forward, and took Marcelino to one side. Out of earshot, the two men talked in hushed tones, casting surreptitious glances at Adam. Finally, nodding in an obvious gesture of agreement, the mariachi took a small handset out of his jacket pocket, and pressed a sequence of keys.

"What are you up to?" Adam asked Stern.

"Three mariachis are not enough. Marcelino's calling for reinforcements. Nothing like massed mariachis to get someone's attention."

The mariachis soon arrived from all over Mama Fiestas, complaining at being called away from their performances, and surprised since they usually only played together for the final set of the evening. After handing Stern a chromed 1950s style wireless microphone, Marcelino marshalled the twenty musicians into a cohesive larger band of guitars, guitarrons, trumpets, violins, and vihuelas, before proudly taking his place at the front.

Displaying effortless agility, Stern leapt onto the table and struck a dynamic pose. Without waiting for the crowds to notice, he simply clicked his fingers and the mariachis burst into a lively well-rehearsed rendition of El Ray (The King). The effect was immediate, the crowd quickly gathering around, jostling for a good view of the spectacle. Even on the far side of the plaza, the luchadores stopped their fighting, and leaned against the ropes, enjoying the entertaining respite.

Tilting the microphone at the optimum crooning angle, Stern sang out in a powerful vibrato-rich baritone - his Spanish enunciation never less than perfect. Swaying, bumping, and grinding like some seductive Latin gigolo, Stern mesmerised the audience with his epic vocal talent, well-toned physique, and natural passion.

"Ass-dude's got some voice," said Joshua. "Ain't too keen on the way he's dancin' though. Looks like he's gonna get his dick out. I heard he does stuff like that. I wouldn't wanna see that."

"I doubt it," said Adam, astounded by Stern's singing ability, but uncertain about any imminent genital exposure.

"Just to be safe, I aint gonna watch. I'm gonna stand right here, looking away with my arms crossed, and you can tell me when it's all over."

After three minutes of pure musical magic, the song ended to rapturous applause, and the mariachis fell silent. Letting out a high-pitched ranchero yelp, Stern stamped his boot hard on the tabletop, and addressed the audience:

"Señors and señoritas, I have an important announcement! An announcement of such awesome magnitude that you will always remember this day, no matter how long eternity might be! As many of you are no doubt aware, I am Stern Lovass. Yes, Stern Lovass, the most celebrated of all the 21st century hind-readers. I am not just a red-hot sex machine, I am a man of serious skill, a man of integrity. But most of all, I am able to dig into a person's deepest darkest hiding places to sniff out their most treasured secrets."

Stern clicked his fingers once more, and the mariachis launched into a frantic 30 second burst of the up-tempo La Negra. Whooping and yelping, the glistening hind-reader clapped his hands and proceeded to dance in a clipped energetic breakdancing flamenco. Once the music stopped, Stern stamped his boot hard on the tabletop and continued his speech:

"So, it is ironic that I, Stern Lovass, have been keeping a secret for the past two years. A secret that I am now finally permitted to reveal to you here today. When I have finished, if you need further proof of what has been said, then please talk to the man in the grey suit. That's Joshua Daniels, founder of 'The Hidden Innocence' Organisation, and he is a well-respected pillar of our community—a very honest, straightforward man. He will confirm everything I am about to say."

Joshua stared forward, unflinching, steadfastly refusing to acknowledge Stern's words. Adam, realising what Stern was about to announce, sidled over and tapped him hard on the boot. To his surprise, Stern reached down, grabbed his hand, and hauled him up onto the table.

"What the hell are you doing?" whispered Adam through clenched teeth. "I thought we'd tell a few people privately. Not like this."

"Hah, too late, muchacho. Just stand by me and look serious. I'll do the talking."

Like a best buddy, Stern put an arm around Adam's shoulder. Not wishing to create an embarrassing public scene, Adam stood silent and serious – the expression came naturally, since he was seething. Stern addressed the transfixed audience once more:

"Señors and señoritas, witness this ordinary, some might say puny looking man. He is not a man of sophistication or great wit, nor a man given to public speaking. However, this man is my neighbour, and I will proudly admit that he is also my friend, perhaps my best friend. His name is Adam Eden, and every Thursday night, without fail, I call on him, and wish him good luck for the following day. You see, my fellow Mama Fiestans, every Friday, Adam faces an ordeal that would make the strongest of us quake and shiver like spineless cowards. To me, Adam Eden is my best buddy, my hero, my ... inspiration. But to all of us, he is the fearless warrior who takes on the psychopaths on their home turf! This is the mighty Copacabana, the one who fights for us on Fridays!"

Rather than the anticipated ecstatic cheering, there was a loud collective gasp, followed by a pregnant silence peppered with low mutterings of disbelief. Desperate not to lose the moment, Stern dramatically gestured towards Joshua. In unison, the entire crowd immediately switched their expectant gaze to the imposing besuited Texan. Arms still crossed, Joshua casually nodded, and said, "Yep, It's him."

The response was explosive. Joshua's simple remark ignited the crowd into a frenzy of unrestrained exaltation—the thunderous whooping and cheering almost unbearable in its intensity. As the crowd went crazy, Adam covered his ears, whilst Stern stood, arms outstretched, soaking up every second of the sonic blast wave. From atop the table, Adam could see the gossiped revelation spreading wavelike beyond the plaza, and into the alleys and buildings beyond.

More people poured into the plaza, and the valiant mariachis, using their sombreros as shields, struggled to hold back the surging crowd. As the line broke, a group of men and women rushed forward—many dressed similarly to Adam in bright pink aloha shirts and white trousers.

"Who the Hell are these people?" exclaimed Adam, anxiously. "They're dressed like me! I'm not feeling too safe up here!"

"Remember earlier, when I called you a Nut? said Stern, ready to leap from the table. "This is what I meant. They're Copanuts. You find them in almost every viro these days. You could call them the unofficial Copacabana fan club. They ... err ... wanna be like you."

Both men's safety concerns were unfounded as the Copanuts linked arms and formed a protective circle around Adam. After seeking permission, the burliest two of the group hoisted him carefully, almost reverentially, onto their broad shoulders. With a cheer, the Copanuts began moving away to parade their most sacred idol around the plaza. Marcelino rallied the bruised and battered mariachis into a musical rear-guard, and along with Joshua, fell in behind the colourful group. Stern, left standing alone on the table, shouted to Adam:

"Enjoy this day, my friend. And, don't worry about a thing. Once the craziness has died down, I'll be there to get you through this."

"Good luck with the vote, Stern," Adam shouted back, as the Copanuts carried him into the heaving throng.

"Hah, are you kidding? I doubt if there'll even be a vote! There's no way anyone's gonna vote against me! Didn't you hear? Copacabana's my best buddy!"

Jumping from the table, Stern began dancing his way to the guild meeting.

The procession advanced slowly through the crowd, Adam sitting majestically above his adoring followers, looking out over a shifting sombrero sea. Unable to decide whether to offer a polite royal wave or a full-blooded arm heave, he finally settled on a cautious combination of the two. Many in the crowd punched their hands in the air and chanted the name, Copa, whilst others just screamed with delirious abandon - mirroring Adam's experience in the psychoviro the previous week. Adopting the role of a marching band, the mariachis launched into a punchy, brass dominant version of Manilow's 'Copacabana', and within moments, it seemed to Adam that the whole world was singing along.

The deafening noise of the crowd blocked out any thoughts of his long tortured journey to this point. Unable to reminisce on the months of pain, fear, and brutality that had stamped his ticket, Adam afforded his fans a genuine smile. Whether the multitudes knew him as Copacabana or Adam Eden mattered little. He had an eternity to understand and come to terms with his new status. Throughout the generations, across tens of millions of viros, Adam was a living legend, the first legend of the Viroverse.

Beginning a second circuit of the plaza, all past-life fear and doubt now veiled by a temporary haze of the sweetest vanity and triumphal pride, Adam had only one nagging regret … he never got to eat those damn burritos.

FRIDAY MOURNING?

It felt great, waking up happy and refreshed in his own bed on a Friday morning without the prospect of a gruesome death and the unwanted discomfort of resurrection. Stretching out his legs and wiggling his toes to enjoy the cool smoothness of the crisp cotton sheets, Adam had no regrets about breaking the Genie's deal. Not fighting the psychos meant never learning how to leave the Viroverse, but yesterday's startling revelations in Mama Fiestas left Adam with a the promise of a contented life back in the bosom of his family, with the respect and authority born of his newly discovered status.

Opening the lounge curtains, Adam stood a moment basking in the warm glow of the artificial early morning sun. He felt reborn, as if disconnected from all the burdens of his past. Perhaps for the last time, Adam chose to wear the evolved Aloha clothing. Within a matter of days, he would gain full dispenser access and consign the tropical ensemble to the back of the wardrobe along with the horrific memories it evoked.

Yesterday, at Mama Fiestas, Stern had lived up to his promise, and moved in as soon as the parade ended. The hind-reader was in an exceptionally joyful mood due to Stinkerella calling off the vote once she learned of Sterns close friendship with Copacabana. With the easy way of a seasoned professional, Stern safely guided Adam through over an hour of glad-handing and celebrity small-talk. Then, with Marcelino's assistance, Adam was surreptitiously disguised as a mariachi, complete with false gaucho moustache, and swiftly moved to the apartment above 'Platos Carnosos', where he spent the rest of the day with an extremely amazed and questioning Scarlett.

There was a sharp rap at the door, and Adam recognised a familiar voice, albeit softer, and more friendly in tone than usual, "Adam, are you in there? This is your father."

"Hi Dad, won't be a minute." Adam slipped into his deck shoes, took a deep breath, and opened the door.

Harry Eden, without his threatening cane, looked unusually relaxed in a pair of faded blue jeans and a multi-coloured hippy style t-shirt.

Harry extended his hand, "Son, your mother and I are so relieved that you're not a murderer. The whole Eden clan is over the moon. Welcome back to the Garden, son." After a firm handshake and the warmest of smiles, he arched an eyebrow and said, "I see you're still planning that trip to Hawaii?"

"And from the look of your clothes I guess you'll be there too, selling beads and bracelets on the beach."

Harry leant forward and gave Adam a big hug, saying, "Oh Son, I'm like a man reborn. Out of the blue, Stern's agreed to stop his embarrassing nude walks and go easy on the racing ... and you're not a child-killer. These were the clothes the AI originally picked out for me when I was resurrected. I never figured myself the hippy type, but now I finally get it."

"Have you spoken to Stern this morning?"

Harry winked, tapping his nose:

"No, I haven't seen him. I guess he's reading one of his books in the glade."

"So, you don't know where I go on Fridays?"

"Oh that, yes of course. Stern told me months ago that you go to a self-help group to discuss your problems. Will you still go to that, now that you know you're innocent?"

Adam shook his head, and carefully considered the words to explain his Friday visits to the psychoviro and his newfound fame as Copacabana. Before Adam was able to speak, Harry said with a furtive grin:

"In fact, I wanted to talk to you about the self-help group. Come over to the Manor with me for breakfast. You haven't already eaten have you?"

Standing under the huge regency portico, Adam realised he had never set foot inside his parent's house. In fact, he had no idea what lay behind the front doors. With a dramatic 'ta-da!' Harry swung open the white double doors, revealing an expansive entrance hall.

The décor was lavish chintz, with huge crystal chandeliers and blue Georgian stripe walls. Everything seemed gilt framed, from Renaissance oil paintings to a large four-seat white leather recliner. Michelangelo's 'Creation of Adam' adorned the wide ceiling, and pink-veined marble floors gave way to an elegantly curved staircase, resplendent with delicately filigreed gold balustrades.

"Your mother's choice, I'm afraid," laughed Harry. "I like to call it Louis IVX meets Scarface. Somewhat tacky if you ask me, but don't let your mother know I said that. Watch your step, the floor's a damned ice rink. I spent a few days sliding around the house and doing the splits before I switched to soft grippy soles. Kitchen's through the door over there."

To Adam's relief, his deck shoes provided adequate grip.

Unlike the gaudy entrance hall, the huge kitchen was sleek and sophisticated—stainless steel and glass utilities contrasted with black lacquered Chinoiserie furniture and a faintly rustic stone tiled floor. It reminded Adam of an early 21st century trendy bistro.

Adam sat at the table, whilst Harry produced a couple of mugs of tea from the dispenser. Joining his son, Harry said:

"First, let me apologise."

"What, for banishing me from the family? asked Adam, taking a sip of the hot milky brew. "Of course, I accept …"

"No, no, not that. It's those criminals need to apologise for that. No one here needs to apologise for the lies they spread. What I want to apologise for, is sneaking into your maisonette whilst you were out with Robert the other day, and taking a little peek at your computer."

"What? Why did you do that?"

Taking a large gulp of tea, Harry explained, "When Stern told me that Scarlett had irrefutable evidence that you didn't murder the Kennans, you can appreciate how overjoyed I was. I racked my brains to come up with some sort of celebration to welcome you back into the family. Now, we've a big family get together planned in a few weeks' time at the Goodwood Picnic and Pims Hub – they can cover 212 years of Edens, so expect a huge crowd - but I thought you needed something sooner, and a bit more personal."

Adam became worried, and asked:

"What do you mean 'a bit more personal'? For god's sake, what have you done? Does Stern know about this?"

"No, this is strictly my idea. I didn't want Stern sticking his nose in and taking over. You see, I knew you wouldn't be going to the self-help group this Friday, so I thought it would be nice to invite your friends over for a surprise party in your honour."

"My friends?"

"I looked through the visit log on your computer, and wrote down the address you go to on Fridays—'Groover's 1970s Glam Rock Theme Party'. Then I used mine, your mother's, and Robert's allowances, and posted an open invitation for six people to come over for drinks and snacks. I heard nothing all week, but then late last night they confirmed. Strange bunch of names, but I guess they use aliases … because of their embarrassing problems."

Adam spoke slowly and coldly, "Rampage, Ziggy, Rhapsody, Dynamite, Stardust, and … Groover."

"Yes, that's them," laughed Harry. "Your mother's gone over to the wake-up building to welcome them. Hope she doesn't scare them. You know how formidable she looks when she's wearing that posh pink frock and the beehive hairdo."

"Dad, these people aren't my friends, they're psychopaths!"

"Oh I know they probably have a few problems … skeletons in the closet so to speak … but I'm sure we'll all get on fine."

"No, you aren't listening! They are ruthless, cold-hearted killers! That 'Glam Theme Party' name is just a cover to lure unsuspecting noobs into their psychoviro! They hunt people down and murder them! They're psychopaths, Dad, real psychopaths!"

"Psychoviro? Oh dear God … I've heard of those places. Maybe … oh God … they won't kill anyone today. Isn't it that psychoviro inmates can only leave their viro if invited? Maybe, just maybe, they'll behave themselves in the hope we'll invite them back."

"They have come to kill us. That's what they do. It's their nature."

All the colour seemed to drain from Harry's face:

"But you go there every week. Why would you …"

Suddenly, the door flung open, and Edna stood there, wild-eyed and shaking, sweating profusely, mascara running down her face. Seeing Harry and Adam did nothing to calm her nerves, and she spoke breathlessly:

"I … I … ran all the way here! They were laughing and joking! Laughing about the horrible horrible things they were going to do to us! The man in the silver suit said he's going to skin me alive! And, he meant it! My skin, my beautiful young skin! What are we going to do? What are we going to do?"

Harry immediately leapt to his feet and tried to comfort his hysterical wife. Turning to Adam, he suggested, "What if we lock ourselves in one of the bedrooms, barricade the door and window?"

"No good. They love a challenge. Anyway, I have a better idea. Dad, I want you to get a pair of binoculars, go upstairs, and watch those psychos.

Get a good look at what they're wearing and any weapons they're carrying. If they head for the Manor then let me know immediately."

Kissing Edna tenderly on the cheek, Harry promised to return soon, and then hurried out the room.

"But what about me?" wailed Edna. "What about me?"

"Calm down, Mum, I have this under control." Adam went over to the sink, opened the cutlery drawer, and then ran some cold water. "Come, you need a drink of water."

"Who are those people, they …?"

Edna was unable to finish the sentence due to the kitchen knives that Adam had thrust into her neck and chest. Without removing the blades, looking straight into her unblinking eyes, Adam gently cradled his mother to the stone floor—her face a startled rictus of disbelief and mortal terror. Reassuring words were unnecessary. She would not remember this tomorrow.

Adam realised providence had granted him one final chance to defeat the psychopaths. The location of the hunt was never specified as part of the deal, and being on his own turf perhaps gave Adam the advantage he needed. Killing his mother was an unfortunate necessity. To put it simply, screaming and panicking, she would have definitely got in his way and ruined any prospect of victory.

Hoping to contain the blood, Adam packed kitchen towels around his mother's wounds, and then pulled out the knives. However, within seconds the towels were saturated, and the warm blood quickly spread out around the body, creating a crimson grid along the grout-lines on the kitchen floor. Adam was considering whether to mop up the mess, and hide his mother's body in one of the kitchen cabinets, when unexpectedly, Harry walked in:

"Adam, do you think we should contact Stern? I think …"

Suddenly noticing the body on the floor and the blood, Harry shuddered and quietly asked, "Did you just kill your mother? Why did you just kill your mother?"

Thinking quickly, not wanting his father to know his true motive, Adam lied, "Dad, this way those evil bastards won't be able to torture her. They do that … to women, and they'd make you watch. I … err … love you both too much to let that happen. I wanted you out the way to spare you the decision."

Harry slouched down beside his wife, oblivious to the blood soaking into his jeans, and gently stroked her Elnett reinforced beehive. With a stony gaze, he looked up at his blood-spattered son:

"What kind of monster are you? I arrange a simple get-together to celebrate you not being a murderer, and the first thing you do is kill your mother. What's going on, Adam?"

"Dad, we have no time for recriminations or explanations. You need to do exactly as I say or we're all dead. Now, I know you and Stern contact each other with walkie-talkies. We will need to warn him about the psychos, and get him to warn Kaylee."

"Oh my God, Kaylee … I forgot all about her."

"First though, I need you to get me a few things from the dispenser. Is this the only one, or do you have another?"

"Err … we have a few," muttered Harry. "There's one in the hall, next to the sofa. But, why do you need me to use the dispenser? Why can't you do it yourself?"

"No time to explain, Dad. Just trust me on this."

Harry flinched as Adam walked over and hauled him to his feet. Escorting his father into the hall, out of sight of the bloody corpse, Adam closed the kitchen door.

Within a few minutes, all the items Adam requested were dispensed, and laid out on a small side-table next to the leather sofa—including a clean pair of jeans for Harry. After changing into the new trousers, Harry picked up the closed Benchmade combat knife:

"I can understand you needing a scary looking knife like this, and the machete, but why did you want the aftershave? At a time like this, you shouldn't really care what you smell like."

"I don't; I'm just playing a hunch. If the right one turns up, then it could prove useful."

Inadvertently, Harry pressed the release button on the knife, and the blade flicked open. Startled, he dropped the weapon and it hit the marble floor then slid right under the sofa. Harry apologised profusely as Adam crawled behind the large piece of furniture to retrieve the knife.

Grabbing the fallen weapon, Adam heard the sound of familiar footsteps stomping into the hall. Sluggish and heavy, with an uneven rhythm, he knew it must be Ziggy clopping along on his platform boots. Hidden from the psycho's sight, Adam quietly altered his position and covertly peered around the side of the sofa. Harry stood back from the side-table, and slowly moved into the centre of the hall, drawing the lumbering giant away from Adam's hiding place. As Ziggy passed his position, Adam gripped his weapon and waited for the optimum moment to strike. Stopping in front of Harry, Ziggy tipped his mirrored top hat in greeting:

"Hah, hah, you look … like … Copacabana! You his … father! You invite … us to … party!"

Forcing a smile, a marked note of fear in his voice, Harry said, "Yes, I did, and you're all very welcome. It … it's nice to see you."

"Hah, hah … you … not see me … anymore!" Ziggy squealed in delight, and tightly clamped Harry's head in his huge brutish hands, before thrusting his gnarly nailed thumbs deep into the eye sockets."

Laughing dementedly, Ziggy let go his grip, and punched Harry in the head, knocking him to the floor. Creeping out from behind the sofa, Adam moved up behind his prey, his approach masked by his father's screams. Unaware of the danger, Ziggy stamped hard on Harry's head with the heel of his platform boot, cracking open the skull. With cold calculating skill and precision, Adam raised the knife, and forcefully drove the blade into the back of Ziggy's thick neck, adding a final lethal twist – like the crack of a lobster shell, the sound of splitting vertebrae was immediately reassuring.

Heaving Ziggy's dead weight out of the way, Adam attended to his father. It took only a quick glance to realise Harry was beyond saving: moaning in pain, his eye sockets streaming blood, and grey matter squeezing out of a gaping gash in his scalp. Out of kindness, or perhaps unconscious self-preservation, Adam deftly slit open Harry's jugular with the tip of his blade, and let him bleed out.

Despite the carnage, Adam maintained a cool presence of mind, and remembered to contact Stern using the walkie-talkie:

"Stern … Stern … are you there … um, over?"

After a few seconds of static, Stern replied:

"Hey, that sounds like my best buddy, Adam? Good to hear from you muchacho. Don't worry about the 'over' shit, 'cause these babies work both ways at once. Hah, kinda like me with the ladies."

"Stern, cut the jokes, and listen. Where are you right now?"

"Kickin' back in the woods, enjoying my new book, Nathaniel Hawthorne's 'The Scarlet Letter'. Ignored it when we studied it at school, but thought it was time for a step up from the usual erotic romance."

"Hmm, I saw the movie - Demi Moore and Gary Oldman, pretty good. Look, Dad invited some people over for a surprise party."

"Whoa, another party day? Adam, my man, you are such an animal!" Stern proceeded to make loud monkey and tiger noises.

"I said cut the jokes! You're not going to like this. The people he invited are from my … Friday self-help group."

After another few seconds of static, Stern sombrely replied:

"You mean the psychoviro?"

"Yeah, Dad stupidly invited the whole damn gang, and they're out for blood. I suggest you contact Kaylee straight away. Get her to join you in the glade. Stay low, and I'll get over there as quickly as I can. I've got to fetch a couple of things from my place, and … deal with Robert."

"But you can beat them, right?"

"Well, I've got a crazy idea of a plan, but if I do beat them, it will be the first time."

"Oh no no no, just when everything was taking a turn for the better," choked Stern, obviously breaking down in tears. "Can't we reason with them? Surely it doesn't have to end in violence?"

Adam stepped away from the blood spurting from Harry's twitching body, and steeled his reserve:

"Too late, my friend; I'm afraid that bird has already flown."

KEEPING IT IN THE FAMILY

D ynamite stood ready, tomahawk raised, as Stardust cautiously peered into the entrance hall of the kitsch Georgian edifice. Decked out in their usual glam finery, Dynamite in shades and furs, and Stardust in his glitter and leather, both killers evoked an image of a clichéd 1970's rock couple visiting their country retreat. Ziggy had lumbered on ahead with his mutant stamina and numbness to pain, doggedly ignoring the protests and warnings from his less physically endowed colleagues. Wearily, slowly, Dynamite and Stardust had followed.

In a break from the usual tactics, Groover decided to split the group in to two, and he, along with Rampage and Rhapsody headed in the opposite direction, up the high meadow to another large dwelling. Unlike the flat land back in the psychoviro, the terrain here was gently sloped and hard going on platform heels. Even with slightly lower heels than usual, ankle pain had forced a stop and a rest every few yards.

As Dynamite and Stardust moved into the hall, the carnage was immediately evident. Ziggy lay face down on the floor, his blood stained cricket bat by his side. Next to him lay another body, dressed in jeans and a t-shirt, the head completely pulped. As Stardust inspected the unrecognizable corpse, Dynamite asked:

"Do you think it's Copacabana? Same colour hair and I reckon the same height. If Ziggy took him out already, then we've got an easy day."

Turning his attention to Ziggy's neck wound, Stardust shook his head:

"Unlikely I'm afraid. This was skilful blade-work; the spine's cleanly severed. Unless there's someone here Groover didn't know about, then I'd say Copa got the jump on our brutish friend. If I was to hazard a guess, I would say this other fellow is Copacabana's father."

A swift, though vigilant scout through the rest of the downstairs revealed another body in the kitchen. As before, the head was completely flattened, and Stardust stifled a retch:

"Ugh, what an absolutely sickening sight! Just look at that dreadful pink dress, and the starchy beehive. This is the frightful harridan that met us at the visitor building. Copa's mother I believe. Who would believe such a devilish harpy could spawn such a wonderful son."

"At least Ziggy took out a couple of people before he was killed. And look, the backdoor's open. Perhaps Copa's moved on."

Stardust looked out the backdoor and carefully surveyed the landscape. Two destinations looked likely – either a large woodland bisected by the central stream, or a ruined chapel further up the hill, beyond a line of trees. Deciding that the chapel looked quite exposed and probably difficult to defend, Stardust concluded that Copacabana was in the woods. However, before leaving the house, they needed to check upstairs.

Almost before they reached the first floor landing, Stardust detected a familiar smell. 'Number 88,' he excitedly exclaimed and hurried to find the source, his perfume-ensnared nostrils leading the way. Following close behind, Dynamite guarded against possible ambush.

At the end of the long landing, they found a self-contained apartment. The lounge area was strewn with oversize child's toys, whilst a half-eaten BK Whopper and large fries revealed the room had been recently vacated. Tentatively, with Dynamite watching his back, Stardust pushed open the door to a small bedroom. He gasped in horror at the scene inside.

Obviously dead, head smashed flat, a huge body lay back on a king-size bed. The monstrously large corpse was muscular, naked, and extremely bloody. Passing over the frighteningly pancaked head and gore, it was the corpse's monster penis that the psychopaths found most disturbing. Disappearing back into the lounge for a moment, Dynamite retuned with the BK Whopper Meal bag and tucked it over the offending organ.

"What kind of people are these," she said, clearly disgusted. "Why would Ziggy leave it exposed like this? It's obscene!"

Stardust, preoccupied with the tabletop contents of a small dresser by the window, muttered:

"I know, it's absolutely disgusting, but unfortunately there's no understanding our Ziggy. Come here, and see what I've discovered."

Proudly, Stardust held up his find, a squat grey glass bottle with No.88 embossed in silver, and offered the cap for Dynamite to smell. She nodded in appreciation:

"Now this is special. I'm getting a gorgeous rose, and something ... refreshingly medicinal. If this is what you've been babbling on about for last few months, then I admire your taste."

"And it's British."

"All the better. But, what's that on the table? Is it another fragrance?" Dynamite pointed at a small misshapen blue object on the dresser top.

Stardust picked up the mysterious container, and it immediately sprang to life as if triggered by his touch. The shimmering blue fish-scale material felt strangely soft, and gently pulsated in Stardust's hand. Hovering holographically above the surface was the word 'Chalut'. Stardust was fascinated:

"My word, this is an unexpected find," he marvelled, shaking the container. "I'm guessing it's another fragrance, but I'm not sure how you dispense the juice."

"I've heard of these. It's a perfume bio-bag from the late 21st century. Those fish eyes are probably the activators. Give them a little squeeze, but don't point that ugly pink nozzle anywhere near me."

Stardust eagerly squeezed the 'eyes' and a gob of liquid spat out of the labia-like nozzle onto his wrist. Taking a deep sniff, Stardust screwed up his face in disgust:

"Oh no, this is terrible ... just terrible. I'm getting fish, fish, and more fish. Smells like a dirty tart's unwashed knickers."

Dynamite, always hard to read behind her dark shades, offered the most ephemeral of smiles:

"Stardust, I believe you've found your signature scent."

Suddenly, taking both psychos completely by surprise, the huge naked corpse raised itself up off the bed, and stumbled quickly towards them – arms swinging lifelessly by its sides, the flattened head hanging down like a hairy flesh-bag over the chest.

Stardust shrieked in terror and tripped backwards, landing awkwardly on the floor next to the dresser. Dynamite also screamed, and lashed out with her tomahawk, chopping deep into the corpse's shoulder. The vicious blow did nothing to halt the frightening advance, or the grisly impact, which sent Dynamite crashing backwards through the window, deadly shards of glass following her down to the slabbed patio area below. With the tomahawk still embedded in its shoulder, the hideous corpse turned towards Stardust.

Quaking with fear and still screaming, the black-clad psycho was back on his feet, struggling desperately to unsheathe his rapier.

Stardust pulled out his weapon, and the corpse halted, swaying unnaturally. With a sickening squelch, and a heaving groan, the giant dead body flopped to the floor, revealing its gory secret. His fraternal meat suit now discarded, Adam stood quivering with unholy adrenalin, machete in hand, and covered head to toe in his brother's still warm blood.

Without waiting to ask questions, Stardust lunged at Adam with his sword. Adam easily parried, and followed through, hammering Stardust hard in the face with the hilt of his machete. Stardust staggered back, blood streaming from a broken nose, and tried to adopt a defensive posture. Under a rain of vicious blows, each crudely but successfully parried, Stardust was driven back across the room. A final, concerted attack by Adam saw Stardust lose his footing and he fell backwards into a large open wardrobe. Slamming shut the wardrobe door, and jamming a chair under the handle, Adam imprisoned his foppish adversary.

After about a minute of silence, Stardust nervously asked:

"That smell? Oh my god, what's that putrid smell? And this heap of … ugh … argh! Argh!"

Adam tolerated the screaming for only a few seconds, before knocking forcefully on the wardrobe door:

"Leave that heap alone, you shit! That's my brother's insides, wrapped in a sheet. Show the slightest disrespect, and I'll flay you alive with his spinal cord."

"You're going to kill me anyway. At least Ziggy smashed a few heads for our team."

Adam put his mouth up close to the door and whispered coldly:

"Well Rosebud, just so you know, I killed them all. Once I saw you and Dynamite heading this way, I knew my plan might work. I smashed in everyone's heads to make it look like Ziggy's work. Lured you dumbasses into a false sense of security. Failing that, I knew you couldn't resist the cologne."

Weeping softly, Stardust said, "You're so right, Copa. I can't resist the refined pleasures of the senses. I sometimes wonder if that is the source of my psychosis. Maybe, just maybe, if my childhood had been less …"

"Shut up, Stardust," ordered Adam. "This is a fucking wardrobe, not a confessional!"

"So, what now? What are you going to do to me?"

"I'm giving you a choice. I'm going to open the door, just a bit, and I want you to throw out your sword and your dagger. If you do that, then I'll kill you quickly with a stab to the heart. If you don't throw out your weapons, then I'm going to open this door, disable you, and kill you in the most painful way that skill and time allows. Your choice."

Quietly sobbing, Stardust threw out his blades. Adam flung open the wardrobe door, machete poised to strike, but then hesitated. Taking pity on the snivelling figure cowering in the shadows, he fetched the bottle of No.88. Handing it to the shaking psycho, he said:

"Here, at least you can go out smelling of roses. I'll give you a moment to enjoy the smell."

Nodding appreciatively, Stardust sprayed the No.88 all around, surrounding himself in a fragrant cloud. Adam watched as Stardust closed his eyes and inhaled deeply, savouring his own personal fleeting breathe of paradise. Without warning, Adam lunged forward, stabbing him cleanly through the ribs. A few minutes later, Adam dragged Stardust across the room by his hair, and then unceremoniously heaved him out of the window to join his dead compatriot.

Surveying the carnage, Adam was struck by deep feelings of sorrow and guilt. Laying down his machete, he carried his brother's hollowed out carcass onto the bed, and placed the sodden sheet-bag of bones and offal alongside. Finally, overcome by emotion, Adam gently smoothed out his brother's flap of face and kissed him tenderly on the cheek:

"Thanks for all your help, little brother; we made a damned good team. And, whatever happens today, I promise you we'll have the best time ever in the park tomorrow."

DEAD END?

Exhausted from the violent events at the Manor, Adam dropped to his knees by the fast flowing stream, and looked down at his rippling reflection. His hair and face were slick with his brother's blood, his eyes stinging with crimson drips and sliding clots. Leaning forward, Adam cupped his hands in the cool fresh water, and splashed the remnants of Robert from his face.

Only ten minutes earlier, before leaving the manor, Adam had scanned the viro from an upstairs window using his father's binoculars, looking for any sign of the three surviving psychopaths. Far away on the high meadow, a small prone motionless figure caught his attention. The choice of attire – bright red split-thigh cocktail dress and matching stilettos – revealed the identity as Kaylee, whilst copious amounts of blood and an arrow jutting from an eye socket meant she was certainly dead. Adam now knew that he and Stern were the only ones left to face Groover, Rampage, and Rhapsody. Concerned that the muscular hind-reader might actually take-out one of the psychos, and thereby destroy any chance of fulfilling the Genie's deal, Adam hurried to the woods. Choosing the quickest route to the woodland glade, he headed for the stream. Following its path led deep into the woodland, close to the glade's entrance, but it meant getting wet.

With his face now clear of unwanted fraternal residue, Adam waded into the stream. Once in the middle, about waist high, Adam fully immersed himself, allowing the firm flow to wash away the blood from his evolved clothing. Keeping a vigilant eye on the high meadow, Adam then laid back in the water, holding his weapon satchel across his chest for extra buoyancy, and let the current carry him into the woodland.

By the time Adam reached the glade, his hair was still wet, though his clothes were miraculously dry. Stern, who had been hiding behind one of the log benches, emerged wielding a couple of broken beer bottles. Adam nodded approvingly at the hind-reader's choice of weapon, and placed his satchel on the table.

"Excellent improvisation, Stern, but I think you need something a little more effective to take on these bastards. You see, unfortunately for us, these bastards aren't your average bar-room brawlers."

Unzipping the satchel, Adam took out Dynamite's tomahawk and handed it to Stern.

"Nice weight, eh? Just remember that the hilt is a weapon too. I don't know how long we've got before they get here, but I advise you to practise a few swings, and get a feel for the weapon. Don't actually chop anything though. That would be noisy, and we don't want to give our position away."

Stern swung the weapon a couple of times, feeling the weight. With a tone of real concern he asked, "What about Kaylee, and the others. Do you have weapons for them too? With the trees being so dense around here, the path's the only way in. Hey, if we were all armed, we could make quite a stand. It'd be like the Alamo but without the overwhelming numbers of Mexicans."

Adam put a hand on Stern's shoulder and grimly replied, "They're all dead. It's just you and me now."

"What about Kaylee? How would you know if ..."

"I saw her body up on the high meadow. Trust me, she's dead."

Adam could see that the news had devastated Stern, and sought to bring a small measure of hope:

"The good news is that I've taken out three of the enemy. Pretty much evens the odds."

"Evens the odds, my ass! That still leaves three of them out there. We're totally outgunned, especially since I have zero skill and experience. I probably couldn't chop shit with this axe."

Adam shook his head:

"One of them's a Genie, and they never fight unless in self-defence; goes against their code. If we leave him alone, then he'll give us no trouble ... well apart from a bit of verbal abuse I suspect."

"How will I know who's who?"

"Well unless they're wearing something different than usual, the Genie's the one in the silver jumpsuit with dark hair. Don't confuse him with the blonde guy who also wears a silver suit; he's a mean bastard."

"And, the other one, how's he dressed?"

"She wears turquoise, and carries a bow. And, don't you underestimate her just because she's a woman. Whatever she aims at, she hits. So, you see, that means it's one each. Or, as you might say, 'mano a mano, muchacho'."

Stern finally allowed himself a smile:

"Hmm, fighting alongside Copacabana. Should keep me in celebrity invitations for a few years."

"Err, that's something we need to get straight, before the action starts. We're not fighting alongside each other. You stay back, behind the picnic table, and let me handle them first. I only want you to get involved if I'm out of action. Don't worry, they probably won't attack you if I'm still fighting."

"What, are you crazy? You're going to get double-teamed. Whatever happened to the fuckin' mano a mano crap? Adam, I'll tell you right now, if I get the chance, I'm taking my revenge on those bastards."

Adam pointed his machete threateningly at Stern:

"This is not up for discussion. If you join in whilst I'm still able to fight, then I'll kill you myself. You just stay back!"

"What the fuck? Why are you threatening me?"

"Just don't get involved unless you're sure I'm out of the game. This is something I have to do for myself."

Stern showed no fear as he squared up to Adam, and replied with questioning revulsion:

"What is this? Have you got some arrangement with these psychos? You don't fight for honour or revenge, do you? This is all part of some fuckin' game. I'll bet you have some deal with the Genie. What is it, you kill them all and get to win the Grand Prize?"

Lowering his machete, Adam said nothing. Stern continued:

"Please don't say you sacrificed us all just for some shitty deal. Surely, you can't be that cold. Whatever the payoff, this can't be worth it."

"Everyone one gets resurrected. They'll all be back tomorrow."

"Fuck you! I'd rather someone break every bone in my body than go through that Hell again."

"Then you'd better stay back and let me do my job. Either I'll take them out, or I'll fall and then you get your shot at revenge. Is that understood?"

Stern nodded, and grudgingly agreed to stay back once the fighting started. Adam walked a few feet away and began practising his machete moves and combat stances. Looking back, he noticed Stern still scowling.

"Hey Stern, a friendly word of advice. If you do get the chance, then exact your revenge without vengeance in your heart. Take it from someone who knows; too much emotion will destroy any hope you have of success."

"And what about too little emotion? Tell me Adam, what hope does that destroy?"

Ignoring the question, Adam turned away and carried on practising.

Less than half an hour later, both men were shaken by a sudden female shriek from the direction of the pathway. More out of fear than reluctant obedience, Stern took position behind the picnic table, whilst Adam stood forward, machete at the ready. With a fearsome cry of 'you killed my sister and now you will pay', Rhapsody charged across the glade like a glittering turquoise banshee, a small bladed knife in her hand.

Steeling himself for the fight, Adam found the situation strange and perplexing. Not only did Rhapsody appear to be alone, but without her bow and the advantage of long-range engagement, she would be a pushover. Inexperienced in a close combat situation, her blade was the weapon of last resort. Unless Rhapsody's behaviour was part of some ingenious plan, the fight would over in a matter of seconds.

As the former twin approached, her expression changed from one of rage to one of pleading desperation. She seemed to be mouthing words, but Adam could not tell what they were. Moving to swiftly end the confrontation, he raised his machete and struck out, aiming for Rhapsody's blade arm. To his surprise, she made little effort to parry or evade the blow, and the blade cleanly severed her hand.

Reeling in agony, blood spurting from the stump, she pleaded quietly:

"Please listen. Please listen. I need your help. I swear this isn't a trick ... I desperately need your help. Make it look like we're still fighting, but please listen."

Wondering if he would regret the decision, Adam lowered his machete— passing up a gift decapitation—and instead kicked Rhapsody roughly to the ground.

Pinning her face down, his knee firmly in her back, Adam had one hand tight around the stump to help staunch the blood, and the other holding a knife to her throat. Leaning in close, he whispered:

"I'm listening, Rhapsody. I'll warn you though, any move I don't like and you're dead."

Her voice straining with pain, Rhapsody explained, "I'm no longer a psychopath. I know it's hard to believe, but when I came back as one person, the sickness was gone from my mind. I ... I ... guess the AI filtered it out when my personalities were merged. I'm revolted by the terrible things I did in my past-life and the murders I've committed since."

"But you're still one of the gang. You're still a murderer."

"I can't let them know I've changed. Have you any idea how vicious they'll be if they knew I wasn't one of them. You've ... got to ... help me."

"How can I help you? That psychoviro is your home for eternity, and there's nothing I can do about that."

Rhapsody's words began to slur through loss of blood:

"I just ... need to get out of that ... wi ... wicked place. Once a week ... twice if possible. Need ... peace and ... nor ... normality. I don't ... want to ... lose my ... sanity. I don't want ... to go back ... to the way ..."

As her voice ebbed into silence, Stern shouted a warning to Adam that the psychos were approaching. Taking the pressure off Rhapsody's stump, Adam carefully nicked her jugular, and left her to die. He decided there and then to do his best to honour her dying wish. Her redemption may have been an accident of science, but Adam could not help thinking that the Sarge had been right all those months ago—perhaps God dared to show his face.

Now Adam's attention turned to Groover and Rampage, facing him on the other side of the glade. Out of their gritty urban environment, glittering in their silver suits and boots, they looked odd and out of place in the tranquil verdant glade - like misplaced spacemen from some camp 1960's sci-fi TV series. In an uncharacteristic gesture of support, Groover slapped his glittering General on the back and wished him good luck. Perhaps out of concern for his own safety, Groover stayed close to the woodland path, whilst Rampage strolled forward, his face simmering with anger and arrogance. If he was at all scared, he did not show it.

Stopping about fifteen feet away from Adam, Rampage unsheathed his gladius short sword and stood ready to fight.

"You surprise me Copa. I didn't expect to meet you face to face like this, especially after our last encounter. I thought you'd be sneaking around in the shadows like the coward you are, trying to pick us off one by one."

"Your pals have been well and truly picked off, but I see no reason to take any special measures with you. With Rhapsody out of action, you don't have a pretty girl with her bow and arrows to watch your back. You're all alone now, Sparklepants. Come on, remind me just how crap you are."

"Oh, you are so dead again!" seethed Rampage through clenched teeth, storming forward to attack.

Even at the first clash of blades, Adam knew he was outclassed. Every fight between him and Rampage had ended with Adam's abrupt death, but those memories were always lost. Now, as many times before, Rampage reacquainted Adam with his ferocious speed, strength, and mastery of the blade. Back-footed and wrong-footed, weaving and reeling, Adam struggled to parry the organic combination of attacks dealt by his silver-clad attacker. With an eye on a quick resolution to the fight, Rampage constantly upped the pressure, his razor-sharp steel whipping and thrusting with devilish speed and precision.

Haunted by the mental scars of his first-life failures, Adam became gripped by morbid self-doubt, sapping his will to win. Narrowly avoiding a deadly slice to the neck, he crashed back into the picnic table. Offering only a half-hearted defence, believing his demise to be imminent … he did not give a damn.

Sensing an early victory, Rampage performed a perfect feint; drawing away Adam's guard and leaving him wide open to attack. With the elegant poise of a master swordsman, Rampage thrust his blade at Adam's heart.

It should have been all over there and then, with Adam destined for another date with resurrection, if not for the unexpected and forever un-credited intervention of … 'The Scarlet Letter'. Before the tip of the blade pierced his flesh, Adam inadvertently stepped on the glossy cover of the paperback book, which had fallen off the picnic table during the fight. As the book creased under the weight, it slid slightly, subtly moving Adam sideways. Nobody noticed Adam's change in position, and the sword missed its intended target—but so close that his beating heart whispered a kiss to the edge of the blade.

Rampage pulled out the sword, and Adam immediately fell to the ground clutching his bloody chest.

"How humiliating," said Rampage, shaking his head. "Yet again, the mighty Copacabana dies. Even with the home advantage, he cannot win. Enjoy the darkness, loser."

Turning his back on his fallen enemy, Rampage noticed Stern quietly sneaking across the glade.

"Not so fast, pretty boy. That's Dynamite's tomahawk you have there isn't it? Come here, and I'll honour you with a brief display of my skill and … ugh …ugh …"

Blood began pouring down the psycho's face, his eyes rolling up in their sockets, as Adam's machete split his skull from behind. Once more, with tremendous force, Adam chopped into the head, totally cleaving the face apart. Now it was Rampage's turn to fall to the ground, but unlike Adam, he was definitely not getting up again.

For two years, Adam had wondered about this moment: how he would feel once the gang were defeated. He always imagined he would make a witty remark—clichéd of course—or punch his fist into the air with triumphant elation. But now, with the blood of loved ones on his hands, he felt tainted, bewildered, and somewhat ashamed.

Stern came running over, and helped Adam over to the log bench. Using a belt, t-shirt, and some pages from 'The Scarlet Letter', Adam fashioned a makeshift compress for his chest wound, which Stern applied and tightened.

"Thanks for not intervening," said Adam. "When I was on the floor, I was worried you'd jump in and take revenge."

"Are you kidding me, Adam? No way was I taking on that guy. I was shitting myself the moment that psycho 70's chick came running over. And, the speed they move on those heels … it's scary. I wasn't going to intervene anything. My heart's still racing even now. To use a tired old phrase, 'I'm a lover not a fighter'."

Referencing their earlier altercation, Stern asked, "Do you win the Grand Prize now? There's just gotta be some payback for all this blood. The Genie made a run for it the moment the fight started. He could be hiding anywhere."

Using Stern for support, Adam slowly rose to his feet.

"Probably find him hiding in one of the wake-up cubicles. I saw your buggy parked along the track, but I think you'll find he's taken it. We'll probably have to walk."

After a slow and gruelling journey across the viro, they found Groover. Just as Adam predicted, the Genie had shut himself into one of the wake-up cubicles behind the utility cottage, and was refusing to come out or even discuss the matter of 'the deal'. Adam spent over half an hour fruitlessly hammering at the door, and attempting to appeal to Groover's sense of honour. Eventually, exhaustion and his painful chest wound got the better of Adam, and he decided to get fixed up before carrying on the confrontation.

Entering the utility building for the first time since that fateful Indian meal two years ago, the décor was dramatically transformed. Unlike then, the interior was now reconfigured as a traditional English cottage, complete with Tudor oak furniture, and a roaring log fire—artificial but very realistic—flaming and crackling in a wrought iron grate.

Adam let Frederick and Amelia, the viro androids, tend to his wound. After carefully cleaning the festering scabbed hole, they applied antiseptic pads and bandaged up the whole chest. Amelia warned Adam that he might have some minor internal bleeding, but that as long as he stayed away from any heavy exertion, he should make it to midnight. Stern, glad to be off his feet, sat quietly drinking a cold beer.

An hour later, after a much-needed rest, Adam was back, banging on the wake-up cubicle door. Groover seemed to be enjoying Adam's growing frustration, and changed his tactics from crude obfuscation to blatant lies:

"My Environment, not 'ere!" he cried scornfully. "That was the deal. I don't know what's goin' wrong with your memory, but you were supposed to kill the gang … in my Environment. Killin' them 'ere don't count."

"You never specified a location. I fulfilled my end of the bargain."

"Well I did specify a location, and it ain't 'ere. Us Originals don't make mistakes … and that be the end of it."

Quietly ushering Adam to one side, Stern rhythmically rapped at the door. Clearing his throat for effect, he addressed the Genie in a serious and business-like tone:

"Mr Groover, not that I for one moment doubt your sincerity, but I've heard that all the Originals monitor and record any deals they make. Maybe you should check the recording to see if you've made a mistake."

"That be one of those stupid rumours. There be no such recording. Now, why don't you both piss off and leave me be."

"That's very strange; I have it on very good authority that such recordings exist. Part of the Original's Code I believe."

"Accusing me of lying are you? Careful what you say, 'cause us Originals ain't too forgiving when it comes to personal insults. We can make things 'appen … bad things."

"Is that so? Well what if one of the other Originals was to hear about this conversation. If it turned out you were lying, and have broken the code, how long do you think it would be before you started losing your privileges?"

"Hah, hah, don't try and threaten me," Groover laughed. "You ain't got the ear of any of the Originals. I've 'eard of your kind; you ain't nothing but a hind-reader."

"The best hind-reader. Mr Groover, I take it you've heard of Taghela Solar, the 22nd century corporate dictator?"

"That's bollocks! No way do you know her. She was the first of us. She'd 'ave you skinned alive if you set foot in her Environment."

"On the contrary, she is a great believer in my gift, and treats me with total respect whenever I visit. You see, someone very dear to me lives in her psychoviro, and in return for this person's guaranteed safety, I perform a personal reading for Taghela once every few months. In fact, our next meeting is only three weeks from now. If you think I'm lying then just carry on being a jerk."

There was about a minute of silence before the door of the cubicle slightly opened and Groover, solemn faced, peered through the gap.

"I suppose it's possible I be mistaken," he said, glowering at Stern. "But what I have to say is for Copa's ears only. I made no deal with you."

"Fair enough," agreed Stern. "I'll … err … piss off and get back to my beer."

Stern walked back to the cottage, and Groover opened the door fully. Before divulging the secret information, Groover had two conditions:

"Well, I don't want you tellin' anybody else the secret. It's not something I shoulda agreed to in the first place, and I don't want any of the other Originals snooping through my recordings."

"I agree. What's your other condition?"

"I wanna borrow your friends cart again so I can go around collectin' the heads … for the trophy shelf."

"But you can't take anything back with you."

"I can. It be one of the privileges of being an Original. One of many I don't want to lose."

"Ok, fine, but only your gang. You leave our people alone."

Groover agreed, and attempted a smile—which at best looked like a manic grin—and invited Adam into the cubicle:

"Come on in, Copa. I guess two years of dying is worth a Genie's secret. We'll share a jug of scrumpy, and I'll tell you what you want to know."

DECISION

Back in the utility cottage, Adam relaxed in a comfortable armchair by the fire, whilst Stern sat playing cards with Amelia and Frederick at a sturdy oak dining table. Unnerved by the day's carnage both men decided to stay in the cottage until the sleep of midnight sent them home again.

Adam wondered about the identity of the 'someone dear to me' that Stern mentioned to Groover. Who was the person living in Taghela Solar's psychoviro: Stern's ex-wife, his father ... maybe Sofia? Thinking it best to leave the hind-reader to his secrets, and grateful for all his help, Adam never broached the subject. After all, Adam was now in possession of the most precious secret of all: how to escape the viro.

Unknown to anyone but himself, Adam also had another secret. Over two years of constant dying, his mind had learned to cope with the dark place's painful effect. Adam had no idea how this phenomenon occurred, but gradually, especially in the past few months, the trauma of resurrection had faded to little more than a faint headache. Coupled with not remembering his deaths, it gave him a fearless edge on the battlefield. However, there were a couple of downsides to his 'super-power'. Firstly, when facing extreme odds, instead of rising to the challenge, it was easy to just give up and wait to fight another day. Secondly, it made him cold and indifferent to other people's fear of the dark place – a trait so dreadfully demonstrated by the events at the manor. Now the deal was over, Adam wondered if he could ever step back from the abyss, and regain his humanity. However, did he really want to step back?

Sipping from a small glass of Islay malt whisky, Adam watched the flames busily licking around the logs, and mulled over his options.

Only a week ago he had given up all hope of escape, and resigned himself to an eternity quietly standing in the shadows, but now everything was turned around. This day's gruesome success, and yesterday's revelation at Mama Fiestas, defined two possible futures: live the celebrity life of a legend in the closed confines of the Viroverse, or eschew stardom to venture out to an uncertain destiny.

Perhaps Stern had been right to call it the 'Grand Prize'. Adam felt very much like a successful contestant in a primetime TV game show facing the final decision: take the money or open the mystery box. Putting aside any questions about the depraved nature of his win, or whether the price was right, he concentrated on his 50/50 future. Without the pressure of a countdown, screaming audience, or a pushy game show host, Adam had an eternity to make up his mind. Only, he did not need an eternity. The choice was already made.

He was going to open the mystery box. It was time to see what lay outside the viro walls.

Printed in Great Britain
by Amazon.co.uk, Ltd.,
Marston Gate.